More Far Eastern Tales

William Somerset Maugham was born in 1874 and lived in Paris until he was ten. He was educated at King's School, Canterbury, and at Heidelberg University. He spent some time at St Thomas's Hospital with the idea of practising medicine, but the success of his first novel, *Liza of Lambeth*, published in 1897, won him over to letters. *Of Human Bondage*, the first of his masterpieces, came out in 1915, and with the publication in 1919 of *The Moon and Sixpence* his reputation as a novelist was established. His position as a successful playwright was being consolidated at the same time. His first play, *A Man of Honour*, was followed by a series of successes just before and after World War I, and his career in the theatre did not end until 1933 with *Sheppey*.

His fame as a short-story writer began with *The Trembling of a Leaf*, sub-titled *Little Stories of the South Sea Islands* in 1921, after which he published more than ten collections. His other works include travel books such as *On a Chinese Screen* and *Don Fernando*, essays, criticism, and the autobiographical *The Summing Up* and *A Writer's Notebook*.

In 1927 Somerset Maugham settled in the South of France and lived there until his death in 1965.

*Also by W. Somerset Maugham
and available in paperback*

Of Human Bondage
The Moon and Sixpence
The Narrow Corner
The Razor's Edge
Cakes and Ale
The Summing Up
Short Stories Vol. 1
Short Stories Vol. 2
Short Stories Vol. 3
Short Stories Vol. 4
Ashenden
Far Eastern Tales
South Sea Tales
For Services Rendered
The Merry-Go-Round
Don Fernando
On a Chinese Screen
Catalina
The Painted Veil
Up at the Villa
Mrs Craddock
Ten Novels and their Authors
A Writer's Notebook
The Casuarina Tree
Christmas Holiday
Liza of Lambeth
The Magician
Points of View
Selected Plays
Theatre
Then and Now
The Vagrant Mood

W. Somerset Maugham

More
Far Eastern Tales

Mandarin

This edition published in the United Kingdom in 1998 by
Mandarin Paperbacks

1 3 5 7 9 10 8 6 4 2

This collection copyright © The Royal Literary Fund

The right of W. Somerset Maugham to be identified as the author
of this work has been asserted by him in accordance with
the Copyright, Designs and Patents Act, 1988

The stories in this collection have been selected by John Whitehead from
Cosmopolitans, The Casuarina Tree, Ah King, Creatures of Circumstance,
and *Collected Short Stories.*

Mandarin Paperbacks
Random House UK Limited
20 Vauxhall Bridge Road, London SW1V 2SA

Random House Australia (Pty) Limited
20 Alfred Street, Milsons Point, Sydney, New South Wales 2061, Australia

Random House New Zealand Limited
18 Poland Road, Glenfield, Auckland 10, New Zealand

Random House South Africa (Pty) Limited
Endulini, 5a Jubilee Road, Parktown 2193, South Africa

Random House UK Limited Reg. No. 954009

A CIP catalogue record for this book is available from the British Library

Papers used by Random House UK Limited
are natural, recyclable products made from wood grown in
sustainable forests. The manufacturing processes conform to
the environmental regulations of the country of origin

Printed and bound in the United Kingdom by
Cox & Wyman Ltd, Reading, Berkshire

ISBN 0 7493 2403 1

Contents

The Letter

Outside on the quay the sun beat fiercely. A stream of motors, lorries and buses, private cars and hirelings, sped up and down the crowded thoroughfare, and every chauffeur blew his horn; rickshaws threaded their nimble path amid the throng, and the panting coolies found breath to yell at one another; coolies, carrying heavy bales, sidled along with their quick jog-trot and shouted to the passer-by to make way; itinerant vendors proclaimed their wares. Singapore is the meeting-place of a hundred peoples; and men of all colours, black Tamils, yellow Chinks, brown Malays, Armenians, Jews and Bengalis, called to one another in raucous tones. But inside the office of Messrs Ripley, Joyce and Naylor it was pleasantly cool; it was dark after the dusty glitter of the street and agreeably quiet after its unceasing din. Mr. Joyce sat in his private room, at the table, with an electric fan turned full on him. He was leaning back, his elbows on the arms of the chair, with the tips of the outstretched fingers of one hand resting neatly against the tips of the outstretched fingers of the other. His gaze rested on the battered volumes of the Law Reports which stood on a long shelf in front of him. On the top of a cupboard were square boxes of japanned tin, on which were painted the names of various clients.

There was a knock at the door.

'Come in.'

A Chinese clerk, very neat in his white ducks, opened it.

'Mr. Crosbie is here, sir.'

He spoke beautiful English, accenting each word with precision, and Mr. Joyce had often wondered at the extent of his vocabulary. Ong Chi Seng was a Cantonese, and he had studied law at Gray's Inn. He was spending a year or two with Messrs Ripley, Joyce and Naylor in order to prepare himself for practice on his own account. He was industrious, obliging, and of exemplary character.

'Show him in,' said Mr. Joyce.

He rose to shake hands with his visitor and asked him to sit down. The light fell on him as he did so. The face of Mr. Joyce remained in shadow. He was by nature a silent man, and now he looked at Robert Crosbie for quite a minute without speaking. Crosbie was a big fellow, well over six feet high, with broad shoulders, and muscular. He was a rubber-planter, hard with the constant exercise of walking over the estate, and with the tennis which was his relaxation when the day's work was over. He was deeply sunburned. His hairy hands, his feet in clumsy boots, were enormous, and Mr. Joyce found himself thinking that a blow of that great fist would easily kill the fragile Tamil. But there was no fierceness in his blue eyes; they were confiding and gentle; and his face, with its big, undistinguished features, was open, frank and honest. But at this moment it bore a look of deep distress. It was drawn and haggard.

'You look as though you hadn't had much sleep the last night or two,' said Mr. Joyce.

'I haven't.'

Mr. Joyce noticed now the old felt hat, with its broad double brim, which Crosbie had placed on the table; and then his eyes travelled to the khaki shorts he wore, showing his red hairy thighs, the tennis shirt open at the neck, without a tie, and the dirty khaki jacket with the ends of the sleeves turned up. He looked as though

2

he had just come in from a long tramp among the rubber trees. Mr. Joyce gave a slight frown.

'You must pull yourself together, you know. You must keep your head.'

'Oh, I'm all right.'

'Have you seen your wife today?'

'No, I'm to see her this afternoon. You know, it is a damned shame that they should have arrested her.'

'I think they had to do that,' Mr. Joyce answered in his level, soft tone.

'I should have thought they'd have let her out on bail.'

'It's a very serious charge.'

'It's damnable. She did what any decent woman would do in her place. Only, nine women out of ten wouldn't have the pluck. Leslie's the best woman in the world. She wouldn't hurt a fly. Why, hang it all, man, I've been married to her for twelve years, do you think I don't know her? God, if I'd got hold of the man I'd have wrung his neck, I'd have killed him without a moment's hesitation. So would you.'

'My dear fellow, everybody's on your side. No one has a good word to say for Hammond. We're going to get her off. I don't suppose either the assessors or the judge will go into court without having already made up their minds to bring in a verdict of not guilty.'

'The whole thing's a farce,' said Crosbie violently. 'She ought never to have been arrested in the first place, and then it's terrible, after all the poor girl's gone through, to subject her to the ordeal of a trial. There's not a soul I've met since I've been in Singapore, man or woman, who hasn't told me that Leslie was absolutely justified. I think it's awful to keep her in prison all these weeks.'

'The law is the law. After all, she confesses that she killed the man. It is terrible, and I'm dreadfully sorry for both you and for her.'

'I don't matter a hang,' interrupted Crosbie.

'But the fact remains that murder has been committed, and in a civilised community a trial is inevitable.'

'Is it murder to exterminate noxious vermin? She shot him as she would have shot a mad dog.'

Mr. Joyce leaned back again in his chair and once more placed the tips of his ten fingers together. The little construction he formed looked like the skeleton of a roof. He was silent for a moment.

'I should be wanting in my duty as your legal adviser,' he said at last, in an even voice, looking at his client with his cool, brown eyes, 'if I did not tell you that there is one point which causes me just a little anxiety. If your wife had only shot Hammond once, the whole thing would be absolutely plain sailing. Unfortunately she fired six times.'

'Her explanation is perfectly simple. In the circumstances anyone would have done the same.'

'I daresay,' said Mr. Joyce, 'and of course I think the explanation is very reasonable. But it's no good closing our eyes to the facts. It's always a good plan to put yourself in another man's place, and I can't deny that if I were prosecuting for the Crown that is the point on which I should centre my enquiry.'

'My dear fellow, that's perfectly idiotic.'

Mr. Joyce shot a sharp glance at Robert Crosbie. The shadow of a smile hovered over his shapely lips. Crosbie was a good fellow, but he could hardly be described as intelligent.

'I daresay it's of no importance,' answered the lawyer. 'I just thought it was a point worth mentioning. You haven't got very long to wait now, and when it's all over I recommend you to go off somewhere with your wife on a trip, and forget all about it. Even though we are almost dead certain to get an acquittal, a trial of that sort is anxious work, and you'll both want a rest.'

For the first time Crosbie smiled, and his smile strangely changed his face. You forgot the uncouthness and saw only the goodness of his soul.

'I think I shall want it more than Leslie. She's borne up wonderfully. By God, there's a plucky little woman for you.'

'Yes, I've been very much struck by her self-control,' said the lawyer. 'I should never have guessed that she was capable of such determination.'

His duties as her counsel had made it necessary for him to have a good many interviews with Mrs. Crosbie since her arrest. Though things had been made as easy as could be for her, the fact remained that she was in jail, awaiting her trial for murder, and it would not have been surprising if her nerves had failed her. She appeared to bear her ordeal with composure. She read a great deal, took such exercise as was possible, and by favour of the authorities worked at the pillow lace which had always formed the entertainment of her long hours of leisure. When Mr. Joyce saw her, she was neatly dressed in cool, fresh, simple frocks, her hair was carefully arranged, and her nails were manicured. Her manner was collected. She was able even to jest upon the little inconveniences of her position. There was something casual about the way in which she spoke of the tragedy, which suggested to Mr. Joyce that only her good breeding prevented her from finding something a trifle ludicrous in a situation which was eminently serious. It surprised him, for he had never thought that she had a sense of humour.

He had known her off and on for a good many years. When she paid visits to Singapore she generally came to dine with his wife and himself, and once or twice she had passed a weekend with them at their bungalow by the sea. His wife had spent a fortnight with her on the estate, and had met Geoffrey Hammond several times.

The two couples had been on friendly, if not on intimate, terms, and it was on this account that Robert Crosbie had rushed over to Singapore immediately after the catastrophe and begged Mr. Joyce to take charge personally of his unhappy wife's defence.

The story she told him the first time he saw her, she had never varied in the smallest detail. She told it as coolly then, a few hours after the tragedy, as she told it now. She told it connectedly, in a level, even voice, and her only sign of confusion was when a slight colour came into her cheeks as she described one or two of its incidents. She was the last woman to whom one would have expected such a thing to happen. She was in the early thirties, a fragile creature, neither short nor tall, and graceful rather than pretty. Her wrists and ankles were very delicate, but she was extremely thin, and you could see the bones of her hands through the white skin, and the veins were large and blue. Her face was colourless, slightly sallow, and her lips were pale. You did not notice the colour of her eyes. She had a great deal of light brown hair, and it had a slight natural wave; it was the sort of hair that with a little touching-up would have been very pretty, but you could not imagine that Mrs. Crosbie would think of resorting to any such device. She was a quiet, pleasant, unassuming woman. Her manner was engaging, and if she was not very popular it was because she suffered from a certain shyness. This was comprehensible enough, for the planter's life is lonely, and in her own house, with people she knew, she was in her quiet way charming. Mrs. Joyce, after her fortnight's stay, had told her husband that Leslie was a very agreeable hostess. There was more in her, she said, than people thought; and when you came to know her you were surprised how much she had read and how entertaining she could be.

She was the last woman in the world to commit murder.

Mr. Joyce dismissed Robert Crosbie with such reassuring words as he could find and, once more alone in his office, turned over the pages of the brief. But it was a mechanical action, for all its details were familiar to him. The case was the sensation of the day, and it was discussed in all the clubs, at all the dinner tables, up and down the Peninsula, from Singapore to Penang. The facts that Mrs. Crosbie gave were simple. Her husband had gone to Singapore on business, and she was alone for the night. She dined by herself, late, at a quarter to nine, and after dinner sat in the sitting-room working at her lace. It opened on the verandah. There was no one in the bungalow, for the servants had retired to their own quarters at the back of the compound. She was surprised to hear a step on the gravel path in the garden, a booted step, which suggested a white man rather than a native, for she had not heard a motor drive up, and she could not imagine who could be coming to see her at that time of night. Someone ascended the few stairs that led up to the bungalow, walked across the verandah, and appeared at the door of the room in which she sat. At the first moment she did not recognise the visitor. She sat with a shaded lamp, and he stood with his back to the darkness.

'May I come in?' he said.

She did not even recognise the voice.

'Who is it?' she asked.

She worked with spectacles, and she took them off as she spoke.

'Geoff Hammond.'

'Of course. Come in and have a drink.'

She rose and shook hands with him cordially. She was a little surprised to see him, for though he was a neighbour neither she nor Robert had been lately on very

7

intimate terms with him, and she had not seen him for some weeks. He was the manager of a rubber estate nearly eight miles from theirs, and she wondered why he had chosen this late hour to come and see them.

'Robert's away,' she said. 'He had to go to Singapore for the night.'

Perhaps he thought his visit called for some explanation, for he said:

'I'm sorry. I felt rather lonely tonight, so I thought I'd just come along and see how you were getting on.'

'How on earth did you come? I never heard a car.'

'I left it down the road. I thought you might both be in bed and asleep.'

This was natural enough. The planter gets up at dawn in order to take the roll-call of the workers, and soon after dinner he is glad to go to bed. Hammond's car was in point of fact found next day a quarter of a mile from the bungalow.

Since Robert was away there was no whisky and soda in the room. Leslie did not call the boy, who was probably asleep, but fetched it herself. Her guest mixed himself a drink and filled his pipe.

Geoff Hammond had a host of friends in the colony. He was at this time in the late thirties, but he had come out as a lad. He had been one of the first to volunteer on the outbreak of war, and had done very well. A wound in the knee caused him to be invalided out of the army after two years, but he returned to the Federated Malay States with a D.S.O. and an M.C. He was one of the best billiard-players in the colony. He had been a beautiful dancer and a fine tennis player, but though able no longer to dance, and his tennis, with a stiff knee, was not so good as it had been, he had the gift of popularity and was universally liked. He was a tall, good-looking fellow, with attractive blue eyes and a fine head of black, curling hair. Old stagers said his only fault was that he was too fond of the girls, and after the catastrophe they shook their heads and vowed that they had always known this would get him into trouble.

He began now to talk to Leslie about the local affairs, the forthcoming races in Singapore, the price of rubber, and his chances of killing a tiger which had been lately seen in the neighbourhood. She was anxious to finish by a certain date the piece of lace on which she was working, for she wanted to send it home for her mother's birthday, and so put on her spectacles again, and drew towards her chair the little table on which stood the pillow.

'I wish you wouldn't wear those great horn-spectacles,' he said. 'I don't know why a pretty woman should do her best to look plain.'

She was a trifle taken aback at this remark. He had never used that tone with her before. She thought the best thing was to make light of it.

'I have no pretensions to being a raving beauty, you know, and if you ask me point blank, I'm bound to tell you that I don't care two pins if you think me plain or not.'

'I don't think you're plain. I think you're awfully pretty.'

'Sweet of you,' she answered, ironically. 'But in that case I can only think you half-witted.'

He chuckled. But he rose from his chair and sat down in another by her side.

'You're not going to have the face to deny that you have the prettiest hands in the world,' he said.

He made a gesture as though to take one of them. She gave him a little tap.

'Don't be an idiot. Sit down where you were before and talk sensibly, or else I shall send you home.'

He did not move.

'Don't you know that I'm awfully in love with you?' he said.

She remained quite cool.

'I don't. I don't believe it for a minute, and even if it were true I don't want you to say it.'

She was the more surprised at what he was saying, since during the seven years she had known him he had never paid her any particular attention. When he came back from the war they had seen a good deal of one another, and once when he was ill Robert had gone over and brought him back to their bungalow in his car. He had stayed with them then for a fortnight. But their interests were dissimilar, and the acquaintance had never ripened into friendship. For the last two or three years they had seen little of him. Now and then he came over to play tennis, now and then they met him at some planter's who was giving a party, but it often happened that they did not set eyes on him for a month at a time.

Now he took another whisky and soda. Leslie wondered if he had been drinking before. There was something odd about him, and it made her a trifle uneasy. She watched him help himself with disapproval.

'I wouldn't drink any more if I were you,' she said, good-humouredly still.

He emptied his glass and put it down.

'Do you think I'm talking to you like this because I'm drunk?' he asked abruptly.

'That is the most obvious explanation, isn't it?'

'Well, it's a lie. I've loved you ever since I first knew you. I've held my tongue as long as I could, and now it's got to come out. I love you, I love you, I love you.'

She rose and carefully put aside the pillow.

'Goodnight,' she said.

'I'm not going now.'

At last she began to lose her temper.

'But, you poor fool, don't you know that I've never loved anyone but Robert, and even if I didn't love

Robert you're the last man I should care for.'

'What do I care? Robert's away.'

'If you don't go away this minute I shall call the boys, and have you thrown out.'

'They're out of earshot.'

She was very angry now. She made a movement as though to go on to the verandah from which the house-boy would certainly hear her, but he seized her arm.

'Let me go,' she cried furiously.

She opened her mouth and called 'Boy, boy,' but with a quick gesture he put his hand over it. Then before she knew what he was about he had taken her in his arms and was kissing her passionately. She struggled, turning her lips away from his burning mouth.

'No, no, no,' she cried. 'Leave me alone. I won't.'

She grew confused about what happened then. All that had been said before she remembered accurately, but now his words assailed her ears through a mist of horror and fear. He seemed to plead for her love. He broke into violent protestations of passion. And all the time he held her in his tempestuous embrace. She was helpless, for he was a strong, powerful man, and her arms were pinioned to her sides; her struggles were unavailing, and she felt herself grow weaker; she was afraid she would faint, and his hot breath on her face made her feel desperately sick. He kissed her mouth, her eyes, her cheeks, her hair. The pressure of his arms was killing her. He lifted her off her feet. She tried to kick him, but he only held her more closely. He was carrying her now. He wasn't speaking any more, but she knew that his face was pale and his eyes hot with desire. He was taking her into the bedroom. He was no longer a civilised man, but a savage. And as he ran he stumbled against a table which was in the way. His stiff knee made him a little awkward on his feet, and with the burden of the woman in his arms he fell. In a moment she had snatched herself away from him. She ran round the sofa. He was up in a flash, and flung himself towards her. There was a revolver on the desk. She was not a nervous woman, but Robert was to be away for the night, and she had meant to take it into her room when she went to bed. That was why it happened to be there. She was frantic with terror now. She did not know what she was doing. She heard a report. She saw Hammond stagger. He gave a cry. He said something, she didn't know what. He lurched out of the room on to the verandah. She was in a frenzy now, she was beside herself, she followed him out, yes, that was it, she must have followed him out, though she remembered nothing of it, she followed firing automatically, shot after shot, till the six chambers were empty. Hammond fell down on the floor of the verandah. He crumpled up into a bloody heap.

When the boys, startled by the reports, rushed up, they found her standing over Hammond with the revolver still in her hand, and Hammond lifeless. She looked at them for a moment without speaking. They stood in a frightened, huddled bunch. She let the revolver fall from her hand, and without a word turned and went into the sitting-room. They watched her go into her bedroom and turn the key in the lock. They dared not touch the dead body, but looked at it with terrified eyes, talking excitedly to one another in undertones. Then the head-boy collected himself; he had been with them for many years, he was Chinese and a level-headed fellow. Robert had gone into Singapore on his motor-cycle, and the car stood in the garage. He told the seis to get it out; they must go at once to the Assistant District Officer and tell him what had happened. He picked up the revolver and put it in his pocket. The A.D.O., a man called Withers, lived on the outskirts of the nearest town, which was about thirty-five miles away. It took them an hour and a half to reach him. Everyone was asleep, and they had to rouse the boys. Presently Withers came out and they told him their errand. The head-boy showed him the revolver in proof of what he said. The A.D.O. went into his room to dress, sent for his car, and in a little while was following them back along the deserted road. The dawn was just breaking as he reached the Crosbies' bungalow. He ran up the steps of the verandah, and stopped short as he saw Hammond's body lying where he fell. He touched the face. It was quite cold.

'Where's mem?' he asked the house-boy.

The Chinese pointed to the bedroom. Withers went to the door and knocked. There was no answer. He knocked again.

'Mrs. Crosbie,' he called.

'Who is it?'

'Withers.'

There was another pause. Then the door was unlocked and slowly opened. Leslie stood before him. She had not been to bed, and wore the tea-gown in which she had dined. She stood and looked silently at the A.D.O.

'Your house-boy fetched me,' he said. 'Hammond. What have you done?'

'He tried to rape me, and I shot him.'

'My God. I say, you'd better come out here. You must tell me exactly what happened.'

'Not now. I can't. You must give me time. Send for my husband.'

Withers was a young man, and he did not know exactly what to do in an emergency which was so out of the run of his duties. Leslie refused to say anything till at last Robert arrived. Then she told the two men the story, from which since then, though she had repeated it over and over again, she had never in the slightest degree diverged.

The point to which Mr. Joyce recurred was the shooting. As a lawyer he was bothered that Leslie had fired not once, but six times, and the examination of the dead man showed that four of the shots had been fired close to the body. One might almost have thought that when the man fell she stood over him and emptied the contents of the revolver into him. She confessed that her memory, so accurate for all that had preceded, failed her here. Her mind was blank. It pointed to an uncontrollable fury; but uncontrollable fury was the last thing you would have expected from this quiet and demure woman. Mr. Joyce had known her a good many years, and had always thought her an unemotional person; during the weeks that had passed since the tragedy her composure had been amazing.

Mr. Joyce shrugged his shoulders.

'The fact is, I suppose,' he reflected, 'that you can never tell what hidden possibilities of savagery there are in the most respectable of women.'

There was a knock at the door.

'Come in.'

The Chinese clerk entered and closed the door behind him. He closed it gently, with deliberation, but decidedly, and advanced to the table at which Mr. Joyce was sitting.

'May I trouble you, sir, for a few words private conversation?' he said.

The elaborate accuracy with which the clerk expressed himself always faintly amused Mr. Joyce, and now he smiled.

'It's no trouble, Chi Seng,' he replied.

'The matter on which I desire to speak to you, sir, is delicate and confidential.'

'Fire away.'

Mr. Joyce met his clerk's shrewd eyes. As usual Ong

Chi Seng was dressed in the height of local fashion. He wore very shiny patent leather shoes and gay silk socks. In his black tie was a pearl and ruby pin, and on the fourth finger of his left hand a diamond ring. From the pocket of his neat white coat protruded a gold fountain pen and a gold pencil. He wore a gold wrist-watch, and on the bridge of his nose invisible pince-nez. He gave a little cough.

'The matter has to do with the case R. *v*. Crosbie, sir.'

'Yes?'

'A circumstance has come to my knowledge, sir, which seems to put a different complexion on it.'

'What circumstance?'

'It has come to my knowledge, sir, that there is a letter in existence from the defendant to the unfortunate victim of the tragedy.'

'I shouldn't be at all surprised. In the course of the last seven years I have no doubt that Mrs. Crosbie often had occasion to write to Mr. Hammond.'

Mr. Joyce had a high opinion of his clerk's intelligence and his words were designed to conceal his thoughts.

'That is very probable, sir. Mrs. Crosbie must have communicated with the deceased frequently, to invite him to dine with her for example, or to propose a tennis game. That was my first thought when the matter was brought to my notice. This letter, however, was written on the day of the late Mr. Hammond's death.'

Mr. Joyce did not flicker an eyelash. He continued to look at Ong Chi Seng with the smile of faint amusement with which he generally talked to him.

'Who has told you this?'

'The circumstances were brought to my knowledge, sir, by a friend of mine.'

Mr. Joyce knew better than to insist.

'You will no doubt recall, sir, that Mrs. Crosbie has

stated that until the fatal night she had had no communication with the deceased for several weeks.'

'Have you got the letter?'

'No, sir.'

'What are its contents?'

'My friend gave me a copy. Would you like to peruse it, sir?'

'I should.'

Ong Chi Seng took from an inside pocket a bulky wallet. It was filled with papers, Singapore dollar notes and cigarette cards. From the confusion he presently extracted a half sheet of thin notepaper and placed it before Mr. Joyce. The letter read as follows:

> *R. will be away for the night. I absolutely must*
> *see you. I shall expect you at eleven. I am desperate,*
> *and if you don't come I won't answer for the*
> *consequences. Don't drive up. – L.*

It was written in the flowing hand which the Chinese were taught at the foreign schools. The writing, so lacking in character, was oddly incongruous with the ominous words.

'What makes you think that this note was written by Mrs. Crosbie?'

'I have every confidence in the veracity of my informant, sir,' replied Ong Chi Seng. 'And the matter can very easily be put to the proof. Mrs. Crosbie will, no doubt, be able to tell you at once whether she wrote such a letter or not.'

Since the beginning of the conversation Mr. Joyce had not taken his eyes off the respectable countenance of his clerk. He wondered now if he discerned in it a faint expression of mockery.

'It is inconceivable that Mrs. Crosbie should have written such a letter,' said Mr. Joyce.

'If that is your opinion, sir, the matter is of course

ended. My friend spoke to me on the subject only because he thought, as I was in your office, you might like to know of the existence of this letter before a communication was made to the Deputy Public Prosecutor.'

'Who has the original?' asked Mr. Joyce sharply.

Ong Chi Seng made no sign that he perceived in this question and its manner a change of attitude.

'You will remember, sir, no doubt, that after the death of Mr. Hammond it was discovered that he had had relations with a Chinese woman. The letter is at present in her possession.'

That was one of the things which had turned public opinion most vehemently against Hammond. It came to be known that for several months he had had a Chinese woman living in his house.

For a moment neither of them spoke. Indeed everything had been said and each understood the other perfectly.

'I'm obliged to you, Chi Seng. I will give the matter my consideration.'

'Very good, sir. Do you wish me to make a communication to that effect to my friend?'

'I daresay it would be as well if you kept in touch with him,' Mr. Joyce answered with gravity.

'Yes, sir.'

The clerk noiselessly left the room, shutting the door again with deliberation, and left Mr. Joyce to his reflections. He stared at the copy, in its neat, impersonal writing, of Leslie's letter. Vague suspicions troubled him. They were so disconcerting that he made an effort to put them out of his mind. There must be a simple explanation of the letter, and Leslie without doubt could give it at once, but, by heaven, an explanation was needed. He rose from his chair, put the letter in his pocket, and took his topee. When he went out Ong Chi Seng was busily writing at his desk.

'I'm going out for a few minutes, Chi Seng,' he said.

'Mr. George Reed is coming by appointment at twelve o'clock, sir. Where shall I say you've gone?'

Mr. Joyce gave him a thin smile.

'You can say that you haven't the least idea.'

But he knew perfectly well that Ong Chi Seng was aware that he was going to the jail. Though the crime had been committed in Belanda and the trial was to take place at Belanda Bharu, since there was in the jail no convenience for the detention of a white woman Mrs. Crosbie had been brought to Singapore.

When she was led into the room in which he waited she held out her thin, distinguished hand, and gave him a pleasant smile. She was as ever neatly and simply dressed, and her abundant, pale hair was arranged with care.

'I wasn't expecting to see you this morning,' she said, graciously.

She might have been in her own house, and Mr. Joyce almost expected to hear her call the boy and tell him to bring the visitor a gin pahit.

'How are you?' he asked.

'I'm in the best of health, thank you.' A flicker of amusement flashed across her eyes. 'This is a wonderful place for a rest cure.'

The attendant withdrew and they were left alone.

'Do sit down,' said Leslie.

He took a chair. He did not quite know how to begin. She was so cool that it seemed almost impossible to say to her the thing he had come to say. Though she was not pretty there was something agreeable in her appearance. She had elegance, but it was the elegance of good breeding in which there was nothing of the artifice of society. You had only to look at her to know what sort of people she had and what kind of surroundings she had lived in. Her fragility gave her a singular refinement. It was impossible to associate her with the vaguest idea of grossness.

'I'm looking forward to seeing Robert this afternoon,' she said, in her good-humoured, easy voice. (It was a pleasure to hear her speak, her voice and her accent were so distinctive of her class.) 'Poor dear, it's been a great trial to his nerves. I'm thankful it'll all be over in a few days.'

'It's only five days now.'

'I know. Each morning when I awake I say to myself, "one less."' She smiled then. 'Just as I used to do at school and the holidays were coming.'

'By the way, am I right in thinking that you had no communication whatever with Hammond for several weeks before the catastrophe?'

'I'm quite positive of that. The last time we met was at a tennis-party at the MacFarrens'. I don't think I said more than two words to him. They have two courts, you know, and we didn't happen to be in the same sets.'

'And you haven't written to him?'

'Oh, no.'

'Are you quite sure of that?'

'Oh, quite,' she answered, with a little smile. 'There was nothing I should write to him for except to ask him to dine or to play tennis, and I hadn't done either for months.'

'At one time you'd been on fairly intimate terms with him. How did it happen that you had stopped asking him to anything?'

Mrs. Crosbie shrugged her thin shoulders.

'One gets tired of people. We hadn't anything very much in common. Of course, when he was ill Robert and I did everything we could for him, but the last year or two he'd been quite well, and he was very popular. He had a good many calls on his time, and there didn't seem to be any need to shower invitations upon him.'

'Are you quite certain that was all?'

Mrs. Crosbie hesitated for a moment.

'Well, I may just as well tell you. It had come to our ears that he was living with a Chinese woman, and Robert said he wouldn't have him in the house. I had seen her myself.'

Mr. Joyce was sitting in a straight-backed armchair, resting his chin on his hand, and his eyes were fixed on Leslie. Was it his fancy that, as she made this remark, her black pupils were filled on a sudden, for the fraction of a second, with a dull red light? The effect was startling. Mr. Joyce shifted in his chair. He placed the tips of his ten fingers together. He spoke very slowly, choosing his words.

'I think I should tell you that there is in existence a letter in your handwriting to Geoff Hammond.'

He watched her closely. She made no movement, nor did her face change colour, but she took a noticeable time to reply.

'In the past I've often sent him little notes to ask him to something or other, or to get me something when I knew he was going to Singapore.'

'This letter asks him to come and see you because Robert was going to Singapore.'

'That's impossible. I never did anything of the kind.'

'You'd better read it for yourself.'

He took it out of his pocket and handed it to her. She gave it a glance and with a smile of scorn handed it back to him.

'That's not my handwriting.'

'I know, it's said to be an exact copy of the original.'

She read the words now, and as she read a horrible change came over her. Her colourless face grew dreadful to look at. It turned green. The flesh seemed on a sudden to fall away and her skin was tightly stretched over the bones. Her lips receded, showing her teeth, so that she had the appearance of making a grimace. She stared at Mr. Joyce with eyes that started from their sockets. He was looking now at a gibbering death's head.

'What does it mean?' she whispered.

Her mouth was so dry that she could utter no more than a hoarse sound. It was no longer a human voice.

'That is for you to say,' he answered.

'I didn't write it. I swear I didn't write it.'

'Be very careful what you say. If the original is in your handwriting it would be useless to deny it.'

'It would be a forgery.'

'It would be difficult to prove that. It would be easy to prove that it was genuine.'

A shiver passed through her lean body. But great beads of sweat stood on her forehead. She took a handkerchief from her bag and wiped the palms of her hands. She glanced at the letter again and gave Mr. Joyce a sidelong look.

'It's not dated. If I had written it and forgotten all about it, it might have been written years ago. If you'll give me time, I'll try and remember the circumstances.'

'I noticed there was no date. If this letter were in the hands of the prosecution they would cross-examine the boys. They would soon find out whether someone took a letter to Hammond on the day of his death.'

Mrs. Crosbie clasped her hands violently and swayed in her chair so that he thought she would faint.

'I swear to you that I didn't write that letter.'

Mr. Joyce was silent for a little while. He took his eyes from her distraught face, and looked down on the floor. He was reflecting.

'In these circumstances we need not go into the matter further,' he said slowly, at last breaking the silence. 'If the possessor of this letter sees fit to place it in the hands of the prosecution you will be prepared.'

His words suggested that he had nothing more to say to her, but he made no movement of departure. He waited. To himself he seemed to wait a very long time. He did not look at Leslie, but he was conscious that she sat very still. She made no sound. At last it was he who spoke.

'If you have nothing more to say to me I think I'll be getting back to my office.'

'What would anyone who read the letter be inclined to think that it meant?' she asked then.

'He'd know that you had told a deliberate lie,' answered Mr. Joyce sharply.

'When?'

'You have stated definitely that you had had no communication with Hammond for at least three months.'

'The whole thing has been a terrible shock to me. The events of that dreadful night have been a nightmare. It's not very strange if one detail has escaped my memory.'

'It would be unfortunate when your memory has reproduced so exactly every particular of your interview with Hammond, that you should have forgotten so important a point as that he came to see you in the bungalow on the night of his death at your express desire.'

'I hadn't forgotten. After what happened I was afraid to mention it. I thought you'd none of you believe my story if I admitted that he'd come at my invitation. I daresay it was stupid of me; but I lost my head, and after I'd said once that I'd had no communication with Hammond I was obliged to stick to it.'

By now Leslie has recovered her admirable composure, and she met Mr. Joyce's appraising glance with candour. Her gentleness was very disarming.

'You will be required to explain, then, *why* you asked Hammond to come and see you when Robert was away for the night.'

She turned her eyes full on the lawyer. He had been mistaken in thinking them insignificant, they were rather fine eyes, and unless he was mistaken they were bright now with tears. Her voice had a little break in it.

'It was a surprise I was preparing for Robert. His birthday is next month. I knew he wanted a new gun and you know I'm dreadfully stupid about sporting things. I wanted to talk to Geoff about it. I thought I'd get him to order it for me.'

'Perhaps the terms of the letter are not very clear to your recollection. Will you have another look at it?'

'No, I don't want to,' she said quickly.

'Does it seem to you the sort of letter a woman would write to a somewhat distant acquaintance because she wanted to consult him about buying a gun?'

'I daresay it's rather extravagant and emotional. I do express myself like that, you know. I'm quite prepared to admit it's very silly.' She smiled. 'And after all, Geoff Hammond wasn't quite a distant acquaintance. When he was ill I'd nursed him like a mother. I asked him to come when Robert was away, because Robert wouldn't have him in the house.'

Mr. Joyce was tired of sitting so long in the same position. He rose and walked once or twice up and down the room, choosing the words he proposed to say; then he leaned over the back of the chair in which he had been sitting. He spoke slowly in a tone of deep gravity.

'Mrs. Crosbie, I want to talk to you very, very seriously. This case was comparatively plain sailing. There was only one point which seemed to me to require explanation: as far as I could judge, you had fired no less than four shots into Hammond when he was lying on the ground. It was hard to accept the possibility that a delicate, frightened, and habitually self-controlled woman, of gentle nature and refined instincts, should have surrendered to an absolutely uncontrolled frenzy.

But of course it was admissible. Although Geoffrey Hammond was much liked and on the whole thought highly of, I was prepared to prove that he was the sort of man who might be guilty of the crime which in justification of your act you accused him of. The fact, which was discovered after his death, that he had been living with a Chinese woman gave us something very definite to go upon. That robbed him of any sympathy which might have been felt for him. We made up our minds to make use of the odium which such a connection cast upon him in the minds of all respectable people. I told your husband this morning that I was certain of an acquittal, and I wasn't just telling him that to give him heart. I do not believe the assessors would have left the court.'

They looked into one another's eyes. Mrs. Crosbie was strangely still. She was like a little bird paralysed by the fascination of a snake. He went on in the same quiet tones.

'But this letter has thrown an entirely different complexion on the case. I am your legal adviser, I shall represent you in Court. I take your story as you tell it me, and I shall conduct your defence according to its terms. It may be that I believe your statements, and it may be that I doubt them. The duty of counsel is to persuade the Court that the evidence placed before it is not such as to justify it in bringing in a verdict of guilty, and any private opinion he may have of the guilt or innocence of his client is entirely beside the point.'

He was astonished to see in Leslie's eyes the flicker of a smile. Piqued, he went on somewhat dryly.

'You're not going to deny that Hammond came to your house at your urgent, and I may even say, hysterical invitation?'

Mrs. Crosbie, hesitating for an instant, seemed to consider.

'They can prove that the letter was taken to his bungalow by one of the house-boys. He rode over on his bicycle.'

'You mustn't expect other people to be stupider than you. The letter will put them on the track of suspicions which have entered nobody's head. I will not tell you what I personally thought when I saw the copy. I do not wish you to tell me anything but what is needed to save your neck.'

Mrs. Crosbie gave a shrill cry. She sprang to her feet, white with terror.

'You don't think they'd hang me?'

'If they came to the conclusion that you hadn't killed Hammond in self-defence, it would be the duty of the assessors to bring in a verdict of guilty. The charge is murder. It would be the duty of the judge to sentence you to death.'

'But what can they prove?' she gasped.

'I don't know what they can prove. You know. I don't want to know. But if their suspicions are aroused, if they begin to make inquiries, if the natives are questioned – what is it that can be discovered?'

She crumpled up suddenly. She fell on the floor before he could catch her. She had fainted. He looked round the room for water, but there was none there, and he did not want to be disturbed. He stretched her out on the floor, and kneeling beside her waited for her to recover. When she opened her eyes he was disconcerted by the ghastly fear that he saw in them.

'Keep quite still,' he said. 'You'll be better in a moment.'

'You won't let them hang me,' she whispered.

She began to cry, hysterically, while in undertones he sought to quieten her.

'For goodness sake pull yourself together,' he said.

'Give me a minute.'

Her courage was amazing. He could see the effort she made to regain her self-control, and soon she was once more calm.

'Let me get up now.'

He gave her his hand and helped her to her feet. Taking her arm, he led her to the chair. She sat down wearily.

'Don't talk to me for a minute or two,' she said.

'Very well.'

When at last she spoke it was to say something which he did not expect. She gave a little sigh.

'I'm afraid I've made rather a mess of things,' she said.

He did not answer, and once more there was a silence.

'Isn't it possible to get hold of the letter?' she said at last.

'I do not think anything would have been said to me about it, if the person in whose possession it is was not prepared to sell it.'

'Who's got it?'

'The Chinese woman who was living in Hammond's house.'

A spot of colour flickered for an instant on Leslie's cheek-bones.

'Does she want an awful lot for it?'

'I imagine that she has a very shrewd idea of its value. I doubt if it would be possible to get hold of it except for a very large sum.'

'Are you going to let me be hanged?'

'Do you think it's so simple as all that to secure possession of an unwelcome piece of evidence? It's no different from suborning a witness. You have no right to make any such suggestion to me.'

'Then what is going to happen to me?'

'Justice must take its course.'

She grew very pale. A little shudder passed through her body.

26

'I put myself in your hands. Of course I have no right to ask you to do anything that isn't proper.'

Mr. Joyce had not bargained for the little break in her voice which her habitual self-restraint made quite intolerably moving. She looked at him with humble eyes, and he thought that if he rejected their appeal they would haunt him for the rest of his life. After all, nothing could bring poor Hammond back to life again. He wondered what really was the explanation of that letter. It was not fair to conclude from it that she had killed Hammond without provocation. He had lived in the East a long time and his sense of professional honour was not perhaps so acute as it had been twenty years before. He stared at the floor. He made up his mind to do something which he knew was unjustifiable, but it stuck in his throat and he felt dully resentful towards Leslie. It embarrassed him a little to speak.

'I don't know exactly what your husband's circumstances are?'

Flushing a rosy red, she shot a swift glance at him.

'He has a good many tin shares and a small share in two or three rubber estates. I suppose he could raise money.'

'He would have to be told what it was for.'

She was silent for a moment. She seemed to think.

'He's in love with me still. He would make any sacrifice for me. Is there any need for him to see the letter?'

Mr. Joyce frowned a little, and, quick to notice, she went on.

'Robert is an old friend of yours. I'm not asking you to do anything for me, I'm asking you to save a rather simple, kind man who never did you any harm from all the pain that's possible.'

Mr. Joyce did not reply. He rose to go and Mrs. Crosbie, with the grace that was natural to her, held out her hand. She was shaken by the scene, and her look was haggard, but she made a brave attempt to speed him with courtesy.

'It's so good of you to take all this trouble for me. I can't begin to tell you how grateful I am.'

Mr. Joyce returned to his office. He sat in his own room, quite still, attempting to do no work, and pondered. His imagination brought him many strange ideas. He shuddered a little. At last there was the discreet knock on the door which he was expecting. Ong Chi Seng came in.

'I was just going out to have my tiffin, sir,' he said.

'All right.'

'I didn't know if there was anything you wanted before I went, sir.'

'I don't think so. Did you make another appointment for Mr. Reed?'

'Yes, sir. He will come at three o'clock.'

'Good.'

Ong Chi Seng turned away, walked to the door, and put his long slim fingers on the handle. Then, as though on an afterthought, he turned back.

'Is there anything you wish me to say to my friend, sir?'

Although Ong Chi Seng spoke English so admirably he had still a difficulty with the letter R, and he pronounced it 'fliend'.

'What friend?'

'About the letter Mrs. Crosbie wrote to Hammond deceased, sir.'

'Oh! I'd forgotten about that. I mentioned it to Mrs. Crosbie and she denies having written anything of the sort. It's evidently a forgery.'

Mr. Joyce took the copy from his pocket and handed it to Ong Chi Seng. Ong Chi Seng ignored the gesture.

'In that case, sir, I suppose there would be no objection if my fliend delivered the letter to the Deputy Public Prosecutor.'

'None. But I don't quite see what good that would do your friend.'

'My fliend, sir, thought it was his duty in the interests of justice.'

'I am the last man in the world to interfere with anyone who wishes to do his duty, Chi Seng.'

The eyes of the lawyer and of the Chinese clerk met. Not the shadow of a smile hovered on the lips of either, but they understood each other perfectly.

'I quite understand, sir,' said Ong Chi Seng, 'but from my study of the case R. *v.* Crosbie I am of opinion that the production of such a letter would be damaging to our client.'

'I have always had a very high opinion of your legal acumen, Chi Seng.'

'It has occurred to me, sir, that if I could persuade my fliend to induce the Chinese woman who has the letter to deliver it into our hands it would save a great deal of trouble.'

Mr. Joyce idly drew faces on his blotting-paper.

'I suppose your friend is a business man. In what circumstances do you think he would be induced to part with the letter?'

'He has not got the letter. The Chinese woman has the letter. He is only a relation of the Chinese woman. She is an ignorant woman; she did not know the value of that letter till my fliend told her.'

'What value did he put on it?'

'Ten thousand dollars, sir.'

'Good God! Where on earth do you suppose Mrs. Crosbie can get ten thousand dollars! I tell you the letter's a forgery.'

He looked up at Ong Chi Seng as he spoke. The clerk was unmoved by the outburst. He stood at the side of the desk, civil, cool and observant.

'Mr. Crosbie owns an eighth share of the Betong

Rubber Estate and a sixth share of the Selantan River Rubber Estate. I have a fliend who will lend him the money on the security of his property.'

'You have a large circle of acquaintance, Chi Seng.'

'Yes, sir.'

'Well, you can tell them all to go to hell. I would never advise Mr. Crosbie to give a penny more than five thousand for a letter that can be very easily explained.'

'The Chinese woman does not want to sell the letter, sir. My fliend took a long time to persuade her. It is useless to offer her less than the sum mentioned.'

Mr. Joyce looked at Ong Chi Seng for at least three minutes. The clerk bore the searching scrutiny without embarrassment. He stood in a respectful attitude with downcast eyes. Mr Joyce knew his man. Clever fellow, Chi Seng, he thought, I wonder how much he's going to get out of it.

'Ten thousand dollars is a very large sum.'

'Mr. Crosbie will certainly pay it rather than see his wife hanged, sir.'

Again Mr. Joyce paused. What more did Chi Seng know than he had said? He must be pretty sure of his ground if he was obviously so unwilling to bargain. That sum had been fixed because whoever it was that was managing the affair knew it was the largest amount that Robert Crosbie could raise.

'Where is the Chinese woman now?' asked Mr. Joyce.

'She is staying at the house of my fliend, sir.'

'Will she come here?'

'I think it more better if you go to her, sir. I can take you to the house tonight and she will give you the letter. She is a very ignorant woman, sir, and she does not understand cheques.'

'I wasn't thinking of giving her a cheque. I will bring banknotes with me.'

'It would only be waste of valuable time to bring less

than ten thousand dollars, sir.'

'I quite understand.'

'I will go and tell my fliend after I have had my tiffin, sir.'

'Very good. You'd better meet me outside the club at ten o'clock tonight.'

'With pleasure, sir,' said Ong Chi Seng.

He gave Mr. Joyce a little bow and left the room. Mr. Joyce went out to have luncheon, too. He went to the club and here, as he had expected, he saw Robert Crosbie. He was sitting at a crowded table, and as he passed him, looking for a place, Mr. Joyce touched him on the shoulder.

'I'd like a word or two with you before you go,' he said.

'Right you are. Let me know when you're ready.'

Mr. Joyce had made up his mind how to tackle him. He played a rubber of bridge after luncheon in order to allow time for the club to empty itself. He did not want on this particular matter to see Crosbie in his office. Presently Crosbie came into the card-room and looked on till the game was finished. The other players went on their various affairs, and the two were left alone.

'A rather unfortunate thing has happened, old man,' said Mr. Joyce, in a tone which he sought to render as casual as possible. 'It appears that your wife sent a letter to Hammond asking him to come to the bungalow on the night he was killed.'

'But that's impossible,' cried Crosbie. 'She's always stated that she had had no communication with Hammond. I know from my own knowledge that she hadn't set eyes on him for a couple of months.'

'The fact remains that the letter exists. It's in the possession of the Chinese woman Hammond was living with. Your wife meant to give you a present on your birthday, and she wanted Hammond to help her to get it. In the emotional excitement that she suffered from after the tragedy, she forgot all about it, and having once denied having any communication with Hammond she was afraid to say that she had made a mistake. It was, of course, very unfortunate, but I daresay it was not un-natural.'

Crosbie did not speak. His large, red face bore an expression of complete bewilderment, and Mr. Joyce was at once relieved and exasperated by his lack of com-prehension. He was a stupid man, and Mr. Joyce had no patience with stupidity. But his distress since the catastrophe had touched a soft spot in the lawyer's heart; and Mrs. Crosbie had struck the right note when she asked him to help her, not for her sake, but for her husband's.

'I need not tell you that it would be very awkward if this letter found its way into the hands of the prosecu-tion. Your wife has lied, and she would be asked to explain the lie. It alters things a little if Hammond did not intrude, an unwanted guest, but came to your house by invitation. It would be easy to arouse in the assessors a certain indecision of mind.'

Mr. Joyce hesitated. He was face to face now with his decision. If it had been a time for humour, he could have smiled at the reflection that he was taking so grave a step, and that the man for whom he was taking it had not the smallest conception of its gravity. If he gave the matter a thought, he probably imagined that what Mr. Joyce was doing was what any lawyer did in the ordin-ary run of business.

'My dear Robert, you are not only my client, but my friend. I think we must get hold of that letter. It'll cost a good deal of money. Except for that I should have pre-ferred to say nothing to you about it.'

'How much?'

'Ten thousand dollars.'

'That's a devil of a lot. With the slump and one thing and another it'll take just about all I've got.'

'Can you get it at once?'

'I suppose so. Old Charlie Meadows will let me have it on my tin shares and on those two estates I'm interested in.'

'Then will you?'

'Is it absolutely necessary?'

'If you want your wife to be acquitted.'

Crosbie grew very red. His mouth sagged strangely. 'But . . .' He could not find words, his face now was purple. 'But I don't understand. She can explain. You don't mean to say they'd find her guilty? They couldn't hang her for putting a noxious vermin out of the way.'

'Of course they wouldn't hang her. They might only find her guilty of manslaughter. She'd probably get off with two or three years.'

Crosbie started to his feet and his red face was distraught with horror.

'Three years.'

Then something seemed to dawn in that slow intelligence of his. His mind was darkness across which shot suddenly a flash of lightning, and though the succeeding darkness was as profound, there remained the memory of something not seen but perhaps just descried. Mr. Joyce saw that Crosbie's big red hands, coarse and hard with all the odd jobs he had set them to, trembled.

'What was the present she wanted to make me?'

'She says she wanted to give you a new gun.'

Once more that great red face flushed a deeper red.

'When have you got to have the money ready?'

There was something odd in his voice now. It sounded as though he spoke with invisible hands clutching at his throat.

'At ten o'clock tonight. I thought you could bring it to my office at about six.'

33

'Is the woman coming to you?'

'No, I'm going to her.'

'I'll bring the money. I'll come with you.'

Mr. Joyce looked at him sharply.

'Do you think there's any need for you to do that? I think it would be better if you left me to deal with this matter by myself.'

'It's my money, isn't it? I'm going to come.'

Mr. Joyce shrugged his shoulders. They rose and shook hands. Mr. Joyce looked at him curiously.

At ten o'clock they met in the empty club.

'Everything all right?' asked Mr. Joyce.

'Yes. I've got the money in my pocket.'

'Let's go then.'

They walked down the steps. Mr. Joyce's car was waiting for them in the square, silent at that hour, and as they came to it Ong Chi Seng stepped out of the shadow of a house. He took his seat beside the driver and gave him a direction. They drove past the Hotel de l'Europe and turned up by the Sailors' Home to get into Victoria Street. Here the Chinese shops were still open, idlers lounged about, and in the roadway rickshaws and motor-cars and gharries gave a busy air to the scene. Suddenly their car stopped and Chi Seng turned round.

'I think it more better if we walk here, sir,' he said.

They got out and he went on. They followed a step or two behind. Then he asked them to stop.

'You wait here, sir. I go in and speak to my fliend.'

He went into a shop, open to the street, where three or four Chinese were standing behind the counter. It was one of those strange shops where nothing was on view, and you wondered what it was they sold there. They saw him address a stout man in a duck suit with a large gold chain across his breast, and the man shot a quick glance out into the night. He gave Chi Seng a key and Chi Seng came out. He beckoned to the two men waiting and slid into a doorway at the side of the shop. They followed him and found themselves at the foot of a flight of stairs.

'If you wait a minute I will light a match,' he said, always resourceful. 'You come upstairs, please.'

He held a Japanese match in front of them, but it scarcely dispelled the darkness and they groped their way up behind him. On the first floor he unlocked a door and going in lit a gas-jet.

'Come in, please,' he said.

It was a small square room, with one window, and the only furniture consisted of two low Chinese beds covered with matting. In one corner was a large chest, with an elaborate lock, and on this stood a shabby tray with an opium pipe on it and a lamp. There was in the room the faint, acrid scent of the drug. They sat down and Ong Chi Seng offered them cigarettes. In a moment the door was opened by the fat Chinaman whom they had seen behind the counter. He bade them good-evening in very good English, and sat down by the side of his fellow-countryman.

'The Chinese woman is just coming,' said Chi Seng.

A boy from the shop brought in a tray with a teapot and cups and the Chinaman offered them a cup of tea. Crosbie refused. The Chinese talked to one another in undertones, but Crosbie and Mr. Joyce were silent. At last there was the sound of a voice outside; someone was calling in a low tone; and the Chinaman went to the door. He opened it, spoke a few words, and ushered a woman in. Mr. Joyce looked at her. He had heard much about her since Hammond's death, but he had never seen her. She was a stoutish person, not very young, with a broad, phlegmatic face, she was powdered and rouged and her eyebrows were a thin black line, but she gave you the impression of a woman of character.

She wore a pale blue jacket and a white skirt, her costume was not quite European nor quite Chinese, but on her feet were little Chinese silk slippers. She wore heavy gold chains round her neck, gold bangles on her wrists, gold ear-rings and elaborate gold pins in her black hair. She walked in slowly, with the air of a woman sure of herself, but with a certain heaviness of tread, and sat down on the bed beside Ong Chi Seng. He said something to her and nodding she gave an incurious glance at the two white men.

'Has she got the letter?' asked Mr. Joyce.

'Yes, sir.'

Crosbie said nothing, but produced a roll of five hundred-dollar notes. He counted out twenty and handed them to Chi Seng.

'Will you see if that is correct?'

The clerk counted them and gave them to the fat Chinaman.

'Quite correct, sir.'

The Chinaman counted them once more and put them in his pocket. He spoke again to the woman and she drew from her bosom a letter. She gave it to Chi Seng who cast his eyes over it.

'This is the right document, sir,' he said, and was about to give it to Mr. Joyce when Crosbie took it from him.

'Let me look at it,' he said.

Mr. Joyce watched him read and then held out his hand for it.

'You'd better let me have it.'

Crosbie folded it up deliberately and put it in his pocket.

'No, I'm going to keep it myself. It's cost me enough money.'

Mr. Joyce made no rejoinder. The three Chinese watched the little passage, but what they thought about it, or whether they thought, it was impossible to tell from their impassive countenances. Mr. Joyce rose to his feet.

'Do you want me any more tonight, sir?' said Ong Chi Seng.

'No.' He knew that the clerk wished to stay behind in order to get his agreed share of the money, and he turned to Crosbie. 'Are you ready?'

Crosbie did not answer, but stood up. The Chinaman went to the door and opened it for them. Chi Seng found a bit of candle and lit it in order to light them down, and the two Chinese accompanied them to the street. They left the woman sitting quietly on the bed smoking a cigarette. When they reached the street the Chinese left them and went once more upstairs.

'What are you going to do with that letter?' asked Mr. Joyce.

'Keep it.'

They walked to where the car was waiting for them and here Mr. Joyce offered his friend a lift. Crosbie shook his head.

'I'm going to walk.' He hesitated a little and shuffled his feet. 'I went to Singapore on the night of Hammond's death partly to buy a new gun that a man I knew wanted to dispose of. Good-night.'

He disappeared quickly into the darkness.

Mr. Joyce was quite right about the trial. The assessors went into court fully determined to acquit Mrs. Crosbie. She gave evidence on her own behalf. She told her story simply and with straightforwardness. The D.P.P. was a kindly man and it was plain that he took no great pleasure in his task. He asked the necessary questions in a deprecating manner. His speech for the prosecution might really have been a speech for the defence, and the assessors took less than five minutes to consider their popular verdict. It was impossible to prevent the great outburst of applause with which it was received by the crowd that packed the court house. The judge congratulated Mrs. Crosbie and she was a free woman.

No one had expressed a more violent disapprobation of Hammond's behaviour than Mrs. Joyce; she was a woman loyal to her friends and she had insisted on the Crosbies staying with her after the trial, for she in common with everyone else had no doubt of the result, till they could make arrangements to go away. It was out of the question for poor, dear, brave Leslie to return to the bungalow at which the horrible catastrophe had taken place. The trial was over by half-past twelve and when they reached the Joyce's house a grand luncheon was awaiting them. Cocktails were ready, Mrs. Joyce's million dollar cocktail was celebrated through all the Malay States, and Mrs. Joyce drank Leslie's health. She was a talkative, vivacious woman, and now she was in the highest spirits. It was fortunate, for the rest of them were silent. She did not wonder, her husband never had much to say, and the other two were naturally exhausted from the long strain to which they had been subjected. During luncheon she carried on a bright and spirited monologue. Then coffee was served.

'Now, children,' she said in her gay, bustling fashion, 'you must have a rest and after tea I shall take you both for a drive to the sea.'

Mr. Joyce, who lunched at home only by exception, had of course to go back to his office.

'I'm afraid I can't do that, Mrs. Joyce,' said Crosbie. 'I've got to get back to the estate at once.'

'Not today?' she cried.

'Yes, now. I've neglected it for too long and I have urgent business. But I shall be very grateful if you will keep Leslie until we have decided what to do.'

Mrs. Joyce was about to expostulate, but her husband prevented her.

'If he must go, he must, and there's an end of it.'

There was something in the lawyer's tone which made her look at him quickly. She held her tongue and there was a moment's silence. Then Crosbie spoke again.

'If you'll forgive me, I'll start at once so that I can get there before dark.' He rose from the table. 'Will you come and see me off, Leslie!'

'Of course.'

They went out of the dining-room together.

'I think that's rather inconsiderate of him,' said Mrs. Joyce. 'He must know that Leslie wants to be with him just now.'

'I'm sure he wouldn't go if it wasn't absolutely necessary.'

'Well, I'll just see that Leslie's room is ready for her. She wants a complete rest, of course, and then amusement.'

Mrs. Joyce left the room and Joyce sat down again. In a short time he heard Crosbie start the engine of his motor-cycle and then noisily scrunch over the gravel of the garden path. He got up and went into the drawing-room. Mrs. Crosbie was standing in the middle of it, looking into space, and in her hand was an open letter. He recognised it. She gave him a glance as he came in and he saw that she was deathly pale.

'He knows,' she whispered.

Mr. Joyce went up to her and took the letter from her hand. He lit a match and set the paper afire. She watched it burn. When he could hold it no longer he dropped it on the tiled floor and they both looked at the paper curl and blacken. Then he trod it into ashes with his foot.

'What does he know?'

She gave him a long, long stare and into her eyes came a strange look. Was it contempt or despair? Mr. Joyce could not tell.

'He knows that Geoff was my lover.'

Mr. Joyce made no movement and uttered no sound.

'He'd been my lover for years. He became my lover almost immediately after he came back from the war. We knew how careful we must be. When we became lovers I pretended I was tired of him, and he seldom came to the house when Robert was there. I used to drive out to a place we knew and he met me, two or three times a week, and when Robert went to Singapore he used to come to the bungalow late, when the boys had gone for the night. We saw one another constantly, all the time, and not a soul had the smallest suspicion of it. And then lately, a year ago, he began to change. I didn't know what was the matter. I couldn't believe that he didn't care for me any more. He always denied it. I was frantic. I made him scenes. Sometimes I thought he hated me. Oh, if you knew what agonies I endured. I passed through hell. I knew he didn't want me any more and I wouldn't let him go. Misery! Misery! I loved him. I'd given him everything. He was all my life. And then I heard he was living with a Chinese woman. I couldn't believe it. I wouldn't believe it. At last I saw her, I saw her with my own eyes, walking in the village, with her gold bracelets and her necklaces, an old, fat, Chinese woman. She was older than I was. Horrible! They all knew in the kampong that she was his mistress. And when I passed her, she looked at me and I knew that she knew I was his mistress too. I sent for him. I told him I must see him. You've read the letter. I was mad to write it. I didn't know what I was doing. I didn't care. I hadn't seen him for ten days. It was a lifetime. And when last we'd parted he took me in his arms and kissed me, and told me not to worry. And he went straight from my arms to hers.'

She had been speaking in a low voice, vehemently, and now she stopped and wrung her hands.

40

'That damned letter. We'd always been so careful. He always tore up any word I wrote to him the moment he'd read it. How was I to know he'd leave that one? He came, and I told him I knew about the Chinawoman. He denied it. He said it was only scandal. I was beside myself. I don't know what I said to him. Oh, I hated him then. I tore him limb from limb. I said everything I could to wound him. I insulted him. I could have spat in his face. And at last he turned on me. He told me he was sick and tired of me and never wanted to see me again. He said I bored him to death. And then he acknowledged that it was true about the Chinawoman. He said he'd known her for years, before the war, and she was the only woman who really meant anything to him, and the rest was just pastime. And he said he was glad I knew, and now at last I'd leave him alone. And then I don't know what happened, I was beside myself, I saw red. I seized the revolver and I fired. He gave a cry and I saw I'd hit him. He staggered and rushed for the verandah. I ran after him and fired again. He fell, and then I stood over him and I fired and fired till the revolver went click, click, and I knew there were no more cartridges.'

At last she stopped, panting. Her face was no longer human, it was distorted with cruelty, and rage and pain. You would never have thought that this quiet, refined woman was capable of such fiendish passion. Mr. Joyce took a step backwards. He was absolutely aghast at the sight of her. It was not a face, it was a gibbering, hideous mask. Then they heard a voice calling from another room, a loud, friendly, cheerful voice. It was Mrs. Joyce.

'Come along, Leslie darling, your room's ready. You must be dropping with sleep.'

Mrs. Crosbie's features gradually composed themselves. Those passions, so clearly delineated, were smoothed away as with your hand you would smooth a crumpled paper, and in a minute the face was cool and calm and unlined. She was a trifle pale, but her lips broke into a pleasant, affable smile. She was once more the well-bred and even distinguished woman.

'I'm coming, Dorothy dear. I'm sorry to give you so much trouble.'

The Four Dutchmen

The Van Dorth Hotel at Singapore was far from grand. The bedrooms were dingy and the mosquito nets patched and darned; the bath-houses, all in a row and detached from the bedrooms, were dank and smelly. But it had character. The people who stayed there, masters of tramps whose round ended at Singapore, mining engineers out of a job and planters taking a holiday, to my mind bore a more romantic air than the smart folk, globe-trotters, government officials and their wives, wealthy merchants, who gave luncheon parties at the Europe and played golf and danced and were fashionable. The Van Dorth had a billiard-room, with a table with a threadbare cloth, where ships' engineers and clerks in insurance offices played snooker. The dining-room was large and bare and silent. Dutch families on the way to Sumatra ate solidly through their dinner without exchanging a word with one another, and single gentlemen on a business trip from Batavia devoured a copious meal while they intently read their paper. On two days a week there was *rysttafel* and then a few residents of Singapore who had a fancy for this dish came for tiffin. The Van Dorth Hotel should have been a depressing place, but somehow it wasn't; its quaintness saved it. It had a faint aroma of something strange and half-forgotten. There was a scrap of garden facing the street where you could sit in the shade of trees and drink cold beer. In that crowded and busy city, though motors whizzed past and rickshaws passed continuously, the coolies' feet pattering on the road and their bells ringing, it had the remote peacefulness of a corner of Holland. It was the third time I had stayed at the Van Dorth. I had been told about it first by the skipper of a Dutch tramp, the S.S. *Utrecht*, on which I had travelled from Merauke in New Guinea to Macassar. The journey took the best part of a month, since the ship stopped at a number of islands in the Malay Archipelago, the Aru and the Kei Islands, Banda-Neira, Amboina and others of which I have even forgotten the names, sometimes for an hour or two, sometimes for a day, to take on or discharge cargo. It was a charming, monotonous and diverting trip. When we dropped anchor the agent came out in his launch, and generally the Dutch Resident, and we gathered on deck under the awning and the captain ordered beer. The news of the island was exchanged for the news of the world. We brought papers and mail. If we were staying long enough the Resident asked us to dinner and, leaving the ship in charge of the second officer, we all (the captain, the chief officer, the engineer, the super-cargo and I) piled into the launch and went ashore. We spent a merry evening. These little islands, one so like another, allured my fancy just because I knew that I should never see them again. It made them strangely unreal, and as we sailed away and they vanished into the sea and sky it was only by an effort of the imagination that I could persuade myself that they did not with my last glimpse of them cease to exist.

But there was nothing illusive, mysterious or fantastic about the captain, the chief officer, the chief engineer and the supercargo. Their solidity was amazing. They were the four fattest men I ever saw. At first I had great difficulty in telling them apart, for though one, the supercargo, was dark and the others were fair, they looked astonishingly alike. They were all big, with large round bare red faces, with large fat arms and large fat legs and large fat bellies. When they went ashore they buttoned up their stengah-shifters and then their great double chins bulged over the collars and they looked as though they would choke. But generally they wore them unbuttoned. They sweated freely and wiped their shiny faces with bandanas and vigorously fanned themselves with palm-leaf fans.

It was a treat to see them at tiffin. Their appetites were enormous. They had *rysttafel* every day, and each seemed to vie with the other how high he could pile his plate. They loved it hot and strong.

'In dis country you can't eat a ting onless it's tasty,' said the skipper.

'De only way to keep yourself up in dis country is to eat hearty,' said the chief.

They were the greatest friends, all four of them; they were like schoolboys together, playing absurd little pranks with one another. They knew each other's jokes by heart and no sooner did one of them start the familiar lines than he would splutter with laughter so violently, the heavy shaking laughter of the fat man, that he could not go on, and then the others began to laugh too. They rolled about in their chairs, and grew redder and redder, hotter and hotter, till the skipper shouted for beer, and each, gasping but happy, drank his bottle in one enchanted draught. They had been on this run together for five years and when a little time before the chief officer had been offered a ship of his own he refused it. He would not leave his companions. They had made up their minds that when the first of them retired they would all retire.

'All friends and a good ship. Good grub and good beer. Vot can a sensible man vant more?'

At first they were a little standoffish with me. Although the ship had accommodation for half a dozen passengers, they did not often get any, and never one whom they did not know. I was a stranger and a foreigner. They liked their bit of fun and did not want anyone to interfere with it. But they were all of them very fond of bridge, and on occasion the chief and the engineer had duties that prevented one or the other from playing. They were willing to put up with me when they discovered that I was ready to make a fourth whenever I was wanted. Their bridge was as incredibly fantastic as they were. They played for infinitesimal stakes, five cents a hundred: they did not want to win one another's money, they said, it was the game they liked. But what a game! Each was wildly determined to play the hand and hardly one was dealt without at least a small slam being declared. The rule was that if you could get a peep at somebody else's cards you did and if you could get away with a revoke you told your partner when there was no danger it could be claimed and you both roared with laughter till the tears rolled down your fat cheeks. But if your partner had insisted on taking the bid away from you and had called a grand slam on five spades to the queen, whereas you were positive on your seven little diamonds you could have made it easily, you could always score him off by redoubling without a trick in your hand. He went down two or three thousand and the glasses on the table danced with the laughter that shook your opponents.

I could never remember their difficult Dutch names, but knowing them anonymously as it were, only by the duties they performed, as one knows the characters, Pantaloon, Harlequin and Punchinello, of the old Italian comedy, added grotesquely to their drollery. The mere sight of them, all four together, set you laughing, and I think they got a good deal of amusement from the astonishment they caused in strangers. They boasted that they were the four most famous Dutchmen in the East Indies. To me not the least comic part of them was their serious side. Sometimes late at night, when they had given up all pretence of still wearing their uniforms, and one or the other of them lay by my side on a long chair in a pyjama jacket and a sarong he would grow sentimental. The chief engineer, due to retire soon, was meditating marriage with a widow whom he had met when last he was home and spending the rest of his life in a little town with old red brick houses on the shores of the Zuyder Zee. But the captain was very susceptible to the charms of the native girls and his thick English became almost unintelligible from emotion when he described to me the effect they had on him. One of these days he would buy himself a house on the hills in Java and marry a pretty little Javanese. They were so small and so gentle and they made no noise, and he would dress her in silk sarongs and give her gold chains to wear round her neck and gold bangles to put on her arms. But the chief mocked him.

'Silly all dat is. Silly. She goes mit all your friends and de houseboys and everybody. By de time you retire, my dear, vot you'll vant vill be a nurse, not a vife.'

'Me?' cried the skipper. 'I shall want a vife ven I'm eighty!'

He had picked up a little thing last time the ship was at Macassar and as we approached that port he began to be all of a flutter. The chief officer shrugged fat and indulgent shoulders. The captain was always losing his head over one brazen hussy after another, but his passion never survived the interval between one stop at a port and the next, and then the chief was called in to smooth out the difficulties that ensued. And so it would be this time.

'De old man suffers from fatty degeneration of de heart. But so long as I'm dere to look after him not much harm comes of it. He vastes his money and dat's a pity, but as long as he's got it to vaste, why shouldn't he?'

The chief officer had a philosophic soul.

At Macassar then I disembarked, and bade farewell to my four fat friends.

'Make another journey with us,' they said. 'Come back next year or the year after. You'll find us all here just the same as ever.'

A good many months had passed since then and I had wandered through more than one strange land. I had been to Bali and Java and Sumatra; I had been to Cambodia and Annam; and now, feeling as though I were home again, I sat in the garden of the Van Dorth Hotel. It was cool in the very early morning and having had breakfast I was looking at back numbers of the *Straits Times* to find out what had been happening in the world since last I had been within reach of papers. Nothing very much. Suddenly my eyes caught a head-line: *The Utrecht Tragedy. Supercargo and Chief Engineer. Not Guilty.* I read the paragraph carelessly and then I sat up. The *Utrecht* was the ship of my four fat Dutchmen and apparently the supercargo and the chief engineer had been on trial for murder. It couldn't be my two fat friends. The names were given, but the names meant nothing to me. The trial had taken place in Batavia. No details were given in this paragraph; it was only a brief announcement that after the judges had considered the speeches of the prosecution and of the defence their verdict was as stated. I was astounded. It was incredible that the men I knew could have committed a murder. I could not find out who had been murdered. I looked through back numbers of the paper. Nothing.

I got up and went to the manager of the hotel, a genial Dutchman, who spoke admirable English, and showed him the paragraph.

'That's the ship I sailed on. I was in her for nearly a month. Surely these fellows aren't the men I knew. The men I knew were enormously fat.'

'Yes, that's right,' he answered. 'They were celebrated all through the Dutch East Indies, the four fattest men in the service. It's been a terrible thing. It made a great sensation. And they were friends. I knew them all. The best fellows in the world.'

'But what happened?'

He told me the story and answered my horrified questions. But there were things I wanted to know that he couldn't tell me. It was all confused. It was unbelievable. What actually had happened was only conjecture. Then someone claimed the manager's attention and I went back to the garden. It was getting hot now and I went up to my room. I was strangely shattered.

It appeared that on one of the trips the captain took with him a Malay girl that he had been carrying on with and I wondered it if was the one he had been so eager to see when I was on board. The other three had been against her coming – what did they want with a woman in the ship? it would spoil everything – but the captain insisted and she came. I think they were all jealous of her. On that journey they didn't have the fun they generally had. When they wanted to play bridge the skipper was dallying with the girl in his cabin; when they touched at a port and went ashore the time seemed long to him till he could get back to her. He was crazy about her. It was the end of all their larks. The chief officer was more bitter against her than anybody: he was the captain's particular chum, they had been shipmates ever since they first came out from Holland; more than once high words passed between them on the subject of the captain's infatuation. Presently those old friends spoke to one another only when their duties demanded it. It was the end of the good fellowship that had so long obtained between the four fat men. Things went from bad to worse. There was a feeling among the junior officers that something untoward was pending.

49

Uneasiness. Tension. Then one night the ship was aroused by the sound of a shot and the screams of the Malay girl. The supercargo and the chief engineer tumbled out of their bunks and they found the captain, a revolver in his hand, at the door of the chief officer's cabin. He pushed past them and went on deck. They entered and found the chief officer dead and the girl cowering behind the door. The captain had found them in bed together and had killed the chief. How he had discovered what was going on didn't seem to be known, nor what was the meaning of the intrigue. Had the chief induced the girl to come to his cabin in order to get back on the captain, or had she, knowing his ill will and anxious to placate him, lured him to become her lover? It was a mystery that would never be solved. A dozen possible explanations flashed across my mind. While the engineer and the supercargo were in the cabin, horror-struck at the sight before them, another shot was heard. They knew at once what had happened. They rushed up the companion. The captain had gone to his cabin and blown his brains out. Then the story grew dark and enigmatic. Next morning the Malay girl was nowhere to be found and when the second officer who had taken command of the ship reported this to the supercargo, the supercargo said: 'She's probably jumped overboard. It's the best thing she could have done. Good riddance to bad rubbish.' But one of the sailors on the watch, just before dawn, had seen the supercargo and the chief engineer carry something up on deck, a bulky package, about the size of a native woman, look about them to see that they were unobserved, and drop it overboard; and it was said all over the ship that these two to avenge their friends had sought the girl out in her cabin and strangled her and flung her body into the sea. When the ship arrived at Macassar they were arrested and taken to Batavia to be tried for murder. The evidence was flimsy and they were acquitted. But all through the East Indies they knew that the supercargo and the chief engineer had executed justice on the trollop who had caused the death of the two men they loved.

And thus ended the comic and celebrated friendship of the four fat Dutchmen.

The Outstation

The new assistant arrived in the afternoon. When the Resident, Mr. Warburton, was told that the prahu was in sight he put on his solar topee and went down to the landing-stage. The guard, eight little Dyak soldiers, stood to attention as he passed. He noted with satisfaction that their bearing was martial, their uniforms neat and clean, and their guns shining. They were a credit to him. From the landing-stage he watched the bend of the river round which in a moment the boat would sweep. He looked very smart in his spotless ducks and white shoes. He held under his arm a gold-headed Malacca cane which had been given him by the Sultan of Perak. He awaited the newcomer with mingled feelings. There was more work in the district than one man could properly do, and during his periodical tours of the country under his charge it had been inconvenient to leave the station in the hands of a native clerk, but he had been so long the only white man there that he could not face the arrival of another without misgiving. He was accustomed to loneliness. During the war he had not seen an English face for three years; and once when he was instructed to put up an afforestation officer he was seized with panic, so that when the stranger was due to arrive, having arranged everything for his reception, he wrote a note telling him he was obliged to go up river, and fled; he remained away till he was informed by a messenger that his guest had left.

Now the prahu appeared in the broad reach. It was manned by prisoners, Dyaks under various sentences, and a couple of warders were waiting on the landing-stage to take them back to jail. They were sturdy fellows, used to the river, and they rowed with a powerful stroke. As the boat reached the side a man got out from under the attap awning and stepped on shore. The guard presented arms.

'Here we are at last. By God, I'm as cramped as the devil. I've brought you your mail.'

He spoke with exuberant joviality. Mr. Warburton politely held out his hand.

'Mr. Cooper, I presume?'

'That's right. Were you expecting anyone else?'

The question had a facetious intent, but the Resident did not smile.

'My name is Warburton. I'll show you your quarters. They'll bring your kit along.'

He preceded Cooper along the narrow pathway and they entered a compound in which stood a small bungalow.

'I've had it made as habitable as I could, but of course no one has lived in it for a good many years.'

It was built on piles. It consisted of a long living-room which opened on to a broad verandah, and behind, on each side of a passage, were two bedrooms.

'This'll do me all right,' said Cooper.

'I daresay you want to have a bath and a change. I shall be very much pleased if you'll dine with me to-night. Will eight o'clock suit you?'

'Any old time will do for me.'

The Resident gave a polite but slightly disconcerted smile, and withdrew. He returned to the Fort where his own residence was. The impression which Allen Cooper had given him was not very favourable, but he was a fair man, and he knew that it was unjust to form an opinion on so brief a glimpse. Cooper seemed to be about thirty. He was a tall, thin fellow, with a sallow face in which there was not a spot of colour. It was a face all in one tone. He had a large, hooked nose and blue eyes. When, entering the bungalow, he had taken off his topee and flung it to a waiting boy, Mr. Warburton noticed that his large skull, covered with short, brown hair, contrasted somewhat oddly with a weak, small chin. He was dressed in khaki shorts and a khaki shirt, but they were shabby and soiled; and his battered topee had not been cleaned for days. Mr. Warburton reflected that the young man had spent a week on a coasting steamer and had passed the last forty-eight hours lying in the bottom of a prahu.

'We'll see what he looks like when he comes in to dinner.'

He went into his room where his things were as neatly laid out as if he had an English valet, undressed, and, walking down the stairs to the bathhouse, sluiced himself with cool water. The only concession he made to the climate was to wear a white dinner-jacket; but otherwise, in a boiled shirt and a high collar, silk socks and patent-leather shoes, he dressed as formally as though he were dining at his club in Pall Mall. A careful host, he went into the dining-room to see that the table was properly laid. It was gay with orchids, and the silver shone brightly. The napkins were folded into elaborate shapes. Shaded candles in silver candlesticks shed a soft light. Mr. Warburton smiled his approval and returned to the sitting-room to await his guest. Presently he appeared. Cooper was wearing the khaki shorts, the khaki shirt, and the ragged jacket in which he had landed. Mr. Warburton's smile of greeting froze on his face.

'Hulloa, you're all dressed up,' said Cooper. 'I didn't know you were going to do that. I very nearly put on a sarong.'

'It doesn't matter at all. I daresay your boys were busy.'

'You needn't have bothered to dress on my account, you know.'

'I didn't. I always dress for dinner.'

'Even when you're alone?'

'Especially when I'm alone,' replied Mr. Warburton, with a frigid stare.

He saw a twinkle of amusement in Cooper's eyes, and he flushed an angry red. Mr. Warburton was a hot-tempered man; you might have guessed that from his red face with its pugnacious features and from his red hair now growing white; his blue eyes, cold as a rule and observing, could flash with a sudden wrath; but he was a man of the world and he hoped a just one. He must do his best to get on with this fellow.

'When I lived in London I moved in circles in which it would have been just as eccentric not to dress for dinner every night as not to have a bath every morning. When I came to Borneo I saw no reason to discontinue so good a habit. For three years during the war I never saw a white man. I never omitted to dress on a single occasion on which I was well enough to come in to dinner. You have not been very long in this country; believe me, there is no better way to maintain the proper pride which you should have in yourself. When a white man surrenders in the slightest degree to the influences that surround him he very soon loses his self-respect, and when he loses his self-respect you may be quite sure that the natives will soon cease to respect him.'

'Well, if you expect me to put on a boiled shirt and a stiff collar in this heat I'm afraid you'll be disappointed.'

'When you are dining in your own bungalow you will, of course, dress as you think fit, but when you do me the pleasure of dining with me, perhaps you will come to the conclusion that it is only polite to wear the costume usual in civilised society.'

Two Malay boys, in sarongs and songkoks, with

smart white coats and brass buttons, came in, one bearing gin pahits, and the other a tray on which were olives and anchovies. Then they went in to dinner. Mr. Warburton flattered himself that he had the best cook, a Chinese, in Borneo, and he took great trouble to have as good food as in the difficult circumstances was possible. He exercised much ingenuity in making the best of his materials.

'Would you care to look at the menu?' he said, handing it to Cooper.

It was written in French and the dishes had resounding names. They were waited on by the two boys. In opposite corners of the room two more waved immense fans, and so gave movement to the sultry air. The fare was sumptuous and the champagne excellent.

'Do you do yourself like this every day?' said Cooper.

Mr. Warburton gave the menu a careless glance.

'I have not noticed that the dinner is any different from usual,' he said. 'I eat very little myself, but I make a point of having a proper dinner served to me every night. It keeps the cook in practice and it's good discipline for the boys.'

The conversation proceeded with effort. Mr. Warburton was elaborately courteous, and it may be that he found a slightly malicious amusement in the embarrassment which he thereby occasioned in his companion. Cooper had not been more than a few months in Sembulu, and Mr. Warburton's enquiries about friends of his in Kuala Solor were soon exhausted.

'By the way,' he said presently, 'did you meet a lad called Hennerley? He's come out recently, I believe.'

'Oh yes, he's in the police. A rotten bounder.'

'I should hardly have expected him to be that. His uncle is my friend Lord Barraclough. I had a letter from Lady Barraclough only the other day asking me to look out for him.'

'I heard he was related to somebody or other. I suppose that's how he got the job. He's been to Eton and Oxford and he doesn't forget to let you know it.'

'You surprise me,' said Mr. Warburton. 'All his family have been at Eton and Oxford for a couple of hundred years. I should have expected him to take it as a matter of course.'

'I thought him a damned prig.'

'To what school did you go?'

'I was born in Barbados. I was educated there.'

'Oh, I see.'

Mr. Warburton managed to put so much offensiveness into his brief reply that Cooper flushed. For a moment he was silent.

'I've had two or three letters from Kuala Solor,' continued Mr. Warburton, 'and my impression was that young Hennerley was a great success. They say he's a first-rate sportsman.'

'Oh, yes, he's very popular. He's just the sort of fellow they would like in K.S. I haven't got much use for the first-rate sportsman myself. What does it amount to in the long run that a man can play golf and tennis better than other people? And who cares if he can make a break of seventy-five at billiards? They attach a damned sight too much importance to that sort of thing in England.'

'Do you think so? I was under the impression that the first-rate sportsman had come out of the war certainly no worse than anyone else.'

'Oh, if you're going to talk of the war then I do know what I'm talking about. I was in the same regiment as Hennerley and I can tell you that the men couldn't stick him at any price.'

'How do you know?'

'Because I was one of the men.'

'Oh, you hadn't got a commission.'

'A fat chance I had of getting a commission. I was what was called a Colonial. I hadn't been to a public school and I had no influence. I was in the ranks the whole damned time.'

Cooper frowned. He seemed to have difficulty in preventing himself from breaking out into violent invective. Mr. Warburton watched him, his little blue eyes narrowed, watched him and formed his opinion. Changing the conversation, he began to speak to Cooper about the work that would be required of him, and as the clock struck ten he rose.

'Well, I won't keep you any more. I daresay you're tired by your journey.'

They shook hands.

'Oh, I say, look here,' said Cooper, 'I wonder if you can find me a boy. The boy I had before never turned up when I was starting from K.S. He took my kit on board and all that, and then disappeared. I didn't know he wasn't there till we were out of the river.'

'I'll ask my head-boy. I have no doubt he can find you someone.'

'All right. Just tell him to send the boy along and if I like the look of him I'll take him.'

There was a moon, so that no lantern was needed. Cooper walked across from the Fort to his bungalow.

'I wonder why on earth they've sent me a fellow like that?' reflected Mr. Warburton. 'If that's the kind of man they're going to get out now I don't think much of it.'

He strolled down his garden. The Fort was built on the top of a little hill and the garden ran down to the river's edge; on the bank was an arbour, and hither it was his habit to come after dinner to smoke a cheroot. And often from the river that flowed below him a voice was heard, the voice of some Malay too timorous to venture into the light of day, and a complaint or an accusation was softly wafted to his ears, a piece of information was whispered to him or a useful hint, which otherwise would never have come into his official ken. He threw himself heavily into a long rattan chair. Cooper! An envious, ill-bred fellow, bumptious, self-assertive and vain. But Mr. Warburton's irritation could not withstand the silent beauty of the night. The air was scented with the sweet-smelling flowers of a tree that grew at the entrance to the arbour, and the fireflies, sparkling dimly, flew with their slow and silvery flight. The moon made a pathway on the broad river for the light feet of Siva's bride, and on the further bank a row of palm trees was delicately silhouetted against the sky. Peace stole into the soul of Mr. Warburton.

He was a queer creature and he had had a singular career. At the age of twenty-one he had inherited a considerable fortune, a hundred thousand pounds, and when he left Oxford he threw himself into the gay life, which in those days (now Mr. Warburton was a man of four and fifty) offered itself to the young man of good family. He had his flat in Mount Street, his private hansom, and his hunting-box in Warwickshire. He went to all the places where the fashionable congregate. He was handsome, amusing, and generous. He was a figure in the society of London in the early nineties, and society then had not lost its exclusiveness nor its brilliance. The Boer War which shook it was unthought of; the Great War which destroyed it was prophesied only by the pessimists. It was no unpleasant thing to be a rich young man in those days, and Mr. Warburton's chimney-piece during the season was packed with cards for one great function after another. Mr. Warburton displayed them with complacency. For Mr. Warburton was a snob. He was not a timid snob, a little ashamed of being impressed by his betters, nor a snob who sought the intimacy of persons who had acquired celebrity in politics or notoriety in the arts, nor the snob who was dazzled by riches; he was the naked, unadulterated common snob who dearly loved a lord. He was touchy and quick-tempered, but he would much rather have been snubbed by a person of quality than flattered by a commoner. His name figured insignificantly in *Burke's Peerage*, and it was marvellous to watch the ingenuity he used to mention his distant relationship to the noble family he belonged to; but never a word did he say of the honest Liverpool manufacturer from whom, through his mother, a Miss Gubbins, he had come by his fortune. It was the terror of his fashionable life that at Cowes, maybe, or at Ascot, when he was with a duchess or even with a prince of the blood, one of these relatives would claim acquaintance with him.

His failing was too obvious not soon to become notorious, but its extravagance saved it from being merely despicable. The great whom he adored laughed at him, but in their hearts felt his adoration not unnatural. Poor Warburton was a dreadful snob, of course, but after all he was a good fellow. He was always ready to back a bill for an impecunious nobleman, and if you were in a tight corner you could safely count on him for a hundred pounds. He gave good dinners. He played whist badly, but never minded how much he lost if the company was select. He happened to be a gambler, an unlucky one, but he was a good loser, and it was impossible not to admire the coolness with which he lost five hundred pounds at a sitting. His passion for cards, almost as strong as his passion for titles, was the cause of his undoing. The life he led was expensive and his gambling losses were formidable. He began to plunge more heavily, first on horses, and then on the Stock Exchange. He had a certain simplicity of character, and the unscrupulous found him an ingenuous prey. I do not know if he ever realised that his smart friends laughed at him behind his back, but I think he had an obscure instinct that he could not afford to appear other than careless of his money. He got into the hands of money-lenders. At the age of thirty-four he was ruined.

He was too much imbued with the spirit of his class to hesitate in the choice of his next step. When a man in his set had run through his money, he went out to the colonies. No one heard Mr. Warburton repine. He made no complaint because a noble friend had advised a disastrous speculation, he pressed nobody to whom he had lent money to repay it, he paid his debts (if he had only known it, the despised blood of the Liverpool manufacturer came out in him there), sought help from no one, and, never having done a stroke of work in his life, looked for a means of livelihood. He remained cheerful, unconcerned and full of humour. He had no wish to make anyone with whom he happened to be uncomfortable by the recital of his misfortune. Mr. Warburton was a snob, but he was also a gentleman.

The only favour he asked of any of the great friends in whose daily company he had lived for years was a recommendation. The able man who was at that time Sultan of Sembulu took him into his service. The night before he sailed he dined for the last time at his club.

'I hear you're going away, Warburton,' the old Duke of Hereford said to him.

'Yes, I'm going to Borneo.'

'Good God, what are you going there for?'

'Oh, I'm broke.'

'Are you? I'm sorry. Well, let us know when you come back. I hope you have a good time.'

'Oh yes. Lots of shooting, you know.'

The Duke nodded and passed on. A few hours later Mr. Warburton watched the coast of England recede into the mist, and he left behind everything which to him made life worth living.

Twenty years had passed since then. He kept up a

busy correspondence with various great ladies and his letters were amusing and chatty. He never lost his love for titled persons and paid careful attention to the announcements in *The Times* (which reached him six weeks after publication) of their comings and goings. He perused the column which records births, deaths, and marriages, and he was always ready with his letter of congratulation or condolence. The illustrated papers told him how people looked and on his periodical visits to England, able to take up the threads as though they had never been broken, he knew all about any new person who might have appeared on the social surface. His interest in the world of fashion was as vivid as when himself had been a figure in it. It still seemed to him the only thing that mattered.

But insensibly another interest had entered into his life. The position he found himself in flattered his vanity; he was no longer the sycophant craving the smiles of the great, he was the master whose word was law. He was gratified by the guard of Dyak soldiers who presented arms as he passed. He liked to sit in judgement on his fellow men. It pleased him to compose quarrels between rival chiefs. When the head-hunters were troublesome in the old days he set out to chastise them with a thrill of pride in his own behaviour. He was too vain not to be of dauntless courage, and a pretty story was told of his coolness in adventuring single-handed into a stockaded village and demanding the surrender of a bloodthirsty pirate. He became a skilful administrator. He was strict, just and honest.

And little by little he conceived a deep love for the Malays. He interested himself in their habits and customs. He was never tired of listening to their talk. He admired their virtues, and with a smile and a shrug of the shoulders condoned their vices.

'In my day,' he would say, 'I have been on intimate

terms with some of the greatest gentlemen in England, but I have never known finer gentlemen than some well-born Malays whom I am proud to call my friends.'

He liked their courtesy and their distinguished manners, their gentleness and their sudden passions. He knew by instinct exactly how to treat them. He had a genuine tenderness for them. But he never forgot that he was an English gentleman, and he had no patience with the white men who yielded to native customs. He made no surrenders. And he did not imitate so many of the white men in taking a native woman to wife, for an intrigue of this nature, however sanctified by custom, seemed to him not only shocking but undignified. A man who had been called George by Albert Edward, Prince of Wales could hardly be expected to have any connection with a native. And when he returned to Borneo from his visits to England it was now with something like relief. His friends, like himself, were no longer young, and there was a new generation which looked upon him as a tiresome old man. It seemed to him that the England of today had lost a good deal of what he had loved in the England of his youth. But Borneo remained the same. It was home to him now. He meant to remain in the service as long as was possible, and the hope in his heart was that he would die before at last he was forced to retire. He had stated in his will that wherever he died he wished his body to be brought back to Sembulu, and buried among the people he loved within the sound of the softly flowing river.

But these emotions he kept hidden from the eyes of men; and no one, seeing this spruce, stout, well-set up man, with his clean-shaven strong face and his whitening hair, would have dreamed that he cherished so profound a sentiment.

He knew how the work of the station should be done, and during the next few days he kept a suspicious eye on his assistant. He saw very soon that he was painstaking and competent. The only fault he had to find with him was that he was brusque with the natives.

'The Malays are shy and very sensitive,' he said to him. 'I think you will find that you will get much better results if you take care always to be polite, patient and kindly.'

Cooper gave a short, grating laugh.

'I was born in Barbados and I was in Africa in the war. I don't think there's much about niggers that I don't know.'

'I know nothing,' said Mr. Warburton acidly. 'But we were not talking of them. We were talking of Malays.'

'Aren't they niggers?'

'You are very ignorant,' replied Mr. Warburton.

He said no more.

On the first Sunday after Cooper's arrival he asked him to dinner. He did everything ceremoniously, and though they had met on the previous day in the office and later, on the Fort verandah where they drank a gin and bitters together at six o'clock, he sent a polite note across to the bungalow by a boy. Cooper, however, unwillingly, came in evening dress and Mr. Warburton, though gratified that his wish was respected, noticed with disdain that the young man's clothes were badly cut and his shirt ill-fitting. But Mr. Warburton was in a good temper that evening.

'By the way,' he said to him, as he shook hands, 'I've talked to my head-boy about finding you someone and he recommends his nephew. I've seen him and he seems a bright and willing lad. Would you like to see him?'

'I don't mind.'

'He's waiting now.'

Mr. Warburton called his boy and told him to send for his nephew. In a moment a tall, slender youth of twenty appeared. He had large dark eyes and a good profile. He was very neat in his sarong, a little white coat, and a fez, without a tassel, of plum coloured velvet. He answered to the name of Abas. Mr. Warburton looked on him with approval, and his manner insensibly softened as he spoke to him in fluent and idiomatic Malay. He was inclined to be sarcastic with white people, but with the Malays he had a happy mixture of condescension and kindliness. He stood in the place of the Sultan. He knew perfectly how to preserve his own dignity, and at the same time put a native at his ease.

'Will he do?' said Mr. Warburton, turning to Cooper.

'Yes, I daresay he's no more of a scoundrel than any of the rest of them.'

Mr. Warburton informed the boy that he was engaged, and dismissed him.

'You're very lucky to get a boy like that,' he told Cooper. 'He belongs to a very good family. They came over from Malacca nearly a hundred years ago.'

'I don't much mind if the boy who cleans my shoes and brings me a drink when I want it has blue blood in his veins or not. All I ask is that he should do what I tell him and look sharp about it.'

Mr. Warburton pursed his lips, but made no reply.

They went in to dinner. It was excellent, and the wine was good. Its influence presently had its effect on them, and they talked not only without acrimony, but even with friendliness. Mr. Warburton liked to do himself well, and on Sunday night he made it a habit to do himself even a little better than usual. He began to think he was unfair to Cooper. Of course he was not a gentleman, but that was not his fault, and when you got to know him it might be that he would turn out a very good fellow. His faults, perhaps, were faults of manner. And he was certainly good at his work, quick, conscientious and thorough. When they reached the dessert Mr. Warburton was feeling kindly disposed towards all mankind.

'This is your first Sunday, and I'm going to give you a very special glass of port. I've only got about two dozen of it left and I keep it for special occasions.'

He gave his boy instructions and presently the bottle was brought. Mr. Warburton watched the boy open it.

'I got this port from my old friend Charles Hollington. He'd had it for forty years, and I've had it for a good many. He was well-known to have the best cellar in England.'

'Is he a wine merchant?'

'Not exactly,' smiled Mr. Warburton. 'I was speaking of Lord Hollington of Castle Reagh. He's one of the richest peers in England. A very old friend of mine. I was at Eton with his brother.'

This was an opportunity that Mr. Warburton could never resist, and he told a little anecdote of which the only point seemed to be that he knew an Earl. The port was certainly very good; he drank a glass and then a second. He lost all caution. He had not talked to a white man for months. He began to tell stories. He showed himself in the company of the great. Hearing him, you would have thought that at one time ministries were formed and policies decided on his suggestion whispered into the ear of a duchess or thrown over the dinner-table to be gratefully acted on by the confidential adviser of the sovereign. The old days at Ascot, Goodwood and Cowes lived again for him. Another glass of port. There were the great house-parties in Yorkshire and in Scotland to which he went every year.

'I had a man called Foreman then, the best valet I ever had, and why do you think he gave me notice? You know in the Housekeeper's Room the ladies' maids and the gentlemen's gentlemen sit according to the precedence of their masters. He told me he was sick of going to party after party at which I was the only commoner. It meant that he always had to sit at the bottom of the table, and all the best bits were taken before a dish reached him. I told the story to the old Duke of Hereford, and he roared. "By God, sir," he said, "if I were King of England, I'd make you a Viscount just to give your man a chance." "Take him yourself, Duke," I said. "He's the best valet I've ever had." "Well, Warburton," he said, "if he's good enough for you he's good enough for me. Send him along." '

Then there was Monte Carlo were Mr. Warburton and the Grand Duke Fyodor, playing in partnership, had broken the bank one evening; and there was Marienbad. At Marienbad Mr. Warburton had played baccarat with Edward VII.

'He was only Prince of Wales then, of course. I remember him saying to me, "George, if you draw on a five you'll lose your shirt." He was right; I don't think he ever said a truer word in his life. He was a wonderful man. I always said he was the greatest diplomatist in Europe. But I was a young fool in those days, I hadn't the sense to take his advice. If I had, if I'd never drawn on a five, I daresay I shouldn't be here today.'

Cooper was watching him. His brown eyes, deep in their sockets, were hard and supercilious, and on his lips was a mocking smile. He had heard a good deal about Mr. Warburton in Kuala Solor, not a bad sort, and he ran his district like clockwork, they said, but by heaven, what a snob! They laughed at him good-naturedly, for it was impossible to dislike a man who was so generous and so kindly, and Cooper had already heard the story of the Prince of Wales and the game of baccarat. But Cooper listened without indulgence. From the beginning he had resented the Resident's manner. He was very sensitive, and he writhed under Mr. Warburton's polite sarcasms. Mr. Warburton had a knack of receiving a remark of which he disapproved with a devastating silence. Cooper had lived little in

England and he had a peculiar dislike of the English. He resented especially the public-school boy since he always feared that he was going to patronise him. He was so much afraid of others putting on airs with him that, in order as it were to get in first, he put on such airs as to make everyone think him insufferably conceited.

'Well, at all events the war has done one good thing for us,' he said at last. 'It's smashed up the power of the aristocracy. The Boer War started it, and 1914 put the lid on.'

'The great families of England are doomed,' said Mr. Warburton with the complacent melancholy of an *émigré* who remembered the court of Louis XV. 'They cannot afford any longer to live in their splendid palaces and their princely hospitality will soon be nothing but a memory.'

'And a damned good job too in my opinion.'

'My poor Cooper, what can you know of the glory that was Greece and the grandeur that was Rome?'

Mr. Warburton made an ample gesture. His eyes for an instant grew dreamy with a vision of the past.

'Well, believe me, we're fed up with all that rot. What we want is a business government by business men. I was born in a Crown Colony, and I've lived practically all my life in the colonies. I don't give a row of pins for a lord. What's wrong with England is snobbishness. And if there's anything that gets my goat it's a snob.'

A snob! Mr. Warburton's face grew purple and his eyes blazed with anger. That was a word that had pursued him all his life. The great ladies whose society he had enjoyed in his youth were not inclined to look upon his appreciation of themselves as unworthy, but even great ladies are sometimes out of temper and more than once Mr. Warburton had had the dreadful word flung in his teeth. He knew, he could not help knowing, that there were odious people who called him a snob. How unfair it was! Why, there was no vice he found so detestable as snobbishness. After all, he liked to mix with people of his own class, he was only at home in their company, and how in heaven's name could anyone say that was snobbish? Birds of a feather.

'I quite agree with you,' he answered. 'A snob is a man who admires or despises another because he is of a higher social rank than his own. It is the most vulgar failing of our English middle-class.'

He saw a flicker of amusement in Cooper's eyes. Cooper put up his hand to hide the broad smile that rose to his lips, and so made it more noticeable. Mr. Warburton's hands trembled a little.

Probably Cooper never knew how greatly he had offended his chief. A sensitive man himself he was strangely insensitive to the feelings of others.

Their work forced them to see one another for a few minutes now and then during the day, and they met at six to have a drink on Mr. Warburton's verandah. This was an old-established custom of the country which Mr. Warburton would not for the world have broken. But they ate their meals separately, Cooper in his bungalow and Mr. Warburton at the Fort. After the office work was over they walked till dusk fell, but they walked apart. There were but few paths in this country where the jungle pressed close upon the plantations of the village, and when Mr. Warburton caught sight of his assistant passing along with his loose stride, he would make a circuit in order to avoid him. Cooper, with his bad manners, his conceit in his own judgment and his intolerance, had already got on his nerves; but it was not till Cooper had been on the station for a couple of months that an incident happened which turned the Resident's dislike into bitter hatred.

Mr. Warburton was obliged to go up country on a tour

of inspection, and he left the station in Cooper's charge with more confidence, since he had definitely come to the conclusion that he was a capable fellow. The only thing he did not like was that he had no indulgence. He was honest, just and painstaking, but he had no sympathy for the natives. It bitterly amused Mr. Warburton to observe that this man who looked upon himself as every man's equal, should look upon so many men as his own inferiors. He was hard, he had no patience with the native mind, and he was a bully. Mr. Warburton very quickly realised that the Malays disliked and feared him. He was not altogether displeased. He would not have liked it very much if his assistant had enjoyed a popularity which might rival his own. Mr. Warburton made his elaborate preparations, set out on his expedition, and in three weeks returned. Meanwhile the mail had arrived. The first thing that struck his eyes when he entered his sitting-room was a great pile of open newspapers. Cooper had met him, and they went into the room together. Mr. Warburton turned to one of the servants who had been left behind, and sternly asked him what was the meaning of those open papers. Cooper hastened to explain.

'I wanted to read all about the Wolverhampton murder, and so I borrowed your *Times*. I brought them back again. I knew you wouldn't mind.'

Mr. Warburton turned on him, white with anger.

'But I do mind. I mind very much.'

'I'm sorry,' said Cooper, with composure. 'The fact is, I simply couldn't wait till you came back.'

'I wonder you didn't open my letters as well.'

Cooper, unmoved, smiled at his chief's exasperation.

'Oh, that's not quite the same thing. After all, I couldn't imagine you'd mind my looking at your newspapers. There's nothing private in them.'

'I very much object to anyone reading my paper before

me.' He went up to the pile. There were nearly thirty numbers there. 'I think it extremely impertinent of you. They're all mixed up.'

'We can easily put them in order,' said Cooper, joining him at the table.

'Don't touch them,' cried Mr. Warburton.

'I say, it's childish to make a scene about a little thing like that.'

'How dare you speak to me like that?'

'Oh, go to hell,' said Cooper, and he flung out of the room.

Mr. Warburton, trembling with passion, was left contemplating his papers. His greatest pleasure in life had been destroyed by those callous, brutal hands. Most people living in out of the way places when the mail comes tear open impatiently their papers and taking the last ones first glance at the latest news from home. Not so Mr. Warburton. His newsagent had instructions to write on the outside of the wrapper the date of each paper he despatched, and when the great bundle arrived Mr. Warburton looked at these dates and with his blue pencil numbered them. His head-boy's orders were to place one on the table every morning in the verandah with the early cup of tea, and it was Mr. Warburton's especial delight to break the wrapper as he sipped his tea, and read the morning paper. It gave him the illusion of living at home. Every Monday morning he read the Monday *Times* of six weeks back, and so went through the week. On Sunday he read the *Observer*. Like his habit of dressing for dinner it was a tie to civilisation. And it was his pride that no matter how exciting the news was he had never yielded to the temptation of opening a paper before its allotted time. During the war the suspense sometimes had been intolerable, and when he read one day that a push was begun he had undergone agonies of suspense which he might have saved himself by the simple expedient of opening a later paper which lay waiting for him on a shelf. It had been the severest trial to which he had ever exposed himself, but he victoriously surmounted it. And that clumsy fool had broken open those neat tight packages because he wanted to know whether some horrid woman had murdered her odious husband.

Mr. Warburton sent for his boy and told him to bring wrappers. He folded up the papers as neatly as he could, placed a wrapper round each and numbered it. But it was a melancholy task.

'I shall never forgive him,' he said. 'Never.'

Of course his boy had been with him on his expedition; he never travelled without him, for his boy knew exactly how he liked things, and Mr. Warburton was not the kind of jungle traveller who was prepared to dispense with his comforts; but in the interval since their arrival he had been gossiping in the servants' quarters. He had learnt that Cooper had had trouble with his boys. All but the youth Abas had left him. Abas had desired to go too, but his uncle had placed him there on the instructions of the Resident, and he was afraid to leave without his uncle's permission.

'I told him he had done well, Tuan,' said the boy. 'But he is unhappy. He says it is not a good house, and he wishes to know if he may go as the others have gone.'

'No, he must stay. The Tuan must have servants. Have those who went been replaced?'

'No, Tuan, no one will go.'

Mr. Warburton frowned. Cooper was an insolent fool, but he had an official position and must be suitably provided with servants. It was not seemly that his house should be improperly conducted.

'Where are the boys who ran away?'

'They are in the kampong, Tuan.'

'Go and see them tonight, and tell them that I expect

them to be back in Tuan Cooper's house at dawn tomorrow.'

'They say they will not go, Tuan.'

'On my order?'

The boy had been with Mr. Warburton for fifteen years, and he knew every intonation of his master's voice. He was not afraid of him, they had gone through too much together, once in the jungle the Resident had saved his life, and once, upset in some rapids, but for him the Resident would have been drowned; but he knew when the Resident must be obeyed without question.

'I will go to the kampong,' he said.

Mr. Warburton expected that his subordinate would take the first opportunity to apologise for his rudeness, but Cooper had the ill-bred man's inability to express regret; and when they met next morning in the office he ignored the incident. Since Mr. Warburton had been away for three weeks it was necessary for them to have a somewhat prolonged interview. At the end of it, Mr. Warburton dismissed him.

'I don't think there's anything else, thank you.' Cooper turned to go, but Mr. Warburton stopped him. 'I understand you've been having some trouble with your boys.'

Cooper gave a harsh laugh.

'They tried to blackmail me. They had the damned cheek to run away, all except that incompetent fellow Abas – he knew when he was well off – but I just sat tight. They've all come to heel again.'

'What do you mean by that?'

'This morning they were all back on their jobs, the Chinese cook and all. There they were, as cool as cucumbers; you would have thought they owned the place. I suppose they'd come to the conclusion that I wasn't such a fool as I looked.'

73

'By no means. They came back on my express order.'
Cooper flushed slightly.

'I should be obliged if you wouldn't interfere with my private concerns.'

'They're not your private concerns. When your servants run away it makes you ridiculous. You are perfectly free to make a fool of yourself, but I cannot allow you to be made a fool of. It is unseemly that your house should not be properly staffed. As soon as I heard that your boys had left you, I had them told to be back in their places at dawn. That'll do.'

Mr. Warburton nodded to signify that the interview was at an end. Cooper took no notice.

'Shall I tell you what I did? I called them and gave the whole bally lot the sack. I gave them ten minutes to get out of the compound.'

Mr. Warburton shrugged his shoulders.

'What makes you think you can get others?'

'I've told my own clerk to see about it.'

Mr. Warburton reflected for a moment.

'I think you behaved very foolishly. You will do well to remember in future that good masters make good servants.'

'Is there anything else you want to teach me?'

'I should like to teach you manners, but it would be an arduous task, and I have not the time to waste. I will see that you get boys.'

'Please don't put yourself to any trouble on my account. I'm quite capable of getting them for myself.'

Mr. Warburton smiled acidly. He had an inkling that Cooper disliked him as much as he disliked Cooper, and he knew that nothing is more galling than to be forced to accept the favours of a man you detest.

'Allow me to tell you that you have no more chance of getting Malay or Chinese servants here now than you have of getting an English butler or a French chef. No one will come to you except on an order from me. Would you like me to give it?'

'No.'

'As you please. Good morning.'

Mr. Warburton watched the development of the situation with acrid humour. Cooper's clerk was unable to persuade Malay, Dyak or Chinese to enter the house of such a master. Abas, the boy who remained faithful to him, knew how to cook only native food, and Cooper, a coarse feeder, found his gorge rise against the everlasting rice. There was no water-carrier, and in that great heat he needed several baths a day. He cursed Abas, but Abas opposed him with sullen resistance and would not do more than he chose. It was galling to know that the lad stayed with him only because the Resident insisted. This went on for a fortnight and then, one morning, he found in his house the very servants whom he had previously dismissed. He fell into a violent rage, but he had learnt a little sense, and this time, without a word, he let them stay. He swallowed his humiliation, but the impatient contempt he had felt for Mr. Warburton's idiosyncrasies changed into a sullen hatred: the Resident with this malicious stroke had made him the laughing stock of all the natives.

The two men now held no communication with one another. They broke the time-honoured custom of sharing, notwithstanding personal dislike, a drink at six o'clock with any white man who happened to be at the station. Each lived in his own house as though the other did not exist. Now that Cooper had fallen into the work, it was necessary for them to have little to do with one another in the office. Mr. Warburton used his orderly to send any message he had to give his assistant, and his instructions he sent by formal letter. They saw one another constantly, that was inevitable, but did not exchange half a dozen words in a week. The fact that they could not avoid catching sight of one another got on their nerves. They brooded over their antagonism, and Mr. Warburton, taking his daily walk, could think of nothing but how much he detested his assistant.

And the dreadful thing was that in all probability they would remain thus, facing each other in deadly enmity, till Mr. Warburton went on leave. It might be three years. He had no reason to send in a complaint to head-quarters: Cooper did his work very well, and at that time men were hard to get. True, vague complaints reached him and hints that the natives found Cooper harsh. There was certainly a feeling of dissatisfaction among them. But when Mr. Warburton looked into specific cases, all he could say was that Cooper had shown severity where mildness would not have been misplaced, and had been unfeeling when himself would have been sympathetic. He had done nothing for which he could be taken to task. But Mr. Warburton watched him. Hatred will often make a man clear-sighted, and he had a suspicion that Cooper was using the natives without consideration, yet keeping within the law, because he felt that thus he could exasperate his chief. One day perhaps he would go too far. None knew better than Mr. Warburton how irritable the incessant heat could make a man and how difficult it was to keep one's self-control after a sleepless night. He smiled softly to himself. Sooner or later Cooper would deliver himself into his hand.

When at last the opportunity came, Mr. Warburton laughed aloud. Cooper had charge of the prisoners; they made roads, built sheds, rowed when it was necessary to send the prahu up or down stream, kept the town clean and otherwise usefully employed themselves. If well-behaved they even on occasion served as house-boys. Cooper kept them hard at it. He liked to see them work. He took pleasure in devising tasks for them; and seeing quickly enough that they were being made to do useless things the prisoners worked badly. He punished them by lengthening their hours. This was contrary to regulations, and as soon as it was brought to the attention of Mr. Warburton, without referring the matter back to his subordinate, he gave instructions that the old hours should be kept; Cooper, going out for his walk, was astounded to see the prisoners strolling back to the jail; he had given instructions that they were not to knock off till dusk. When he asked the warder in charge why they had left off work he was told that it was the Resident's bidding.

White with rage he strode to the Fort. Mr. Warburton, in his spotless white ducks and his neat topee, with a walking-stick in his hand, followed by his dogs, was on the point of starting out on his afternoon stroll. He had watched Cooper go, and knew that he had taken the road by the river. Cooper jumped up the steps and went straight up to the Resident.

'I want to know what the hell you mean by countermanding my order that the prisoners were to work till six,' he burst out, beside himself with fury.

Mr. Warburton opened his cold blue eyes very wide and assumed an expression of great surprise.

'Are you out of your mind? Are you so ignorant that you do not know that that is not the way to speak to your official superior?'

'Oh, go to hell. The prisoners are my pidgin, and you've got no right to interfere. You mind your business and I'll mind mine. I want to know what the devil you mean by making a damned fool of me. Everyone in the place will know that you've countermanded my order.'

Mr. Warburton kept very cool.

'You had no power to give the order you did. I countermanded it because it was harsh and tyrannical. Believe me, I have not made half such a damned fool of you as you have made of yourself.'

'You disliked me from the first moment I came here. You've done everything you could to make the place impossible for me because I wouldn't lick your boots for you. You got your knife into me because I wouldn't flatter you.'

Cooper, spluttering with rage, was nearing dangerous ground, and Mr. Warburton's eyes grew on a sudden colder and more piercing.

'You are wrong. I thought you were a cad, but I was perfectly satisfied with the way you did your work.'

'You snob. You damned snob. You thought me a cad because I hadn't been to Eton. Oh, they told me in K.S. what to expect. Why, don't you know that you're the laughing-stock of the whole country? I could hardly help bursting into a roar of laughter when you told your celebrated story about the Prince of Wales. My God, how they shouted at the club when they told it. By God, I'd rather be the cad I am than the snob you are.'

He got Mr. Warburton on the raw.

'If you don't get out of my house this minute I shall knock you down,' he cried.

The other came a little closer to him and put his face in his.

'Touch me, touch me,' he said. 'By God, I'd like to see you hit me. Do you want me to say it again? Snob. Snob.'

Cooper was three inches taller than Mr. Warburton, a strong, muscular young man. Mr. Warburton was fat and fifty-four. His clenched fist shot out. Cooper caught him by the arm and pushed him back.

'Don't be a damned fool. Remember I'm not a gentleman. I know how to use my hands.'

He gave a sort of hoot, and grinning all over his pale, sharp face jumped down the verandah steps. Mr. Warburton, his heart in his anger pounding against his ribs, sank exhausted into a chair. His body tingled as though he had prickly heat. For one horrible moment he thought he was going to cry. But suddenly he was conscious that his head-boy was on the verandah and instinctively regained control of himself. The boy came forward and filled him a glass of whisky and soda. Without a word Mr. Warburton took it and drank it to the dregs.

'What do you want to say to me?' asked Mr. Warburton, trying to force a smile on to his strained lips.

'Tuan, the assistant tuan is a bad man. Abas wishes again to leave him.'

'Let him wait a while. I shall write to Kuala Solor and ask that Tuan Cooper should go elsewhere.'

'Tuan Cooper is not good with the Malays.'

'Leave me.'

The boy silently withdrew. Mr. Warburton was left alone with his thoughts. He saw the club at Kuala Solor, the men sitting round the table in the window in their flannels, when the night had driven them in from golf and tennis, drinking whiskies and gin pahits, and laughing when they told the celebrated story of the Prince of Wales and himself at Marienbad. He was hot with shame and misery. A snob! They all thought him a snob. And he had always thought them very good fellows, he had always been gentleman enough to let it make no difference to him that they were of very second-rate position. He hated them now. But his hatred for them was nothing compared with his hatred for Cooper. And if it had come to blows Cooper could have thrashed him. Tears of mortification ran down his red, fat face. He sat there for a couple of hours smoking cigarette after cigarette, and he wished he were dead.

At last the boy came back and asked him if he would dress for dinner. Of course! He always dressed for dinner. He rose wearily from his chair and put on his stiff shirt and the high collar. He sat down at the prettily decorated table, and was waited on as usual by the two boys while two others waved their great fans. Over there in the bungalow, two hundred yards away, Cooper was eating a filthy meal clad only in a sarong and a baju. His feet were bare and while he ate he probably read a detective story. After dinner Mr. Warburton sat down to write a letter. The Sultan was away, but he wrote, privately and confidentially, to his representative. Cooper did his work very well, he said, but the fact was that he couldn't get on with him. They were getting dreadfully on each other's nerves and he would look upon it as a great favour if Cooper could be transferred to another post.

He despatched the letter next morning by special messenger. The answer came a fortnight later with the month's mail. It was a private note, and ran as follows:

'My dear Warburton,

I do not want to answer your letter officially, and so I am writing you a few lines myself. Of course if you insist I will put the matter up to the Sultan, but I think you would be much wiser to drop it. I know Cooper is a rough diamond, but he is capable, and he had a pretty thin time in the war, and I think he should be given every chance. I think you are a little too much inclined to attach importance to a man's social position. You must remember that times have changed. Of course it's a very good thing for a man to be a gentleman, but it's better that he should be competent and hard-working. I think if you'll exercise a little tolerance you'll get on very well with Cooper.

Yours very sincerely,

Richard Temple.'

The letter dropped from Mr. Warburton's hand. It was easy to read between the lines. Dick Temple, whom he had known for twenty years, Dick Temple who came from quite a good county family, thought him a snob, and for that reason had no patience with his request. Mr. Warburton felt on a sudden discouraged with life. The world of which he was a part had passed away and the future belonged to a meaner generation. Cooper represented it and Cooper he hated with all his heart. He stretched out his hand to fill his glass, and at the gesture his head-boy stepped forward.

'I didn't know you were there.'

The boy picked up the official letter. Ah, that was why he was waiting.

'Does Tuan Cooper go, Tuan?'

'No.'

'There will be a misfortune.'

For a moment the words conveyed nothing to his lassitude. But only for a moment. He sat up in his chair and looked at the boy. He was all attention.

'What do you mean by that?'

'Tuan Cooper is not behaving rightly with Abas.'

Mr. Warburton shrugged his shoulders. How should a man like Cooper know how to treat servants? Mr. Warburton knew the type: he would be grossly familiar with them at one moment and rude and inconsiderate the next.

'Let Abas go back to his family.'

'Tuan Cooper holds back his wages so that he may not run away. He has paid him nothing for three months. I tell him to be patient. But he is angry, he will not listen to reason. If the Tuan continues to use him ill there will be a misfortune.'

'You were right to tell me.'

The fool! Did he know so little of the Malays as to think he could safely injure them? It would serve him damned well right if he got a kriss in his back. A kriss. Mr. Warburton's heart seemed on a sudden to miss a beat. He had only to let things take their course and one fine day he would be rid of Cooper. He smiled faintly as the phrase, a masterly inactivity, crossed his mind. And now his heart beat a little quicker, for he saw the man he hated lying on his face in a pathway of the jungle with a knife in his back. A fit end for the cad and the bully. Mr. Warburton sighed. It was his duty to warn him, and of course he must do it. He wrote a brief and formal note to Cooper asking him to come to the Fort at once.

In ten minutes Cooper stood before him. They had not spoken to one another since the day when Mr. Warburton had nearly struck him. He did not now ask him to sit down.

'Do you wish to see me?' asked Cooper.

He was untidy and none too clean. His face and hands were covered with little red blotches where mosquitoes had bitten him and he had scratched himself till the blood came. His long, thin face bore a sullen look.

'I understand that you are again having trouble with your servants. Abas, my head-boy's nephew, complains that you have held back his wages for three months. I consider it a most arbitrary proceeding. The lad wishes to leave you, and I certainly do not blame him. I must insist on your paying what is due to him.'

'I don't choose that he should leave me. I am holding back his wages as a pledge of his good behaviour.'

'You do not know the Malay character. The Malays are very sensitive to injury and ridicule. They are passionate and revengeful. It is my duty to warn you that if you drive this boy beyond a certain point you run a great risk.'

Cooper gave a contemptuous chuckle.

'What do you think he'll do?'

'I think he'll kill you.'

'Why should you mind?'

'Oh, I wouldn't,' replied Mr. Warburton, with a faint laugh. 'I should bear it with the utmost fortitude. But I feel the official obligation to give you a proper warning.'

'Do you think I'm afraid of a damned nigger?'

'It's a matter of entire indifference to me.'

'Well, let me tell you this, I know how to take care of myself; that boy Abas is a dirty, thieving rascal, and if he tries any monkey tricks on me, by God, I'll wring his bloody neck.'

'That was all I wished to say to you,' said Mr. Warburton. 'Good evening.'

Mr. Warburton gave him a little nod of dismissal. Cooper flushed, did not for a moment know what to say or do, turned on his heel and stumbled out of the room. Mr. Warburton watched him go with an icy smile on his lips. He had done his duty. But what would he have thought had he known that when Cooper got back to his bungalow, so silent and cheerless, he threw himself down on his bed and in his bitter loneliness on a sudden lost all control of himself? Painful sobs tore his chest and heavy tears rolled down his thin cheeks.

After this Mr. Warburton seldom saw Cooper, and never spoke to him. He read his *Times* every morning, did his work at the office, took his exercise, dressed for dinner, dined and sat by the river smoking his cheroot. If by chance he ran across Cooper he cut him dead. Each, though never for a moment unconscious of the propinquity, acted as though the other did not exist. Time did nothing to assuage their animosity. They watched one another's actions and each knew what the other did. Though Mr. Warburton had been a keen shot in his youth, with age he had acquired a distaste for killing the wild things of the jungle, but on Sundays and holidays Cooper went out with his gun: if he got something it was a triumph over Mr. Warburton; if not, Mr. Warburton shrugged his shoulders and chuckled. These counter-jumpers trying to be sportsmen! Christmas was a bad time for both of them: they ate their dinners alone, each in his own quarters, and they got deliberately drunk. They were the only white men within two hundred miles and they lived within shouting distance of each other. At the beginning of the year Cooper went down with fever, and when Mr. Warburton caught sight of him again he was surprised to see how thin he had grown. He looked ill and worn. The solitude, so much more unnatural because it was due to no necessity, was getting on his nerves. It was getting on Mr. Warburton's too, and often he could not sleep at night. He lay awake brooding. Cooper was drinking heavily and surely the breaking point was near; but in his dealings with the natives he took care to do nothing that might expose him to his chief's rebuke. They fought a grim and silent battle with one another. It was a test of endurance. The months passed, and neither gave sign of weakening. They were like men dwelling in regions of eternal night, and their souls were oppressed with the knowledge that never would the day dawn for them. It looked as though their lives would continue for ever in this dull and hideous monotony of hatred.

And when at last the inevitable happened it came upon Mr. Warburton with all the shock of the unexpected. Cooper accused the boy Abas of stealing some of his clothes, and when the boy denied the theft took him by the scruff of the neck and kicked him down the steps of the bungalow. The boy demanded his wages and Cooper flung at his head every word of abuse he knew. If he saw him in the compound in an hour he would hand him over to the police. Next morning the boy waylaid him outside the Fort when he was walking over to his office, and again demanded his wages. Cooper struck him in the face with his clenched fist. The boy fell to the ground and got up with blood streaming from his nose.

Cooper walked on and set about his work. But he could not attend to it. The blow had calmed his irritation, and he knew that he had gone too far. He was worried. He felt ill, miserable and discouraged. In the adjoining office sat Mr. Warburton, and his impulse was to go and tell him what he had done; he made a movement in his chair, but he knew with what icy scorn he would listen to the story. He could see his patronising smile. For a moment he had an uneasy fear of what Abas might do. Warburton had warned him all right. He sighed. What a fool he had been! But he shrugged his shoulders impatiently. He did not care; a fat lot he had to live for. It was all Warburton's fault; if he hadn't put his back up nothing like this would have happened. Warburton had made life a hell for him from the start. The snob. But they were all like that: it was because he was a Colonial. It was a damned shame that he had never got his commission in the war; he was as good as anyone else. They were a lot of dirty snobs. He was damned if he was going to knuckle under now. Of course Warburton would hear of what had happened; the old devil knew everything. He wasn't afraid. He wasn't afraid of any Malay in Borneo, and Warburton could go to blazes.

He was right in thinking that Mr. Warburton would know what had happened. His head-boy told him when he went in to tiffin.

'Where is your nephew now?'

'I do not know, Tuan. He has gone.'

Mr. Warburton remained silent. After luncheon as a rule he slept a little, but to-day he found himself very wide awake. His eyes involuntarily sought the bungalow where Cooper was now resting.

The idiot! Hesitation for a little was in Mr. Warburton's mind. Did the man know in what peril he was? He supposed he ought to send for him. But each time he had tried to reason with Cooper, Cooper had insulted him. Anger, furious anger welled up suddenly in Mr. Warburton's heart, so that the veins on his temples stood out and he clenched his fists. The cad had had his warning. Now let him take what was coming to him. It was no business of his, and if anything happened it was not his fault. But perhaps they would wish in Kuala Solor that they had taken his advice and transferred Cooper to another station.

He was strangely restless that night. After dinner he walked up and down the verandah. When the boy went away to his own quarters, Mr. Warburton asked him whether anything had been seen of Abas.

'No, Tuan, I think maybe he has gone to the village of his mother's brother.'

Mr. Warburton gave him a sharp glance, but the boy was looking down, and their eyes did not meet. Mr. Warburton went down to the river and sat in his arbour. But peace was denied him. The river flowed ominously silent. It was like a great serpent gliding with sluggish movement towards the sea. And the trees of the jungle over the water were heavy with a breathless menace. No bird sang. No breeze ruffled the leaves of the cassias. All around him it seemed as though something waited.

He walked across the garden to the road. He had Cooper's bungalow in full view from there. There was a light in his sitting-room, and across the road floated the sound of rag-time. Cooper was playing his gramophone. Mr. Warburton shuddered; he had never got over his instinctive dislike of that instrument. But for that he would have gone over and spoken to Cooper. He turned and went back to his own house. He read late into the night, and at last he slept. But he did not sleep very long, he had terrible dreams, and he seemed to be awakened by a cry. Of course that was a dream too, for no cry – from the bungalow for instance – could be heard in his room. He lay awake till dawn. Then he heard hurried steps and the sound of voices, his head-boy burst suddenly into the room without his fez, and Mr. Warburton's heart stood still.

'Tuan, Tuan.'

Mr. Warburton jumped out of bed.

'I'll come at once.'

He put on his slippers, and in his sarong and pyjama-jacket walked across his compound and into Cooper's. Cooper was lying in bed, with his mouth open, and a kriss sticking in his heart. He had been killed in his sleep. Mr. Warburton started, but not because he had not expected to see just such a sight, he started because he felt in himself a sudden glow of exultation. A great burden had been lifted from his shoulders.

Cooper was quite cold. Mr. Warburton took the kriss out of the wound, it had been thrust in with such force that he had to use an effort to get it out, and looked at it. He recognised it. It was a kriss that a dealer had offered him some weeks before, and which he knew Cooper had bought.

'Where is Abas?' he asked sternly.

'Abas is at the village of his mother's brother.'

The sergeant of the native police was standing at the foot of the bed.

'Take two men and go to the village and arrest him.'

Mr. Warburton did what was immediately necessary. With set face he gave orders. His words were short and peremptory. Then he went back to the Fort. He shaved and had his bath, dressed and went into the dining-room. By the side of his plate *The Times* in its wrapper lay waiting for him. He helped himself to some fruit. The head-boy poured out his tea while the second handed him a dish of eggs. Mr. Warburton ate with a good appetite. The head-boy waited.

'What is it?' asked Mr. Warburton.

'Tuan, Abas, my nephew, was in the house of his mother's brother all night. It can be proved. His uncle will swear that he did not leave the kampong.'

Mr. Warburton turned upon him with a frown.

'Tuan Cooper was killed by Abas. You know it as well as I know it. Justice must be done.'

'Tuan, you would not hang him?'

Mr. Warburton hesitated an instant, and though his voice remained set and stern a change came into his eyes. It was a flicker which the Malay was quick to notice and across his own eyes flashed an answering look of understanding.

'The provocation was very great. Abas will be sentenced to a term of imprisonment.' There was a pause while Mr. Warburton helped himself to marmalade. 'When he has served a part of his sentence in prison I will take him into this house as a boy. You can train him in his duties. I have no doubt that in the house of Tuan Cooper he got into bad habits.'

'Shall Abas give himself up, Tuan?'

'It would be wise of him.'

The boy withdrew. Mr. Warburton took his *Times* and neatly slit the wrapper. He loved to unfold the heavy, rustling pages. The morning, so fresh and cool, was delicious and for a moment his eyes wandered out over the garden with a friendly glance. A great weight had been lifted from his mind. He turned to the columns in which were announced the births, deaths, and marriages. That was what he always looked at first. A name he knew caught his attention. Lady Ormskirk had had a son at last. By George, how pleased the old dowager must be! He would write her a note of congratulation by the next mail.

Abas would make a very good house-boy.

That fool Cooper!

The Vessel of Wrath

There are few books in the world that contain more meat than the 'Sailing Directions' published by the Hydrographic Department by order of the Lords Commissioners of the Admiralty. They are handsome volumes, bound (very flimsily) in cloth of different colours, and the most expensive of them is cheap. For four shillings you can buy the 'Yangste Kiang Pilot,' 'containing a description of, and sailing directions for, the Yangste Kiang from the Wusung river to the highest navigable point, including the Han Kiang, the Kialing Kiang, and the Min Kiang'; and for three shillings you can get Part III of the 'Eastern Archipelago Pilot,' 'comprising the N.E. end of Celebes, Molucca and Gilolo passages, Banda and Arafura Seas, and North, West, and South-West coasts of New Guinea.' But it is not very safe to do so if you are a creature of settled habits that you have no wish to disturb or if you have an occupation that holds you fast to one place. These business-like books take you upon enchanted journeys of the spirit; and their matter-of-fact style, the admirable order, the concision with which the material is set before you, the stern sense of the practical that informs every line, cannot dim the poetry that, like the spice-laden breeze that assails your senses with a more than material languor when you approach some of those magic islands of the Eastern seas, blows with so sweet a fragrance through the printed pages. They tell you the anchorages and the landing-places, what supplies you can get at each spot, and where you can get water; they tell you the lights and buoys, tides, winds and weather that you will find there. They give you brief information about the population and the trade. And it is strange when you think how sedately it is all set down, with no words wasted, that so much else is given you besides. What? Well, mystery and beauty, romance and the glamour of the unknown. It is no common book that offers you casually turning its pages such a paragraph as this: 'Supplies. A few jungle fowl are preserved, the island is also the resort of vast numbers of sea birds. Turtle are found in the lagoon, as well as quantities of various fish, including grey mullet, shark, and dog-fish; the seine cannot be used with any effect; but there is a fish which may be taken on a rod. A small store of tinned provisions and spirits is kept in a hut for the relief of shipwrecked persons. Good water may be obtained from a well near the landing-place.' Can the imagination want more material than this to go on a journey through time and space?

In the volume from which I have copied this passage, the compilers with the same restraint have described the Alas Islands. They are composed of a group or chain of islands, 'for the most part low and wooded, extending about 75 miles east and west, and 40 miles north and south.' The information about them, you are told, is very slight; there are channels between the different groups, and several vessels have passed through them, but the passages have not been thoroughly explored, and the positions of many of the dangers not yet determined; it is therefore advisable to avoid them. The population of the group is estimated at about 8000, of whom 200 are Chinese and 400 Mohammedans. The rest are heathen. The principal island is called Baru, it is surrounded by a reef, and here lives a Dutch Contrôleur. His white house with its red roof on the top of a little hill is the most prominent object that the vessels of the

Royal Netherlands Steam Packet Company see when every other month on their way up to Macassar and every four weeks on their way down to Merauke in Dutch New Guinea they touch at the island.

At a certain moment of the world's history the Contrôleur was Mynheer Evert Gruyter and he ruled the people who inhabited the Alas Islands with firmness tempered by a keen sense of the ridiculous. He had thought it a very good joke to be placed at the age of twenty-seven in a position of such consequence and at thirty he was still amused by it. There was no cable communication between his islands and Batavia, and the mail arrived after so long a delay that even if he asked advice, by the time he received it, it was useless, and so he equably did what he thought best and trusted to his good fortune to keep out of trouble with the authorities. He was very short, not more than five feet four in height, and extremely fat; he was of a florid complexion. For coolness' sake he kept his head shaved and his face was hairless. It was round and red. His eyebrows were so fair that you hardly saw them; and he had little twinkling blue eyes. He knew that he had no dignity, but for the sake of his position made up for it by dressing very dapperly. He never went to his office, nor sat in court, nor walked abroad but in spotless white. His stengah-shifter, with its bright brass buttons, fitted him very tightly and displayed the shocking fact that, young though he was, he had a round and protruding belly. His good-humoured face shone with sweat and he constantly fanned himself with a palm-leaf fan.

But in his house Mr. Gruyter preferred to wear nothing but a sarong and then with his white podgy little body he looked like a fat funny boy of sixteen. He was an early riser and his breakfast was always ready for him at six. It never varied. It consisted of a slice of papaia, three cold fried eggs, Edam cheese, sliced thin, and a cup of black coffee. When he had eaten it, he smoked a large Dutch cigar, read the papers if he had not read them through and through already, and then dressed to go down to his office.

One morning while he was thus occupied his head-boy came into his bedroom and told him that Tuan Jones wanted to know if he could see him. Mr. Gruyter was standing in front of a looking-glass. He had his trousers on and was admiring his smooth chest. He arched his back in order to throw it out and throw in his belly and with a good deal of satisfaction gave his breast three or four resounding slaps. It was a manly chest. When the boy brought the message he looked at his own eyes in the mirror and exchanged a slightly ironic smile with them. He asked himself what the devil his visitor could want. Evert Gruyter spoke English, Dutch and Malay with equal facility, but he thought in Dutch. He liked to do this. It seemed to him a pleasantly ribald language.

'Ask the Tuan to wait and say I shall come directly.' He put on his tunic, over his naked body, buttoned it up, and strutted into the sitting-room. The Rev. Owen Jones got up.

'Good morning, Mr. Jones,' said the Contrôleur. 'Have you come in to have a peg with me before I start my day's work?'

Mr. Jones did not smile.

'I've come to see you upon a very distressing matter, Mr. Gruyter,' he answered.

The Contrôleur was not disconcerted by his visitor's gravity nor depressed by his words. His little blue eyes beamed amiably.

'Sit down, my dear fellow, and have a cigar.'

Mr. Gruyter knew quite well that the Rev. Owen Jones neither drank nor smoked, but it tickled something prankish in his nature to offer him a drink and a smoke whenever they met. Mr. Jones shook his head.

Mr. Jones was in charge of the Baptist Mission on the Alas Islands. His headquarters were at Baru, the largest of them, with the greatest population, but he had meeting-houses under the care of native helpers in several other islands of the group. He was a tall, thin melancholy man, with a long face, sallow and drawn, of about forty. His brown hair was already white on the temples and it receded from the forehead. This gave him a look of somewhat vacuous intellectuality. Mr. Gruyter both disliked and respected him. He disliked him because he was narrow-minded and dogmatic. Himself a cheerful pagan who liked the good things of the flesh and was determined to get as many of them as his circumstances permitted, he had no patience with a man who disapproved of them all. He thought the customs of the country suited its inhabitants and had no patience with the missionary's energetic efforts to destroy a way of life that for centuries had worked very well. He respected him because he was honest, zealous and good. Mr. Jones, an Australian of Welsh descent, was the only qualified doctor in the group and it was a comfort to know that if you fell ill you need not rely only on a Chinese practitioner, and none knew better than the Contrôleur how useful to all Mr. Jones's skill had been and with what charity he had given it. On the occasion of an epidemic of influenza the missionary had done the work of ten men and no storm short of a typhoon could prevent him from crossing to one island or another if his help was needed.

He lived with his sister in a little white house about half a mile from the village and when the Contrôleur had arrived, came on board to meet him and begged him to stay till he could get his own house in order. The Contrôleur had accepted and soon saw for himself with what simplicity the couple lived. It was more than he could stand. Tea at three sparse meals a day and when

93

he lit his cigar Mr. Jones politely but firmly asked him to be good enough not to smoke, since both his sister and he strongly disapproved of it. In twenty-four hours Mr. Gruyter moved into his own house. He fled, with panic in his heart, as though from a plague-stricken city. The Contrôleur was fond of a joke and he liked to laugh; to be with a man who took your nonsense in deadly earnest and never even smiled at your best story was more than flesh and blood could stand. The Rev. Owen Jones was a worthy man, but as a companion he was impossible. His sister was worse. Neither had a sense of humour, but whereas the missionary was of a melancholy turn, doing his duty so conscientiously, with the obvious conviction that everything in the world was hopeless, Miss Jones was resolutely cheerful. She grimly looked on the bright side of things. With the ferocity of an avenging angel she sought out the good in her fellow-men. Miss Jones taught in the mission school and helped her brother in his medical work. When he did operations she gave the anæsthetic and was matron, dresser and nurse of the tiny hospital which on his own initiative Mr. Jones had added to the mission. But the Contrôleur was an obstinate little fellow and he never lost his capacity of extracting amusement from the Rev. Owen's dour struggle with the infirmities of human nature, and Miss Jones's ruthless optimism. He had to get his fun where he could. The Dutch boats came in three times in two months for a few hours and then he could have a good old crack with the captain and chief engineer, and once in a blue moon a pearling lugger came in from Thursday Island or Port Darwin and for two or three days he had a grand time. They were rough fellows, the pearlers, for the most part, but they were full of guts, and they had plenty of liquor on board, and good stories to tell, and the Contrôleur had them up to his house and gave them a fine dinner and the party was only counted a success if they were all too drunk to get back on the lugger again that night. But beside the missionary the only white man who lived on Baru was Ginger Ted, and he, of course, was a disgrace to civilisation. There was not a single thing to be said in his favour. He cast discredit on the white race. All the same, but for Ginger Ted the Contrôleur sometimes thought he would find life on the island of Baru almost more than he could bear.

Oddly enough it was on account of this scamp that Mr. Jones, when he should have been instructing the pagan young in the mysteries of the Baptist faith, was paying Mr. Gruyter this early visit.

'Sit down, Mr. Jones,' said the Contrôleur. 'What can I do for you?'

'Well, I've come to see you about the man they call Ginger Ted. What are you going to do now?'

'Why, what's happened?'

'Haven't you heard? I thought the sergeant would have told you.'

'I don't encourage the members of my staff to come to my private house unless the matter is urgent,' said the Contrôleur rather grandly. 'I am unlike you, Mr. Jones, I only work in order to have leisure and I like to enjoy my leisure without disturbance.'

But Mr. Jones did not care much for small talk and he was not interested in general reflections.

'There was a disgraceful row in one of the Chinese shops last night. Ginger Ted wrecked the place and half killed a Chinaman.'

'Drunk again, I suppose,' said the Contrôleur placidly.

'Naturally. When is he anything else? They sent for the police and he assaulted the sergeant. They had to have six men to get him to the jail.'

'He's a hefty fellow,' said the Contrôleur.

'I suppose you'll send him to Macassar.'

Evert Gruyter returned the missionary's outraged look with a merry twinkle. He was no fool and he knew already what Mr. Jones was up to. It gave him considerable amusement to tease him a little.

'Fortunately my powers are wide enough to enable me to deal with the situation myself,' he answered.

'You have power to deport anyone you like, Mr. Gruyter, and I'm sure it would save a lot of trouble if you got rid of the man altogether.'

'I have the power of course, but I am sure you would be the last person to wish me to use it arbitrarily.'

'Mr. Gruyter, the man's presence here is a public scandal. He's never sober from morning till night; it's notorious that he has relations with one native woman after another.'

'That is an interesting point, Mr. Jones. I had always heard that alcoholic excess, though it stimulated sexual desire, prevented its gratification. What you tell me about Ginger Ted does not seem to bear out this theory.'

The missionary flushed a dull red.

'These are physiological matters which at the moment I have no wish to go into,' he said, frigidly. 'The behaviour of this man does incalculable damage to the prestige of the white race, and his example seriously hampers the efforts that are made in other quarters to induce the people of these islands to lead a less vicious life. He's an out-and-out bad lot.'

'Pardon my asking, but have you made any attempts to reform him?'

'When he first drifted here I did my best to get in touch with him. He repelled all my advances. When there was that first trouble I went to him and talked to him straight from the shoulder. He swore at me.'

'No one has a greater appreciation than I of the excellent work that you and other missionaries do on these islands, but are you sure that you always exercise your calling with all the tact possible?'

The Contrôleur was rather pleased with this phrase. It was extremely courteous and yet contained a reproof that he thought worth administering. The missionary looked at him gravely. His sad brown eyes were full of sincerity.

'Did Jesus exercise tact when he took a whip and drove the money-changers from the Temple? No, Mr. Gruyter. Tact is the subterfuge the lax avail themselves of to avoid doing their duty.'

Mr. Jones's remark made the Contrôleur feel suddenly that he wanted a bottle of beer. The missionary leaned forward earnestly.

'Mr. Gruyter, you know this man's transgressions just as well as I do. It's unnecessary for me to remind you of them. There are no excuses for him. Now he really has overstepped the limit. You'll never have a better chance than this. I beg you to use the power you have and turn him out once for all.'

The Contrôleur's eyes twinkled more brightly than ever. He was having a lot of fun. He reflected that human beings were much more amusing when you did not feel called upon in dealing with them to allot praise or blame.

'But, Mr. Jones, do I understand you right? Are you asking me to give you an assurance to deport this man before I've heard the evidence against him and listened to his defence?'

'I don't know what his defence can be.'

The Contrôleur rose from his chair and really he managed to get quite a little dignity into his five feet four inches.

'I am here to administer justice according to the laws of the Dutch Government. Permit me to tell you that I am exceedingly surprised that you should attempt to influence me in my judicial functions.'

The missionary was a trifle flustered. It had never occurred to him that this little whipper-snapper of a boy, ten years younger than himself, would dream of adopting such an attitude. He opened his mouth to explain and apologise, but the Contrôleur raised a podgy little hand.

'It is time for me to go to my office, Mr. Jones. I wish you good-morning.'

The missionary, taken aback, bowed and without another word walked out of the room. He would have been surprised to see what the Contrôleur did when his back was turned. A broad grin broke on his lips and he put his thumb to his nose and cocked a snook at the Rev. Owen Jones.

A few minutes later he went down to his office. His head clerk, who was a Dutch half-caste, gave him his version of the previous night's row. It agreed pretty well with Mr. Jones's. The Court was sitting that day.

'Will you take Ginger Ted first, sir?' asked the clerk.

'I see no reason to do that. There are two or three cases held over from the last sitting. I will take him in his proper order.'

'I thought perhaps as he was a white man you would like to see him privately, sir.'

'The majesty of the law knows no difference between white and coloured, my friend,' said Mr. Gruyter, somewhat pompously.

The Court was a big square room with wooden benches on which, crowded together, sat natives of all kinds, Polynesians, Bugis, Chinese, Malays, and they all rose when a door was opened and a sergeant announced the arrival of the Contrôleur. He entered with his clerk and took his place on a little dais at a table of varnished pitch pine. Behind him was a large engraving of Queen Wilhelmina. He despatched half a dozen cases and then

Ginger Ted was brought in. He stood in the dock, hand-cuffed, with a warder on either side of him. The Contrôleur looked at him with a grave face, but he could not keep the amusement out of his eyes.

Ginger Ted was suffering from a hang-over. He swayed a little as he stood and his eyes were vacant. He was a man still young, thirty perhaps, of somewhat over the middle height, rather fat, with a bloated red face and a shock of curly red hair. He had not come out of the tussle unscathed. He had a black eye and his mouth was cut and swollen. He wore khaki shorts, very dirty and ragged, and his singlet had been almost torn off his back. A great rent showed the thick mat of red hair with which his chest was covered, but showed also the astonishing whiteness of his skin. The Contrôleur looked at the charge sheet. He called the evidence. When he had heard it, when he had seen the Chinaman whose head Ginger Ted had broken with a bottle, when he had heard the agitated story of the sergeant who had been knocked flat when he tried to arrest him, when he had listened to the tale of the havoc wrought by Ginger Ted who in his drunken fury had smashed everything he could lay hands on, he turned and addressed the accused in English.

'Well, Ginger, what have you got to say for yourself?'

'I was blind. I don't remember a thing about it. If they say I half killed 'im I suppose I did. I'll pay the damage if they'll give me time.'

'You will, Ginger,' said the Contrôleur, 'but it's me who'll give you time.'

He looked at Ginger Ted for a minute in silence. He was an unappetising object. A man who had gone completely to pieces. He was horrible. It made you shudder to look at him and if Mr. Jones had not been so officious, at that moment the Contrôleur would certainly have ordered him to be deported.

'You've been a trouble ever since you came to the islands, Ginger. You're a disgrace. You're incorrigibly idle. You've been picked up in the street dead drunk time and time again. You've kicked up row after row. You're hopeless. I told you the last time you were brought here that if you were arrested again I should deal with you severely. You've gone the limit this time and you're for it. I sentence you to six months' hard labour.'

'Me?'

'You.'

'By God, I'll kill you when I come out.'

He burst into a string of oaths both filthy and blasphemous. Mr. Gruyter listened scornfully. You can swear much better in Dutch than in English and there was nothing that Ginger Ted said that he could not have effectively capped.

'Be quiet,' he ordered. 'You make me tired.'

The Contrôleur repeated his sentence in Malay and the prisoner was led struggling away.

Mr. Gruyter sat down to tiffin in high good humour. It was astonishing how amusing life could be if you exercised a little ingenuity. There were people in Amsterdam, and even in Batavia and Surabaya, who looked upon his island home as a place of exile. They little knew how agreeable it was and what fun he could extract from unpromising material. They asked him whether he did not miss the club and the races and the cinema, the dances that were held once a week at the Casino and the society of Dutch ladies. Not at all. He liked comfort. The substantial furniture of the room in which he sat had a satisfying solidity. He liked reading French novels of a frivolous nature and he appreciated the sensation of reading one after the other without the uneasiness occasioned by the thought that he was wasting his time. It seemed to him a great luxury to waste time. When his young man's fancy turned to thoughts of love his head-boy brought to the house a little dark-skinned bright-eyed creature in a sarong. He took care to form no connection of a permanent nature. He thought that change kept the heart young. He enjoyed freedom and was not weighed down by a sense of responsibility. He did not mind the heat. It made a sluice over with cold water half a dozen times a day a pleasure that had almost an æsthetic quality. He played the piano. He wrote letters to his friends in Holland. He felt no need for the conversation of intellectual persons. He liked a good laugh, but he could get that out of a fool just as well as out of a professor of philosophy. He had a notion that he was a very wise little man.

Like all good Dutchmen in the Far East he began his lunch with a small glass of Hollands gin. It has a musty acrid flavour, and the taste for it must be acquired, but Mr. Gruyter preferred it to any cocktail. When he drank it he felt besides that he was upholding the traditions of his race. Then he had *rysttafel*. He had it every day. He heaped a soup-plate high with rice, and then, his three boys waiting on him, helped himself to the curry that one handed him, to the fried egg that another brought, and to the condiment presented by the third. Then each one brought another dish, of bacon, or bananas, or pickled fish, and presently his plate was piled high in a huge pyramid. He stirred it all together and began to eat. He ate slowly and with relish. He drank a bottle of beer.

He did not think while he was eating. His attention was applied to the mass in front of him and he consumed it with a happy concentration. It never palled on him. And when he had emptied the great plate it was a compensation to think that next day he would have *rysttafel* again. He grew tired of it as little as the rest of us grow tired of bread. He finished his beer and lit his cigar. The boy brought him a cup of coffee. He leaned back in his chair then and allowed himself the luxury of reflection.

It tickled him to have sentenced Ginger Ted to the richly deserved punishment of six months' hard labour, and he smiled when he thought of him working on the roads with the other prisoners. It would have been silly to deport from the island the one man with whom he could occasionally have a heart-to-heart talk, and besides, the satisfaction it would have given the missionary would have been bad for that gentleman's character. Ginger Ted was a scamp and a scallywag, but the Contrôleur had a kindly feeling for him. They had drunk many a bottle of beer in one another's company and when the pearl fishers from Port Darwin came in and they all made a night of it, they had got gloriously tight together. The Contrôleur liked the reckless way in which Ginger Ted squandered the priceless treasure of life.

Ginger Ted had wandered in one day on the ship that was going up from Merauke to Macassar. The captain did not know how he had found his way there, but he had travelled steerage with the natives, and he stopped off at the Alas Islands because he liked the look of them. Mr. Gruyter had a suspicion that their attraction consisted perhaps in their being under the Dutch flag and so out of British jurisdiction. But his papers were in order, so there was no reason why he should not stay. He said that he was buying pearl-shell for an Australian firm, but it soon appeared that his commercial undertakings were not serious. Drink, indeed, took up so much of his time that he had little left over for other pursuits. He was in receipt of two pounds a week, paid monthly, which came regularly to him from England. The Contrôleur guessed that this sum was paid only so long as he kept well away from the persons who sent it. It was anyway too small to permit him any liberty of movement. Ginger Ted was reticent. The Contrôleur discovered that he was an Englishman, this he learnt from his passport, which described him as Edward Wilson, and that he had been in Australia. But why he had left England and what he had done in Australia he had no notion. Nor could he ever quite tell to what class Ginger Ted belonged. When you saw him in a filthy singlet and a pair of ragged trousers, a battered topee on his head, with the pearl-fishers and heard his conversation, coarse, obscene and illiterate, you thought he must be a sailor before the mast who had deserted his ship, or a labourer, but when you saw his handwriting you were surprised to find that it was that of a man not without at least some education, and on occasion when you got him alone, if he had had a few drinks but was not yet drunk, he would talk of matters that neither a sailor nor a labourer would have been likely to know anything about. The Contrôleur had a certain sensitiveness and he realised that Ginger Ted did not speak to him as an inferior to a superior but as an equal. Most of his remittance was mortgaged before he received it, and the Chinamen to whom he owed money were standing at his elbow when the monthly letter was delivered to him, but with what was left he proceeded to get drunk. It was then that he made trouble, for when drunk he grew violent and was then likely to commit acts that brought him into the hands of the police. Hitherto Mr. Gruyter had contented himself with keeping him in jail till he was sober and giving him a talking to. When he was out of money he cadged what drink he could from anyone who would give it him. Rum, brandy, arak, it was all the same to him. Two or three times Mr. Gruyter had got him work on plantations run by Chinese in one or other of the islands, but he could not stick to it, and in a few weeks was back again at Baru on the beach. It was a miracle how he kept body and soul

together. He had, of course, a way with him. He picked
up the various dialects spoken on the islands, and knew
how to make the natives laugh. They despised him, but
they respected his physical strength, and they liked his
company. He was as a result never at a loss for a meal
or a mat to sleep on. The strange thing was, and it was
this that chiefly outraged the Rev. Owen Jones, that he
could do anything he liked with a woman. The
Contrôleur could not imagine what it was they saw in
him. He was casual with them and rather brutal. He
took what they gave him, but seemed incapable of
gratitude. He used them for his pleasure and then flung
them indifferently away. Once or twice this had got
him into trouble, and Mr. Gruyter had had to sentence
an angry father for sticking a knife in Ginger Ted's back
one night, and a Chinese woman had sought to poison
herself by swallowing opium because he had deserted
her. Once Mr. Jones came to the Contrôleur in a great
state because the beachcomber had seduced one of his
converts. The Contrôleur agreed that it was very
deplorable, but could only advise Mr. Jones to keep a
sharp eye on these young persons. The Contrôleur liked
it less when he discovered that a girl whom he fancied
a good deal himself and had been seeing for several
weeks had all the time been according her favours also
to Ginger Ted. When he thought of this particular incident he smiled again at the thought of Ginger Ted doing
six months' hard labour. It is seldom in this life that in
the process of doing your bounden duty you can get
back on a fellow who has played you a dirty trick.

A few days later Mr. Gruyter was taking a walk,
partly for exercise and partly to see that some job he
wanted done was being duly proceeded with, when he
passed a gang of prisoners working under the charge of
a warder. Among them he saw Ginger Ted. He wore the
prison sarong, a dingy tunic called in Malay a baju, and

his own battered topee. They were repairing the road, and Ginger Ted was wielding a heavy pick. The way was narrow and the Contrôleur saw that he must pass within a foot of him. He remembered his threats. He knew that Ginger Ted was a man of violent passion and the language he had used in the dock made it plain that he had not seen what a good joke it was of the Contrôleur's to sentence him to six months' hard labour. If Ginger Ted suddenly attacked him with the pick, nothing on God's earth could save him. It was true that the warder would immediately shoot him down, but meanwhile the Contrôleur's head would be bashed in. It was with a funny little feeling in the pit of his stomach that Mr. Gruyter walked through the gang of prisoners. They were working in pairs a few feet from one another. He set his mind on neither hastening his pace nor slackening it. As he passed Ginger Ted, the man swung his pick into the ground and looked up at the Contrôleur and as he caught his eye winked. The Contrôleur checked the smile that rose to his lips and with official dignity strode on. But that wink, so lusciously full of sardonic humour, filled him with satisfaction. If he had been the Caliph of Bagdad instead of a junior official in the Dutch Civil Service, he would forthwith have released Ginger Ted, sent slaves to bath and perfume him, and having clothed him in a golden robe entertained him to a sumptuous repast.

Ginger Ted was an exemplary prisoner and in a month or two the Contrôleur, having occasion to send a gang to do some work on one of the outlying islands, included him in it. There was no jail there, so the ten fellows he sent, under the charge of a warder, were billeted on the natives and after their day's work lived like free men. The job was sufficient to take up the rest of Ginger Ted's sentence. The Contrôleur saw him before he left.

'Look here, Ginger,' he said to him, 'here's ten guilder for you so that you can buy yourself tobacco when you're gone.'

'Couldn't you make it a bit more? There's eight pounds a month coming in regularly.'

'I think that's enough. I'll keep the letters that come for you, and when you get back you'll have a tidy sum. You'll have enough to take you anywhere you want to go.'

'I'm very comfortable here,' said Ginger Ted.

'Well, the day you come back, clean yourself up and come over to my house. We'll have a bottle of beer together.'

'That'll be fine. I guess I'll be ready for a good crack then.'

Now chance steps in. The island to which Ginger Ted had been sent was called Maputiti, and like all the rest of them it was rocky, heavily wooded and surrounded by a reef. There was a village among coconuts on the sea-shore opposite the opening of the reef and another village on a brackish lake in the middle of the island. Of this some of the inhabitants had been converted to Christianity. Communication with Baru was effected by a launch that touched at the various islands at irregular intervals. It carried passengers and produce. But the villagers were seafaring folk, and if they had to communicate urgently with Baru, manned a prahu and sailed the fifty miles or so that separated them from it. It happened that when Ginger Ted's sentence had but another fortnight to run the Christian headman of the village on the lake was taken suddenly ill. The native remedies availed him nothing and he writhed in agony. Messengers were sent to Baru imploring the missionary's help; but as ill luck would have it Mr. Jones was suffering at the moment from an attack of malaria. He was in bed and unable to move. He talked the matter over with his sister.

'It sounds like acute appendicitis,' he told her.

'You can't go, Owen,' she said.

'I can't let the man die.'

Mr. Jones had a temperature of a hundred and four. His head was aching like mad. He had been delirious all night. His eyes were shining strangely and his sister felt that he was holding on to his wits by a sheer effort of will.

'You couldn't operate in the state you're in.'

'No, I couldn't. Then Hassan must go.'

Hassan was the dispenser.

'You couldn't trust Hassan. He'd never dare to do an operation on his own responsibility. And they'd never let him. I'll go. Hassan can stay here and look after you.'

'You can't remove an appendix?'

'Why not? I've seen you do it. I've done lots of minor operations.'

Mr. Jones felt he didn't quite understand what she was saying.

'Is the launch in?'

'No, it's gone to one of the islands. But I can go in the prahu the men came in.'

'You? I wasn't thinking of you. You can't go.'

'I'm going, Owen.'

'Going where?' he said.

She saw that his mind was wandering already. She put her hand soothingly on his dry forehead. She gave him a dose of medicine. He muttered something and she realised that he did not know where he was. Of course she was anxious about him, but she knew that his illness was not dangerous, and she could leave him safely to the mission boy who was helping her nurse him and to the native dispenser. She slipped out of the room. She put her toilet things, a night-dress, and a change of clothes into a bag. A little chest with surgical instruments, bandages and antiseptic dressings was kept always ready. She gave them to the two natives who had come over from Maputiti, and telling the dispenser what she was going to do gave him instructions to inform her brother when he was able to listen. Above all he was not to be anxious about her. She put on her topee and sallied forth. The mission was about half a mile from the village. She walked quickly. At the end of the jetty the prahu was waiting. Six men manned it. She took her place in the stern and they set off with a rapid stroke. Within the reef the sea was calm, but when they crossed the bar they came upon a long swell. But this was not the first journey of the sort Miss Jones had taken and she was confident in the seaworthiness of the boat she was in. It was noon and the sun beat down from a sultry sky. The only thing that harassed her was that they could not arrive before dark, and if she found it necessary to operate at once she could count only on the light of hurricane lamps.

Miss Jones was a woman of hard on forty. Nothing in her appearance would have prepared you for such determination as she had just shown. She had an odd drooping gracefulness, which suggested that she might be swayed by every breeze; it was almost an affectation; and it made the strength of character which you soon discovered in her seem positively monstrous. She was flat-chested, tall and extremely thin. She had a long sallow face and she was much afflicted with prickly heat. Her lank brown hair was drawn back straight from her forehead. She had rather small eyes, grey in colour, and because they were somewhat too close they gave her face a shrewish look. Her nose was long and thin and a trifle red. She suffered a good deal from indigestion. But this infirmity availed nothing against her ruthless determination to look upon the bright side of things. Firmly persuaded that the world was evil and

men unspeakably vicious, she extracted any little piece
of decency she could find in them with the modest
pride with which a conjurer extracts a rabbit from a hat.
She was quick, resourceful and competent. When she
arrived on the island she saw that there was not a
moment to lose if she was to save the headman's life.
Under the greatest difficulties, showing a native how to
give the anæsthetic, she operated, and for the next three
days nursed the patient with anxious assiduity.
Everything went very well and she realised that her
brother could not have made a better job of it. She
waited long enough to take out the stitches and then
prepared to go home. She could flatter herself that she
had not wasted her time. She had given medical attention to such as needed it, she had strengthened the
small Christian community in its faith, admonished
such as were lax and cast the good seed in places where
it might be hoped under divine providence to take root.

The launch, coming from one of the other islands, put
in somewhat late in the afternoon, but it was full moon
and they expected to reach Baru before midnight. They
brought her things down to the wharf and the people
who were seeing her off stood about repeating their
thanks. Quite a little crowd collected. The launch was
loaded with sacks of copra, but Miss Jones was used to
its strong smell and it did not incommode her. She
made herself as comfortable a place to sit in as she
could, and waiting for the launch to start, chatted with
her grateful flock. She was the only passenger. Suddenly
a group of natives emerged from the trees that em-
bowered the little village on the lagoon and she saw
that among them was a white man. He wore a prison
sarong and a baju. He had long red hair. She at once
recognised Ginger Ted. A policeman was with him.
They shook hands and Ginger Ted shook hands with
the villagers who accompanied him. They bore bundles

of fruit and a jar which Miss Jones guessed contained native spirit, and these they put in the launch. She discovered to her surprise that Ginger Ted was coming with her. His term was up and instructions had arrived that he was to be returned to Baru in the launch. He gave her a glance, but did not nod – indeed Miss Jones turned away her head – and stepped in. The mechanic started his engine and in a moment they were jug-jugging through the channel in the lagoon. Ginger Ted clambered on to a pile of sacks and lit a cigarette.

Miss Jones ignored him. Of course she knew him very well. Her heart sank when she thought that he was going to be once more in Baru, creating a scandal and drinking, a peril to the women and a thorn in the flesh of all decent people. She knew the steps her brother had taken to have him deported and she had no patience with the Contrôleur, who would not see a duty that stared him so plainly in the face. When they had crossed the bar and were in the open sea Ginger Ted took the stopper out of the jar of arak and putting his mouth to it took a long pull. Then he handed the jar to the two mechanics who formed the crew. One was a middle-aged man and the other a youth.

'I do not wish you to drink anything while we are on the journey,' said Miss Jones sternly to the elder one.

He smiled at her and drank.

'A little arak can do no one any harm,' he answered. He passed the jar to his companion, who drank also.

'If you drink again I shall complain to the Contrôleur,' said Miss Jones.

The elder man said something she could not understand, but which she suspected was very rude, and passed the jar back to Ginger Ted. They went along for an hour or more. The sea was like glass and the sun set radiantly. It set behind one of the islands and for a few minutes changed it into a mystic city of the skies. Miss

Jones turned round to watch it and her heart was filled with gratitude for the beauty of the world.

'And only man is vile,' she quoted to herself.

They went due east. In the distance was a little island which she knew they passed close by. It was un-inhabited. A rocky islet thickly grown with virgin forest. The boatman lit his lamps. The night fell and immediately the sky was thick with stars. The moon had not yet risen. Suddenly there was a slight jar and the launch began to vibrate strangely. The engine rattled. The head mechanic, calling to his mate to take the helm, crept under the housing. They seemed to be going more slowly. The engine stopped. She asked the youth what was the matter, but he did not know. Ginger Ted got down from the top of the copra sacks and slipped under the housing. When he reappeared she would have liked to ask him what had happened, but her dignity prevented her. She sat still and occupied her-self with her thoughts. There was a long swell and the launch rolled slightly. The mechanic emerged once more into view and started the engine. Though it rattled like mad they began to move. The launch vibrated from stem to stern. They went very slowly. Evidently something was amiss, but Miss Jones was exasperated rather than alarmed. The launch was supposed to do six knots, but now it was just crawling along; at that rate they would not get into Baru till long, long after midnight. The mechanic, still busy under the housing, shouted out something to the man at the helm. They spoke in Bugi, of which Miss Jones knew very little. But after a while she noticed that they had changed their course and seemed to be heading for the little uninhabited island a good deal to the lee of which they should have passed.

'Where are we going?' she asked the helmsman with sudden misgiving.

He pointed to the islet. She got up and went to the

housing and called to the man to come out.

'You're not going there? Why? What's the matter?'

'I can't get to Baru,' he said.

'But you must. I insist. I order you to go to Baru.'

The man shrugged his shoulders. He turned his back on her and slipped once more under the housing. Then Ginger Ted addressed her.

'One of the blades of the propeller has broken off. He thinks he can get as far as that island. We shall have to stay the night there and he'll put on a new propeller in the morning when the tide's out.'

'I can't spend the night on an uninhabited island with three men,' she cried.

'A lot of women would jump at it.'

'I insist on going to Baru. Whatever happens we must get there tonight.'

'Don't get excited, old girl. We've got to beach the boat to put a new propeller on, and we shall be all right on the island.'

'How dare you speak to me like that. I think you're very insolent.'

'You'll be O.K. We've got plenty of grub and we'll have a snack when we land. You have a drop of arak and you'll feel like a house on fire.'

'You're an impertinent man. If you don't go to Baru I'll have you all put in prison.'

'We're not going to Baru. We can't. We're going to that island and if you don't like it you can get out and swim.'

'Oh, you'll pay for this.'

'Shut up, you old cow,' said Ginger Ted.

Miss Jones gave a gasp of anger. But she controlled herself. Even out there, in the middle of the ocean, she had too much dignity to bandy words with that vile wretch. The launch, the engine rattling horribly, crawled on. It was pitch dark now, and she could no longer see the island they were making for. Miss Jones, deeply incensed, sat with lips tight shut and a frown on her brow; she was not used to being crossed. Then the moon rose and she could see the bulk of Ginger Ted sprawling on the top of the piled sacks of copra. The glimmer of his cigarette was strangely sinister. Now the island was vaguely outlined against the sky. They reached it and the boatman ran the launch on to the beach. Suddenly Miss Jones gave a gasp. The truth had dawned on her and her anger changed to fear. Her heart beat violently. She shook in every limb. She felt dreadfully faint. She saw it all. Was the broken propeller a put-up job or was it an accident? She could not be certain; anyhow, she knew that Ginger Ted would seize the opportunity. Ginger Ted would rape her. She knew his character. He was mad about women. That was what he had done, practically, to the girl at the mission, such a good little thing she was and an excellent sempstress; they would have prosecuted him for that and he would have been sentenced to years of imprisonment only very unfortunately the innocent child had gone back to him several times and indeed had only complained of his ill usage when he left her for somebody else. They had gone to the Contrôleur about it, but he had refused to take any steps, saying in that coarse way of his that even if what the girl said was true, it didn't look very much as though it had been an altogether unpleasant experience. Ginger Ted was a scoundrel. And she was a white woman. What chance was there that he would spare her? None. She knew men. But she must pull herself together. She must keep her wits about her. She must have courage. She was determined to sell her virtue dearly, and if he killed her – well, she would rather die than yield. And if she died she would rest in the arms of Jesus. For a moment a great light blinded her eyes and she saw the mansions of her

Heavenly Father. They were a grand and sumptuous mixture of a picture palace and a railway station. The mechanics and Ginger Ted jumped out of the launch and, waist-deep in water, gathered round the broken propeller. She took advantage of their preoccupation to get her case of surgical instruments out of the box. She took out the four scalpels it contained and secreted them in her clothing. If Ginger Ted touched her she would not hesitate to plunge a scalpel in his heart.

'Now then, miss, you'd better get out,' said Ginger Ted. 'You'll be better off on the beach than in the boat.'

She thought so too. At least there she would have freedom of action. Without a word she clambered over the copra sacks. He offered her his hand.

'I don't want your help,' she said coldly.

'You can go to hell,' he answered.

It was a little difficult to get out of the boat without showing her legs, but by the exercise of considerable ingenuity she managed it.

'Damned lucky we've got something to eat. We'll make a fire and then you'd better have a snack and a nip of arak.'

'I want nothing. I only want to be left alone.'

'It won't hurt me if you go hungry.'

She did not answer. She walked, with head erect, along the beach. She held the largest scalpel in her closed fist. The moon allowed her to see where she was going. She looked for a place to hide. The thick forest came down to the very edge of the beach; but, afraid of its darkness (after all, she was but a woman), she dared not plunge into its depth. She did not know what animals lurked there or what dangerous snakes. Besides, her instinct told her that it was better to keep those three bad men in sight; then if they came towards her she would be prepared. Presently she found a little hollow. She looked round. They seemed to be occupied with their own affairs and they could not see her. She slipped in. There was a rock between them and her so that she was hidden from them and yet could watch them. She saw them go to and from the boat carrying things. She saw them build a fire. It lit them luridly and she saw them sit around it and eat, and she saw the jar of arak passed from one to the other. They were all going to get drunk. What would happen to her then? It might be that she could cope with Ginger Ted, though his strength terrified her, but against three she would be powerless. A mad idea came to her to go to Ginger Ted and fall on her knees before him and beg him to spare her. He must have some spark of decent feeling in him and she had always been so convinced that there was good even in the worst of men. He must have had a mother. Perhaps he had a sister. Ah, but how could you appeal to a man blinded with lust and drunk with arak? She began to feel terribly weak. She was afraid she was going to cry. That would never do. She needed all her self-control. She bit her lip. She watched them, like a tiger watching his prey; no, not like that, like a lamb watching three hungry wolves. She saw them put more wood on the fire and Ginger Ted, in his sarong, silhouetted by the flames. Perhaps after he had had his will of her he would pass her on to the others. How could she go back to her brother when such a thing had happened to her? Of course he would be sympathetic, but would he ever feel quite the same to her again? It would break his heart. And perhaps he would think that she ought to have resisted more. For his sake perhaps it would be better if she said nothing about it. Naturally the men would say nothing. It would mean twenty years in prison for them. But then supposing she had a baby. Miss Jones instinctively clenched her hands with horror and nearly cut herself with the scalpel. Of course it would only infuriate them if she resisted.

'What shall I do?' she cried. 'What have I done to deserve this?'

She flung herself down on her knees and prayed to God to save her. She prayed long and earnestly. She reminded God that she was a virgin and just mentioned, in case it had slipped the divine memory, how much St. Paul had valued that excellent state. And then she peeped round the rock again. The three men appeared to be smoking and the fire was dying down. Now was the time that Ginger Ted's lewd thoughts might be expected to turn to the woman who was at his mercy. She smothered a cry, for suddenly he got up and walked in her direction. She felt all her muscles grow taut, and though her heart was beating furiously she clenched the scalpel firmly in her hand. But it was for another purpose that Ginger Ted had got up. Miss Jones blushed and looked away. He strolled slowly back to the others and sitting down again raised the jar of arak to his lips. Miss Jones, crouching behind the rock, watched with straining eyes. The conversation round the fire grew less and presently she divined, rather than saw, that the two natives wrapped themselves in blankets and composed themselves to slumber. She understood. This was the moment Ginger Ted had been waiting for. When they were fast asleep he would get up cautiously and without a sound, in order not to wake the others, creep stealthily towards her. Was it that he was unwilling to share her with them or did he know that his deed was so dastardly that he did not wish them to know of it? After all, he was a white man and she was a white woman. He could not have sunk so low as to allow her to suffer the violence of natives. But his plan, which was so obvious to her, had given her an idea; when she saw him coming she would scream, she would scream so loudly that it would wake the two mechanics. She remembered now that the elder, though he had only one eye, had a kind face. But Ginger Ted did not move. She was feeling terribly tired. She began to fear that she would not have the strength now to resist him. She had gone through too much. She closed her eyes for a minute.

When she opened them it was broad daylight. She must have fallen asleep and, so shattered was she by emotion, have slept till long after dawn. It gave her quite a turn. She sought to rise, but something caught in her legs. She looked and found that she was covered with two empty copra sacks. Someone had come in the night and put them over her. Ginger Ted! She gave a little scream. The horrible thought flashed through her mind that he had outraged her in her sleep. No. It was impossible. And yet he had had her at his mercy. Defenceless. And he had spared her. She blushed furiously. She raised herself to her feet, feeling a little stiff, and arranged her disordered dress. The scalpel had fallen from her hand and she picked it up. She took the two copra sacks and emerged from her hiding-place. She walked towards the boat. It was floating in the shallow water of the lagoon.

'Come on, Miss Jones,' said Ginger Ted. 'We've finished. I was just going to wake you up.'

She could not look at him, but she felt herself as red as a turkey cock.

'Have a banana?' he said.

Without a word she took it. She was very hungry, and ate it with relish.

'Step on this rock and you'll be able to get in without wetting your feet.'

Miss Jones felt as though she could sink into the ground with shame, but she did as he told her. He took hold of her arm – good heavens! his hand was like an iron vice, never, never could she have struggled with him – and helped her into the launch. The mechanic started the engine and they slid out of the lagoon. In three hours they were at Baru.

That evening, having been officially released, Ginger Ted went to the Contrôleur's house. He wore no longer the prison uniform, but the ragged singlet and the khaki shorts in which he had been arrested. He had had his hair cut and it fitted his head now like a little curly red cap. He was thinner. He had lost his bloated flabbiness and looked younger and better. Mr. Gruyter, a friendly grin on his round face, shook hands with him and asked him to sit down. The boy brought two bottles of beer.

'I'm glad to see you hadn't forgotten my invitation, Ginger,' said the Contrôleur.

'Not likely. I've been looking forward to this for six months.'

'Here's luck, Ginger Ted.'

'Same to you, Contrôleur.'

They emptied their glasses and the Contrôleur clapped his hands. The boy brought two more bottles.

'Well, you don't bear me any malice for the sentence I gave you, I hope.'

'No bloody fear. I was mad for a minute, but I got over it. I didn't have half a bad time, you know. Nice lot of girls on that island, Contrôleur. You ought to give 'em a look over one of these days.'

'You're a bad lot, Ginger.'

'Terrible.'

'Good beer, isn't it?'

'Fine.'

'Let's have some more.'

Ginger Ted's remittance had been arriving every month and the Contrôleur now had fifty pounds for him. When the damage he had done to the Chinaman's shop was paid for there would still be over thirty.

'That's quite a lot of money, Ginger. You ought to do something useful with it.'

'I mean to,' answered Ginger. 'Spend it.'

The Contrôleur sighed.

'Well, that's what money's for, I guess.'

The Contrôleur gave his guest the news. Not much had happened during the last six months. Time on the Alas Islands did not matter very much and the rest of the world did not matter at all.

'Any wars anywhere?' asked Ginger Ted.

'No. Not that I've noticed. Harry Jervis found a pretty big pearl. He says he's going to ask a thousand quid for it.'

'I hope he gets it.'

'And Charlie McCormack's married.'

'He always was a bit soft.'

Suddenly the boy appeared and said Mr. Jones wished to know if he might come in. Before the Contrôleur could give an answer Mr. Jones walked in.

'I won't detain you long,' he said. 'I've been trying to get hold of this good man all day and when I heard he was here I thought you wouldn't mind my coming.'

'How is Miss Jones?' asked the Contrôleur politely. 'None the worse for her night in the open, I trust.'

'She's naturally a bit shaken. She had a temperature and I've insisted on her going to bed, but I don't think it's serious.'

The two men had got up on the missionary's entrance, and now the missionary went up to Ginger Ted and held out his hand.

'I want to thank you. You did a great and noble thing. My sister is right, one should always look for the good in their fellow-men; I am afraid I misjudged you in the past: I beg your pardon.'

He spoke very solemnly. Ginger Ted looked at him with amazement. He had not been able to prevent the missionary taking his hand. He still held it.

'What the hell are you talking about?'

'You had my sister at your mercy and you spared her. I thought you were all evil and I am ashamed. She was defenceless. She was in your power. You had pity on her. I thank you from the bottom of my heart. Neither my sister nor I will ever forget. God bless and guard you always.'

Mr. Jones's voice shook a little and he turned his head away. He released Ginger Ted's hand and strode quickly to the door. Ginger Ted watched him with a blank face.

'What the blazes does he mean?' he asked.

The Contrôleur laughed. He tried to control himself, but the more he did the more he laughed. He shook and you saw the folds of his fat belly ripple under the sarong. He leaned back in his long chair and rolled from side to side. He did not laugh only with his face, he laughed with his whole body, and even the muscles of his podgy legs shook with mirth. He held his aching ribs. Ginger Ted looked at him frowning, and because he did not understand what the joke was he grew angry. He seized one of the empty beer bottles by the neck.

'If you don't stop laughing, I'll break your bloody head open,' he said.

The Contrôleur mopped his face. He swallowed a mouthful of beer. He sighed and groaned because his sides were hurting him.

'He's thanking you for having respected the virtue of Miss Jones,' he spluttered at last.

'Me?' cried Ginger Ted.

The thought took quite a long time to travel through his head, but when at last he got it he flew into a violent rage. There flowed from his mouth such a stream of blasphemous obscenities as would have startled a marine.

'That old cow,' he finished. 'What does he take me for?'

'You have the reputation of being rather hot stuff

with the girls, Ginger,' giggled the little Contrôleur.

'I wouldn't touch her with the fag-end of a barge-pole. It never entered my head. The nerve. I'll wring his blasted neck. Look here, give me my money, I'm going to get drunk.'

'I don't blame you,' said the Contrôleur.

'That old cow,' repeated Ginger Ted. 'That old cow.'

He was shocked and outraged. The suggestion really shattered his sense of decency.

The Contrôleur had the money at hand and having got Ginger Ted to sign the necessary papers gave it to him.

'Go and get drunk, Ginger Ted,' he said, 'but I warn you, if you get into mischief it'll be twelve months' next time.'

'I shan't get into mischief,' said Ginger Ted sombrely. He was suffering from a sense of injury. 'It's an insult,' he shouted at the Contrôleur. 'That's what it is, it's a bloody insult.'

He lurched out of the house, and as he went he muttered to himself: 'dirty swine, dirty swine.' Ginger Ted remained drunk for a week. Mr. Jones went to see the Contrôleur again.

'I'm very sorry to hear that poor fellow has taken up his evil course again,' he said. 'My sister and I are dreadfully disappointed. I'm afraid it wasn't very wise to give him so much money at once.'

'It was his own money. I had no right to keep it back.'

'Not a legal right, perhaps, but surely a moral right.'

He told the Contrôleur the story of that fearful night on the island. With her feminine instinct, Miss Jones had realised that the man, inflamed with lust, was determined to take advantage of her, and, resolved to defend herself to the last, had armed herself with a scalpel. He told the Contrôleur how she had prayed and wept and how she had hidden herself. Her agony was indescribable, and she knew that she could never have survived the shame. She rocked to and fro and every moment she thought he was coming. And there was no help anywhere and at last she had fallen asleep; she was tired out, poor thing, she had undergone more than any human being could stand, and then when she awoke she found that he had covered her with copra sacks. He had found her asleep, and surely it was her innocence, her very helplessness that had moved him, he hadn't the heart to touch her; he covered her gently with two copra sacks and crept silently away.

'It shows you that deep down in him there is something sterling. My sister feels it's our duty to save him. We must do something for him.'

'Well, in your place I wouldn't try till he's got through all his money,' said the Contrôleur, 'and then if he's not in jail you can do what you like.'

But Ginger Ted didn't want to be saved. About a fortnight after his release from prison he was sitting on a stool outside a Chinaman's shop looking vacantly down the street when he saw Miss Jones coming along. He stared at her for a minute and once more amazement seized him. He muttered to himself and there can be little doubt that his mutterings were disrespectful. But then he noticed that Miss Jones had seen him and he quickly turned his head away; he was conscious, notwithstanding, that she was looking at him. She was walking briskly, but she sensibly diminished her pace as she approached him. He thought she was going to stop and speak to him. He got up quickly and went into the shop. He did not venture to come out for at least five minutes. Half an hour later Mr. Jones himself came along and he went straight up to Ginger Ted with outstretched hand.

'How do you do, Mr. Edward? My sister told me I should find you here.'

Ginger Ted gave him a surly look and did not take the proffered hand. He made no answer.

'We'd be so very glad if you'd come to dinner with us next Sunday. My sister's a capital cook and she'll make you a real Australian dinner.'

'Go to hell,' said Ginger Ted.

'That's not very gracious,' said the missionary, but with a little laugh to show that he was not affronted. 'You go and see the Contrôleur from time to time, why shouldn't you come and see us? It's pleasant to talk to white people now and then. Won't you let bygones be bygones? I can assure you of a very cordial welcome.'

'I haven't got clothes fit to go out in,' said Ginger Ted sulkily.

'Oh, never mind about that. Come as you are.'

'I won't.'

'Why not? You must have a reason.'

Ginger Ted was a blunt man. He had no hesitation in saying what we should all like to when we receive unwelcome invitations.

'I don't want to.'

'I'm sorry. My sister will be very disappointed.'

Mr. Jones, determined to show that he was not in the least offended, gave him a breezy nod and walked on. Forty-eight hours later there mysteriously arrived at the house in which Ginger Ted lodged a parcel containing a suit of ducks, a tennis shirt, a pair of socks and some shoes. He was unaccustomed to receiving presents and next time he saw the Contrôleur asked him if it was he who had sent the things.

'Not on your life,' replied the Contrôleur. 'I'm perfectly indifferent to the state of your wardrobe.'

'Well, then, who the hell can have?'

'Search me.'

It was necessary from time to time for Miss Jones to see Mr. Gruyter on business and shortly after this she came to see him one morning in his office. She was a capable woman and though she generally wanted him to do something he had no mind to, she did not waste his time. He was a little surprised then to discover that she had come on a very trivial errand. When he told her that he could not take cognizance of the matter in question, she did not as was her habit try to convince him, but accepted his refusal as definite. She got up to go and then as though it were an afterthought said:

'Oh, Mr. Gruyter, my brother is very anxious that we should have the man they call Ginger Ted to supper with us and I've written him a little note inviting him for the day after to-morrow. I think he's rather shy, and I wonder if you'd come with him.'

'That's very kind of you.'

'My brother feels that we ought to do something for the poor fellow.'

'A woman's influence and all that sort of thing.' said the Contrôleur demurely.

'Will you persuade him to come? I'm sure he will if you make a point of it, and when he knows the way he'll come again. It seems such a pity to let a young man like that go to pieces altogether.'

The Contrôleur looked up at her. She was several inches taller than he. He thought her very unattractive. She reminded him strangely of wet linen hung on a clothes-line to dry. His eyes twinkled, but he kept a straight face.

'I'll do my best,' he said.

'How old is he?' she asked.

'According to his passport he's thirty-one.'

'And what is his real name?'

'Wilson.'

'Edward Wilson,' she said softly.

'It's astonishing that after the life he's led he should be so strong,' murmured the Contrôleur. 'He has the strength of an ox.'

'Those red-headed men sometimes are very power-ful,' said Miss Jones, but she spoke as though she were choking.

'Quite so,' said the Contrôleur.

Then for no obvious reason Miss Jones blushed. She hurriedly said good-bye to the Contrôleur and left his office.

'*Godverdomme!*' said the Contrôleur.

He knew now who had sent Ginger Ted the new clothes.

He met him during the course of the day and asked him whether he had heard from Miss Jones. Ginger Ted took a crumpled ball of paper out of his pocket and gave it to him. It was the invitation. It ran as follows:

Dear Mr. Wilson, –
My brother and I would be so very glad if you
would come and have supper with us next
Thursday at 7.30. The Contrôleur has kindly
promised to come. We have some new records from
Australia which I am sure you will like. I am
afraid I was not very nice to you last time we met,
but I did not know you so well then, and I am big
enough to admit it when I have committed an
error. I hope you will forgive me and let me be your
friend.

Yours sincerely,
Martha Jones.

The Contrôleur noticed that she addressed him as Mr. Wilson and referred to his own promise to go, so that when she told him she had already invited Ginger Ted she had a little anticipated the truth.

'What are you going to do?'

'I'm not going, if that's what you mean. Damned nerve.'

'You must answer the letter.'

'Well, I won't.'

'Now look here, Ginger, you put on those new clothes and you come as a favour to me. I've got to go, and damn it all, you can't leave me in the lurch. It won't hurt you just once.'

Ginger Ted looked at the Contrôleur suspiciously, but his face was serious and his manner sincere: he could not guess that within him the Dutchman bubbled with laughter.

'What the devil do they want me for?'

'I don't know. The pleasure of your society, I suppose.'

'Will there be any booze?'

'No, but come up to my house at seven, and we'll have a tiddly before we go.'

'Oh, all right,' said Ginger Ted sulkily.

The Contrôleur rubbed his little fat hands with joy. He was expecting a great deal of amusement from the party. But when Thursday came and seven o'clock Ginger Ted was dead drunk and Mr. Gruyter had to go alone. He told the missionary and his sister the plain truth. Mr. Jones shook his head.

'I'm afraid it's no good, Martha, the man's hopeless.'

For a moment Miss Jones was silent and the Contrôleur saw two tears trickle down her long thin nose. She bit her lip.

'No one is hopeless. Everyone has some good in him. I shall pray for him every night. It would be wicked to doubt the power of God.'

Perhaps Miss Jones was right in this, but the divine providence took a very funny way of effecting its ends. Ginger Ted began to drink more heavily than ever. He was so troublesome that even Mr. Gruyter lost patience with him. He made up his mind that he could not have the fellow on the islands any more and resolved to deport him on the next boat that touched at Baru. Then a man died under mysterious circumstances after having been for a trip to one of the islands and the Contrôleur learnt that there had been several deaths on the same island. He sent the Chinese who was the official doctor of the group to look into the matter, and very soon received intelligence that the deaths were due to cholera. Two more took place at Baru and the certainty was forced upon him that there was an epidemic.

The Contrôleur cursed freely. He cursed in Dutch, he cursed in English and he cursed in Malay. Then he drank a bottle of beer and smoked a cigar. After that he took thought. He knew the Chinese doctor would be useless. He was a nervous little man from Java and the natives would refuse to obey his orders. The Contrôleur was efficient and knew pretty well what must be done, but he could not do everything single-handed. He did not like Mr. Jones, but just then he was thankful that he was at hand, and he sent for him at once. In ten minutes Mr. Jones was in the office. He was accompanied by his sister.

'You know what I want to see you about, Mr. Jones,' he said abruptly.

'Yes. I've been expecting a message from you. That is why my sister has come with me. We are ready to put all our resources at your disposal. I need not tell you that my sister is as competent as a man.'

'I know. I shall be very glad of her assistance.'

They set to without further delay to discuss the steps that must be taken. Hospital huts would have to be erected and quarantine stations. The inhabitants of the various villages on the islands must be forced to take proper precautions. In a good many cases the infected villages drew their water from the same well as the uninfected, and in each case this difficulty would have to be dealt with according to circumstances. It was necessary to send round people to give orders and make sure that they were carried out. Negligence must be ruthlessly punished. The worst of it was that the natives would not obey other natives, and orders given by native policemen, themselves unconvinced of their efficacy, would certainly be disregarded. It was advisable for Mr. Jones to stay at Baru where the population was largest and his medical attention most wanted; and what with the official duties that forced him to keep in touch with his headquarters, it was impossible for Mr. Gruyter to visit all the other islands himself. Miss Jones must go; but the natives of some of the outlying islands were wild and treacherous; the Contrôleur had had a good deal of trouble with them. He did not like the idea of exposing her to danger.

'I'm not afraid,' she said.

'I daresay. But if you have your throat cut I shall get into trouble, and besides, we're so short-handed I don't want to risk losing your help.'

'Then let Mr. Wilson come with me. He knows the natives better than anyone and can speak all their dialects.'

'Ginger Ted?' The Contrôleur stared at her. 'He's just getting over an attack of D.Ts.'

'I know,' she answered.

'You know a great deal, Miss Jones.'

Even though the moment was so serious Mr. Gruyter could not but smile. He gave her a sharp look, but she met it coolly.

'There's nothing like responsibility for bringing out what there is in a man, and I think something like this may be the making of him.'

'Do you think it would be wise to trust yourself for days at a time to a man of such infamous character?' said the missionary.

'I put my trust in God,' she answered gravely.

'Do you think he'd be any use?' asked the Contrôleur. 'You know what he is.'

'I'm convinced of it.' Then she blushed. 'After all, no one knows better than I that he's capable of self-control.'

The Contrôleur bit his lip.

'Let's send for him.'

He gave a message to the sergeant and in a few minutes Ginger Ted stood before them. He looked ill. He had evidently been much shaken by his recent attack and his nerves were all to pieces. He was in rags and he had not shaved for a week. No one could have looked more disreputable.

'Look here, Ginger,' said the Contrôleur, 'it's about this cholera business. We've got to force the natives to take precautions and we want you to help us.'

'Why the hell should I?'

'No reason at all. Except philanthropy.'

'Nothing doing, Contrôleur. I'm not a philanthropist.'

'That settles that. That was all. You can go.'

But as Ginger Ted turned to the door Miss Jones stopped him.

'It was my suggestion, Mr. Wilson. You see, they want me to go to Labobo and Sakunchi, and the natives there are so funny I was afraid to go alone. I thought if you came I should be safer.'

He gave her a look of extreme distaste.

'What do you suppose I care if they cut your throat?'

Miss Jones looked at him and her eyes filled with tears. She began to cry. He stood and watched her stupidly.

'There's no reason why you should.' She pulled herself together and dried her eyes. 'I'm being silly. I shall be all right. I'll go alone.'

'It's damned foolishness for a woman to go to Labobo.'

She gave him a little smile.

'I daresay it is, but you see, it's my job and I can't help myself. I'm sorry if I offended you by asking you. You must forget about it. I daresay it wasn't quite fair to ask you to take such a risk.'

For quite a minute Ginger Ted stood and looked at her. He shifted from one foot to the other. His surly face seemed to grow black.

'Oh, hell, have it your own way,' he said at last. 'I'll come with you. When d'you want to start?'

They set out next day, with drugs and disinfectants, in the Government launch. Mr. Gruyter as soon as he had put the necessary work in order was to start off in a prahu in the other direction. For four months the epidemic raged. Though everything possible was done to localise it one island after another was attacked. The Contrôleur was busy from morning to night. He had no sooner got back to Baru from one or other of the islands to do what was necessary there than he had to set off again. He distributed food and medicine. He cheered the terrified people. He supervised everything. He worked like a dog. He saw nothing of Ginger Ted, but he heard from Mr. Jones that the experiment was working out beyond all hopes. The scamp was behaving himself. He had a way with the natives; and by cajolery, firmness and on occasion the use of his fist, managed to make them take the steps necessary for their own safety. Miss Jones could congratulate herself on the success of the scheme. But the Contrôleur was too tired to be amused. When the epidemic had run its course he rejoiced because out of a population of eight thousand only six hundred had died.

Finally he was able to give the district a clean bill of health.

One evening he was sitting in his sarong on the verandah of his house and he read a French novel with the happy consciousness that once more he could take things easy. His head-boy came in and told him that Ginger Ted wished to see him. He got up from his chair and shouted to him to come in. Company was just what he wanted. It had crossed the Contrôleur's mind that it would be pleasant to get drunk that night, but it is dull to get drunk alone, and he had regretfully put the thought aside. And heaven had sent Ginger Ted in the nick of time. By God, they would make a night of it. After four months they deserved a bit of fun. Ginger Ted entered. He was wearing a clean suit of white ducks. He was shaved. He looked another man.

'Why, Ginger, you look as if you'd been spending a month at a health resort instead of nursing a pack of natives dying of cholera. And look at your clothes. Have you just stepped out of a band-box?'

Ginger Ted smiled rather sheepishly. The head-boy brought two bottles of beer and poured them out.

'Help yourself, Ginger,' said the Contrôleur as he took his glass.

'I don't think I'll have any, thank you.'

The Contrôleur put down his glass and looked at Ginger Ted with amazement.

'Why, what's the matter? Aren't you thirsty?'

'I don't mind having a cup of tea.'

'A cup of what?'

'I'm on the wagon. Martha and I are going to be married.'

'Ginger!'

The Contrôleur's eyes popped out of his head. He scratched his shaven pate.

'You can't marry Miss Jones,' he said. 'No one could marry Miss Jones.'

'Well, I'm going to. That's what I've come to see you about. Owen's going to marry us in chapel, but we want to be married by Dutch law as well.'

'A joke's a joke, Ginger. What's the idea?'

'She wanted it. She fell for me that night we spent on the island when the propeller broke. She's not a bad old girl when you get to know her. It's her last chance, if you understand what I mean, and I'd like to do something to oblige her. And she wants someone to take care of her, there's no doubt about that.'

'Ginger, Ginger, before you can say knife she'll make you into a damned missionary.'

'I don't know that I'd mind that so much if we had a little mission of our own. She says I'm a bloody marvel with the natives. She says I can do more with a native in five minutes than Owen can do in a year. She says she's never known anyone with the magnetism I have. It seems a pity to waste a gift like that.'

The Contrôleur looked at him without speaking and slowly nodded his head three or four times. She'd nobbled him all right.

'I've converted seventeen already,' said Ginger Ted.

'You? I didn't know you believed in Christianity.'

'Well, I don't know that I did exactly, but when I talked to 'em and they just came into the fold like a lot of blasted sheep, well, it gave me quite a turn. Blimey, I said, I daresay there's something in it after all.'

'You should have raped her, Ginger. I wouldn't have been hard on you. I wouldn't have given you more than three years' and three years' is soon over.'

'Look here, Contrôleur, don't you ever let on that the thought never entered my head. Women are touchy, you know, and she'd be as sore as hell if she knew that.'

'I guessed she'd got her eye on you, but I never thought it would come to this.' The Contrôleur in an agitated manner walked up and down the verandah. 'Listen to me, old boy,' he said after an interval of reflection, 'we've had some grand times together and a friend's a friend. I'll tell you what I'll do, I'll lend you the launch and you can go and hide on one of the islands till the next ship comes along and then I'll get 'em to slow down and take you on board. You've only got one chance now and that's to cut and run.'

Ginger Ted shook his head.

'It's no good, Contrôleur, I know you mean well, but I'm going to marry the blasted woman, and that's that. You don't know the joy of bringing all them bleeding sinners to repentance, and Christ! that girl can make a treacle pudding. I haven't eaten a better one since I was a kid.'

The Contrôleur was very much disturbed. The drunken scamp was his only companion on the islands and he did not want to lose him. He discovered that he had even a certain affection for him. Next day he went to see the missionary.

'What's this I hear about your sister marrying Ginger Ted?' he asked him. 'It's the most extraordinary thing I've ever heard in my life.'

'It's true nevertheless.'

'You must do something about it. It's madness.'

'My sister is of full age and entitled to do as she pleases.'

'But you don't mean to tell me you approve of it. You know Ginger Ted. He's a bum and there are no two ways about it. Have you told her the risk she's running? I mean, bringing sinners to repentance and all that sort of thing's all right, but there are limits. And does the leopard ever change his spots?'

Then for the first time in his life the Contrôleur saw a twinkle in the missionary's eye.

'My sister is a very determined woman, Mr. Gruyter,' he replied. 'From that night they spent on the island he never had a chance.'

The Contrôleur gasped. He was as surprised as the prophet when the Lord opened the mouth of the ass, and she said unto Balaam, What have I done unto thee, that thou hast smitten me these three times? Perhaps Mr. Jones was human after all.

'*Allejesus!*' muttered the Contrôleur.

Before anything more could be said Miss Jones swept into the room. She was radiant. She looked ten years younger. Her cheeks were flushed and her nose was hardly red at all.

'Have you come to congratulate me, Mr. Gruyter?' she cried, and her manner was sprightly and girlish. 'You see, I was right after all. Everyone has some good in them. You don't know how splendid Edward has been all through this terrible time. He's a hero. He's a saint. Even I was surprised.'

'I hope you'll be very happy, Miss Jones.'

'I know I shall. Oh, it would be wicked of me to doubt it. For it is the Lord who has brought us together.'

'Do you think so?'

'I know it. Don't you see? Except for the cholera Edward would never have found himself. Except for the cholera we should never have learnt to know one another. I have never seen the hand of God more plainly manifest.'

The Contrôleur could not but think that it was rather a clumsy device to bring those two together that necessitated the death of six hundred innocent persons, but not being well versed in the ways of omnipotence he made no remark.

'You'll never guess where we're going for our honeymoon,' said Miss Jones, perhaps a trifle archly.

'Java?'

'No, if you'll lend us the launch, we're going to that island where we were marooned. It has very tender recollections for both of us. It was there that I first guessed how fine and good Edward was. It's there I want him to have his reward.'

The Contrôleur caught his breath. He left quickly, for he thought that unless he had a bottle of beer at once he would have a fit. He was never so shocked in his life.

Flotsam and Jetsam

Norman Grange was a rubber-planter. He was up before daybreak to take the roll-call of his labour and then walked over the estate to see that the tapping was properly done. This duty performed, he came home, bathed and changed, and now with his wife opposite him he was eating the substantial meal, half breakfast and half luncheon, which in Borneo is called brunch. He read as he ate. The dining-room was dingy. The worn electro-plate, the shabby cruet, the chipped dishes betokened poverty, but a poverty accepted with apathy. A few flowers would have brightened the table, but there was apparently no one to care how things looked. When Grange had finished he belched, filled his pipe and lit it, rose from the table and went out on to the verandah. He took no more notice of his wife than if she had not been there. He lay down in a long rattan chair and went on reading. Mrs. Grange reached over for a tin of cigarettes and smoked while she sipped her tea. Suddenly she looked out, for the house-boy came up the steps and accompanied by two men went up to her husband. One was a Dyak and the other Chinese. Strangers seldom came and she could not imagine what they wanted. She got up and went to the door to listen. Though she had lived in Borneo for so many years she knew no more Malay than was necessary to get along with the boys, and she only vaguely understood what was said. She gathered from her husband's tone that something had happened to annoy him. He seemed to be asking questions first of the Chink and then of the

Dyak; it looked as though they were pressing him to do something he didn't want to do; at length, however, with a frown on his face he raised himself from his chair and followed by the men walked down the steps. Curious to see where he was going she slipped out on to the verandah. He had taken the path that led down to the river. She shrugged her thin shoulders and went to her room. Presently she gave a violent start, for she heard her husband call her.

'Vesta.'

She came out.

'Get a bed ready. 'There's a white man in a prahu at the landing-stage. He's damned ill.'

'Who is he?'

'How the hell should I know? They're just bringing him up.'

'We can't have anyone to stay here.'

'Shut up and do as I tell you.'

He left her on that and again went down to the river. Mrs. Grange called the boy and told him to put sheets on the bed in the spare room. Then she stood at the top of the steps and waited. In a little while she saw her husband coming back and behind him a huddle of Dyaks carrying a man on a mattress. She stood aside to let them pass and caught a glimpse of a white face.

'What shall I do?' she asked her husband.

'Get out and keep quiet.'

'Polite, aren't you?'

The sick man was taken into the room, and in two or three minutes the Dyaks and Grange came out.

'I'm going to see about his kit. I'll have it brought up. His boy's looking after him and there's no cause for you to butt in!'

'What's the matter with him?'

'Malaria. His boatmen are afraid he's going to die and won't take him on. His name's Skelton.'

'He isn't going to die, is he?'

'If he does we'll bury him.'

But Skelton didn't die. He woke next morning to find himself in a room, in bed and under a mosquito-net. He couldn't think where he was. It was a cheap iron bed and the mattress was hard, but to lie on it was a relief after the discomfort of the prahu. He could see nothing of the room but a chest of drawers, roughly made by a native carpenter, and a wooden chair. Opposite was a doorway, with a blind down, and this he guessed led on to a verandah.

'Kong,' he called.

The blind was drawn aside and his boy came in. The Chinaman's face broke into a grin when he saw that his master was free from fever.

'You more better, Tuan. Velly glad.'

'Where the devil am I?'

Kong explained.

'Luggage all right?' asked Skelton.

'Yes, him all right.'

'What's the name of this fellow – the tuan whose house this is?'

'Mr. Norman Glange.'

To confirm what he said he showed Skelton a little book in which the owner's name was written. It was Grange. Skelton noticed that the book was Bacon's *Essays*. It was curious to find it in a planter's house away up a river in Borneo.

'Tell him I'd be glad to see him.'

'Tuan out. Him come presently.'

'What about my having a wash? And by God, I want a shave.'

He tried to get out of bed, but his head swam and with a bewildered cry he sank back. But Kong shaved and washed him, and changed the shorts and singlet in which he had been lying ever since he fell ill for a sarong and a baju. After that he was glad to lie still. But presently Kong came in and said that the tuan of the house was back. There was a knock on the door and a large stoutish man stepped in.

'I hear you're better,' he said.

'Oh, much. It's terribly kind of you to have taken me in like this. It seems awful, planting myself on you.'

Grange answered a trifle harshly.

'That's all right. You were pretty bad, you know. No wonder those Dyaks wanted to get rid of you.'

'I don't want to impose myself on you longer than I need. If I could hire a launch here, or a prahu, I could get off this afternoon.'

'There's no launch to hire. You'd better stay a bit. You must be as weak as a rat.'

'I'm afraid I shall be a frightful bother.'

'I don't see why. You've got your own boy and he'll look after you.'

Grange had just come in from his round of the estate and wore dirty shorts, a khaki shirt open at the neck and an old, battered terai hat. He looked as shabby as a beachcomber. He took off his hat to wipe his sweating brow; he had close-cropped grey hair; his face was red, a broad, fleshy face, with a large mouth under a stubble of grey moustache, a short, pugnacious nose and small, mean eyes.

'I wonder if you could let me have something to read,' said Skelton.

'What sort of thing?'

'I don't mind so long as it's lightish.'

'I'm not much of a novel reader myself, but I'll send you in two or three books. My wife can provide you with novels. They'll be trash, because that's all she reads. But it may suit you.'

With a nod he withdrew. Not a very likeable man. But he was obviously very poor, the room in which

Skelton lay, something in Grange's appearance, indicated that; he was probably manager of an estate on a cut salary, and it was not unlikely that the expense of a guest and his servant was unwelcome. Living in that remote spot, and so seeing white men but seldom, it might be that he was ill at ease with strangers. Some people improve unbelievably on acquaintance. But his hard, shifty little eyes were disconcerting; they gave the lie to the red face and the massive frame which otherwise might have persuaded you that this was a jolly sort of fellow with whom you could quickly make friends.

After a while the house-boy came in with a parcel of books. There were half a dozen novels by authors he had never heard of, and a glance told him they were slop; these must be Mrs. Grange's; and then there was a Boswell's *Johnson*, Borrow's *Lavengro* and Lamb's *Essays*. It was an odd choice. They were not the books you would have expected to find in a planter's house. In most planter's houses there is not more than a shelf or two of books and for the most part they're detective stories. Skelton had a disinterested curiosity in human creatures, and he amused himself now by trying to make out from the books Norman Grange had sent, from the look of him and from the few words they had exchanged, what sort of a man he could be. Skelton was a little surprised that his host did not come to see him again that day; it looked as though he were going to content himself with giving his uninvited guest board and lodging, but were not sufficiently interested in him to seek his company. Next morning he felt well enough to get up, and with Kong's help settled himself in a long chair on the verandah. It badly needed a coat of paint. The bungalow stood on the brow of a hill, about fifty yards from the river; and on the opposite bank, looking very small across that great stretch of water, you could see native houses on piles nestling among the greenery.

Skelton had not yet the activity of mind to read steadily, and after a page or two, his thoughts wandering, he found himself content to watch idly the sluggish flow of the turbid stream. Suddenly he heard a step. He saw a little elderly woman come towards him, and knowing that this must be Mrs. Grange tried to get up.

'Don't move,' she said. 'I only came to see if you had everything you wanted.'

She wore a blue cotton dress, simple enough, but more suited to a young girl than to a woman of her age; her short hair was tousled, as though on getting out of bed she had scarcely troubled to pass a comb through it, and dyed a vivid yellow, but badly, and the roots showed white. Her skin was raddled and dry, and there was a great dab of rouge on each cheekbone, put on however so clumsily that you could not for a moment take it for a natural colour, and a smear of lipstick on her mouth. But the strangest thing about her was a tic she had that made her jerk her head as though she were beckoning you to an inner room. It seemed to come at regular intervals, perhaps three times a minute, and her left hand was in almost constant movement; it was not quite a tremble, it was a rapid twirl as though she wanted to draw your attention to something behind her back. Skelton was startled by her appearance and embarrassed by her tic.

'I hope I'm not making myself too great a nuisance,' he said. 'I think I shall be well enough to make a move to-morrow or the day after.'

'It's not often we see anybody in a place like this, you know. It's a treat to have someone to talk to.'

'Won't you sit down? I'll tell my boy to bring you a chair.'

'Norman said I was to leave you alone.'

'I haven't spoken to a white person for two years. I've been longing for a good old talk.'

Her head twitched violently, more quickly than usual, and her hand gave that queer spasmodic gesture.

'He won't be back for another hour. I'll get a chair.'

Skelton told her who he was and what he had been doing, but he discovered that she had questioned his boy and already knew all about him.

'You must be crazy to get back to England?' she asked.

'I shan't be sorry.'

Suddenly Mrs. Grange seemed to be attacked by what one could only describe as a nerve storm. Her head twitched so madly, her hand shook with such fury, that it was disconcerting. You could only look away.

'I haven't been to England for sixteen years,' she said.

'You don't mean that? Why, I thought all you planters went home every five years at the longest.'

'We can't afford it; we're broke to the wide. Norman put all the money he had into this plantation, and it hasn't really paid for years. It only just brings in enough to keep us from starvation. Of course it doesn't matter to Norman. He isn't English really.'

'He looks English enough.'

'He was born in Sarawak. His father was in the government service. If he's anything he's a native of Borneo.'

Then, without warning, she began to cry. It was horribly painful to see the tears running down the raddled, painted cheeks of that woman with the constant tic. Skelton knew neither what to say nor what to do. He did what was probably the best thing, he kept silent. She dried her eyes.

'You must think me a silly old fool. I sometimes wonder that after all these years I can still cry. I suppose it's in my nature. I always could cry very easy when I was on the stage.'

'Oh, were you on the stage?'

'Yes, before I married. That's how I met Norman. We were playing in Singapore and he was there on holiday. I don't suppose I shall ever see England any more. I shall stay here till I die and every day of my life I shall look at that beastly river. I shall never get away now. Never.'

'How did you happen to find yourself in Singapore?'

'Well, it was soon after the war, I couldn't get anything to suit me in London, I'd been on the stage a good many years and I was fed up with playing small parts; the agents told me a fellow called Victor Palace was taking a company out East. His wife was playing lead, but I could play seconds. They'd got half a dozen plays, comedies, you know, and farces. The salary wasn't much, but they were going to Egypt and India, the Malay States and China and then down to Australia. It was a chance to see the world and I accepted. We didn't do badly in Cairo and I think we made money in India, but Burma wasn't much good, and Siam was worse; Penang was a disaster and so were the rest of the Malay States. Well, one day Victor called us together and said he was bust, he hadn't got the money for our fares on to Hong Kong, and the tour was a wash-out and he was very sorry but we'd have to get back home as best we could. Of course we told him he couldn't do that to us. You never heard such a row. Well, the long and short of it was that he said we could have the scenery and the props if we thought they was any good to us, but as to money it was no use asking for it because he damned well hadn't got it. And next day we found out that him and his wife, without saying a word to anybody, had got on a French boat and skipped. I was in a rare state, I can tell you. I had a few pounds I'd saved out of me salary, and that was all; somebody told me if we was absolutely stranded the government would have to send us home, but only steerage, and I didn't much fancy that. We got the Press to put our plight before the public and someone came along with the proposition that we should give a benefit performance. Well, we did, but it wasn't much without Victor or his wife, and by the time we'd paid the expenses we weren't any better off than we'd been before. I was at my wits' end, I don't mind telling you. It was then that Norman proposed to me. The funny thing is that I hardly knew him. He'd taken me for a drive round the island and we'd had tea two or three times at the Europe and danced. Men don't often do things for you without wanting something in return, and I thought he expected to get a little bit of fun, but I'd had a good deal of experience and I thought he'd be clever if he got round me. But when he asked me to marry him, well, I was so surprised, I couldn't hardly believe me own ears. He said he'd got his own estate in Borneo and it only wanted a little patience and he'd make a packet. And it was on the banks of a fine river and all round was the jungle. He made it sound very romantic. I was getting on, you know, I was thirty, it wasn't going to be any easier to get work as time went on, and it was tempting to have a house of me own and all that. Never to have to hang around agents' offices no more. Never to have to lay awake no more and wonder how you was going to pay next week's rent. He wasn't a bad-looking chap in those days, brown and big and virile. No one could say I was willing to marry anybody just to . . .' Suddenly she stopped. 'There he is. Don't say you've seen me.'

She picked up the chair she had been sitting in and quickly slipped away with it into the house. Skelton was bewildered. Her grotesque appearance, the painful tears, her story told with that incessant twitching; and then her obvious fear when she heard her husband's voice in the compound, and her hurried escape; he could make nothing of it.

In a few minutes Norman Grange stumped along the verandah.

'I hear you're better,' he said.

'Much, thanks.'

'If you care to join us at brunch I'll have a place laid for you.'

'I'd like it very much.'

'All right. I'm just going to have a bath and a change.'

He walked away. Presently a boy came along and told Skelton his tuan was waiting for him. Skelton followed him into a small sitting-room, with the jalousies drawn to keep out the heat, an uncomfortable, overcrowded room with a medley of furniture, English and Chinese, and occasional tables littered with worthless junk. It was neither cosy nor cool. Grange had changed into a sarong and baju and in the native dress looked coarse but powerful. He introduced Skelton to his wife. She shook hands with him as though she had never seen him before and uttered a few polite words of greeting. The boy announced that their meal was ready and they went into the dining-room.

'I hear that you've been in this bloody country for some time,' said Grange.

'Two years. I'm an anthropologist, and I wanted to study the manners and customs of tribes that haven't had any contact with civilisation.'

Skelton felt that he should tell his host how it had come about that he had been forced to accept a hospitality which he could not but feel was grudgingly offered. After leaving the village that had been his head-quarters he had journeyed by land for ten days till he reached the river. There he had engaged a couple of prahus, one for himself and his luggage and the other for Kong, his Chinese servant, and the camp equipment, to take him to the coast. The long trek across country had been hard going and he found it very comfortable to lie on a mattress under an awning of rattan matting and take his ease. All the time he had been away Skelton had been in perfect health, and as he travelled down the river he could not but think that he was very lucky; but even as the thought passed through his mind, it occurred to him that if he happened just then to congratulate himself on his good fortune in this respect, it was because he did not feel quite so well as usual. It was true that he had been forced to drink a great deal of arak the night before at the long-house where he had put up, but he was used to it and that hardly accounted for his headache. He had a general sense of malaise. He was wearing nothing but shorts and a singlet, and he felt chilly; it was curious because the sun was shining fiercely and when he put his head on the gunwale of the prahu the heat was hardly bearable. If he had had a coat handy he would have put it on. He grew colder and colder and presently his teeth began to chatter; he huddled up on his mattress, shivering all over, in a desperate effort to get warm. He could not fail to guess what was the matter.

'Christ,' he groaned. 'Malaria.'

He called the headman, who was steering the prahu.

'Get Kong.'

The headman shouted to the second prahu and ordered his own paddlers to stop. In a moment the two boats were side by side and Kong stepped in.

'I've got fever, Kong,' gasped Skelton. 'Get me the medicine chest and, for God's sake, blankets. I'm freezing to death.'

Kong gave his master a big dose of quinine and piled on him what coverings they had. They started off again.

Skelton was too ill to be taken ashore when they tied up for the night and so passed it in the prahu. All next day and the day after he was very ill. Sometimes one or other of the crew came and looked at him, and often the headman stayed for quite a long while staring at him thoughtfully.

'How many days to the coast?' Skelton asked the boy.

'Four, five.' He paused for a minute. 'Headman, he no go coast. He say, he wantchee go home.'

'Tell him to go to hell.'

'Headman say, you velly sick, you die. If you die and he go coast he catchee trouble.'

'I'm not thinking of dying,' said Skelton. 'I shall be all right. It's just an ordinary go of malaria.'

Kong did not answer. The silence irritated Skelton. He knew that the Chinese had something in mind that he did not like to say.

'Spit it out, you fool,' he cried.

Skelton's heart sank when Kong told him the truth. When they reached their resting-place that night the headman was going to demand his money and slip away with the two prahus before dawn. He was too frightened to carry a dying man farther. Skelton had no strength to take the determined attitude that might have availed him; he could only hope by the offer of more money to persuade the headman to carry out his agreement. The day passed in long arguments between Kong and the headman, but when they tied up for the night the head-man came to Skelton and told him sulkily that he would go no farther. There was a long-house nearby where he might get lodging till he grew better. He began to unload the baggage. Skelton refused to move. He got Kong to give him his revolver and swore to shoot any-one who came near him.

Kong, the crew and the headman went up to the long-house and Skelton was left alone. Hour after hour he lay there, the fever burning his body and his mouth parched, while muddled thoughts hammered away in his brain. Then there were lights and the sound of men talking. The Chinese boy came with the headman and another man, whom Skelton had not yet seen, from the neighbouring long-house. He did his best to understand what Kong was telling him. It appeared that a few hours downstream there lived a white man, and to his house, if that would satisfy Skelton, the headman was willing to take him.

'More better you say yes,' said Kong. 'Maybe white man has launch, then we go down to coast chop-chop.'

'Who is he?'

'Planter,' said Kong. 'This fellow say, him have rubber estate.'

Skelton was too tired to argue further. All he wanted just then was to sleep. He accepted the compromise.

'To tell you the truth,' he finished, 'I don't remember much more till I woke up yesterday morning to find myself an uninvited guest in your house.'

'I don't blame those Dyaks, you know,' said Grange. 'When I came down to the prahu and saw you, I thought you were for it.'

Mrs. Grange sat silent while Skelton told his story, her head and her hand twitching regularly, as though by the action of some invisible clockwork, but when her husband addressed her, asking for the Worcester sauce, and that was the only time he spoke to her, she was seized with such a paroxysm of involuntary movement that it was horrible to see. She passed him what he asked for without a word. Skelton got an uncomfortable impression that she was terrified of Grange. It was odd, because to all appearance he was not a bad sort. He was knowledgeable and far from stupid; and though you could not have said that his manner was cordial, it was plain that he was ready to be of what service he could.

They finished their meal and separated to rest through the heat of the day.

'See you again at six for a sundowner,' said Grange.

When Skelton had had a good sleep, a bath and a read,

he went out on to the verandah. Mrs. Grange came up to him. It looked as though she had been waiting.

'He's back from the office. Don't think it's funny if I don't speak to you. If he thought I liked having you here he'd turn you out tomorrow.'

She said these words in a whisper and slipped back into the house. Skelton was startled. It was a strange house he had come into in a strange manner. He went into the overcrowded sitting-room and there found his host. He had been worried by the evident poverty of the establishment and he felt that the Granges could ill afford even the small expense he must be putting them to. But he had already formed the impression that Grange was a quick-tempered, susceptible man and he did not know how he would take an offer to help. He made up his mind to risk it.

'Look here,' he said to him, 'it looks as though I might have to inflict myself on you for several days, I'd be so much more comfortable if you'd let me pay for my board and lodging.'

'Oh, that's all right, your lodging costs nothing, the house belongs to the mortgagees, and your board doesn't come to much.'

'Well, there are drinks anyway and I've had to come down on your stores of tobacco and cigarettes.'

'It's not more than once a year that anyone comes up here, and then it's only the D.O. or someone like that – besides, when one's as broke as I am nothing matters much.'

'Well, then, will you take my camp equipment? I shan't be wanting it any more, and if you'd like one of my guns, I'd be only too glad to leave it with you.'

Grange hesitated. There was a glimmer of cupidity in those small, cunning eyes of his.

'If you'd let me have one of your guns you'd pay for your board and lodging over and over again.'

'That's settled, then.'

They began to talk over the whisky and sparkler with which, following the Eastern habit, they celebrated the setting of the sun. Discovering that they both played chess they had a game. Mrs. Grange did not join them till dinner. The meal was dull. An insipid soup, a tasteless river fish, a tough piece of steak and a caramel pudding. Norman Grange and Skelton drank beer; Mrs. Grange water. She never of her own will uttered a word. Skelton had again the uncomfortable impression that she was scared to death of her husband. Once or twice, Skelton from common politeness sought to bring her into the conversation, addressing himself to her, telling her a story or asking her a question, but it evidently distressed her so much, her head twitched so violently, her hand was agitated by gestures so spasmodic that he thought it kinder not to insist. When the meal was over she got up.

'I'll leave you gentlemen to your port,' she said.

Both the men got up as she left the room. It was rather absurd, and somehow sinister, to see this social pretence in those poverty-stricken surroundings on a Borneo river.

'I may add that there is no port. There might be a little Benedictine left.'

'Oh, don't bother.'

They talked for a while and Grange began to yawn. He got up every morning before sunrise and by nine o'clock at night could hardly keep his eyes open.

'Well, I'm going to turn in,' he said.

He nodded to Skelton and without further ceremony left him. Skelton went to bed, but he could not sleep. Though the heat was oppressive, it was not the heat that kept him awake. There was something horrible about that house and those two people who lived in it. He didn't know what it was that affected him with this peculiar uneasiness, but this he knew, that he would be heartily thankful to be out of it and away from them. Grange had talked a good deal about himself, but he knew no more of him than he had learned at the first glance. To all appearances he was just the commonplace planter who had fallen upon evil days. He had bought his land immediately after the war and had planted trees; but by the time they were bearing the slump had come and since then it had been a constant struggle to keep going. The estate and the house were heavily mortgaged, and now that rubber was once more selling profitably all he made went to the mortgagees. That was an old story in Malaya. What made Grange somewhat unusual was that he was a man without a country. Born in Borneo, he had lived there with his parents till he was old enough to go to school in England; at seventeen he had come back and had never left it since except to go to Mesopotamia during the war. England meant nothing to him. He had neither relations nor friends there. Most planters, like civil servants, have come from England, go back on leave now and then, and look forward to settling down there when they retire. But what had England to offer Norman Grange?

'I was born here,' he said, 'and I shall die here. I'm a stranger in England. I don't like their ways over there and I don't understand the things they talk about. And yet I'm a stranger here too. To the Malays and the Chinese I'm a white man, though I speak Malay as well as they do, and a white man I shall always be.' Then he said a significant thing. 'Of course if I'd had any sense I'd have married a Malay girl and had half a dozen half-caste kids. That's the only solution really for us chaps who were born and bred here.'

Grange's bitterness was greater than could be explained by his financial embarrassment. He had little good to say of any of the white men in the colony. He seemed to think that they despised him because he was native-born. He was a sour, disappointed fellow, and a conceited one. He had shown Skelton his books. There were not many of them, but they were the best on the whole that English literature can show; he had read them over and over again; but it looked as though he had learnt from them neither charity nor loving-kindness, it looked as though their beauty had left him unmoved; and to know them so well had only made him self-complacent. His exterior, which was so hearty and English, seemed to have little relation to the man within; you could not resist the suspicion that it masked a very sinister being.

Early next morning, to enjoy the cool of the day, Skelton, with his pipe and a book, was sitting on the verandah outside his room. He was still very weak, but felt much better. In a little while Mrs. Grange joined him. She held in her hand a large album.

'I thought I'd like to show you some of me old photos and me notices. You mustn't think I always looked like what I do now. He's off on his round and he won't be back for two or three hours yet.'

Mrs. Grange, in the same blue dress she had worn the day before, her hair as untidy, appeared strangely excited.

'It's all I have to remind me of the past. Sometimes when I can't bear life any more I look at my album.'

She sat by Skelton's side as he turned the pages. The notices were from provincial papers, and the references to Mrs. Grange, whose stage name had been apparently Vesta Blaise, were carefully underlined. From the photographs you could see that she had been pretty enough in an undistinguished way. She had acted in musical comedy and revue, in farce and comedy, and taking the photographs and the notices together it was easy to tell that here had been the common, dreary, rather vulgar career of the girl with no particular talent who has taken to the stage on the strength of a pretty face and a good figure. Her head twitching, her hand shaking, Mrs. Grange looked at the photographs and read the notices with as much interest as if she had never seen them before.

'You've got to have influence on the stage, and I never had any,' she said. 'If I'd only had my chance I know I'd have made good. I had bad luck, there's no doubt about that.'

It was all sordid and somewhat pathetic.

'I daresay you're better off as you are,' said Skelton.

She snatched the book from him and shut it with a bang. She had a paroxysm so violent that it was really frightening to look at her.

'What d'you mean by that? What d'you know about the life I lead here? I'd have killed myself years ago only I know he wants me to die. That's the only way I can get back on him, by living, and I'm going to live; I'm going to live as long as he does. Oh, I hate him. I've often thought I'd poison him, but I was afraid. I didn't know how to do it really, and if he died the Chinks would foreclose and I'd be turned out. And where should I go then? I haven't a friend in the world.'

Skelton was aghast. It flashed through his mind that she was crazy. He hadn't a notion what to say. She gave him a keen look.

'I suppose it surprises you to hear me talk like that. I mean it, you know, every word of it. He'd like to kill me too, but he daren't either. And he knows how to do it all right. He knows how the Malays kill people. He was born here. There's nothing he doesn't know about the country.'

Skelton forced himself to speak.

'You know, Mrs. Grange, I'm a total stranger. Don't

you think it's rather unwise to tell me all sorts of things there's no need for me to know? After all, you live a very solitary life. I daresay you get on one another's nerves. Now that things are looking up perhaps you'll be able to take a trip to England.'

'I don't want to go to England. I'd be ashamed to let them see me like I am now. D'you know how old I am? Forty-six. I look sixty and I know it. That's why I showed you those photos, so as you might see I wasn't always like what I am now. Oh, my God, how I've wasted my life! They talk of the romance of the East. They can have it. I'd rather be a dresser in a provincial theatre, I'd rather be one of the sweepers that keep it clean, than what I am now. Until I came here I'd never been alone in me life, I'd always lived in a crowd; you don't know what it is to have nobody to talk to from year's end to year's end. To have to keep it all bottled up. How would you like to see no one, week in and week out, day after day for sixteen years, except the man you hate most in the world? How would you like to live for sixteen years with a man who hates you so he can't bear to look at you?'

'Oh come, it can't be as bad as that.'

'I'm telling you the truth. Why should I tell you a lie? I shall never see you again; what do I care what you think of me? And if you tell them what I've said when you get down to the coast, what's the odds? They'll say: "God, you don't mean to say you stayed with those people? I pity you. He's an outsider and she's crazy; got a tic; they say it looks as if she was always trying to wipe the blood off her dress. They were mixed up in a damned funny business, but no one ever really knew the ins and outs of it; it all happened a long time ago and the country was pretty wild in those days". A damned funny business and no mistake. I'd tell you for two pins. That would be a bit of dirt for them at the club. You wouldn't have to pay for a drink for days. Damn them. Oh, Christ, how I hate this country. I hate that river. I hate this house. I hate that damned rubber. I loathe the filthy natives. And that's all I've got to look forward to till I die – till I die without a doctor to take care of me, without a friend to hold me hand.'

She began to cry hysterically. Mrs. Grange had spoken with a dramatic intensity of which Skelton would never have thought her capable. Her coarse irony was as painful as her anguish. Skelton was young, he was not yet thirty, and he did not know how to deal with the difficult situation. But he could not keep silent.

'I'm terribly sorry, Mrs. Grange. I wish I could do something to help you.'

'I'm not asking for your help. No one can help me.'

Skelton was distressed. From what she said he could not but suspect that she had been concerned in a mysterious and perhaps dreadful occurrence, and it might be that to tell him about it without fear of the consequences was just the relief she needed.

'I don't want to butt into what's no business of mine, but, Mrs. Grange, if you think it would ease your mind to tell me – what you were referring to just now, I mean what you said was a damned funny business, I promise you on my word of honour that I'll never repeat it to a living soul.'

She stopped crying quite suddenly and gave him a long, intent look. She hesitated. He had an impression that the desire to speak was almost irresistible. But she shook her head and sighed.

'It wouldn't do any good. Nothing can do me any good.'

She got up and abruptly left him.

The two men sat down to brunch by themselves.

'My wife asks you to excuse her,' said Grange. 'She's got one of her sick headaches and she's staying in bed today.'

'Oh, I'm sorry.'

Skelton had a notion that in the searching look that Grange gave him was mistrust and animosity. It flashed through his mind that somehow he had discovered that Mrs. Grange had been talking to him and perhaps had said things that should have been left unsaid. Skelton made an effort at conversation, but his host was taciturn, and they ended the meal in a silence that was only broken by Grange when he got up.

'You seem pretty fit today and I don't suppose you want to stay in this God-forsaken place longer than you must. I've sent over the river to arrange for a couple of prahus to take you down to the coast. They'll be here at six to-morrow morning.'

Skelton felt sure then that he was right; Grange knew or guessed that his wife had spoken too freely, and he wanted to be rid as soon as possible of the dangerous visitor.

'That's terribly kind of you,' Skelton answered, smiling. 'I'm as fit as a fiddle.'

But in Grange's eyes was no answering smile. They were coldly hostile.

'We might have another game of chess later on,' said he.

'All right. When d'you get back from your office?'

'I haven't got much to do there today. I shall be about the house.'

Skelton wondered if it were only his fancy that there was something very like a threat in the tone in which Grange uttered these words. It looked as though he were going to make sure that his wife and Skelton should not again be left alone. Mrs. Grange did not come to dinner. They drank their coffee and smoked their cheroots. Then Grange, pushing back his chair, said:

'You've got to make an early start tomorrow. I daresay you'd like to turn in. I shall have started out on my round by the time you go, so I'll say goodbye to you now.'

'Let me get my guns. I want you to take the one you like best.'

'I'll tell the boy to fetch them.'

The guns were brought and Grange made his choice. He gave no sign that he was pleased with the handsome gift.

'You quite understand that this gun's worth a damned sight more than what your food and drink and smoke have run me into?' he said.

'For all I know you saved my life. I don't think an old gun is an over-generous return for that.'

'Oh, well, if you like to look at it that way, I suppose it's your own business. Thank you very much all the same.'

They shook hands and parted.

Next morning, while the baggage was being stowed away in the prahus, Skelton asked the house-boy whether, before starting, he could say goodbye to Mrs. Grange. The house-boy said he would go and see. He waited a little while. Mrs. Grange came out of her room on to the verandah. She was wearing a pink dressing-gown, shabby, rumpled and none too clean, of Japanese silk, heavily trimmed with cheap lace. The powder was thick on her face, her cheeks were rouged and her lips scarlet with lipstick. Her head seemed to twitch more violently than usual and her hand was agitated by that strange gesture. When first Skelton saw it he had thought that it suggested a wish to call attention to something behind her back, but now, after what she had told him yesterday, it did indeed look as though she were constantly trying to brush something off her dress. Blood, she had said.

'I didn't want to go without thanking you for all your kindness to me,' he said.

'Oh, that's all right.'

'Well, goodbye.'

'I'll walk down with you to the landing-stage.'

They hadn't far to go. The boatmen were still arranging the luggage. Skelton looked across the river where you could see some native houses.

'I suppose these men come from over there. It looks quite a village.'

'No, only those few houses. There used to be a rubber estate there, but the company went broke and it was abandoned.'

'D'you ever go over there?'

'Me?' cried Mrs. Grange. Her voice rose shrill and her head, her hand, were on a sudden convulsed by a paroxysm of involuntary movement. 'No. Why should I?'

Skelton could not imagine why that simple question, asked merely for something to say, should so greatly upset her. But by now all was in order and he shook hands with her. He stepped into the boat and comfortably settled down. They pushed off. He waved to Mrs. Grange. As the boat slid into the current she cried out with a harsh, strident scream:

'Give my regards to Leicester Square.'

Skelton heaved a great sigh of relief as with their powerful strokes the paddlers took him farther and farther away from that dreadful house and from those two unhappy and yet repellent people. He was glad now that Mrs. Grange had not told him the story that was on the tip of her tongue to tell. He did not want some tragic tale of sin or folly to connect him with them in a recollection that he could not escape. He wanted to forget them as one forgets a bad dream.

But Mrs. Grange watched the two prahus till a bend of the river took them out of sight. She walked slowly up to the house and went into her bedroom. The light was dim because the blinds were drawn to keep out the heat, but she sat down at her dressing-table and stared at herself in the glass. Norman had had the dressing-table made for her soon after they were married. It had been made by a native carpenter, of course, and they had had the mirror sent from Singapore, but it was made to her own design, of the exact size and shape she wanted, with plenty of room for all her toilet things and her make-up. It was the dressing-table she had hankered after for donkey's years and had never had. She remembered still how pleased she was when first she had it. She threw her arms round her husband's neck and kissed him.

'Oh, Norman, you are good to me,' she said. 'I'm a lucky little girl to have caught a chap like you, aren't I?'

But then everything delighted her. She was amused by the river life and the life of the jungle, the teeming growth of the forest, the birds with their gay plumage and the brilliant butterflies. She set about giving the house a woman's touch; she put out all her own photographs and she got vases to put flowers in; she routed around and got a lot of knick-knacks to place here and there. 'They make a room look homey,' she said. She wasn't in love with Norman, but she liked him all right; and it was lovely to be married; it was lovely to have nothing to do from morning till night, except play the gramophone, or patience, and read novels. It was lovely to think one hadn't got to bother about one's future. Of course it was a bit lonely sometimes, but Norman said she'd get used to that, and he'd promised that in a year, or two at the outside, he'd take her to England for three months. It would be a lark to show him off to her friends. She felt that what had caught him was the glamour of the stage and she'd made herself out a good deal more successful than she really had been. She wanted him to realise that she'd made a sacrifice when she'd thrown up her career to become a planter's wife.

She'd claimed acquaintance with a good many stars that in point of fact she'd never even spoken to. That would need a bit of handling when they went home, but she'd manage it; after all, poor Norman knew no more about the stage than a babe unborn; if she couldn't cod a simple fellow like that, after twelve years on the stage, well, she'd wasted her time, that's all she could say. Things went all right the first year. At one moment she thought she was going to have a baby. They were both disappointed when it turned out not to be true. Then she began to grow bored. It seemed to her that she'd done the same damned thing day after day for ever and it frightened her to think that she'd have to go on doing the same damned thing day after day for ever more. Norman said he couldn't leave the plantation that year. They had a bit of a scene. It was then that he'd said something that scared her.

'I hate England,' he said. 'If I had my way I'd never set foot in the damned country again.'

Living this lonely life Mrs. Grange got into the habit of talking out loud to herself. Shut up in her room she could be heard chattering away hour after hour; and now, dipping the puff in her powder and plastering her face with it, she addressed her reflection in the mirror exactly as though she were talking to another person.

'That ought to have warned me. I should have insisted on going by myself, and who knows, I might have got a job when I got to London. With all the experience I had and everything. Then I'd have written to him and said I wasn't coming back.' Her thoughts turned to Skelton. 'Pity I didn't tell him,' she continued. 'I had half a mind to. P'raps he was right, p'raps it would have eased me mind. I wonder what he'd have said.' She imitated his Oxford accent. 'I'm so terribly sorry, Mrs. Grange. I wish I could help you.' She gave a chuckle which was almost a sob. 'I'd have liked to tell him about Jack. Oh, Jack.'

It was when they had been married for two years that they got a neighbour. The price of rubber at that time was so high that new estates were being put under cultivation and one of the big companies had bought a great tract of land on the opposite bank of the river. It was a rich company and everything was done on a lavish scale. The manager they had put in had a launch at his disposal so that it was no trouble for him to pop over and have a drink whenever he felt inclined. Jack Carr his name was. He was quite a different sort of chap from Norman; for one thing he was a gentleman, he'd been to a public school and a university; he was about thirty-five, tall, not beefy like Norman, but slight, he had the sort of figure that looked lovely in evening dress; and he had crisply curling hair and a laughing look in his eyes. Just her type. She took to him at once. It was a treat, having someone you could talk about London to, and the theatre. He was gay and easy. He made the sort of jokes you could understand. In a week or two she felt more at home with him than she did with her husband after two years. There had always been something about Norman that she hadn't quite been able to get to the bottom of. He was crazy about her, of course, and he'd told her a lot about himself, but she had a funny feeling that there was something he kept from her, not because he wanted to, but – well, you couldn't hardly explain it – because it was so alien, you might say, that he couldn't put it into words. Later, when she knew Jack better, she mentioned it to him, and Jack said it was because he was country-born; even though he hadn't a drop of native blood in his veins, something of the country had gone to the making of him so that he wasn't white really; he had an Eastern streak in him. However hard he tried he could never be quite English.

She chattered away aloud, in that empty house, for the two boys, the cook and the house-boy, were in their own quarters, and the sound of her voice, ringing along the wooden floors, piercing the wooden walls, was like the uncanny, unhuman gibber of new wine fermenting in a vat. She spoke just as though Skelton were there, but so incoherently that if he had been, he would have had difficulty in following the story she told. It did not take her long to discover that Jack Carr wanted her. She was excited. She'd never been promiscuous, but in all those years she'd been on the stage naturally there'd been episodes. You couldn't hardly have put up with being on tour month after month if you didn't have a bit of fun sometimes. Of course now she wasn't going to give in too easily, she didn't want to make herself cheap, but what with the life she led, she'd be a fool if she missed the chance; and as far as Norman was concerned, well, what the eye didn't see the heart didn't grieve over. They understood one another all right, Jack and her; they knew it was bound to happen sooner or later, it was only a matter of waiting for the opportunity; and the opportunity came. But then something happened that they hadn't bargained for: they fell madly in love with one another. If Mrs. Grange really had been telling the story to Skelton it might have seemed as unlikely to him as it did to them. They were two very ordinary people, he a jolly, good-natured, commonplace planter, and she a small-part actress far from clever, not even very young, with nothing to recommend her but a neat figure and a prettyish face. What started as a casual affair turned without warning into a devastating passion, and neither of them was of a texture to sustain its exorbitant compulsion. They longed to be with one another; they were restless and miserable apart. She'd been finding Norman a bore for some time, but she'd put up with him because he was her husband; now he

irritated her to frenzy because he stood between her and
Jack. There was no question of their going off together,
Jack Carr had nothing but his salary, and he couldn't
throw up a job he'd been only too glad to get. It was
difficult for them to meet. They had to run awful risks.
Perhaps the chances they had to take, the obstacles they
had to surmount, were fuel to their love; a year passed
and it was as overwhelming as at the beginning; it was
a year of agony and bliss, of fear and thrill. Then she discovered that she was pregnant. She had no doubt that
Jack Carr was the father and she was wildly happy. It
was true life was difficult, so difficult sometimes that
she felt she just couldn't cope with it, but there'd be a
baby, his baby, and that would make everything easy.
She was going to Kuching for her confinement. It
happened about then that Jack Carr had to go to Singapore on business and was to be away for several weeks;
but he promised to get back before she left and he said
he'd send word by a native the moment he arrived.
When at last the message came she felt sick with the
anguish of her joy. She had never wanted him so badly.

'I hear that Jack is back,' she told her husband at
dinner. 'I shall go over tomorrow morning and get the
things he promised to bring me.'

'I wouldn't do that. He's pretty sure to drop in towards sundown and he'll bring them himself.'

'I can't wait. I'm crazy to have them.'

'All right. Have it your own way.'

She couldn't help talking about him. For some time
now they had seemed to have little to say to one
another, Norman and she, but that night, in high spirits,
she chattered away as she had done during the first
months of their marriage. She always rose early, at six,
and next morning she went down to the river and had a
bathe. There was a little dent in the bank just there,
with a tiny sandy beach, and it was delicious to splash

about in the cool, transparent water. A kingfisher stood on the branch of a tree overhanging the pool and its reflection was brilliantly blue in the water. Lovely. She had a cup of tea and then stepped into a dug-out. A boy paddled her across the river. It took a good half-hour. As they got near she scanned the bank; Jack knew she would come at the earliest opportunity; he must be on the look-out. Ah, there he was. The delicious pain in her heart was almost unbearable. He came down to the landing-stage and helped her to get out of the boat. They walked hand in hand up the pathway and when they were out of sight of the boy who had paddled her over and of prying eyes from the house, they stopped. He put his arms round her and she yielded with ecstasy to his embrace. She clung to him. His mouth sought hers. In that kiss was all the agony of their separation and all the bliss of their reunion. The miracle of love transfused them so that they were unconscious of time and place. They were not human any more, but two spirits united by a divine fire. No thought passed through their minds. No words issued from their lips. Suddenly there was a brutal shock, like a blow, and immediately, almost simultaneously, a deafening noise. Horrified, not understanding, she clung to Jack more tightly and his grip on her was spasmodic, so that she gasped; then she felt that he was bearing her over.

'Jack.'

She tried to hold him up. His weight was too great for her and as he fell to the ground she fell with him. Then she gave a great cry, for she felt a gush of heat, and his blood sputtered over her. She began to scream. A rough hand seized her and dragged her to her feet. It was Norman. She was distraught. She could not understand.

'Norman, what have you done?'

'I've killed him.'

She stared at him stupidly. She pushed him aside.

'Jack. Jack.'

'Shut up. I'll go and get help. It was an accident.'

He walked quickly up the pathway. She fell to her knees and took Jack's head in her arms.

'Darling,' she moaned. 'Oh, my darling.'

Norman came back with some coolies and they carried him up to the house. That night she had a miscarriage and was so ill that for days it looked as if she would die. When she recovered she had the nervous tic that she'd had ever since. She expected that Norman would send her away; but he didn't, he had to keep her to allay suspicion. There was some talk among the natives, and after a while the District Officer came up and asked a lot of questions; but the natives were frightened of Norman, and the D.O. could get nothing out of them. The Dyak boy who paddled her over had vanished. Norman said something had gone wrong with his gun and Jack was looking at it to see what was the matter and it went off. They bury people quickly in that country and by the time they might have dug him up there wouldn't have been much left to show that Norman's story wasn't true. The D.O. hadn't been satisfied.

'It all looks damned fishy to me,' he said, 'but in the absence of any evidence, I suppose I must accept your version.'

She would have given anything to get away, but with that nervous affliction she had no ghost of a chance any longer of earning a living. She had to stay – or starve; and Norman had to keep her – or hang. Nothing had happened since then and now nothing ever would happen. The endless years one after another dragged out their weary length.

Mrs. Grange on a sudden stopped talking. Her sharp ears had caught the sound of a footstep on the path and she knew that Norman was back from his round. Her head twitching furiously, her hand agitated by that sinister, uncontrollable gesture, she looked in the untidy mess of her dressing-table for her precious lipstick. She smeared it on her lips, and then, she didn't know why, on a freakish impulse daubed it all over her nose till she looked like a red-nose comedian in a music-hall. She looked at herself in the glass and burst out laughing.

'To hell with life!' she shouted.

The Book-Bag

Some people read for instruction, which is praiseworthy, and some for pleasure, which is innocent, but not a few read from habit, and I suppose that this is neither innocent nor praiseworthy. Of that lamentable company am I. Conversation after a time bores me, games tire me and my own thoughts, which we are told are the unfailing resource of a sensible man, have a tendency to run dry. Then I fly to my book as the opium-smoker to his pipe. I would sooner read the catalogue of the Army and Navy Stores or Bradshaw's Guide than nothing at all, and indeed I have spent many delightful hours over both these works. At one time I never went out without a second-hand bookseller's list in my pocket. I know no reading more fruity. Of course to read in this way is as reprehensible as doping, and I never cease to wonder at the impertinence of great readers who, because they are such, look down on the illiterate. From the standpoint of what eternity is it better to have read a thousand books than to have ploughed a million furrows? Let us admit that reading with us is just a drug that we cannot do without – who of this band does not know the restlessness that attacks him when he has been severed from reading too long, the apprehension and irritability, and the sigh of relief which the sight of a printed page extracts from him? – and so let us be no more vainglorious than the poor slaves of the hypodermic needle or the pint-pot.

And like the dope-fiend who cannot move from place to place without taking with him a plentiful supply of his deadly balm I never venture far without a sufficiency of reading matter. Books are so necessary to me that when in a railway train I have become aware that fellow-travellers have come away without a single one I have been seized with a veritable dismay. But when I am starting on a long journey the problem is formidable. I have learnt my lesson. Once, imprisoned by illness for three months in a hill-town in Java, I came to the end of all the books I had brought with me, and knowing no Dutch was obliged to buy the school-books from which intelligent Javanese, I suppose, acquired knowledge of French and German. So I read again after five-and-twenty years the frigid plays of Goethe, the fables of La Fontaine and the tragedies of the tender and exact Racine. I have the greatest admiration for Racine, but I admit that to read his plays one after the other requires a certain effort in a person who is suffering from colitis. Since then I have made a point of travelling with the largest sack made for carrying soiled linen and filling it to the brim with books to suit every possible occasion and every mood. It weighs a ton and strong porters reel under its weight. Custom-house officials look at it askance, but recoil from it with consternation when I give them my word that it contains nothing but books. Its inconvenience is that the particular work I suddenly hanker to read is always at the bottom and it is impossible for me to get it without emptying the book-bag's entire contents upon the floor. Except for this, however, I should perhaps never have heard the singular history of Olive Hardy.

I was wandering about Malaya, staying here and there, a week or two if there was a rest-house or a hotel, and a day or so if I was obliged to inflict myself on a planter or a District Officer whose hospitality I had no wish to abuse; and at the moment I happened to be at Penang. It is a pleasant little town, with a hotel that has always seemed to me very agreeable, but the stranger finds little to do there and time hung a trifle heavily on my hands. One morning I received a letter from a man I knew only by name. This was Mark Featherstone. He was Acting Resident, in the absence on leave of the Resident, at a place called Tenggarah. There was a sultan there and it appeared that a water festival of some sort was to take place which Featherstone thought would interest me. He said that he would be glad if I would come and stay with him for a few days. I wired to tell him that I should be delighted and next day took the train to Tenggarah. Featherstone met me at the station. He was a man of about thirty-five, I should think, tall and handsome, with fine eyes and a strong, stern face. He had a wiry black moustache and bushy eyebrows. He looked more like a soldier than a government official. He was very smart in white ducks, with a white topee, and he wore his clothes with elegance. He was a little shy, which seemed odd in a strapping fellow of resolute mien, but I surmised that this was only because he was unused to the society of that strange fish, a writer, and I hoped in a little to put him at his ease.

'My boys'll look after your barang,' he said. 'We'll go down to the club. Give them your keys and they'll unpack before we get back.'

I told him that I had a good deal of luggage and thought it better to leave everything at the station but what I particularly wanted. He would not hear of it.

'It doesn't matter a bit. It'll be safer at my house. It's always better to have one's barang with one.'

'All right.'

I gave my keys and the ticket for my trunk and my book-bag to a Chinese boy who stood at my host's elbow. Outside the station a car was waiting for us and we stepped in.

'Do you play bridge?' asked Featherstone.

'I do.'

'I thought most writers didn't.'

'They don't,' I said. 'It's generally considered among authors a sign of deficient intelligence to play cards.'

The club was a bungalow, pleasing but unpretentious; it had a large reading-room, a billiard-room with one table, and a small card-room. When we arrived it was empty but for one or two persons reading the English weeklies, and we walked through to the tennis courts where a couple of sets were being played. A number of people were sitting on the verandah, looking on, smoking and sipping long drinks. I was introduced to one or two of them. But the light was failing and soon the players could hardly see the ball. Featherstone asked one of the men I had been introduced to if he would like a rubber. He said he would. Featherstone looked about for a fourth. He caught sight of a man sitting a little by himself, paused for a second, and went up to him. The two exchanged a few words and then came towards us. We strolled in to the card-room. We had a very nice game. I did not pay much attention to the two men who made up the four. They stood me drinks and I, a temporary member of the club, returned the compliment. The drinks were very small, quarter whiskies, and in the two hours we played each of us was able to show his open-handedness without an excessive consumption of alcohol. When the advancing hour suggested that the next rubber must be the last we changed from whisky to gin pahits. The rubber came to an end. Featherstone called for the book and the winnings and losings of each one of us were set down. One of the men got up.

'Well, I must be going,' he said.

'Going back to the Estate?' asked Featherstone.

'Yes,' he nodded. He turned to me. 'Shall you be here to-morrow?'

'I hope so.'

He went out of the room.

'I'll collect my men and get along home to dinner,' said the other.

'We might be going too,' said Featherstone.

'I'm ready whenever you are,' I replied.

We got into the car and drove to his house. It was a longish drive. In the darkness I could see nothing much, but presently I realised that we were going up a rather steep hill. We reached the Residency.

It had been an evening like any other, pleasant, but not at all exciting, and I had spent I don't know how many just like it. I did not expect it to leave any sort of impression on me.

Featherstone led me into his sitting-room. It looked comfortable, but it was a trifle ordinary. It had large basket arm-chairs covered with cretonne and on the walls were a great many framed photographs; the tables were littered with papers, magazines and official reports, with pipes, yellow tins of straight-cut cigarettes and pink tins of tobacco. In a row of shelves were untidily stacked a good many books, their bindings stained with damp and the ravages of white ants. Featherstone showed me my room and left me with the words:

'Shall you be ready for a gin pahit in ten minutes?'

'Easily,' I said.

I had a bath and changed and went downstairs. Featherstone, ready before me, mixed our drink as he heard me clatter down the wooden staircase. We dined. We talked. The festival which I had been invited to see was the next day but one, but Featherstone told me he had arranged for me before that to be received by the Sultan.

'He's a jolly old boy,' he said. 'And the palace is a sight for sore eyes.'

After dinner we talked a little more, Featherstone put

on the gramophone, and we looked at the latest illustrated papers that had arrived from England. Then we
went to bed. Featherstone came to my room to see that
I had everything I wanted.

'I suppose you haven't any books with you,' he said. 'I
haven't got a thing to read.'

'Books?' I cried.

I pointed to my book-bag. It stood upright, bulging
oddly, so that it looked like a humpbacked gnome
somewhat the worse for liquor.

'Have you got books in there? I thought that was your
dirty linen or a camp-bed or something. Is there anything you can lend me?'

'Look for yourself.'

Featherstone's boys had unlocked the bag, but quail-
ing before the sight that then discovered itself had done
no more. I knew from long experience how to unpack it.
I threw it over on its side, seized its leather bottom and,
walking backwards, dragged the sack away from its contents. A river of books poured on to the floor. A look of
stupefaction came upon Featherstone's face.

'You don't mean to say you travel with as many
books as that? By George, what a snip!'

He bent down and turning them over rapidly looked
at the titles. There were books of all kinds. Volumes of
verse, novels, philosophical works, critical studies (they
say books about books are profitless, but they certainly
make very pleasant reading), biographies, history; there
were books to read when you were ill and books to read
when your brain, all alert, craved for something to
grapple with; there were books that you had always
wanted to read, but in the hurry of life at home had
never found time to; there were books to read at sea
when you were meandering through narrow waters on a
tramp steamer, and there were books for bad weather
when your whole cabin creaked and you had to wedge

yourself in your bunk in order not to fall out; there were books chosen solely for their length, which you took with you when on some expedition you had to travel light, and there were the books you could read when you could read nothing else. Finally Featherstone picked out a life of Byron that had recently appeared.

'Hullo, what's this?' he said. 'I read a review of it some time ago.'

'I believe it's very good,' I replied. 'I haven't read it yet.'

'May I take it? It'll do me for to-night at all events.'

'Of course. Take anything you like.'

'No, that's enough. Well, goodnight. Breakfast at eight-thirty.'

When I came down next morning the head-boy told me that Featherstone, who had been at work since six, would be in shortly. While I waited for him I glanced at his shelves.

'I see you've got a grand library of books on bridge,' I remarked as we sat down to breakfast.

'Yes, I get every one that comes out. I'm very keen on it.'

'That fellow we were playing with yesterday plays a good game.'

'Which? Hardy?'

'I don't know. Not the one who said he was going to collect his wife. The other.'

'Yes, that was Hardy. That was why I asked him to play. He doesn't come to the club very often.'

'I hope he will to-night.'

'I wouldn't bank on it. He has an estate about thirty miles away. It's a longish ride to come just for a rubber of bridge.'

'Is he married?'

'No. Well, yes. But his wife is in England.'

'It must be awfully lonely for those men who live by themselves on those estates,' I said.

'Oh, he's not so badly off as some. I don't think he much cares about seeing people. I think he'd be just as lonely in London.'

There was something in the way Featherstone spoke that struck me as a little strange. His voice had what I can only describe as a shuttered tone. He seemed suddenly to have moved away from me. It was as though one were passing along a street at night and paused for a second to look in at a lighted window that showed a comfortable room and suddenly an invisible hand pulled down a blind. His eyes, which habitually met those of the person he was talking to with frankness, now avoided mine and I had a notion that it was not only my fancy that read in his face an expression of pain. It was drawn for a moment as it might be by a twinge of neuralgia. I could not think of anything to say and Featherstone did not speak. I was conscious that his thoughts, withdrawn from me and what we were about, were turned upon a subject unknown to me. Presently he gave a little sigh, very slight, but unmistakable, and seemed with a deliberate effort to pull himself together.

'I'm going down to the office immediately after breakfast,' he said. 'What are you going to do with yourself?'

'Oh, don't bother about me. I shall slack around. I'll stroll down and look at the town.'

'There's not much to see.'

'All the better. I'm fed up with sights.'

I found that Featherstone's verandah gave me sufficient entertainment for the morning. It had one of the most enchanting views I had seen in the F.M.S. The Residency was built on the top of a hill and the garden was large and well-cared for. Great trees gave it almost the look of an English park. It had vast lawns and there Tamils, black and emaciated, were scything with deliberate and beautiful gestures. Beyond and below, the jungle grew thickly to the bank of a broad, winding and swiftly flowing river, and on the other side of this, as far as the eye could reach, stretched the wooded hills of Tenggarah. The contrast between the trim lawns, so strangely English, and the savage growth of the jungle beyond pleasantly titillated the fancy. I sat and read and smoked. It is my business to be curious about people and I asked myself how the peace of this scene, charged nevertheless with a tremulous and dark significance, affected Featherstone who lived with it. He knew it under every aspect: at dawn when the mist rising from the river shrouded it with a ghostly pall; in the splendour of noon; and at last when the shadowy gloaming crept softly out of the jungle, like an army making its way with caution in unknown country, and presently enveloped the green lawns and the great flowering trees and the flaunting cassias in the silent night. I wondered whether, unbeknownst to him, the tender and yet strangely sinister aspect of the scene, acting on his nerves and his loneliness, imbued him with some mystical quality so that the life he led, the life of the capable administrator, the sportsman and the good fellow, on occasion seemed to him not quite real. I smiled at my own fancies, for certainly the conversation we had had the night before had not indicated in him any stirrings of the soul. I had thought him quite nice. He had been at Oxford and was a member of a good London club. He seemed to attach a good deal of importance to social things. He was a gentleman and slightly conscious of the fact that he belonged to a better class than most of the Englishmen his life brought him in contact with. I gathered from the various silver pots that adorned his dining-room that he excelled in games. He played tennis and billiards. When he went on leave he hunted and, anxious to keep his weight down, he dieted carefully. He talked a good deal of what he would do when he retired. He hankered after the life of a country gentleman. A little house in Leicestershire, a couple of hunters and neighbours to play bridge with. He would have his pension and he had a little money of his own. But meanwhile he worked hard and did his work, if not brilliantly, certainly with competence. I have no doubt that he was looked upon by his superiors as a reliable officer. He was cut upon a pattern that I knew too well to find very interesting. He was like a novel that is careful, honest and efficient, yet a little ordinary, so that you seem to have read it all before, and you turn the pages listlessly, knowing that it will never afford you a surprise or move you to excitement.

But human beings are incalculable and he is a fool who tells himself that he knows what a man is capable of.

In the afternoon Featherstone took me to see the Sultan. We were received by one of his sons, a shy, smiling youth who acted as his A.D.C. He was dressed in a neat blue suit, but round his waist he wore a sarong, white flowers on a yellow ground, on his head a red fez, and on his feet knobby American shoes. The palace, built in the Moorish style, was like a very big doll's house and it was painted bright yellow, which is the royal colour. We were led into a spacious room, furnished with the sort of furniture you would find in an English lodging-house at the seaside, but the chairs were covered with yellow silk. On the floor was a Brussels carpet and on the walls photographs in very grand gilt frames of the Sultan at various state functions. In a cabinet was a large collection of all kinds of fruit done entirely in crochet work. The Sultan came in with several attendants. He was a man of fifty, perhaps, short and stout, dressed in trousers and tunic of a large white-and-yellow check; round his middle he wore a very beautiful yellow sarong and on his head a white fez. He had large handsome friendly eyes. He gave us coffee to drink, sweet cakes to eat and cheroots to smoke. Conversation was not difficult, for he was affable, and he told me that he had never been to a theatre or played cards, for he was very religious, and he had four wives and twenty-four children. The only bar to the happiness of his life seemed to be that common decency obliged him to divide his time equally between his four wives. He said that an hour with one was a month and with another five minutes. I remarked that Professor Einstein – or was it Bergson? – had made similar observations upon time and indeed on this question had given the world much to ponder over. Presently we took our leave and the Sultan presented me with some beautiful white Malaccas.

In the evening we went to the club. One of the men we had played with the day before got up from his chair as we entered.

'Ready for a rubber?' he said.

'Where's our fourth?' I asked.

'Oh, there are several fellows here who'll be glad to play.'

'What about that man we played with yesterday?' I had forgotten his name.

'Hardy? He's not here.'

'It's not worth while waiting for him,' said Featherstone.

'He very seldom comes to the club. I was surprised to see him last night.'

I did not know why I had the impression that behind the very ordinary words of these two men there was an odd sense of embarrassment. Hardy had made no impression on me and I did not even remember what he looked like. He was just a fourth at the bridge table. I had a feeling that they had something against him. It was no business of mine and I was quite content to play with a man who at that moment joined us. We certainly had a more cheerful game than before. A good deal of chaff passed from one side of the table to the other. We played less serious bridge. We laughed. I wondered if it was only that they were less shy of the stranger who had happened in upon them or if the presence of Hardy had caused in the other two a certain constraint. At half-past eight we broke up and Featherstone and I went back to dine at his house.

After dinner we lounged in arm-chairs and smoked cheroots. For some reason our conversation did not flow easily. I tried topic after topic, but could not get Featherstone to interest himself in any of them. I began to think that in the last twenty-four hours he had said all he had to say. I fell somewhat discouraged into silence. It prolonged itself and again, I did not know why, I had a faint sensation that it was charged with a significance that escaped me. I felt slightly uncomfortable. I had that queer feeling that one sometimes has when sitting in an empty room that one is not by oneself. Presently I was conscious that Featherstone was steadily looking at me. I was sitting by a lamp, but he was in shadow so that the play of his features was hidden from me. But he had very large brilliant eyes and in the half darkness they seemed to shine dimly. They were like new boot-buttons that caught a reflected light. I wondered why he looked at me like that. I gave him a glance and catching his eyes insistently fixed upon me faintly smiled.

'Interesting book that one you lent me last night,' he said suddenly, and I could not help thinking his voice did not sound quite natural. The words issued from his lips as though they were pushed from behind.

'Oh, the *Life of Byron*?' I said breezily. 'Have you read it already?'

'A good deal of it. I read till three.'

'I've heard it's very well done. I'm not sure that Byron

interests me so much as all that. There was so much in him that was so frightfully second-rate. It makes one rather uncomfortable.'

'What do you think is the real truth of that story about him and his sister?'

'Augusta Leigh? I don't know very much about it. I've never read *Astarte*.'

'Do you think they were really in love with one another?'

'I suppose so. Isn't it generally believed that she was the only woman he ever genuinely loved?'

'Can you understand it?'

'I can't really. It doesn't particularly shock me. It just seems to me very unnatural. Perhaps "unnatural" isn't the right word. It's incomprehensible to me. I can't throw myself into the state of feeling in which such a thing seems possible. You know, that's how a writer gets to know the people he writes about, by standing himself in their shoes and feeling with their hearts.'

I knew I did not make myself very clear, but I was trying to describe a sensation, an action of the subconscious, which from experience was perfectly familiar to me, but which no words I knew could precisely indicate. I went on.

'Of course she was only his half-sister, but just as habit kills love I should have thought habit would prevent its arising. When two persons have known one another all their lives and lived together in close contact I can't imagine how or why that sudden spark should flash that results in love. The probabilities are that they would be joined by mutual affection and I don't know anything that is more contrary to love than affection.'

I could just see in the dimness the outline of a smile flicker for a moment on my host's heavy, and it seemed to me then, somewhat saturnine face.

'You only believe in love at first sight?'

'Well, I suppose I do, but with the proviso that people may have met twenty times before seeing one another. "Seeing" has an active side and a passive one. Most people we run across mean so little to us that we never bestir ourselves to look at them. We just suffer the impression they make on us.'

'Oh, but one's often heard of couples who've known one another for years and it's never occurred to one they cared two straws for each other and suddenly they go and get married. How do you explain that?'

'Well, if you're going to bully me into being logical and consistent, I should suggest that their love is of a different kind. After all, passion isn't the only reason for marriage. It may not even be the best one. Two people may marry because they're lonely or because they're good friends or for convenience' sake. Though I said that affection was the greatest enemy of love, I would never deny that it's a very good substitute. I'm not sure that a marriage founded on it isn't the happiest.'

'What did you think of Tim Hardy?'

I was a little surprised at the sudden question, which seemed to have nothing to do with the subject of our conversation.

'I didn't think of him very much. He seemed quite nice. Why?'

'Did he seem to you just like everybody else?'

'Yes. Is there anything peculiar about him? If you'd told me that I'd have paid more attention to him.'

'He's very quiet, isn't he? I suppose no one who knew nothing about him would give him a second thought.'

I tried to remember what he looked like. The only thing that had struck me when we were playing cards was that he had fine hands. It passed idly through my mind that they were not the sort of hands I should have expected a planter to have. But why a planter should have different hands from anybody else I did not trouble to ask myself. His were somewhat large, but very well formed, with peculiarly long fingers, and the nails were of an admirable shape. They were virile and yet oddly sensitive hands. I noticed this and thought no more about it. But if you are a writer instinct and the habit of years enable you to store up impressions that you are not aware of. Sometimes of course they do not correspond with the facts and a woman for example may remain in your subconsciousness as a dark, massive and ox-eyed creature when she is indeed rather small and of a nondescript colouring. But that is of no consequence. The impression may very well be more exact than the sober truth. And now, seeking to call up from the depths of me a picture of this man I had a feeling of some ambiguity. He was clean-shaven and his face, oval but not thin, seemed strangely pale under the tan of long exposure to the tropical sun. His features were vague. I did not know whether I remembered it or only imagined now that his rounded chin gave one the impression of a certain weakness. He had thick brown hair, just turning grey, and a long wisp fell down constantly over his forehead. He pushed it back with a gesture that had become habitual. His brown eyes were rather large and gentle, but perhaps a little sad; they had a melting softness which, I could imagine, might be very appealing.

After a pause Featherstone continued:

'It's rather strange that I should run across Tim Hardy here after all these years. But that's the way of the F.M.S. People move about and you find yourself in the same place as a man you'd known years before in another part of the country. I first knew Tim when he had an estate near Sibuku. Have you ever been there?'

'No. Where is it?'

'Oh, it's up north. Towards Siam. It wouldn't be

worth your while to go. It's just like every other place in the F.M.S. But it was rather nice. It had a very jolly little club and there were some quite decent people. There was the schoolmaster and the head of the police, the doctor, the padre and the government engineer. The usual lot, you know. A few planters. Three or four women. I was A.D.O. It was one of my first jobs. Tim Hardy had an estate about twenty-five miles away. He lived there with his sister. They had a bit of money of their own and he'd bought the place. Rubber was pretty good then and he wasn't doing at all badly. We rather cottoned on to one another. Of course it's a toss-up with planters. Some of them are very good fellows, but they're not exactly . . .' he sought for a word or a phrase that did not sound snobbish. 'Well, they're not the sort of people you'd be likely to meet at home. Tim and Olive were of one's own class, if you understand what I mean.'

'Olive was the sister?'

'Yes. They'd had a rather unfortunate past. Their parents had separated when they were quite small, seven or eight, and the mother had taken Olive and the father had kept Tim. Tim went to Clifton, they were West Country people, and only came home for the holidays. His father was a retired naval man who lived at Fowey. But Olive went with her mother to Italy. She was educated in Florence; she spoke Italian perfectly and French too. For all those years Tim and Olive never saw one another once, but they used to write to one another regularly. They'd been very much attached when they were children. As far as I could understand, life when their people were living together had been rather stormy with all sorts of scenes and upsets, you know the sort of thing that happens when two people who are married don't get on together, and that had thrown them on their own resources. They were left a good deal to themselves. Then Mrs. Hardy died and Olive came home to England and went back to her father. She was eighteen then and Tim was seventeen. A year later the war broke out. Tim joined up and his father, who was over fifty, got some job at Portsmouth. I take it he had been a hard liver and a heavy drinker. He broke down before the end of the war and died after a lingering illness. They don't seem to have had any relations. They were the last of a rather old family; they had a fine old house in Dorsetshire that had belonged to them for a good many generations, but they had never been able to afford to live in it and it was always let. I remember seeing photographs of it. It was very much a gentleman's house, of grey stone and rather stately, with a coat of arms carved over the front door and mullioned windows. Their great ambition was to make enough money to be able to live in it. They used to talk about it a lot. They never spoke as though either of them would marry, but always as though it were a settled thing that they would remain together. It was rather funny considering how young they were.'

'How old were they then?' I asked.

'Well, I suppose he was twenty-five or twenty-six and she was a year older. They were awfully kind to me when I first went up to Sibuku. They took a fancy to me at once. You see, we had more in common than most of the people there. I think they were glad of my company. They weren't particularly popular.'

'Why not?' I asked.

'They were rather reserved and you couldn't help seeing that they liked their own society better than other people's. I don't know if you've noticed it, but that always seems to put people's backs up. They resent it somehow if they have a feeling that you can get along very well without them.'

'It's tiresome, isn't it?' I said.

'It was rather a grievance to the other planters that Tim was his own master and had private means. They had to put up with an old Ford to get about in, but Tim had a real car. Tim and Olive were very nice when they came to the club and they played in the tennis tournaments and all that sort of thing, but you had an impression that they were always glad to get away again. They'd dine out with people and make themselves very pleasant, but it was pretty obvious that they'd just as soon have stayed at home. If you had any sense you couldn't blame them. I don't know if you've been much to planters' houses. They're a bit dreary. A lot of gimcrack furniture and silver ornaments and tiger skins. And the food's uneatable. But the Hardys had made their bungalow rather nice. There was nothing very grand in it; it was just easy and homelike and comfortable. Their living-room was like a drawing-room in an English country house. You felt that their things meant something to them and that they had had them a long time. It was a very jolly house to stay at. The bungalow was in the middle of the estate, but it was on the brow of a little hill and you looked right over the rubber trees to the sea in the distance. Olive took a lot of trouble with her garden and it was really topping. I never saw such a show of cannas. I used to go there for week-ends. It was only about half an hour's drive to the sea and we'd take our lunch with us and bathe and sail. Tim kept a small boat there. Those days were grand. I never knew one could enjoy oneself so much. It's a beautiful bit of coast and it was really extraordinarily romantic. Then in the evenings we'd play patience and chess or turn on the gramophone. The cooking was damned good too. It was a change from what one generally got. Olive had taught their cook to make all sorts of Italian dishes and we used to have great wallops of macaroni and risotto and gnocchi and things like that. I couldn't help envying them their life, it was so jolly and peaceful, and when they talked of what they'd do when they went back to England for good I used to tell them they'd always regret what they'd left.

'"We've been very happy here,"' said Olive.

'She had a way of looking at Tim, with a slow, sidelong glance from under her long eyelashes, that was rather engaging.

'In their own house they were quite different from what they were when they went out. They were so easy and cordial. Everybody admitted that and I'm bound to say that people enjoyed going there. They often asked people over. They had the gift of making you feel at home. It was a very happy house, if you know what I mean. Of course no one could help seeing how attached they were to one another. And whatever people said about their being standoffish and self-centred, they were bound to be rather touched by the affection they had for one another. People said they couldn't have been more united if they were married, and when you saw how some couples got on you couldn't help thinking they made most marriages look rather like a wash-out. They seemed to think the same things at the same time. They had little private jokes that made them laugh like children. They were so charming with one another, so gay and happy, that really to stay with them was, well, a spiritual refreshment. I don't know what else you could call it. When you left them, after a couple of days at the bungalow, you felt that you'd absorbed some of their peace and their sober gaiety. It was as though your soul had been sluiced with cool clear water. You felt strangely purified.'

It was singular to hear Featherstone talking in this exalted strain. He looked so spruce in his smart white coat, technically known as a bum-freezer, his moustache was so trim, his thick curly hair so carefully brushed, that his high-flown language made me a trifle un-comfortable. But I realised that he was trying to express in his clumsy way a very sincerely felt emotion.

'What was Olive Hardy like?' I asked.

'I'll show you. I've got quite a lot of snapshots.'

He got up from his chair and going to a shelf brought me a large album. It was the usual thing, indifferent photographs of people in groups and unflattering like-nesses of single figures. They were in bathing dress or in shorts or tennis things, generally with their faces screwed up because the sun blinded them, or puckered by the distortion of laughter. I recognised Hardy, not much changed after ten years, with his wisp of hair hanging across his forehead. I remembered him better now that I saw the snapshots. In them he looked nice and fresh and young. He had an alertness of expression that was attractive and that I certainly had not noticed when I saw him. In his eyes was a sort of eagerness for life that danced and sparkled through the fading print. I glanced at the photographs of his sister. Her bathing dress showed that she had a good figure, well-developed, but slender; and her legs were long and slim.

'They look rather alike,' I said.

'Yes, although she was a year older they might have been twins, they were so much alike. They both had the same oval face and that pale skin without any colour in the cheeks, and they both had those soft brown eyes, very liquid and appealing, so that you felt whatever they did you could never be angry with them. And they both had a sort of careless elegance that made them look charming whatever they wore and however untidy they were. He's lost that now, I suppose, but he certainly had it when I first knew him. They always rather reminded me of the brother and sister in *Twelfth Night*. You know whom I mean.'

'Viola and Sebastian.'

'They never seemed to belong quite to the present. There was something Elizabethan about them. I don't think it was only because I was very young then that I couldn't help feeling they were strangely romantic somehow. I could see them living in Illyria.'

I gave one of the snapshots another glance.

'The girl looks as though she had a good deal more character than her brother,' I remarked.

'She had. I don't know if you'd have called Olive beautiful, but she was awfully attractive. There was something poetic in her, a sort of lyrical quality, as it were, that coloured her movements, her acts and everything about her. It seemed to exalt her above common cares. There was something so candid in her expression, so courageous and independent in her bearing, that – oh, I don't know, it made mere beauty just flat and dull.'

'You speak as if you'd been in love with her,' I interrupted.

'Of course I was. I should have thought you'd guessed that at once. I was frightfully in love with her.'

'Was it love at first sight?' I smiled.

'Yes, I think it was, but I didn't know it for a month or so. When it suddenly struck me that what I felt for her – I don't know how to explain it, it was a sort of shattering turmoil that affected every bit of me – that that was love, I knew I'd felt it all along. It was not only her looks, though they were awfully alluring, the smoothness of her pale skin and the way her hair fell over her forehead and the grave sweetness of her brown eyes, it was more than that; you had a sensation of well-being when you were with her, as though you could relax and be quite natural and needn't pretend to be anything you weren't. You felt she was incapable of meanness. It was impossible to think of her as envious of other people or catty. She seemed to have a natural generosity of soul. One could be silent with her for an hour at a time and yet feel that one had had a good time.'

'A rare gift,' I said.

'She was a wonderful companion. If you made a suggestion to do something she was always glad to fall in with it. She was the least exacting girl I ever knew. You could throw her over at the last minute and however disappointed she was it made no difference. Next time you saw her she was just as cordial and serene as ever.'

'Why didn't you marry her?'

Featherstone's cheroot had gone out. He threw the stub away and deliberately lit another. He did not answer for a while. It may seem strange to persons who live in a highly civilised state that he should confide these intimate things to a stranger; it did not seem strange to me. I was used to it. People who live so desperately alone, in the remote places of the earth, find it a relief to tell someone whom in all probability they will never meet again the story that has burdened perhaps for years their waking thoughts and their dreams at night. And I have an inkling that the fact of your being a writer attracts their confidence. They feel that what they tell you will excite your interest in an impersonal way that makes it easier for them to discharge their souls. Besides, as we all know from our own experience, it is never unpleasant to talk about oneself.

'Why didn't you marry her?' I had asked him.

'I wanted to badly enough,' Featherstone answered at length. 'But I hesitated to ask her. Although she was always so nice to me and so easy to get on with, and we were such good friends, I always felt that there was something a little mysterious in her. Although she was so simple, so frank and natural, you never quite got over the feeling of an inner kernel of aloofness, as if deep in her heart she guarded, not a secret, but a sort of privacy of the soul that not a living person would ever be allowed to know. I don't know if I make myself clear.'

'I think so.'

'I put it down to her upbringing. They never talked of their mother, but somehow I got the impression that she was one of those neurotic, emotional women who wreck their own happiness and are a pest to everyone connected with them. I had a suspicion that she'd led rather a hectic life in Florence and it struck me that Olive owed her beautiful serenity to a disciplined effort of her own will and that her aloofness was a sort of citadel she'd built to protect herself from the knowledge of all sorts of shameful things. But of course that aloofness was awfully captivating. It was strangely exciting to think that if she loved you, and you were married to her, you would at last pierce right into the hidden heart of that mystery; and you felt that if you could share that with her it would be as it were a consummation of all you'd ever desired in your life. Heaven wouldn't be in it. You know, I felt about it just like Bluebeard's wife about the forbidden chamber in the castle. Every room was open to me, but I should never rest till I had gone into that last one that was locked against me.'

My eye was caught by a chik-chak, a little brown house lizard with a large head, high up on the wall. It is a friendly little beast and it is good to see it in a house. It watched a fly. It was quite still. On a sudden it made a dart and then as the fly flew away fell back with a sort of jerk into a strange immobility.

'And there was another thing that made me hesitate. I couldn't bear the thought that if I proposed to her and she refused me she wouldn't let me come to the bungalow in the same old way. I should have hated that, I enjoyed going there so awfully. It made me so happy to be with her. But you know, sometimes one can't help oneself. I did ask her at last, but it was almost by accident. One evening, after dinner, when we were sitting on the verandah by ourselves, I took her hand. She withdrew it at once.

'"Why did you do that?" I asked her.

'"I don't very much like being touched," she said. She turned her head a little and smiled. "Are you hurt? You mustn't mind, it's just a funny feeling I have. I can't help it."

'"I wonder if it's ever occurred to you that I'm frightfully fond of you," I said.

'I expect I was terribly awkward about it, but I'd never proposed to anyone before.' Featherstone gave a little sound that was not quite a chuckle and not quite a sigh. 'For the matter of that, I've never proposed to anyone since. She didn't say anything for a minute. Then she said:

'"I'm very glad, but I don't think I want you to be anything more than that."

'"Why not?" I asked.

'"I could never leave Tim."

'"But supposing he marries?"

'"He never will."

'I'd gone so far then that I thought I'd better go on. But my throat was so dry that I could hardly speak. I was shaking with nervousness.

'"I'm frightfully in love with you, Olive. I want to marry you more than anything in the world."

'She put her hand very gently on my arm. It was like a flower falling to the ground.

'"No, dear, I can't," she said.

'I was silent. It was difficult for me to say what I wanted to. I'm naturally rather shy. She was a girl. I couldn't very well tell her that it wasn't quite the same thing living with a husband and living with a brother. She was normal and healthy; she must want to have babies; it wasn't reasonable to starve her natural instincts. It was such waste of her youth. But it was she who spoke first.

'"Don't let's talk about this any more," she said. "D'you mind? It did strike me once or twice that perhaps you cared for me. Tim noticed it. I was sorry because I was afraid it would break up our friendship. I don't want it to do that, Mark. We do get on so well together, the three of us, and we have such jolly times. I don't know what we should do without you now."

'"I thought of that too," I said.

'"D'you think it need?" she asked me.

'"My dear, I don't want it to," I said. "You must know how much I love coming here. I've never been so happy anywhere before!"

'"You're not angry with me?"

'"Why should I be? It's not your fault. It only means that you're not in love with me. If you were you wouldn't care a hang about Tim."

'"You are rather sweet," she said.

'She put her arm round my neck and kissed me lightly on the cheek. I had a notion that in her mind it settled our relation. She adopted me as a second brother.

'A few weeks later Tim went back to England. The tenant of their house in Dorset was leaving and though there was another in the offing, he thought he ought to be on the spot to conduct negotiations. And he wanted some new machinery for the estate. He thought he'd get it at the same time. He didn't expect to be gone more than three months and Olive made up her mind not to go. She knew hardly anyone in England, and it was practically a foreign country to her, she didn't mind being left alone, and she wanted to look after the estate. Of course they could have put a manager in charge, but that wasn't the same thing. Rubber was falling and in case of accidents it was just as well that one or other of them should be there. I promised Tim I'd look after her and if she wanted me she could always call me up. My proposal hadn't changed anything. We carried on as though nothing had happened. I don't know whether she'd told Tim. He made no sign that he knew. Of course I loved her as much as ever, but I kept it to myself. I have a good deal of self-control, you know. I had a sort of feeling I hadn't a chance. I hoped eventually my love would change into something else and we could just be wonderful friends. It's funny, it never has, you know. I suppose I was hit too badly ever to get quite over it.

'She went down to Penang to see Tim off and when she came back I met her at the station and drove her home. I couldn't very well stay at the bungalow while Tim was away, but I went over every Sunday and had tiffin and we'd go down to the sea and have a bathe. People tried to be kind to her and asked her to stay with them, but she wouldn't. She seldom left the estate. She had plenty to do. She read a lot. She was never bored. She seemed quite happy in her own company, and when she had visitors it was only from a sense of duty. She didn't want them to think her ungracious. But it was an effort and she told me she heaved a sigh of relief when she saw the last of them and could again enjoy without disturbance the peaceful loneliness of the bungalow. She was a very curious girl. It was strange that at her age she should be so indifferent to parties and the other small gaieties the station afforded. Spiritually, if you know what I mean, she was entirely self-supporting. I don't know how people found out that I was in love with her; I thought I'd never given myself away in anything, but I had hints here and there that they knew. I gathered they thought Olive hadn't gone home with her brother on my account. One woman, a Mrs. Sergison, the policeman's wife, actually asked me when they were going to be able to congratulate me. Of course I pretended I didn't know what she was talking about, but it didn't go down very well. I couldn't help being amused. I meant so little to Olive in that way that I really believe she'd entirely forgotten that I'd asked her to marry me. I can't say she was unkind to me, I don't think she could have been unkind to anyone; but she treated me with just the casualness with which a sister might treat a younger brother. She was two or three years older than I. She was always terribly glad to see me, but it never occurred to her to put herself out for me, she was almost amazingly intimate with me; but unconsciously, you know, as you might be with a person you'd known so well all your life that you never thought of putting on frills with him. I might not have been a man at all, but an old coat that she wore all the time because it was easy and comfortable and she didn't mind what she did in it. I should have been crazy not to see that she was a thousand miles away from loving me.

'Then one day, three or four weeks before Tim was due back, when I went to the bungalow I saw she'd been crying. I was startled. She was always so composed. I'd never seen her upset over anything.

'"Hullo, what's the matter?" I said.

'"Nothing."

'"Come off it, darling," I said. "What have you been crying about?"

'She tried to smile.

'"I wish you hadn't got such sharp eyes," she said. "I think I'm being silly. I've just had a cable from Tim to say he's postponed his sailing."

'"Oh, my dear, I am sorry," I said. "You must be awfully disappointed."

'"I've been counting the days. I want him back so badly."

'"Does he say why he's postponing?" I asked.

'"No, he says he's writing. I'll show you the cable."

'I saw that she was very nervous. Her slow quiet eyes were filled with apprehension and there was a little frown of anxiety between her brows. She went into her bedroom and in a moment came back with the cable. I felt that she was watching me anxiously as I read. So far as I remember it ran: *Darling, I cannot sail on the seventh after all. Please forgive me. Am writing fully. Fondest love. Tim.*

'"Well, perhaps the machinery he wanted isn't ready and he can't bring himself to sail without it," I said.

'"What could it matter if it came by a later ship? Anyhow, it'll be hung up at Penang."

'"It may be something about the house."

'"If it is why doesn't he say so? He must know how frightfully anxious I am."

'"It wouldn't occur to him," I said. "After all, when you're away you don't realise that the people you've left behind don't know something that you take as a matter of course."

'She smiled again, but now more happily.

'"I daresay you're right. In point of fact Tim is a little like that. He's always been rather slack and casual. I daresay I've been making a mountain out of a molehill. I must just wait patiently for his letter."

'Olive was a girl with a lot of self-control and I saw her by an effort of will pull herself together. The little line between her eyebrows vanished and she was once more her serene, smiling and kindly self. She was always gentle: that day she had a mildness so heavenly that it was shattering. But for the rest of the time I could see that she kept her restlessness in check only by the deliberate exercise of her common sense. It was as though she had a foreboding of ill. I was with her the day before the mail was due. Her anxiety was all the more pitiful to see because she took such pains to hide it. I was always busy on mail day, but I promised to go up to the estate later on and hear the news. I was just thinking of starting when Hardy's seis came along in the car with a message from the amah asking me to go at once to her mistress. The amah was a decent, elderly woman to whom I had given a dollar or two and said that if anything went wrong on the estate she was to let me know at once. I jumped into my car. When I arrived I found the amah waiting for me on the steps.

'"A letter came this morning," she said.

'I interrupted her. I ran up the steps. The sitting-room was empty.

'"Olive," I called.

'I went into the passage and suddenly I heard a sound that froze my heart. The amah had followed me and now she opened the door of Olive's room. The sound I had heard was the sound of Olive crying. I went in. She was lying on her bed, on her face, and her sobs shook her from head to foot. I put my hand on her shoulder.

'"Olive, what is it?" I asked.

'"Who's that?" she cried. She sprang to her feet suddenly, as though she were scared out of her wits. And then: "Oh, it's you," she said. She stood in front of me, with her head thrown back and her eyes closed, and the tears streamed from them. It was dreadful. "Tim's married," she gasped, and her face screwed up in a sort of grimace of pain.

'I must admit that for one moment I had a thrill of exultation, it was like a little electric shock tingling through my heart; it struck me that now I had a chance, she might be willing to marry me; I know it was terribly selfish of me; you see, the news had taken me by surprise; but it was only for a moment, after that I was melted by her awful distress and the only thing I felt was deep sorrow because she was unhappy. I put my arm round her waist.

'"Oh, my dear, I'm so sorry," I said. "Don't stay here. Come into the sitting-room and sit down and we'll talk about it. Let me give you something to drink."

'She let me lead her into the next room and we sat down on the sofa. I told the amah to fetch the whisky and syphon and I mixed her a good strong stengah and made her drink a little. I took her in my arms and rested her head on my shoulder. She let me do what I liked with her. The great tears streamed down her poor face.

'"How could he?" she moaned. "How could he?"

'"My darling," I said, "it was bound to happen sooner or later. He's a young man. How could you expect him never to marry? It's only natural."

'"No, no, no," she gasped.

'Tight-clenched in her hand I saw that she had a letter and I guessed that it was Tim's.

'"What does he say?" I asked.

'She gave a frightened movement and clutched the letter to her heart as though she thought I would take it from her.

'"He says he couldn't help himself. He says he had to. What does it mean?"

'"Well, you know, in his way he's just as attractive as you are. He has so much charm. I suppose he just fell madly in love with some girl and she with him."

'"He's so weak," she moaned.

'"Are they coming out?" I asked.

'"They sailed yesterday. He says it won't make any difference. He's insane. How *can* I stay here?"

'She began to cry hysterically. It was torture to see that girl, usually so calm, utterly shattered by her emotion. I had always felt that her lovely serenity masked a capacity for deep feeling. But the abandon of her distress simply broke me up. I held her in my arms and kissed her, her eyes and her wet cheek and her hair. I don't think she knew what I was doing. I was hardly conscious of it myself. I was so deeply moved.

'"What shall I do?" she wailed.

'"Why won't you marry me?" I said.

'She tried to withdraw herself from me, but I wouldn't let her go.

'"After all, it would be a way out," I said.

'"How can I marry you?" she moaned. "I'm years older than you are."

'"Oh, what nonsense, two or three. What do I care?"

'"No, no."

'"Why not?" I said.

'"I don't love you," she said.

'"What does that matter? I love you."

'I don't know what I said. I told her that I'd try to make her happy. I said I'd never ask anything from her but what she was prepared to give me. I talked and talked. I tried to make her see reason. I felt that she didn't want to stay there, in the same place as Tim, and I told her that I'd be moved soon to some other district. I thought that might tempt her. She couldn't deny that we'd always got on awfully well together. After a time she did seem to grow a little quieter. I had a feeling that she was listening to me. I had even a sort of feeling that she knew that she was lying in my arms and that it comforted her. I made her drink a drop more whisky. I gave her a cigarette. At last I thought I might be just mildly facetious.

'"You know, I'm not a bad sort really," I said. "You might do worse."

'"You don't know me," she said. "You know nothing whatever about me."

'"I'm capable of learning," I said.

'She smiled a little.

'"You're awfully kind, Mark," she said.

'"Say yes, Olive," I begged.

'She gave a deep sigh. For a long time she stared at the

ground. But she did not move and I felt the softness of her body in my arms. I waited. I was frightfully nervous and the minutes seemed endless.

'"All right," she said at last, as though she were not conscious that any time had passed between my prayer and her answer.

'I was so moved that I had nothing to say. But when I wanted to kiss her lips, she turned her face away, and wouldn't let me. I wanted us to be married at once, but she was quite firm that she wouldn't. She insisted on waiting till Tim came back. You know how sometimes you see so clearly in people's thoughts that you're more certain of them than if they'd spoken them; I saw that she couldn't quite believe that what Tim had written was true and that she had a sort of miserable hope that it was all a mistake and he wasn't married after all. It gave me a pang, but I loved her so much, I just bore it. I was willing to bear anything. I adored her. She wouldn't even let me tell anyone that we were engaged. She made me promise not to say a word till Tim's return. She said she couldn't bear the thought of the congratulations and all that. She wouldn't even let me make any announcement of Tim's marriage. She was obstinate about it. I had a notion that she felt if the fact were spread about it gave it a certainty that she didn't want it to have.

'But the matter was taken out of her hands. News travels mysteriously in the East. I don't know what Olive had said in the amah's hearing when first she received the news of Tim's marriage; anyhow, the Hardys' seis told the Sergisons' and Mrs. Sergison attacked me the next time I went into the club.

'"I hear Tim Hardy's married," she said.

'"Oh?" I answered, unwilling to commit myself.

'She smiled at my blank face, and told me that her amah having told her the rumour she had rung up Olive and asked her if it was true. Olive's answer had been rather odd. She had not exactly confirmed it, but said that she had received a letter from Tim telling her he was married.

'"She's a strange girl," said Mrs. Sergison. "When I asked her for details she said she had none to give and when I said: 'Aren't you thrilled?' she didn't answer."

'"Olive's devoted to Tim, Mrs. Sergison," I said. "His marriage has naturally been a shock to her. She knows nothing about Tim's wife. She's nervous about her."

'"And when are you two going to be married?" she asked me abruptly.

'"What an embarrassing question!" I said, trying to laugh it off.

'She looked at me shrewdly.

'"Will you give me your word of honour that you're not engaged to her?"

'I didn't like to tell her a deliberate lie, nor to ask her to mind her own business, and I'd promised Olive faithfully that I would say nothing till Tim got back. I hedged.

'"Mrs. Sergison," I said, "when there's anything to tell I promise that you'll be the first person to hear it. All I can say to you now is that I do want to marry Olive more than anything in the world."

'"I'm very glad that Tim's married," she answered. "And I hope she'll marry you very soon. It was a morbid and unhealthy life that they led up there, those two, they kept far too much to themselves and they were far too much absorbed in one another."

'I saw Olive practically every day. I felt that she didn't want me to make love to her, and I contented myself with kissing her when I came and when I went. She was very nice to me, kindly and thoughtful; I knew she was glad to see me and sorry when it was time for me to go. Ordinarily, she was apt to fall into silence, but during this time she talked more than I had ever heard her talk before. But never of the future and never of Tim and his wife. She told me a lot about her life in Florence with her mother. She had led a strange lonely life, mostly with servants and governesses, while her mother, I suspected, engaged in one affair after another with vague Italian counts and Russian princes. I guessed that by the time she was fourteen there wasn't much she didn't know. It was natural for her to be quite unconventional: in the only world she knew till she was eighteen conventions weren't mentioned because they didn't exist. Gradually, Olive seemed to regain her serenity and I should have thought that she was beginning to accustom herself to the thought of Tim's marriage if it hadn't been that I couldn't but notice how pale and tired she looked. I made up my mind that the moment he arrived I'd press her to marry me at once. I could get short leave whenever I asked for it, and by the time that was up I thought I could manage a transfer to some other post. What she wanted was change of air and fresh scenes.

'We knew, of course, within a day when Tim's ship would reach Penang, but it was a question whether she'd get in soon enough for him to catch the train and I wrote to the P. & O. agent asking him to telegraph as soon as he had definite news. When I got the wire and took it up to Olive I found that she'd just received one from Tim. The ship had docked early and he was arriving next day. The train was supposed to get in at eight o'clock in the morning, but it was liable to be anything from one to six hours late, and I bore with me an invitation from Mrs. Sergison asking Olive to come back with me to stay the night with her so that she would be on the spot and need not go to the station till the news came through that the train was coming.

'I was immensely relieved. I thought that when the blow at last fell Olive wouldn't feel it so much. She had worked herself up into such a state that I couldn't help thinking that she must have a reaction now. She might take a fancy to her sister-in-law. There was no reason why they shouldn't all three get on very well together. To my surprise Olive said she wasn't coming down to the station to meet them.

'"They'll be awfully disappointed," I said.

'"I'd rather wait here," she answered. She smiled a little. "Don't argue with me, Mark, I've made up my mind."

'"I've ordered breakfast in my house," I said.

'"That's all right. You meet them and take them to your house and give them breakfast, and then they can come along here afterwards. Of course I'll send the car down."

'"I don't suppose they'll want to breakfast if you're not there," I said.

'"Oh, I'm sure they will. If the train gets in on time they wouldn't have thought of breakfasting before it arrived and they'll be hungry. They won't want to take this long drive without anything to eat."

'I was puzzled. She had been looking forward so intensely to Tim's coming, it seemed strange that she should want to wait all by herself while the rest of us were having a jolly breakfast. I supposed she was nervous and wanted to delay as long as possible meeting the strange woman who had come to take her place. It seemed unreasonable, I couldn't see that an hour sooner or an hour later could make any difference, but I knew women were funny, and anyhow I felt Olive wasn't in the mood for me to press it.

'"Telephone when you're starting so that I shall know when to expect you," she said.

'"All right," I said, "but you know I shan't be able to come with them. It's my day for going to Lahad."

'This was a town that I had to go to once a week to take cases. It was a good way off and one had to ferry across a river, which took some time, so that I never got back till late. There were a few Europeans there and a club. I generally had to go on there for a bit to be sociable and see that things were getting along all right.

'"Besides," I added, "with Tim bringing his wife home for the first time I don't suppose he'll want me about. But if you'd like to ask me to dinner I'll be glad to come to that."

'Olive smiled.

'"I don't think it'll be my place to issue any more invitations, will it?" she said. "You must ask the bride."

'She said this so lightly that my heart leaped. I had a feeling that at last she had made up her mind to accept the altered circumstances and, what was more, was accepting them with cheerfulness. She asked me to stay to dinner. Generally I left about eight and dined at home. She was very sweet, almost tender, and I was happier than I'd been for weeks. I had never been more desperately in love with her. I had a couple of gin pahits and I think I was in rather good form at dinner. I know I made her laugh. I felt that at last she was casting away the load of misery that had oppressed her. That was why I didn't let myself be very much disturbed by what happened at the end.

'"Don't you think it's about time you were leaving a presumably maiden lady?" she said.

'She spoke in a manner that was so quietly gay that I answered without hesitation:

'"Oh, my dear, if you think you've got a shred of reputation left you deceive yourself. You're surely not under the impression that the ladies of Sibuku don't know that I've been coming to see you every day for a month. The general feeling is that if we're not married it's high time we were. Don't you think it would be just as well if I broke it to them that we're engaged?'

'"Oh, Mark, you mustn't take our engagement very

seriously," she said.

'I laughed.

'"How else do you expect me to take it? It is serious."

'She shook her head a little.

'"No. I was upset and hysterical that day. You were being very sweet to me. I said yes because I was too miserable to say no. But now I've had time to collect myself. Don't think me unkind. I made a mistake. I've been very much to blame. You must forgive me."

'"Oh, darling, you're talking nonsense. You've got nothing against me."

'She looked at me steadily. She was quite calm. She had even a little smile at the back of her eyes.

'"I can't marry you. I can't marry anyone. It was absurd of me ever to think I could."

'I didn't answer at once. She was in a queer state and I thought it better not to insist.

'"I suppose I can't drag you to the altar by main force," I said.

'I held out my hand and she gave me hers. I put my arm round her, and she made no attempt to withdraw. She suffered me to kiss her as usual on the cheek.

'Next morning I met the train. For once in a way it was punctual. Tim waved to me as his carriage passed the place where I was standing, and by the time I had walked up he had already jumped out and was handing down his wife. He grasped my hand warmly.

'"Where's Olive?" he said, with a glance along the platform. "This is Sally."

'I shook hands with her and at the same time explained why Olive was not there.

'"It was frightfully early, wasn't it?" said Mrs. Hardy.

'I told them that the plan was for them to come and have a bit of breakfast at my house and then drive home.

'"I'd love a bath," said Mrs. Hardy.

'"You shall have one," I said.

'She was really an extremely pretty little thing, very fair, with enormous blue eyes and a lovely little straight nose. Her skin, all milk and roses, was exquisite. A little of the chorus girl type, of course, and you may happen to think that rather namby-pamby, but in that style she was enchanting. We drove to my house, they both had a bath and Tim a shave; I just had two minutes alone with him. He asked me how Olive had taken his marriage. I told her she'd been upset.

'"I was afraid so," he said, frowning a little. He gave a short sigh. "I couldn't do anything else."

'I didn't understand what he meant. At that moment Mrs. Hardy joined us and slipped her arm through her husband's. He took her hand in his and gently pressed it. He gave her a look that had in it something pleased and humorously affectionate, as though he didn't take her quite seriously, but enjoyed his sense of proprietorship and was proud of her beauty. She really was lovely. She was not at all shy, she asked me to call her Sally before we'd known one another ten minutes, and she was quick in the uptake. Of course, just then she was excited at arriving. She'd never been East and everything thrilled her. It was quite obvious that she was head over heels in love with Tim. Her eyes never left him and she hung on his words. We had a jolly breakfast and then we parted. They got into their car to go home and I into mine to go to Lahad. I promised to go straight to the estate from there and in point of fact it was out of my way to pass by my house. I took a change with me. I didn't see why Olive shouldn't like Sally very much, she was frank and gay, and ingenuous; she was extremely young, she couldn't have been more than nineteen, and her wonderful prettiness couldn't fail to appeal to Olive. I was just as glad to have had a reasonable excuse to leave the three of them by themselves for the day, but as I started out from Lahad I had a notion that by the time I arrived they would all be pleased to see me. I drove up to the bungalow and blew my horn two or three times, expecting someone to appear. Not a soul. The place was in total darkness. I was surprised. It was absolutely silent. I couldn't make it out. They must be in. Very odd, I thought. I waited a moment, then got out of the car and walked up the steps. At the top of them I stumbled over something. I swore and bent down to see what it was; it had felt like a body. There was a cry and I saw it was the amah. She shrank back cowering as I touched her and broke into loud wails.

'"What the hell's the matter?" I cried, and then I felt a hand on my arm and heard a voice: Tuan, Tuan. I turned and in the darkness recognised Tim's head-boy. He began to speak in little frightened gasps. I listened to him with horror. What he told me was unspeakable. I pushed him aside and rushed into the house. The sitting-room was dark. I turned on the light. The first thing I saw was Sally huddled up in an armchair. She was startled by my sudden appearance and cried out. I could hardly speak. I asked her if it was true. When she told me it was I felt the room suddenly going round and round me. I had to sit down. As the car that bore Tim and Sally drove up the road that led to the house and Tim sounded the claxon to announce their arrival and the boys and the amah ran out to greet them there was the sound of a shot. They ran to Olive's room and found her lying in front of the looking-glass in a pool of blood. She had shot herself with Tim's revolver.

'"Is she dead?" I said.

'"No, they sent for the doctor, and he took her to the hospital."

'I hardly knew what I was doing. I didn't even trouble to tell Sally where I was going. I got up and staggered to the door. I got into the car and told my seis to drive like hell to the hospital. I rushed in. I asked where she was.

They tried to bar my way, but I pushed them aside. I knew where the private rooms were. Someone clung to my arm, but I shook him off. I vaguely understood that the doctor had given instructions that no one was to go into the room. I didn't care about that. There was an orderly at the door; he put out his arm to prevent me from passing. I swore at him and told him to get out of my way. I suppose I made a row, I was beside myself; the door was opened and the doctor came out.

'"Who's making all this noise?" he said. "Oh, it's you. What do you want?"

'"Is she dead?" I asked.

'"No. But she's unconscious. She never regained consciousness. It's only a matter of an hour or two."

'"I want to see her."

'"You can't."

'"I'm engaged to her."

'"You?" he cried, and even at that moment I was aware that he looked at me strangely. "That's all the more reason."

'I didn't know what he meant. I was stupid with horror.

'"Surely you can do something to save her," I cried.

'He shook his head.

'"If you saw her you wouldn't wish it," he said.

'I stared at him aghast. In the silence I heard a man's convulsive sobbing.

'"Who's that?" I asked.

'"Her brother."

'Then I felt a hand on my arm. I looked round and saw it was Mrs. Sergison.

'"My poor boy," she said, "I'm so sorry for you."

'"What on earth made her do it?" I groaned.

'"Come away, my dear," said Mrs. Sergison. "You can do no good here."

'"No, I must stay," I said.

'"Well, go and sit in my room," said the doctor.

'I was so broken that I let Mrs. Sergison take me by the arm and lead me into the doctor's private room. She made me sit down. I couldn't bring myself to realise that it was true. I thought it was a horrible nightmare from which I must awake. I don't know how long we sat there. Three hours. Four hours. At last the doctor came in.

'"It's all over," he said.

'Then I couldn't help myself, I began to cry. I didn't care what they thought of me. I was so frightfully unhappy.

'We buried her next day.

'Mrs. Sergison came back to my house and sat with me for a while. She wanted me to go to the club with her. I hadn't the heart. She was very kind, but I was glad when she left me by myself. I tried to read, but the words meant nothing to me. I felt dead inside. My boy came in and turned on the lights. My head was aching like mad. Then he came back and said that a lady wished to see me. I asked who it was. He wasn't quite sure, but he thought it must be the new wife of the tuan at Putatan. I couldn't imagine what she wanted. I got up and went to the door. He was right. It was Sally. I asked her to come in. I noticed that she was deathly white. I felt sorry for her. It was a frightful experience for a girl of that age and for a bride a miserable home-coming. She sat down. She was very nervous. I tried to put her at her ease by saying conventional things. She made me very uncomfortable because she stared at me with those enormous blue eyes of hers, and they were simply ghastly with horror. She interrupted me suddenly.

'"You're the only person here I know," she said. "I had to come to you. I want you to get me away from here."

'I was dumbfounded.

'"What *do* you mean?" I said.

'"I don't want you to ask me any questions. I just want you to get me away. At once. I want to go back to England!"

'"But you can't leave Tim like that just now," I said. "My dear, you must pull yourself together. I know it's been awful for you. But think of Tim. I mean, he'll be miserable. If you have any love for him the least you can do is to try and make him a little less unhappy."

'"Oh, you don't know," she cried. "I can't tell you. It's too horrible. I beseech you to help me. If there's a train to-night let me get on it. If I can only get to Penang I can get a ship. I can't stay in this place another night. I shall go mad."

'I was absolutely bewildered.

'"Does Tim know?" I asked her.

'"I haven't seen Tim since last night. I'll never see him again. I'd rather die."

'I wanted to gain a little time.

'"But how can you go without your things? Have you got any luggage?"

'"What does that matter?" she cried impatiently. "I've got what I want for the journey."

'"Have you any money?"

'"Enough. Is there a train to-night?"

'"Yes," I said. "It's due just after midnight."

'"Thank God. Will you arrange everything? Can I stay here till then?"

'"You're putting me in a frightful position," I said. "I don't know what to do for the best. You know, it's an awfully serious step you're taking."

'"If you knew everything you'd know it was the only possible thing to do."

'"It'll create an awful scandal here. I don't know what people'll say. Have you thought of the effect on Tim?" I was worried and unhappy. "God knows I don't want to interfere in what isn't my business. But if you want me to help you I ought to know enough to feel justified in doing so. You must tell me what's happened."

'"I can't. I can only tell you that I know everything."'

'She hid her face with her hands and shuddered. Then she gave herself a shake as though she were recoiling from some frightful sight.

'"He had no right to marry me. It was monstrous."

'And as she spoke her voice rose shrill and piercing. I was afraid she was going to have an attack of hysterics. Her pretty doll-like face was terrified and her eyes stared as though she could never close them again.

'"Don't you love him any more?" I asked.

'"After that?"

'"What will you do if I refuse to help you?" I said.

'"I suppose there's a clergyman here or a doctor. You can't refuse to take me to one of them."

'"How did you get here?"

'"The head-boy drove me. He got a car from somewhere."

'"Does Tim know you've gone?"

'"I left a letter for him."

'"He'll know you're here."

'"He won't try to stop me. I promise you that. He daren't. For God's sake don't you try either. I tell you I shall go mad if I stay here another night."

'I sighed. After all she was of an age to decide for herself.'

I, the writer of this, hadn't spoken for a long time.

'Did you know what she meant?' I asked Featherstone.

He gave me a long, haggard look.

'There was only one thing she could mean. It was unspeakable. Yes, I knew all right. It explained everything. Poor Olive. Poor sweet. I suppose it was unreasonable of me, at that moment I only felt a horror of that little pretty fair-haired thing with her terrified eyes. I hated her. I didn't say anything for a while. Then I told her I'd do as she wished. She didn't even say thank you. I think she knew what I felt about her. When it was dinner-time I made her eat something and then she asked me if there was a room she could go and lie down in till it was time to go to the station. I showed her into my spare room and left her. I sat in the sitting-room and waited. My God, I don't think the time has ever passed so slowly for me. I thought twelve would never strike. I rang up the station and was told the train wouldn't be in till nearly two. At midnight she came back to the sitting-room and we sat there for an hour and a half. We had nothing to say to one another and we didn't speak. Then I took her to the station and put her on the train.'

'Was there an awful scandal?'

Featherstone frowned.

'I don't know. I applied for short leave. After that I was moved to another post. I heard that Tim had sold his estate and bought another. But I didn't know where. It was a shock to me at first when I found him here.'

Featherstone, getting up, went over to a table and mixed himself a whisky and soda. In the silence that fell now I heard the monotonous chorus of the croaking frogs. And suddenly the bird that is known as the fever-bird, perched in a tree close to the house, began to call. First, three notes in a descending, chromatic scale, then five, then four. The varying notes of the scale succeeded one another with maddening persistence. One was compelled to listen and to count them, and because one did not know how many there would be it tortured one's nerves.

'Blast that bird,' said Featherstone. 'That means no sleep for me to-night.'

Raw Material

I have long had in mind a novel in which a card-sharper was the principal character; and, going up and down the world, I have kept my eyes open for members of this profession. Because the idea is prevalent that it is a slightly dishonourable one the persons who follow it do not openly acknowledge the fact. Their reticence is such that it is often not till you have become quite closely acquainted with them, or even have played cards with them two or three times, that you discover in what fashion they earn their living. But even then they have a disinclination to enlarge upon the mysteries of their craft. They have a weakness for passing themselves off for cavalrymen, commercial agents or landed proprietors. This snobbish attitude makes them the most difficult class in the world for the novelist to study. It has been my good fortune to meet a number of these gentlemen, and though I have found them affable, obliging and debonair, I have no sooner hinted, however discreetly, at my curiosity (after all purely professional) in the technique of their calling than they have grown shy and uncommunicative. An airy reference on my part to stacking the cards has made them assume immediately the appearance of a clam. I am not easily discouraged, and learning by experience that I could hope for no good results from a direct method, I have adopted the oblique. I have been childlike with them and bland. I have found that they gave me their attention and even their sympathy. Though they confessed honestly that they had never read a word I had written they were interested by the fact that I was a writer. I suppose they felt obscurely that I too followed a calling that the philistine regarded without indulgence. But I have been forced to gather my facts by a bold surmise. It has needed patience and industry.

It may be imagined with what enthusiasm I made the acquaintance a little while ago of two gentlemen who seemed likely to add appreciably to my small store of information. I was travelling from Haiphong on a French liner going East, and they joined the ship at Hong-Kong. They had gone there for the races and were now on their way back to Shanghai. I was going there too, and thence to Peking. I soon learned that they had come from New York for a trip, were bound for Peking also, and by a happy coincidence meant to return to America in the ship in which I had myself booked a passage. I was naturally attracted to them, for they were pleasant fellows, but it was not till a fellow-passenger warned me that they were professional gamblers that I settled down to complete enjoyment of their acquaintance. I had no hope that they would ever discuss with frankness their interesting occupation, but I expected from a hint here, from a casual remark there, to learn some very useful things.

One – Campbell was his name – was a man in the late thirties, small, but so well built as not to look short, slender, with large melancholy eyes and beautiful hands. But for a premature baldness he would have been more than commonly good-looking. He was neatly dressed. He spoke slowly, in a low voice, and his movements were deliberate. The other was made on another pattern. He was a big, burly man with a red face and crisp black hair, of powerful appearance, strong in the arm and pugnacious. His name was Peterson.

The merits of the combination were obvious. The elegant, exquisite Campbell had the subtle brain, the knowledge of character, and the deft hands; but the hazards of the card-sharper's life are many, and when it came to a scrap Peterson's ready fist must often have proved invaluable. I do not know how it spread through the ship so quickly that a blow of Peterson's would stretch any man out. But during the short voyage from Hong-Kong to Shanghai they never even suggested a game of cards. Perhaps they had done well during the race-week and felt entitled to a holiday. They were certainly enjoying the advantages of not living for the time in a dry country and I do not think I do them an injustice if I say that for the most part they were far from sober. Each one talked little of himself but willingly of the other. Campbell informed me that Peterson was one of the most distinguished mining engineers in New York and Peterson assured me that Campbell was an eminent banker. He said that his wealth was fabulous. And who was I not to accept ingenuously all that was told me? But I thought it negligent of Campbell not to wear jewellery of a more expensive character. It seemed to me that to use a silver cigarette case was rather careless.

I stayed but a day in Shanghai, and though I met the pair again in Peking I was then so much engaged that I saw little of them. I thought it a little odd that Campbell should spend his entire time in the hotel. I do not think he even went to see the Temple of Heaven. But I could quite understand that from his point of view Peking was unsatisfactory and I was not surprised when the pair returned to Shanghai where, I knew, the wealthy merchants played for big money. I met them again in the ship that was to take us across the Pacific and I could not but sympathise with my friends when I saw that the passengers were little inclined to gamble. There were no rich people among them. It was a dull crowd. Campbell indeed suggested a game of poker, but no one would play more than twenty dollar table stakes, and Peterson, evidently not thinking it worth his while, would not join. Although we played afternoon and evening through the journey he sat down with us only on the last day. I suppose he thought he might just as well make his bar chits, and this he did very satisfactorily in a single sitting. But Campbell evidently loved the game for itself. Of course it is only if you have a passion for the business by which you earn your living that you can make a success of it. The stakes were nothing to him and he played all day and every day. It fascinated me to see the way in which he dealt the cards, very slowly, with his delicate hands. His eyes seemed to bore through the back of each one. He drank heavily, but remained quiet and self-controlled. His face was expressionless. I judged him to be a perfect card player and I wished that I could see him at work. It increased my esteem for him to see that he could take what was only a relaxation so seriously.

I parted with the pair at Victoria and concluded that I should never see them again. I set about sorting my impressions and made notes of the various points that I thought would prove useful.

When I arrived in New York I found an invitation to luncheon at the Ritz with an old friend of mine. When I went she said to me:

'It's quite a small party. A man is coming whom I think you'll like. He's a prominent banker; he's bringing a friend with him.'

The words were hardly out of her mouth when I saw coming up to us Campbell and Peterson. The truth flashed across me: Campbell really was an opulent banker; Peterson really was a distinguished engineer; they were not card-sharpers at all. I flatter myself I kept my face, but as I blandly shook hands with them I muttered under my breath furiously:

'Impostors!'

The Yellow Streak

The two prahus were dropping easily down stream, one a few yards ahead of the other, and in the first sat the two white men. After seven weeks on the rivers they were glad to know that they would lodge that night in a civilised house. To Izzart, who had been in Borneo since the war, the Dyak houses and their feasts were of course an old story; but Campion, though new to the country and at first amused by the strangeness, hankered too now for chairs to sit on and a bed to sleep in. The Dyaks were hospitable, but no one could say that there was much comfort to be found in their houses, and there was a monotony in the entertainment they offered a guest which presently grew somewhat wearisome. Every evening, as the travellers reached the landing-place, the headman, bearing a flag, and the more important members of the household, came down to the river to fetch them. They were led up to the long-house – a village really under one roof, built on piles, to which access was obtained by climbing up the trunk of a tree rudely notched into steps – and to the beating of drums and gongs walked up and down the whole length of it in long procession. On both sides serried throngs of brown people sat on their haunches and stared silently as the white men passed. Clean mats were unrolled and the guests seated themselves. The headman brought a live chicken and, holding it by the legs, waved it three times over their heads, called the spirits loudly to witness and uttered an invocation. Then various persons brought eggs. Arak was drunk. A girl, a very small shy thing with the grace of a flower but with something hieratic in her immobile face, held a cup to the white man's lips till it was empty and then a great shout arose. The men began to dance, one after the other, each treading his little measure, with his shield and his parang, to the accompaniment of drum and gong. After this had gone on for some time the visitors were taken into one of the rooms that led off the long platform on which was led the common life of the household and found their supper prepared for them. The girls fed them with Chinese spoons. Then everyone grew a little drunk and they all talked till the early hours of the morning.

But now their journey was done and they were on their way to the coast. They had started at dawn. The river then was very shallow and ran clear and bright over a shingly bottom; the trees leaned over it so that above there was only a strip of blue sky; but now it had broadened out, and the men were poling no longer but paddling. The trees, bamboos, wild sago like huge bunches of ostrich feathers, trees with enormous leaves and trees with feathery foliage like the acacia, coconut trees and areca palms, with their long straight white stems, the trees on the banks were immensely and violently luxuriant. Here and there, gaunt and naked, was the bare skeleton of a tree struck by lightning or dead of old age, and its whiteness against all that green was vivid. Here and there, rival kings of the forest, tall trees soared above the common level of the jungle. Then there were the parasites; in the fork of two branches great tufts of lush green leaves, or flowering creepers that covered the spreading foliage like a bride's veil; sometimes they wound round a tall trunk, a sheath of splendour, and threw long flowering arms from branch to branch. There was something thrilling in the passionate wildness of that eager growth; it had the daring abandon of the nomad rioting in the train of the god.

The day wore on, and now the heat was no longer so oppressive. Campion looked at the shabby silver watch on his wrist. It could not be long now before they reached their destination.

'What sort of a chap is Hutchinson?' he asked.

'I don't know him. I believe he's a very good sort.'

Hutchinson was the Resident in whose house they were to spend the night, and they had sent on a Dyak in a canoe to announce their arrival.

'Well, I hope he's got some whisky. I've drunk enough Arak to last me a lifetime.'

Campion was a mining engineer whom the Sultan on his way to England had met at Singapore, and finding him at a loose end had commissioned to go to Sembulu and see whether he could discover any mineral which might be profitably worked. He sent Willis, the Resident at Kuala Solor, instructions to afford him every facility, and Willis had put him in the care of Izzart because Izzart spoke both Malay and Dyak like a native. This was the third trip they had made into the interior, and now Campion was to go home with his reports. They were to catch the *Sultan Ahmed*, which was due to pass the mouth of the river at dawn on the next day but one, and with any luck should reach Kuala Solor on the same afternoon. They were both glad to get back to it. There was tennis and golf there, and the club with its billiard tables, food which was relatively good, and the comforts of civilisation. Izzart was glad, too, that he would have other society than Campion's. He gave him a sidelong glance. He was a little man with a big, bald head, and though certainly fifty, strong and wiry; he had quick, shining blue eyes and a stubbly, grey moustache. He was seldom without an old briar pipe between his broken and discoloured teeth. He was neither clean nor neat, his khaki shorts were ragged and his singlet torn; he was wearing now a battered topee.

He had knocked about the world since he was eighteen and had been in South Africa, in China and in Mexico. He was good company; he could tell a story well, and he was prepared to drink and drink again with anyone he met. They had got on very well together, but Izzart had never felt quite at home with him. Though they joked and laughed together, got drunk together, Izzart felt that there was no intimacy between them: for all the cordiality of their relations they remained nothing but acquaintances. He was very sensitive to the impression he made on others, and behind Campion's joviality he had felt a certain coolness; those shining blue eyes had summed him up; and it vaguely irritated Izzart that Campion had formed an opinion of him, and he did not quite know what it was. He was exasperated by the possibility that this common little man did not think entirely well of him. He desired to be liked and admired. He wanted to be popular. He wished the people he met to take an inordinate fancy to him, so that he could either reject them or a trifle condescendingly bestow his friendship on them. His inclination was to be familiar with all and sundry, but he was held back by the fear of a rebuff; sometimes he had been uneasily conscious that his effusiveness surprised the persons he lavished it on.

By some chance he had never met Hutchinson, though of course he knew all about him just as Hutchinson knew all about *him*, and they would have many common friends to talk of. Hutchinson had been at Winchester, and Izzart was glad that he could tell him that he had been at Harrow . . .

The prahu rounded a bend in the river and suddenly, standing on a slight eminence, they saw the bungalow. In a few minutes they caught sight of the landing-stage and on it, among a little group of natives, a figure in white waving to them.

Hutchinson was a tall, stout man with a red face. His appearance led you to expect that he was breezy and self-confident, so that it was not a little surprising to discover quickly that he was diffident and even a trifle shy. When he shook hands with his guests – Izzart introduced himself and then Campion – and led them up the pathway to the bungalow, though he was plainly anxious to be civil it was not hard to see that he found it difficult to make conversation. He took them out on to the verandah and here they found on the table glasses and whisky and soda. They made themselves comfortable on long chairs. Izzart, conscious of Hutchinson's slight embarrassment with strangers, expanded; he was very hearty and voluble. He began to speak of their common acquaintances at Kuala Solor, and he managed very soon to slip in casually the information that he had been at Harrow.

'You were at Winchester, weren't you?' he asked.

'Yes.'

'I wonder if you knew George Parker. He was in my regiment. He was at Winchester. I daresay he was younger than you.'

Izzart felt that it was a bond between them that they had been at these particular schools, and it excluded Campion, who obviously had enjoyed no such advantage. They drank two or three whiskies. Izzart in half an hour began to call his host Hutchie. He talked a good deal about 'my regiment' in which he had got his company during the war, and what good fellows his brother officers were. He mentioned two or three names which could hardly be unknown to Hutchinson. They were not the sort of people that Campion was likely to have come across, and he was not sorry to administer to him a neat snub when he claimed acquaintance with someone he spoke of.

'Billie Meadows?' I knew a fellow called Billie

Meadows in Sinaloa many years ago,' said Campion.

'Oh, I shouldn't think it could be the same,' said Izzart, with a smile. 'Billie's by way of being a peer of the realm. He's the Lord Meadows who races. Don't you remember, he owned Spring Carrots?'

Dinner time was approaching, and after a wash and brush-up they drank a couple of gin pahits. They sat down. Hutchinson had not been to Kuala Solor for the best part of a year, and had not seen another white man for three months. He was anxious to make the most of his visitors. He could give them no wine, but there was plenty of whisky and after dinner he brought out a precious bottle of Benedictine. They were very gay. They laughed and talked a great deal. Izzart was getting on famously. He thought he had never liked a fellow more than Hutchinson, and he pressed him to come down to Kuala Solor as soon as he could. They would have a wonderful beano. Campion was left out of the conversation by Izzart with the faintly malicious intention of putting him in his place, and by Hutchinson through shyness; and presently, after yawning a good deal, he said he would go to bed. Hutchinson showed him to his room and when he returned Izzart said to him:

'You don't want to turn in yet, do you?'

'Not on your life. Let's have another drink.'

They sat and talked. They both grew a little drunk. Presently Hutchinson told Izzart that he lived with a Malay girl, and had a couple of children by her. He had told them to keep out of sight while Campion was there.

'I expect she's asleep now,' said Hutchinson, with a glance at the door which Izzart knew led into his room, 'but I'd like you to see the kiddies in the morning.'

Just then a faint wail was heard and Hutchinson with a 'Hulloa, the little devil's awake,' went to the door and opened it. In a moment or two he came out of the room with a child in his arms. A woman followed him.

'He's cutting his teeth,' said Hutchinson. 'It makes him restless.'

The woman wore a sarong and a thin white jacket and she was barefoot. She was young, with fine dark eyes, and she gave Izzart when he spoke to her a bright and pleasant smile. She sat down and lit a cigarette. She answered the civil questions Izzart put to her without embarrassment, but also without effusion. Hutchinson asked her if she would have a whisky and soda, but she refused. When the two men began to talk again in English she sat on quite quietly, faintly rocking herself in her chair, and occupied with none could tell what calm thoughts.

'She's a very good girl,' said Hutchinson. 'She looks after the house and she's no trouble. Of course it's the only thing to do in a place like this.'

'I shall never do it myself,' said Izzart. 'After all, one may want to get married and then it means all sorts of botherations.'

'But who wants to get married? What a life for a white woman. I wouldn't ask a white woman to live here for anything in the world.'

'Of course it's a matter of taste. If I have any kiddies I'm going to see that they have a white mother.'

Hutchinson looked down at the little dark-skinned child he held in his arms. He gave a faint smile.

'It's funny how you get to like them,' he said. 'When they're your own it doesn't seem to matter that they've got a touch of the tar-brush.'

The woman gave the child a look, and getting up said she would take it back to bed.

'I should think we'd all better turn in,' said Hutchinson. 'God knows what the time is.'

Izzart went to his room and threw open the shutters

which his boy Hassan, whom he was travelling with, had closed. Blowing out the candle so that it should not attract the mosquitoes, he sat down at the window and looked at the soft night. The whisky he had drunk made him feel very wide awake, and he was not inclined to go to bed. He took off his ducks, put on a sarong and lit a cheroot. His good-humour was gone. It was the sight of Hutchinson looking fondly at the half-caste child which had upset him.

'They've got no right to have them,' he said to himself. 'They've got no chance in the world. Ever.'

He passed his hands reflectively along his bare and hairy legs. He shuddered a little. Though he had done everything he could to develop the calves, his legs were like broomsticks. He hated them. He was uneasily conscious of them all the time. They were like a native's. Of course they were the very legs for a top-boot. In his uniform he had looked very well. He was a tall, powerful man, over six feet high, and he had a neat black moustache and neat black hair. His dark eyes were fine and mobile. He was a good-looking fellow and he knew it, and he dressed well, shabbily when shabbiness was good form, and smartly when the occasion demanded. He had loved the army, and it was a bitter blow to him when, at the end of the war, he could not remain in it. His ambitions were simple. He wanted to have two thousand a year, give smart little dinners, go to parties and wear a uniform. He hankered after London.

Of course his mother lived there, and his mother cramped his style. He wondered how on earth he could produce her if ever he got engaged to the girl of good family (with a little money) whom he was looking for to make his wife. Because his father had been dead so long and during the later part of his career was stationed in the most remote of the Malay States, Izzart felt fairly sure that no one in Sembulu knew anything about her, but he lived in terror lest someone, running across her in London, should write over to tell people that she was a half-caste. She had been a beautiful creature when Izzart's father, an engineer in the Government Service, had married her; but now she was a fat old woman with grey hair who sat about all day smoking cigarettes. Izzart was twelve years old when his father died and then he could speak Malay much more fluently than English. An aunt offered to pay for his education and Mrs. Izzart accompanied her son to England. She lived habitually in furnished apartments, and her rooms with their Oriental draperies and Malay silver were overheated and stuffy. She was for ever in trouble with her landladies because she would leave cigarette-ends about. Izzard hated the way she made friends with them: she would be shockingly familiar with them for a time, then there would be a falling-out, and after a violent scene she would flounce out of the house. Her only amusement was the pictures, and to these she went every day in the week. At home she wore an old and tawdry dressing-gown, but when she went out she dressed herself – but, oh, how untidily – in extravagant colours, so that it was a mortification to her dapper son. He quarrelled with her frequently, she made him impatient and he was ashamed of her; and yet he felt for her a deep tenderness; it was almost a physical bond between them, something stronger than the ordinary feeling of mother and son, so that notwithstanding the failings that exasperated him she was the only person in the world with whom he felt entirely at home.

It was owing to his father's position and his own knowledge of Malay, for his mother always spoke it to him, that after the war, finding himself with nothing to do, he had managed to enter the service of the Sultan of Sembulu. He had been a success. He played games well, he was strong and a good athlete; in the rest-house at Kuala Solor were the cups which he had won at Harrow for running and jumping, and to these he had added since others for golf and tennis. With his abundant fund of small-talk he was an asset at parties and his cheeriness made things go. He ought to have been happy and he was wretched. He wanted so much to be popular, and he had an impression, stronger than ever at this moment, that popularity escaped him. He wondered whether by any chance the men at Kuala Solor with whom he was so hail fellow well met suspected that he had native blood in him. He knew very well what to expect if they ever found out. They wouldn't say he was gay and friendly then, they would say he was damned familiar; and they would say he was inefficient and careless, as the half-castes were, and when he talked of marrying a white woman they would snigger. Oh, it was so unfair! What difference could it make, that drop of native blood in his veins, and yet because of it they would always be on the watch for the expected failure at the critical moment. Everyone knew that you couldn't rely on Eurasians, sooner or later they would let you down; he knew it too, but now he asked himself whether they didn't fail because failure was expected of them. They were never given a chance, poor devils.

But a cock crew loudly. It must be very late and he was beginning to feel chilly. He got into bed. When Hassan brought him his tea next morning he had a racking headache, and when he went in to breakfast he could not look at the porridge and the bacon and eggs which were set before him. Hutchinson too was feeling none too well.

'I fancy we made rather a night of it,' said his host, with a smile to conceal his faint embarrassment.

'I feel like hell,' said Izzart.

'I'm going to breakfast off a whisky and soda myself,' added Hutchinson.

Izzart asked for nothing better, and it was with distaste that they watched Campion eat with healthy appetite a substantial meal. Campion chaffed them.

'By God, Izzart, you're looking green about the gills,' he said. 'I never saw such a filthy colour.'

Izzart flushed. His swarthiness was always a sensitive point with him. But he forced himself to give a cheery laugh.

'You see, I had a Spanish grandmother,' he answered, 'and when I'm under the weather it always comes out. I remember at Harrow I fought a boy and licked him, because he called me a damned half-caste.'

'You are dark,' said Hutchinson. 'Do Malays ever ask you if you have any native blood in you?'

'Yes, damn their impudence.'

A boat with their kit had started early in the morning in order to get to the mouth of the river before them, and tell the skipper of the *Sultan Ahmed*, if by chance he arrived before he was due, that they were on their way. Campion and Izzart were to set out immediately after tiffin in order to arrive at the place where they were to spend the night before the Bore passed. A Bore is a tidal wave that, by reason of a peculiarity in the lie of the land, surges up certain rivers, and there happened to be one on the river on which they were travelling. Hutchinson had talked to them of it the night before and Campion, who had never seen such a thing, was much interested.

'This is one of the best in Borneo. It's worth looking at,' said Hutchinson.

He told them how the natives, waiting the moment, rode it and were borne up the river on its crest at a breathless and terrifying speed. He had done it once himself.

'Never no more for me,' he said. 'I was scared out of my wits.'

'I should like to try it once,' said Izzart.

'It's exciting enough, but my word, when you're in a flimsy dug-out and you know that if the native doesn't get the right moment you'll be flung in that seething torrent and you won't have a chance in a million . . . no, it's not my idea of sport.'

'I've shot a good many rapids in my day,' said Campion.

'Rapids be damned. You wait till you see the Bore. It's one of the most terrifying things I know. D'you know that at least a dozen natives are drowned in it in this river alone every year?'

They lounged about on the verandah most of the morning and Hutchinson showed them the court-house. Then gin pahits were served. They drank two or three. Izzart began to feel himself, and when at length tiffin was ready he found that he had an excellent appetite. Hutchinson had boasted of his Malay curry and when the steaming, succulent dishes were placed before them they all set to ravenously. Hutchinson pressed them to drink.

'You've got nothing to do but sleep. Why shouldn't you get drunk?'

He could not bear to let them go so soon, it was good after so long to have white men to talk to, and he lingered over the meal. He urged them to eat. They would have a filthy meal that night at the long-house and nothing to drink but arak. They had better make hay while the sun shone. Campion suggested once or twice that they should start, but Hutchinson, and Izzart too, for now he was feeling very happy and comfortable, assured him there was plenty of time. Hutchinson sent for his precious bottle of Benedictine. They had made a hole in it last night; they might as well finish it before they went.

When at last he walked down with them to the river they were all very merry and none of them was quite steady on his legs. Over the middle of the boat was an attap awning, and under this Hutchinson had had a mattress laid. The crew were prisoners who had been marched down from the jail to row the white men, and they wore dingy sarongs with the prison mark. They waited at their oars. Izzart and Campion shook hands with Hutchinson and threw themselves down on the mattress. The boat pushed off. The turbid river, wide and placid, glistened in the heat of that brilliant afternoon like polished brass. In the distance ahead of them they could see the bank with its tangle of green trees. They felt drowsy, but Izzart at least found a curious enjoyment in resisting for a little while the heaviness that was creeping over him, and he made up his mind that he would not let himself fall asleep till he had finished his cheroot. At last the stub began to burn his fingers and he flung it into the river.

'I'm going to have a wonderful snooze,' he said.

'What about the Bore?' asked Campion.

'Oh, that's all right. We needn't worry about that.'

He gave a long and noisy yawn. His limbs felt like lead. He had one moment in which he was conscious of his delicious drowsiness and then he knew nothing more. Suddenly he was awakened by Campion shaking him.

'I say, what's that?'

'What's what?'

He spoke irritably, for sleep was still heavy upon him, but with his eyes he followed Campion's gesture. He could hear nothing, but a good way off he saw two or three white crested waves following one another. They did not look very alarming.

'Oh, I suppose that's the Bore.'

'What are we going to do about it?' cried Campion.

Izzart was scarcely yet quite awake. He smiled at the concern in Campion's voice.

'Don't worry. These fellows know all about it. They know exactly what to do. We may get a bit splashed.'

But while they were saying these few words the Bore came nearer, very quickly, with a roar like the roar of an angry sea, and Izzart saw that the waves were much higher than he had thought. He did not like the look of them and he tightened his belt so that his shorts should not slip down if the boat were upset. In a moment the waves were upon them. It was a great wall of water that seemed to tower over them, and it might have been ten or twelve feet high, but you could measure it only with your horror. It was quite plain that no boat could weather it. The first wave dashed over them, drenching them all, half filling the boat with water, and then immediately another wave struck them. The boatmen began to shout. They pulled madly at their oars and the steersman yelled an order. But in that surging torrent they were helpless, and it was frightening to see how soon they lost all control of the boat. The force of the water turned it broadside on and it was carried along, helter skelter, upon the crest of the Bore. Another great wave dashed over them and the boat began to sink. Izzart and Campion scrambled out of the covered place in which they had been lying and suddenly the boat gave way under their feet and they found themselves struggling in the water. It surged and stormed around them. Izzart's first impulse was to swim for the shore, but his boy, Hassan, shouted to him to cling to the boat. For a minute or two they all did this.

'Are you all right?' Campion shouted to him.

'Yes, enjoying the bath,' said Izzart.

He imagined that the waves would pass by as the Bore ascended the river, and in a few minutes at the outside they would find themselves in calm water once more.

He forgot that they were being carried along on its crest. The waves dashed over them. They clung to the gunwale and the base of the structure which supported the attap awning. Then a larger wave caught the boat and it turned over, falling upon them so that they lost their hold; there seemed nothing but a slippery bottom to cling to and Izzart's hands slithered helplessly on the greasy surface. But the boat continued to turn and he made a desperate grab at the gunwale, only to feel it slip out of his hands as the turn went on, then he caught the framework of the awning, and still it turned, turned slowly right round and once more he sought for a handhold on the bottom. The boat went round and round with a horrible regularity. He thought this must be because everyone was clinging to one side of it, and he tried to make the crew go round to the other. He could not make them understand. Everyone was shouting and the waves beat against them with a dull and angry roar. Each time the boat rolled over on them Izzart was pushed under the water, only to come up again as the gunwale and the framework of the awning gave him something to cling to. The struggle was awful. Presently he began to get terribly out of breath, and he felt his strength leaving him. He knew that he could not hold on much longer, but he did not feel frightened, for his fatigue by now was so great that he did not very much care what happened. Hassan was by his side and he told him he was growing very tired. He thought the best thing was to make a dash for the shore, it did not look more than sixty yards away, but Hassan begged him not to. Still they were being carried along amid those seething, pounding waves. The boat went round and round and they scrambled over it like squirrels in a cage. Izzart swallowed a lot of water. He felt he was very nearly done. Hassan could not help him, but it was a comfort that he was there, for Izzart knew that his boy, used to the water all his life, was a powerful swimmer. Then, Izzart did not know why, for a minute or two the boat held bottom downwards, so that he was able to hold on to the gunwale. It was a precious thing to be able to get his breath. At that moment two dugouts, with Malays in them riding the Bore, passed swiftly by them. They shouted for help, but the Malays averted their faces and went on. They saw the white men, and did not want to be concerned in any trouble that might befall them. It was agonising to see them go past, callous and indifferent in their safety. But on a sudden the boat rolled round again, round and round, slowly, and the miserable, exhausting scramble repeated itself. It took the heart out of you. But the short respite had helped Izzart, and he was able to struggle a little longer. Then once more he found himself so terribly out of breath that he thought his chest would burst. His strength was all gone, and he did not know now whether he had enough to try to swim for the shore. Suddenly he heard a cry.

'Izzart, Izzart. Help. Help.'

It was Campion's voice. It was a scream of agony. It sent a shock all through Izzart's nerves. Campion, Campion, what did he care for Campion? Fear seized him, a blind animal fear, and it gave him a new strength. He did not answer.

'Help me, quick, quick,' he said to Hassan.

Hassan understood him at once. By a miracle one of the oars was floating quite close to them and he pushed it into Izzart's reach. He placed a hand under Izzart's arm and they struck away from the boat. Izzart's heart was pounding and his breath came with difficulty. He felt horribly weak. The waves beat in his face. The bank looked dreadfully far away. He did not think he could ever reach it. Suddenly the boy cried that he could touch bottom and Izzart put down his legs; but he could feel nothing; he swam a few more exhausted strokes, his eyes fixed on the bank, and then, trying again, felt his feet sink into thick mud. He was thankful. He floundered on and there was the bank within reach of his hands, black mud in which he sank to his knees; he scrambled up, desperate to get out of the cruel water, and when he came to the top he found a little flat with tall rank grass all about it. He and Hassan sank down on it and lay for a while stretched out like dead men. They were so tired that they could not move. They were covered with black mud from head to foot.

But presently Izzart's mind began to work, and a pang of anguish on a sudden shook him. Campion was drowned. It was awful. He did not know how he was going to explain the disaster when he got back to Kuala Solor. They would blame him for it; he ought to have remembered the Bore and told the steersman to make for the bank and tie up the boat when he saw it coming. It wasn't his fault, it was the steersman's, he knew the river; why in God's name hadn't he had the sense to get into safety? How could he have expected that it was possible to ride that horrible torrent? Izzart's limbs shook as he remembered the wall of seething water that rushed down upon them. He must get the body and take it back to Kuala Solor. He wondered whether any of the crew were drowned too. He felt too weak to move, but Hassan now rose and wrang the water out of his sarong; he looked over the river and quickly turned to Izzart.

'Tuan, a boat is coming.'

The lalang grass prevented Izzart from seeing anything.

'Shout to them,' he said.

Hassan slipped out of view and made his way along the branch of a tree that overhung the water; he cried out and waved. Presently Izzart heard voices. There was a rapid conversation between the boy and the occupants of the boat, and then the boy came back.

'They saw us capsize, Tuan,' he said, 'and they came as soon as the Bore passed. There's a long-house on the other side. If you will cross the river they will give us sarongs and food and we can sleep there.'

Izzart for a moment felt that he could not again trust himself on the face of the treacherous water.

'What about the other tuan?' he asked.

'They do not know.'

'If he's drowned they must find the body.'

'Another boat has gone up stream.'

Izzart did not know what to do. He was numb. Hassan put his arm round his shoulder and raised him to his feet. He made his way through the thick grass to the edge of the water, and there he saw a dug-out with two Dyaks in it. The river now once more was calm and sluggish; the great wave had passed on and no one would have dreamed that so short a while before the placid surface was like a stormy sea. The Dyaks repeated to him what they had already told the boy. Izzart could not bring himself to speak. He felt that if he said a word he would burst out crying. Hassan helped him to get in, and the Dyaks began to pull across. He fearfully wanted something to smoke, but his cigarettes and his matches, both in a hip-pocket were soaking. The passage of the river seemed endless. The night fell and when they reached the bank the first stars were shining. He stepped ashore and one of the Dyaks took him up to the long-house. But Hassan seized the paddle he had dropped and with the other pushed out into the stream. Two or three men and some children came down to meet Izzart and he climbed to the house amid a babel of conversation. He went up the ladder and was led with greetings and excited comment to the space where the young men slept. Rattan mats were hurriedly laid to make him a couch and he sank down on them.

Someone brought him a jar of arak and he took a long drink; it was rough and fiery, burning his throat, but it warmed his heart. He slipped off his shirt and trousers and put on a dry sarong which someone lent him. By chance he caught sight of the yellow new moon lying on her back, and it gave him a keen, almost a sensual, pleasure. He could not help thinking that he might at that moment be a corpse floating up the river with the tide. The moon had never looked to him more lovely. He began to feel hungry and he asked for rice. One of the women went into a room to prepare it. He was more himself now, and he began to think again of the explanations he would make at Kuala Solor. No one could really blame him because he had gone to sleep; he certainly wasn't drunk, Hutchinson would bear him out there, and how was he to suspect that the steersman would be such a damned fool? It was just rotten luck. But he couldn't think of Campion without a shudder. At last a platter of rice was brought him, and he was just about to start eating when a man ran hurriedly along and came up to him.

'The tuan's come,' he cried.

'What tuan?'

He jumped up. There was a commotion about the doorway and he stepped forward. Hassan was coming quickly towards him out of the darkness, and then he heard a voice.

'Izzart. Are you there?'

Campion advanced towards him.

'Well, here we are again. By God, that was a pretty near thing, wasn't it? You seem to have made yourself nice and comfortable. My heavens, I could do with a drink.'

His dank clothes clung round him, and he was muddy and dishevelled. But he was in excellent spirits.

'I didn't know where the hell they were bringing me.

I'd made up my mind that I should have to spend the night on the bank. I thought you were drowned.'

'Here's some arak,' said Izzart.

Campion put his mouth to the jar and drank and spluttered and drank again.

'Muck, but by God it's strong.' He looked at Izzart with a grin of his broken and discoloured teeth. 'I say, old man, you look as though you'd be all the better for a wash.'

'I'll wash later.'

'All right, so will I. Tell them to get me a sarong. How did you get out?' He did not wait for an answer. 'I thought I was done for. I owe my life to these two sportsmen here.' He indicated with a cheery nod two of the Dyak prisoners whom Izzart vaguely recognised as having been part of their crew. 'They were hanging on to that blasted boat on each side of me and somehow they cottoned on to it that I was down and out. I couldn't have lasted another minute. They made signs to me that we could risk having a shot at getting to the bank, but I didn't think I had the strength. By George, I've never been so blown in all my life. I don't know how they managed it, but somehow they got hold of the mattress we'd been lying on, and they made it into a roll. They're sportsmen they are. I don't know why they didn't just save themselves without bothering about me. They gave it me. I thought it a damned poor lifebelt, but I saw the force of the proverb about a drowning man clutching at a straw. I caught hold of the damned thing and between them somehow or other they dragged me ashore.'

The danger from which he had escaped made Campion excited and voluble; but Izzart hardly listened to what he said. He heard once more, as distinctly as though the words rang now through the air, Campion's agonised cry for help, and he felt sick with terror. The

blind panic raced down his nerves. Campion was talking still, but was he talking to conceal his thoughts?
Izzart looked into those bright blue eyes and sought to
read the sense behind the flow of words. Was there a
hard glint in them or something of cynical mockery?
Did he know that Izzart, leaving him to his fate, had cut
and run? He flushed deeply. After all, what was there
that he could have done? At such a moment it was each
for himself and the devil take the hindmost. But what
would they say in Kuala Solor if Campion told them
that Izzart had deserted him? He ought to have stayed,
he wished now with all his heart that he had, but then,
then it was stronger than himself, he couldn't. Could
anyone blame him? No one who had seen that fierce
and seething torrent. Oh, the water and the exhaustion,
so that he could have cried!

'If you're as hungry as I am you'd better have a tuck
in at this rice,' he said.

Campion ate voraciously, but when Izzart had taken
a mouthful or two he found that he had no appetite.
Campion talked and talked. Izzart listened suspiciously. He felt that he must be alert and he drank
more arak. He began to feel a little drunk.

'I shall get into the devil of a row at K.S.' he said
tentatively.

'I don't know why.'

'I was told off to look after you. They won't think it
was very clever of me to let you get nearly drowned.'

'It wasn't your fault. It was the fault of the damned
fool of a steersman. After all, the important thing is that
we're saved. By George, I thought I was finished once. I
shouted out to you. I don't know if you heard me.'

'No, I didn't hear anything. There was such a devil of
a row wasn't there?'

'Perhaps you'd got away before. I don't know exactly
when you did get away.'

Izzart looked at him sharply. Was it his fancy that there was an odd look in Campion's eyes?

'There was such an awful confusion,' he said. 'I was just about down and out. My boy threw me over an oar. He gave me to understand you were all right. He told me you'd got ashore.'

The oar! He ought to have given Campion the oar and told Hassan, the strong swimmer, to give *him* his help. Was it his fancy again that Campion gave him a quick and searching glance?

'I wish I could have been of more use to you,' said Izzart.

'Oh, I'm sure you had enough to do to look after yourself,' answered Campion.

The headman brought them cups of arak, and they both drank a great deal. Izzart's head began to spin and he suggested that they should turn in. Beds had been prepared for them and mosquito nets fixed. They were to set out at dawn on the rest of their journey down the river. Campion's bed was next to his, and in a few minutes he heard him snoring. He had fallen asleep the moment he lay down. The young men of the long-house and the prisoners of the boat's crew went on talking late into the night. Izzart's head now was aching horribly and he could not think. When Hassan roused him as day broke it seemed to him that he had not slept at all. Their clothes had been washed and dried, but they were bedraggled objects as they walked along the narrow pathway to the river where the prahu was waiting for them. They rowed leisurely. The morning was lovely and the great stretch of placid water gleamed in the early light.

'By George, it's fine to be alive,' said Campion.

He was grubby and unshaved. He took long breaths, and his twisted mouth was half open with a grin. You could tell that he found the air singularly good to breathe. He was delighted with the blue sky and the sunshine and the greenness of the trees. Izzart hated him. He was sure that this morning there was a difference in his manner. He did not know what to do. He had a mind to throw himself on his mercy. He had behaved like a cad, but he was sorry, he would give anything to have the chance again, but anyone might have done what he did, and if Campion gave him away he was ruined. He could never stay in Sembulu; his name would be mud in Borneo and the Straits Settlements. If he made his confession to Campion he could surely get Campion to promise to hold his tongue. But would he keep his promise? He looked at him, a shifty little man: how could he be relied on? Izzart thought of what he had said the night before. It wasn't the truth, of course, but who could know that? At all events who could prove that he hadn't honestly thought that Campion was safe? Whatever Campion said it was only his word against Izzart's; he could laugh and shrug his shoulders and say that Campion had lost his head and didn't know what he was talking about. Besides, it wasn't certain that Campion hadn't accepted his story; in that frightful struggle for life he could be very sure of nothing. He had a temptation to go back to the subject, but was afraid if he did that he would excite suspicion in Campion's mind. He *must* hold his tongue. That was his only chance of safety. And when they got to K.S. he would get in his story first.

'I should be completely happy now,' said Campion, 'if I only had something to smoke.'

'We shall be able to get some stinkers on board.'

Campion gave a little laugh.

'Human beings are very unreasonable,' he said. 'At the first moment I was so glad to be alive that I thought of nothing else, but now I'm beginning to regret the loss of my notes and my photographs and my shaving tackle.'

Izzart formulated the thought which had lurked at the back of his mind, but which all through the night he had refused to admit into his consciousness.

'I wish to God he'd been drowned. Then I'd have been safe.'

'There she is,' cried Campion suddenly.

Izzart looked round. They were at the mouth of the river and there was the *Sultan Ahmed* waiting for them. Izzart's heart sank: he had forgotten that she had an English skipper and that he would have to be told the story of their adventure. What would Campion say? The skipper was called Bredon, and Izzart had met him often at Kuala Solor. He was a little bluff man, with a black moustache, and a breezy manner.

'Hurry up,' he called out to them, as they rowed up, 'I've been waiting for you since dawn.' But when they climbed on board his face fell. 'Hulloa, what's the matter with you?'

'Give us a drink and you shall hear all about it,' said Campion, with his crooked grin.

'Come along.'

They sat down under the awning. On a table were glasses, a bottle of whisky and soda water. The skipper gave an order and in a few minutes they were noisily under way.

'We were caught in the Bore,' said Izzart.

He felt he must say something. His mouth was horribly dry notwithstanding the drink.

'Were you, by Jove? You're lucky not to have been drowned. What happened?'

He addressed himself to Izzart because he knew him, but it was Campion who answered. He related the whole incident, accurately, and Izzart listened with strained attention. Campion spoke in the plural when he told the early part of the story, and then, as he came to the moment when they were thrown into the water,

237

changed to the singular. At first it was what *they* had done and now it was what happened to *him*. He left Izzart out of it. Izzart did not know whether to be relieved or alarmed. Why did not he not mention him? Was it because in that mortal struggle for life he had thought of nothing but himself or – did he *know*?

'And what happened to you?' said Captain Bredon, turning to Izzart.

Izzart was about to answer when Campion spoke.

'Until I got over to the other side of the river I thought he was drowned. I don't know how he got out. I expect he hardly knows himself.'

'It was touch and go,' said Izzart with a laugh.

Why had Campion said that? He caught his eye. He was sure now that there was a gleam of amusement in it. It was awful not to be certain. He was frightened. He was ashamed. He wondered if he could not so guide the conversation, either now or later, as to ask Campion whether that was the story he was going to tell in Kuala Solor. There was nothing in it to excite anyone's suspicions. But if nobody else knew, Campion knew. He could have killed him.

'Well, I think you're both of you damned lucky to be alive,' said the skipper.

It was but a short run to Kuala Solor, and as they steamed up the Sembulu river Izzart moodily watched the banks. On each side were the mangroves and the nipas washed by the water, and behind, the dense green of the jungle; here and there, among fruit trees, were Malay houses on piles. Night fell as they docked. Goring, of the police, came on board and shook hands with them. He was living at the rest-house just then, and as he set about his work of seeing the native passengers he told them they would find another man, Porter by name, staying there too. They would all meet at dinner. The boys took charge of their kit, and

Campion and Izzart strolled along. They bathed and changed, and at half-past eight the four of them assembled in the common room for gin pahits.

'I say, what's this Bredon tells me about your being nearly drowned?' said Goring as he came in.

Izzart felt himself flush, but before he could answer Campion broke in, and it seemed certain to Izzart that he spoke in order to give the story as he chose. He felt hot with shame. Not a word was spoken in disparagement of him, not a word was said of him at all; he wondered if those two men who listened, Goring and Porter, thought it strange that he should be left out. He looked at Campion intently as he proceeded with his narration, he told it rather humorously; he did not disguise the danger in which they had been, but he made a joke of it, so that the two listeners laughed at the quandary in which they had found themselves.

'A thing that's tickled me since,' said Campion, 'is that when I got over to the other bank I was black with mud from head to foot. I felt I really ought to jump in the river and have a wash, but you know I felt I'd been in that damned river as much as ever I wanted, and I said to myself: No, by George, I'll go dirty. And when I got into the long-house and saw Izzart as black as I was, I knew he'd felt just like I did.'

They laughed and Izzart forced himself to laugh too. He noticed that Campion had told the story in precisely the same words as he had used when he told it to the skipper of the *Sultan Ahmed*. There could be only one explanation of that; he knew, he knew everything, and had made up his mind exactly what story to tell. The ingenuity with which Campion gave the facts, and yet left out what must be to Izzart's discredit was devilish. But why was he holding his hand? It wasn't in him not to feel contempt and resentment for the man who had callously deserted him in that moment of dreadful peril.

Suddenly, in a flash of inspiration Izzart understood: he was keeping the truth to tell to Willis, the Resident. Izzart had gooseflesh as he thought of confronting Willis. He could deny, but would his denials serve him? Willis was no fool, and he would get at Hassan; Hassan could not be trusted to be silent; Hassan would give him away. Then he would be done for. Willis would suggest that he had better go home.

He had a racking headache, and after dinner he went to his room, for he wanted to be alone so that he could devise a plan of action. And then a thought came to him which made him go hot and cold; he knew that the secret which he had guarded so long, was a secret to nobody. He was on a sudden certain of it. Why should he have those bright eyes and that swarthy skin? Why should he speak Malay with such ease and have learned Dyak so quickly? Of course they knew. What a fool he was ever to think that they believed that story of his, about the Spanish grandmother! They must have laughed up their sleeves when he told it, and behind his back they had called him a damned nigger. And now another thought came to him, torturing, and he asked himself whether it was on account of that wretched drop of native blood in him that when he heard Campion cry out his nerve failed him. After all, anyone might at that moment have been seized with panic; and why in God's name should he sacrifice his life to save a man's whom he cared nothing for? It was insane. But of course in K.S. they would say it was only what they expected; they would make no allowances.

At last he went to bed, but when, after tossing about recklessly for God knows how long, he fell asleep, he was awakened by a fearful dream; he seemed to be once more in that raging torrent, with the boat turning, turning; and then there was the desperate clutching at the gunwale, and the agony as it slipped out of his hands, and the water that roared over him. He was wide awake before dawn. His only chance was to see Willis and get his story in first; and he thought over carefully what he was going to say, and chose the very words he meant to use.

He got up early, and in order not to see Campion went out without breakfast. He walked along the high road till such time as he knew the Resident would be in his office, and then walked back again. He sent in his name and was ushered into Willis's room. He was a little elderly man with thin grey hair and a long yellow face.

'I'm glad to see you back safe and sound,' he said, shaking hands with Izzart. 'What's this I hear about your being nearly drowned?'

Izzart, in clean ducks, his topee spotless, was a fine figure of a man. His black hair was neatly brushed, and his moustache was trimmed. He had an upright and soldiery bearing.

'I thought I'd better come and tell you at once, sir, as you told me to look after Campion.'

'Fire away.'

Izzart told his story. He made light of the danger. He gave Willis to understand that it had not been very great. They would never have been upset if they had not started so late.

'I tried to get Campion away earlier, but he'd had two or three drinks and the fact is, he didn't want to move.'

'Was he tight?'

'I don't know about that,' smiled Izzart good-humouredly. 'I shouldn't say he was cold sober.'

He went on with his story. He managed to insinuate that Campion had lost his head a little. Of course it was a very frightening business to a man who wasn't a decent swimmer: he, Izzart, had been more concerned for Campion than for himself; he knew the only chance was to keep cool, and the moment they were upset he saw that Campion had got the wind up.

'You can't blame him for that,' said the Resident.

'Of course I did everything I possibly could for him, sir, but the fact is, there wasn't anything much I could do.'

'Well, the great thing is that you both escaped. It would have been very awkward for all of us if he'd been drowned.'

'I thought I'd better come and tell you the facts before you saw Campion, sir. I fancy he's inclined to talk rather wildly about it. There's no use exaggerating.'

'On the whole your stories agree pretty well,' said Willis, with a little smile.

Izzart looked at him blankly.

'Haven't you seen Campion this morning? I heard from Goring that there'd been some trouble, and I looked in last night on my way home from the Fort after dinner. You'd already gone to bed.'

Izzart felt himself trembling, and he made a great effort to preserve his composure.

'By the way, you got away first, didn't you?'

'I don't really know, sir. You see, there was a lot of confusion.'

'You must have if you got over to the other side before he did.'

'I suppose I did then.'

'Well, thanks for coming to tell me,' said Willis, rising from his chair.

As he did so he knocked some books on the floor. They fell with a sudden thud. The unexpected sound made Izzart start violently, and he gave a gasp. The Resident looked at him quickly.

'I say, your nerves are in a pretty state.'

Izzart could not control his trembling.

'I'm very sorry, sir,' he murmured.

'I expect it's been a shock. You'd better take it easy

for a few days. Why don't you get the doctor to give you something?'

'I didn't sleep very well last night.'

The Resident nodded as though he understood. Izzart left the room, and as he passed out some man he knew stopped and congratulated him on his escape. They all knew of it. He walked back to the rest-house. And as he walked, he repeated to himself the story he had told the Resident. Was it really the same story that Campion had told? He had never suspected that the Resident had already heard it from Campion. What a fool he had been to go to bed! He should never have let Campion out of his sight. Why had the Resident listened without telling him that he already knew? Now Izzart cursed himself for having suggested that Campion was drunk and had lost his head. He had said this in order to discredit him, but he knew now that it was a stupid thing to do. And why had Willis said that about his having got away first? Perhaps he was holding his hand too; perhaps he was going to make enquiries; Willis was very shrewd. But what exactly had Campion said? He must know that; at whatever cost he must know. Izzart's mind was seething, so that he felt he could hardly keep a hold on his thoughts, but he must keep calm. He felt like a hunted animal. He did not believe that Willis liked him; once or twice in the office he had blamed him because he was careless; perhaps he was just waiting till he got all the facts. Izzart was almost hysterical.

He entered the rest-house and there, sitting on a long chair, with his legs stretched out, was Campion. He was reading the papers which had arrived during their absence in the jungle. Izzart felt a blind rush of hatred well up in him as he looked at the little, shabby man who held him in the hollow of his hand.

'Hulloa,' said Campion, looking up. 'Where have you been?'

To Izzart it seemed that there was in his eyes a mocking irony. He clenched his hands, and his breath came fast.

'What have you been saying to Willis about me?' he asked abruptly.

The tone in which he put the unexpected question was so harsh that Campion gave him a glance of faint surprise.

'I don't think I've been saying anything very much about you. Why?'

'He came here last night.'

Izzart looked at him intently. His brows were drawn together in an angry frown as he tried to read Campion's thoughts.

'I told him you'd gone to bed with a headache. He wanted to know about our mishap.'

'I've just seen him.'

Izzart walked up and down the large and shaded room; now, though it was still early, the sun was hot and dazzling. He felt himself in a net. He was blind with rage; he could have seized Campion by the throat and strangled him, and yet, because he did not know what he had to fight against, he felt himself powerless. He was tired and ill, and his nerves were shaken. On a sudden the anger which had given him a sort of strength left him, and he was filled with despondency. It was as though water and not blood ran through his veins; his heart sank and his knees seemed to give way. He felt that if did not take care, he would begin to cry. He was dreadfully sorry for himself.

'Damn you, I wish to God I'd never set eyes on you,' he cried pitifully.

'What on earth's the matter?' asked Campion, with astonishment.

'Oh, don't pretend. We've been pretending for two days, and I'm fed up with it.' His voice rose shrilly, it sounded odd in that robust and powerful man. 'I'm fed up with it. I cut and run. I left you to drown. I know I behaved like a skunk. I couldn't help it.'

Campion rose slowly from his chair.

'What *are* you talking about?'

His tone was so genuinely surprised that it gave Izzart a start. A cold shiver ran down his spine.

'When you called for help I was panic-stricken. I just caught hold of an oar and got Hassan to help me get away.'

'That was the most sensible thing you could do.'

'I couldn't help you. There wasn't a thing I could do.'

'Of course not. It was damned silly of me to shout. It was a waste of breath, and breath was the very thing I wanted.'

'Do you mean to say you didn't know?'

'When those fellows got me the mattress, I thought you were still clinging to the boat. I had an idea that I got away before you did.'

Izzart put both his hands to his head, and gave a hoarse cry of despair.

'My God, what a fool I've been.'

The two men stood for a while staring at one another. The silence seemed endless.

'What are you going to do now?' asked Izzart at last.

'Oh, my dear fellow, don't worry. I've been frightened too often myself to blame anyone who shows the white feather. I'm not going to tell a soul.'

'Yes, but you *know*.'

'I promise you, you can trust me. Besides, my job's done here and I'm going home. I want to catch the next boat to Singapore.' There was a pause, and Campion looked for a while reflectively at Izzart. 'There's only one thing I'd like to ask you: I've made a good many friends here, and there are one or two things I'm a little sensitive about; when you tell the story of our upset, I should be grateful if you wouldn't make out that I had behaved badly. I wouldn't like the fellows here to think that I'd lost my nerve.'

Izzart flushed darkly. He remembered what he had said to the Resident. It almost looked as though Campion had been listening over his shoulder. He cleared his throat.

'I don't know why you think I should do that.'

Campion chuckled good-naturedly, and his blue eyes were gay with amusement.

'The yellow streak,' he replied, and then, with a grin that showed his broken and discoloured teeth: 'Have a cheroot, dear boy.'

Masterson

When I left Colombo I had no notion of going to Keng Tung, but on the ship I met a man who told me he had spent five years there. He said it had an important market, held every five days, whither came natives of half a dozen countries and members of half a hundred tribes. It had pagodas darkly splendid and a remoteness that liberated the questing spirit from its anxiety. He said he would sooner live there than anywhere in the world. I asked him what it had offered him and he said, contentment. He was a tall, dark fellow with the aloofness of manner you often find in those who have lived much alone in unfrequented places. Men like this are a little restless in the company of others and though in the smoking-room of a ship or at the club bar they may be talkative and convivial, telling their story with the rest, joking and glad sometimes to narrate their unusual experiences, they seem always to hold something back. They have a life in themselves that they keep apart, and there is a look in their eyes, as it were turned inwards, that informs you that this hidden life is the only one that signifies to them. And now and then their eyes betray their weariness with the social round into which hazard or the fear of seeming odd has for a moment forced them. They seem then to long for the monotonous solitude of some place of their predilection where they can be once more alone with the reality they have found.

It was as much the manner of this chance acquaintance as what he told me that persuaded me to make the journey across the Shan States on which I now set out. From the rail-head in Upper Burma to the rail-head in Siam, whence I could get down to Bangkok, it was between six and seven hundred miles. Kind people had done everything possible to render the excursion easy for me and the Resident at Taunggyi had wired to me that he had made arrangements for mules and ponies to be ready for me on my arrival. I had bought in Rangoon such stores as seemed necessary, folding chairs and a table, a filter, lamps, and I know not what. I took the train from Mandalay to Thazi, intending there to hire a car for Taunggyi, and a man I had met at the club at Mandalay and who lived at Thazi asked me to have brunch (the pleasant meal of Burma that combines breakfast and lunch) with him before I started. His name was Masterson. He was a man in the early thirties, with a pleasant friendly face, curling dark hair speckled with grey, and handsome dark eyes. He spoke with a singularly musical voice, very slowly, and this, I hardly know why, inspired you with confidence. You felt that a man who took such a long time to say what he had to say and had found the world with sufficient leisure to listen to him must have qualities that made him sympathetic to his fellows. He took the amiability of mankind for granted and I suppose he could only have done this because he was himself amiable. He had a nice sense of humour, without of course a quick thrust and parry, but agreeably sarcastic; it was of that agreeable type that applies common sense to the accidents of life and so sees them in a faintly ridiculous aspect. He was engaged in a business that kept him travelling up and down Burma most of the year, and in his journeyings he had acquired the collector's habit. He told me that he spent all his spare money on buying Burmese curiosities and it was especially to see them that he asked me to have a meal with him.

The train got in early in the morning. He had warned me that, having to be at his office, he could not meet me; but brunch was at ten and he told me to go to his house as soon as I was finished with the one or two things I had to do in the town.

'Make yourself at home,' he said, 'and if you want a drink ask the boy for it. I'll get back as soon as I've got through with my business.'

I found out where there was a garage and made a bargain with the owner of a very dilapidated Ford to take me and my baggage to Taunggyi. I left my Madrassi servant to see that everything was stowed in it that was possible and the rest tied on to the footboards, and strolled along to Masterson's house. It was a neat little bungalow in a road shaded by tall trees, and in the early light of a sunny day looked pretty and homelike. I walked up the steps and was hailed by Masterson.

'I got done more quickly than I expected. I shall have time to show you my things before brunch is ready. What will you have? I'm afraid I can only offer you a whisky and soda.'

'Isn't it rather early for that?'

'Rather. But it's one of the rules of the house that nobody crosses the threshold without having a drink.'

'What can I do but submit to the rule?'

He called the boy and in a moment a trim Burmese brought in a decanter, a syphon, and glasses. I sat down and looked about the room. Though it was still so early the sun was hot outside and the jalousies were drawn. The light was pleasant and cool after the glare of the road. The room was comfortably furnished with rattan chairs and on the walls were water-colour paintings of English scenes. They were a little prim and old-fashioned and I guessed that they had been painted in her youth by the maiden and elderly aunt of my host. There were two of a cathedral I did not know, two or three of a rose garden, and one of a Georgian house. When he saw my eyes for an instant rest upon this, he said:

'That was our house at Cheltenham.'

'Oh, is that where you come from?'

Then there was his collection. The room was crowded with Buddhas and with figures, in bronze or wood, of the Buddha's disciples; there were boxes of all shapes, utensils of one kind and another, curiosities of every sort, and although there were far too many they were arranged with a certain taste so that the effect was pleasing. He had some lovely things. He showed them to me with pride, telling me how he had got this object and that, and how he had heard of another and hunted it down and the incredible astuteness he had employed to induce an unwilling owner to part with it. His kindly eyes shone when he described a great bargain and they flashed darkly when he inveighed against the unreasonableness of a vendor who rather than accept a fair price for a bronze dish had taken it away. There were flowers in the room, and it had not the forlorn look that so many bachelors' houses have in the East.

'You've made the place very comfortable,' I said.

He gave the room a sweeping glance.

'It *was* all right. It's not much now.'

I did not quite know what he meant. Then he showed me a long wooden gilt box, decorated with the glass mosaic that I had admired in the palace at Mandalay, but the workmanship was more delicate than anything I had seen there, and this with its gem-like richness had really something of the ornate exquisiteness of the Italian Renaissance.

'They tell me it's about a couple of hundred years old,' he said. 'They've not been able to turn out anything like this for a long time.'

It was a piece made obviously for a king's palace and

you wondered to what uses it had been put and what hands it had passed through. It was a jewel.

'What is the inside like?' I asked.

'Oh, nothing much. It's just lacquered.'

He opened it and I saw that it contained three or four framed photographs.

'Oh, I'd forgotten those were there,' he said.

His soft, musical voice had a queer sound in it, and I gave him a sidelong look. He was bronzed by the sun, but his face notwithstanding flushed a deeper red. He was about to close the box, and then he changed his mind. He took out one of the photographs and showed it to me.

'Some of these Burmese girls are rather sweet when they're young, aren't they?' he said.

The photograph showed a young girl standing somewhat self-consciously against the conventional background of a photographer's studio, a pagoda and a group of palm-trees. She was wearing her best clothes and she had a flower in her hair. But the embarrassment you saw she felt at having her picture taken did not prevent a shy smile from trembling on her lips and her large solemn eyes had nevertheless a roguish twinkle. She was very small and very slender.

'What a ravishing little thing,' I said.

Then Masterson took out another photograph in which she sat with a child standing by her side, his hand timidly on her knee, and a baby in her arms. The child stared straight in front of him with a look of terror on his face; he could not understand what that machine and the man behind it, his head under a black cloth, were up to.

'Are those her children?' I asked.

'And mine,' said Masterson.

At that moment the boy came in to say that brunch was ready. We went into the dining-room and sat down.

'I don't know what you'll get to eat. Since my girl went away everything in the house has gone to blazes.'

A sulky look came into his red honest face and I did not know what to reply.

'I'm so hungry that whatever I get will seem good,' I hazarded.

He did not say anything and a plate of thin porridge was put before us. I helped myself to milk and sugar. Masterson ate a spoonful or two and pushed his plate aside.

'I wish I hadn't looked at those damned photographs,' he said. 'I put them away on purpose.'

I did not wish to be inquisitive or to force a confidence my host had no wish to give, but neither did I desire to seem so unconcerned as to prevent him from telling me something he had in his heart. Often in some lonely post in the jungle or in a stiff grand house, solitary in the midst of a teeming Chinese city, a man has told me stories about himself that I was sure he had never told to a living soul. I was a stray acquaintance whom he had never seen before and would never see again, a wanderer for a moment through his monotonous life, and some starved impulse led him to lay bare his soul. I have in this way learned more about men in a night (sitting over a syphon or two and a bottle of whisky, the hostile, inexplicable world outside the radius of an acetylene lamp) than I could have if I had known them for ten years. If you are interested in human nature it is one of the great pleasures of travel. And when you separate (for you have to be up betimes) sometimes they will say to you:

'I'm afraid I've bored you to death with all this nonsense. I haven't talked so much for six months. But it's done me good to get it off my chest.'

The boy removed the porridge plates and gave each of us a piece of pale fried fish. It was rather cold.

'The fish is beastly, isn't it?' said Masterson. 'I hate river fish, except trout; the only thing is to smother it with Worcester sauce.'

He helped himself freely and passed me the bottle.

'She was a damned good housekeeper, my girl; I used to feed like a fighting-cock when she was here. She'd have had the cook out of the house in a quarter of an hour if he'd sent in muck like this.'

He gave me a smile, and I noticed that his smile was very sweet. It gave him a peculiarly gentle look.

'It was rather a wrench parting with her, you know.'

It was quite evident now that he wished to talk and I had no hesitation in giving him a lead.

'Did you have a row?'

'No. You could hardly call it a row. She lived with me five years and we never had a tiff even. She was the best-tempered little thing that ever was. Nothing seemed to put her out. She was always as merry as a cricket. You couldn't look at her without her lips breaking into a smile. She was always happy. And there was no reason why she shouldn't be. I was very good to her.'

'I'm sure you were,' I answered.

'She was mistress here. I gave her everything she wanted. Perhaps if I'd been more of a brute she wouldn't have gone away.'

'Don't make me say anything so obvious as that women are incalculable.'

He gave me a deprecating glance and there was a trace of shyness in the smile that just flickered in his eyes.

'Would it bore you awfully if I told you about it?'

'Of course not.'

'Well, I saw her one day in the street and she rather took my fancy. I showed you her photograph, but the photograph doesn't begin to do her justice. It sounds silly to say about a Burmese girl, but she was like a rose-bud, not an English rose, you know, she was as little like that as the glass flowers on that box I showed you are like real flowers, but a rose grown in an Eastern garden that had something strange and exotic about it. I don't know how to make myself plain.'

'I think I understand what you mean all the same,' I smiled.

'I saw her two or three times and found out where she lived. I sent my boy to make inquiries about her, and he told me that her parents were quite willing that I should have her if we could come to an arrangement. I wasn't inclined to haggle and everything was settled in no time. Her family gave a party to celebrate the occasion and she came to live here. Of course I treated her in every way as my wife and put her in charge of the house. I told the boys that they'd got to take their orders from her and if she complained of any of them out they went. You know, some fellows keep their girls in the servants' quarters and when they go away on tour the girls have a rotten time. Well, I think that's a filthy thing to do. If you are going to have a girl to live with you the least you can do is to see that she has a good time.

'She was a great success and I was pleased as Punch. She kept the house spotless. She saved me money. She wouldn't let the boys rob me. I taught her to play bridge and, believe me, she learned to play a damned good game.'

'Did she like it?'

'Loved it. When people came here she couldn't have received them better if she'd been a duchess. You know, these Burmese have beautiful manners. Sometimes it would make me laugh to see the assurance with which she would receive my guests, government officials, you know, and soldiers who were passing through. If some young subaltern was rather shy she'd put him at his ease at once. She was never pushing or obtrusive, but just there when she was wanted and doing her best to see that everything went well and everyone had a good time. And I'll tell you what, she could mix the best cocktail you'd get anywhere between Rangoon and Bhamo. People used to say I was lucky.'

'I'm bound to say I think you were,' I said.

The curry was served and I piled my plate with rice and helped myself to chicken and then chose from a dozen little dishes the condiments I fancied. It was a good curry.

'Then she had her babies, three in three years, but one died when it was six weeks old. I showed you a photograph of the two that are living. Funny-looking little things, aren't they? Are you fond of children?'

'Yes. I have a strange and almost unnatural passion for new-born babies.'

'I don't think I am, you know. I couldn't even feel very much about my own. I've often wondered if it showed that I was rather a rotter.'

'I don't think so. I think the passion many people affect for children is merely a fashionable pose. I have a notion that children are all the better for not being burdened with too much parental love.'

'Then my girl asked me to marry her, legally I mean, in the English way. I treated it as a joke. I didn't know how she'd got such an idea in her head. I thought it was only a whim and I gave her a gold bracelet to keep her quiet. But it wasn't a whim. She was quite serious about it. I told her there was nothing doing. But you know what women are, when they once set their mind on getting something they never give you a moment's peace. She wheedled and sulked, she cried, she appealed to my compassion, she tried to extract a promise out of me when I was rather tight, she was on the watch for me when I was feeling amorous, she nearly tripped me when she was ill. She watched me more carefully, I should think, than a stockbroker ever watched the market, and I knew that, however natural she seemed, however occupied with something else, she was always warily alert for the unguarded moment when she could pounce on me and gain her point.'

Masterson gave me once more his slow, ingenuous smile.

'I suppose women are pretty much the same all the world over,' he said.

'I expect so,' I answered.

'A thing I've never been able to understand is why a woman thinks it worth while to make you do something you don't want to. She'd rather you did a thing against the grain than not do it at all. I don't see what satisfaction it can be to them.'

'The satisfaction of triumph. A man convinced against his will may be of the same opinion still, but a woman doesn't mind that. She has conquered. She has proved her power.'

Masterson shrugged his shoulders. He drank a cup of tea.

'You see, she said that sooner or later I was bound to marry an English girl and turn her out. I said I wasn't thinking of marrying. She said she knew all about that. And even if I didn't I should retire some day and go back to England. And where would she be then? It went on for a year. I held out. Then she said that if I wouldn't marry her she'd go and take the kids with her. I told her not to be a silly little fool. She said that if she left me now she could marry a Burman, but in a few years nobody would want her. She began to pack her things. I thought it was only a bluff and I called it: I said: "Well, go if you want to, but if you do you won't come back." I didn't think she'd give up a house like this, and the presents I made her, and all the pickings, to go back to her own family. They were as poor as church mice.

Well, she went on packing her things. She was just as nice as ever to me, she was gay and smiling; when some fellows came to spend the night here she was just as cordial as usual, and she played bridge with us till two in the morning. I couldn't believe she meant to go and yet I was rather scared. I was very fond of her. She was a damned good sort.'

'But if you were fond of her why on earth didn't you marry her? It had been a great success.'

'I'll tell you. If I married her I'd have to stay in Burma for the rest of my life. Sooner or later I shall retire and then I want to go back to my old home and live there. I don't want to be buried out here. I want to be buried in an English churchyard. I'm happy enough here, but I don't want to live here always. I couldn't. I want England. Sometimes I get sick of this hot sunshine and these garish colours. I want grey skies and a soft rain falling and the smell of the country. I shall be a funny fat elderly man when I go back, too old to hunt even if I could afford it, but I can fish. I don't want to shoot tigers, I want to shoot rabbits. And I can play golf on a proper course. I know I shall be out of it, we fellows who've spent our lives out here always are, but I can potter about the local club and talk to retired Anglo-Indians. I want to feel under my feet the grey pavement of an English country town, I want to be able to go and have a row with the butcher because the steak he sent me in yesterday was tough, and I want to browse about second-hand bookshops. I want to be said how d'you do to in the street by people who knew me when I was a boy. And I want to have a walled garden at the back of my house and grow roses. I dare say it all sounds very humdrum and provincial and dull to you, but that's the sort of life my people have always lived and that's the sort of life I want to live myself. It's a dream if you like, but it's all I have, it means everything in the world to me, and I can't give it up.'

He paused for a moment and looked into my eyes.

'Do you think me an awful fool?'

'No.'

'Then one morning she came to me and said that she was off. She had her things put on a cart and even then I didn't think she meant it. Then she put the two children in a rickshaw and came to say good-bye to me. She began to cry. By George, that pretty well broke me up. I asked her if she really meant to go and she said yes, unless I married her. I shook my head. I very nearly yielded. I'm afraid I was crying too. Then she gave a great sob and ran out of the house. I had to drink about half a tumbler of whisky to steady my nerves.'

'How long ago did this happen?'

'Four months. At first I thought she'd come back and then because I thought she was ashamed to make the first step I sent my boy to tell her that if she wanted to come I'd take her. But she refused. The house seemed awfully empty without her. At first I thought I'd get used to it, but somehow it doesn't seem to get any less empty. I didn't know how much she meant to me. She'd twined herself round my heart.'

'I suppose she'll come back if you agree to marry her.'

'Oh, yes, she told the boy that. Sometimes I ask myself if it's worth while to sacrifice my happiness for a dream. It is only a dream, isn't it? It's funny, one of the things that holds me back is the thought of a muddy lane I know, with great clay banks on both sides of it, and above, beech trees bending over. It's got a sort of cold, earthy smell that I can never quite get out of my nostrils. I don't blame her, you know. I rather admire her. I had no idea she had so much character. Sometimes I'm awfully inclined to give way.' He hesitated for a little while. 'I think, perhaps, if I thought she loved me I would. But of course, she doesn't; they never do, these girls who go and live with white men. I think she liked me, but that's all. What would you do in my place?'

'Oh, my dear fellow, how can I tell? Would you ever forget that dream?'

'Never.'

At that moment the boy came in to say that my Madrassi servant with the Ford car had just come up. Masterson looked at his watch.

'You'll want to be getting off, won't you? And I must get back to my office. I'm afraid I've rather bored you with my domestic affairs.'

'Not at all,' I said.

We shook hands, I put on my topee, and he waved to me as the car drove off.

The Back of Beyond

George Moon was sitting in his office. His work was finished, and he lingered there because he hadn't the heart to go down to the club. It was getting on towards tiffin time, and there would be a good many fellows hanging about the bar. Two or three of them would offer him a drink. He could not face their heartiness. Some he had known for thirty years. They had bored him, and on the whole he disliked them, but now that he was seeing them for the last time it gave him a pang. To-night they were giving him a farewell dinner. Everyone would be there and they were presenting him with a silver tea-service that he did not in the least want. They would make speeches in which they would refer eulogistically to his work in the colony, express their regret at his departure and wish him long life to enjoy his well-earned leisure. He would reply suitably. He had prepared a speech in which he surveyed the changes that had taken place in the F.M.S., since first, a raw cadet, he had landed at Singapore. He would thank them for their loyal co-operation with him during the term which it had been his privilege to serve as Resident at Timbang Belud, and draw a glowing picture of the future that awaited the country as a whole and Timbang Belud in particular. He would remind them that he had known it as a poverty-stricken village with a few Chinese shops and left it now a prosperous town with paved streets down which ran trams, with stone houses, a rich Chinese settlement and a club-house second in splendour only to that of Singapore. They would sing 'For he's a jolly good fellow' and 'Auld Lang Syne.' Then they would dance and a good many of the younger men would get drunk. The Malays had already given him a farewell party and the Chinese an interminable feast. Tomorrow a vast concourse would see him off at the station and that would be the end of him. He wondered what they would say of him. The Malays and the Chinese would say that he had been stern, but acknowledge that he had been just. The planters had not liked him. They thought him hard because he would not let them ride roughshod over their labour. His subordinates had feared him. He drove them. He had no patience with slackness or inefficiency. He had never spared himself and saw no reason why he should spare others. They thought him inhuman. It was true that there was nothing come-hither in him. He could not throw off his official position when he went to the club and laugh at bawdy stories, chaff and be chaffed. He was conscious that his arrival cast a gloom, and to play bridge with him (he liked to play every day from six to eight) was looked upon as a privilege rather than an entertainment. When at some other table a young man's four as the evening wore on grew hilarious, he caught glances thrown in his direction and sometimes an older member would stroll up to the noisy ones and in an undertone advise them to be quiet. George Moon sighed a little. From an official standpoint his career had been a success, he had been the youngest Resident ever appointed in the F.M.S., and for exceptional services a C.M.G. had been conferred upon him; but from the human it had perhaps been otherwise. He had earned respect, respect for his ability, industry and trustworthiness, but he was too clear-sighted to think for a moment that he had inspired affection. No one would regret him. In a few months he would be forgotten.

He smiled grimly. He was not sentimental. He had

enjoyed his authority, and it gave him an austere satisfaction to know that he had kept everyone up to the
mark. It did not displease him to think that he had been
feared rather than loved. He saw his life as a problem in
higher mathematics, the working-out of which had
required intense application of all his powers, but of
which the result had not the least practical consequence. Its interest lay in its intricacy and its beauty
in its solution. But like pure beauty it led nowhither.
His future was blank. He was fifty-five, and full of
energy, and to himself his mind seemed as alert as ever,
his experience of men and affairs was wide: all that
remained to him was to settle down in a country town
in England or in a cheap part of the Riviera and play
bridge with elderly ladies and golf with retired colonels.
He had met, when on leave, old chiefs of his, and had
observed with what difficulty they adapted themselves
to the change in their circumstances. They had looked
forward to the freedom that would be theirs when they
retired and had pictured the charming uses to which
they would put their leisure. Mirage. It was not very
pleasant to be obscure after having dwelt in a spacious
residency, to make do with a couple of maids when you
had been accustomed to the service of half a dozen
Chinese boys; and above all, it was not pleasant to
realise that you did not matter a row of beans to anyone
when you had grown used to the delicate flattery of
knowing that a word of praise could delight and a frown
humiliate all sorts and conditions of men.

George Moon stretched out his hand and helped himself to a cigarette from the box on his desk. As he did so
he noticed all the little lines on the back of his hand and
the thinness of his shrivelled fingers. He frowned with
distaste. It was the hand of an old man. There was in his
office a Chinese mirror-picture that he had bought long
ago and that he was leaving behind. He got up and

looked at himself in it. He saw a thin yellow face, wrinkled and tight-lipped, thin grey hair and grey tired eyes. He was tallish, very spare, with narrow shoulders, and he held himself erect. He had always played polo and even now could beat most of the younger men at tennis. When you talked to him he kept his eyes fixed on your face, listening attentively, but his expression did not change, and you had no notion what effect your words had on him. Perhaps he did not realise how disconcerting this was. He seldom smiled.

An orderly came in with a name written on a chit. George Moon looked at it and told him to show the visitor in. He sat down once more in his chair and looked with his cold eyes at the door through which in a moment the visitor would come. It was Tom Saffary, and he wondered what he wanted. Presumably something to do with the festivity that night. It had amused him to hear that Tom Saffary was the head of the committee that had organised it, for their relations during the last year had been far from cordial. Saffary was a planter and one of his Tamil overseers had lodged a complaint against him for assault. The Tamil had been grossly insolent to him and Saffary had given him a thrashing. George Moon realised that the provocation was great, but he had always set his face against the planters taking the law in their own hands, and when the case was tried he sentenced Saffary to a fine. But when the court rose, to show that there was no ill-feeling he asked Saffary to luncheon: Saffary, resentful of what he thought an unmerited affront, curtly refused and since then had declined to have any social relations with the Resident. He answered when George Moon, casually, but resolved not to be affronted, spoke to him; but would neither play bridge nor tennis with him. He was manager of the largest rubber estate in the district, and George Moon asked himself sardonically whether he had arranged the dinner and collected subscriptions for the presentation because he thought his dignity required it or whether, now that his Resident was leaving, it appealed to his sentimentality to make a noble gesture. It tickled George Moon's frigid sense of humour to think that it would fall to Tom Saffary to make the principal speech of the evening, in which he would enlarge upon the departing Resident's admirable qualities, and voice the community's regret at their irreparable loss.

Tom Saffary was ushered in. The Resident rose from his chair, shook hands with him and thinly smiled.

'How do you do? Sit down. Won't you have a cigarette?'

'How do you do?'

Saffary took the chair to which the Resident motioned him, and the Resident waited for him to state his business. He had a notion that his visitor was embarrassed. He was a big, burly, stout fellow, with a red face and a double chin, curly black hair and blue eyes. He was a fine figure of a man, strong as a horse, but it was plain that he did himself too well. He drank a good deal and ate too heartily. But he was a good business man and a hard worker. He ran his estate efficiently. He was popular in the community. He was generally known as a good chap. He was free with his money and ready to lend a helping hand to anyone in distress. It occurred to the Resident that Saffary had come in order before the dinner to compose the difference between them. The emotion that might have occasioned such a desire excited in the Resident's sensibility a very faint, good-humoured contempt. He had no enemies because individuals did not mean enough to him for him to hate any of them, but if he had, he thought, he would have hated them to the end.

'I daresay you're a bit surprised to see me here this

morning, and I expect, as it's your last day and all that, you're pretty busy.'

George Moon did not answer, and the other went on.

'I've come on rather an awkward business. The fact is that my wife and I won't be able to come to the dinner tonight, and after that unpleasantness we had together last year I thought it only right to come and tell you that it has nothing to do with that. I think you treated me very harshly; it's not the money I minded, it was the indignity, but bygones are bygones. Now that you're leaving I don't want you to think that I bear any more ill-feeling towards you.'

'I realised that when I heard that you were chiefly responsible for the send-off you're giving me,' answered the Resident civilly. 'I'm sorry that you won't be able to come tonight.'

'I'm sorry, too. It's on account of Knobby Clarke's death.' Saffary hesitated for a moment. 'My wife and I were very much upset by it.'

'It was very sad. He was a great friend of yours, wasn't he?'

'He was the greatest friend I had in the colony.'

Tears shone in Tom Saffary's eyes. Fat men are very emotional, thought George Moon.

'I quite understand that in that case you should have no heart for what looks like being a rather uproarious party,' he said kindly. 'Have you heard anything of the circumstances?'

'No, nothing but what appeared in the paper.'

'He seemed all right when he left here.'

'As far as I know he'd never had a day's illness in his life.'

'Heart, I suppose. How old was he?'

'Same age as me. Thirty-eight.'

'That's young to die.'

Knobby Clarke was a planter and the estate he

managed was next door to Saffary's. George Moon had liked him. He was a rather ugly man, sandy, with high cheek-bones and hollow temples, large pale eyes in deep sockets and a big mouth. But he had an attractive smile and an easy manner. He was amusing and could tell a good story. He had a careless good humour that people found pleasing. He played games well. He was no fool. George Moon would have said he was somewhat colourless. In the course of his career he had known a good many men like him. They came and went. A fortnight before, he had left for England on leave and the Resident knew that the Saffarys had given a large dinner-party on his last night. He was married and his wife of course went with him.

'I'm sorry for her,' said George Moon. 'It must have been a terrible blow. He was buried at sea, wasn't he?'

'Yes. That's what it said in the paper.'

The news had reached Timbang the night before. The Singapore papers arrived at six, just as people were getting to the club, and a good many men waited to play bridge or billiards till they had had a glance at them. Suddenly one fellow had called out:

'I say, do you see this? Knobby's dead.'

'Knobby who? Not Knobby Clarke?'

There was a three-line paragraph in a column of general intelligence.

'Messrs Star, Mosley & Co. have received a cable informing them that Mr. Harold Clarke of Timbang Batu died suddenly on his way home and was buried at sea.'

A man came up and took the paper from the speaker's hand, and incredulously read the note for himself. Another peered over his shoulder. Such as happened to be reading the paper turned to the page in question and read the three indifferent lines.

'By George,' cried one.

'I say, what tough luck,' said another.

'He was as fit as a fiddle when he left here.'

A shiver of dismay pierced those hearty, jovial, careless men, and each one for a moment remembered that he too was mortal. Other members came in and as they entered, braced by the thought of the six o'clock drink, and eager to meet their friends, they were met by the grim tidings.

'I say, have you heard? Poor Knobby Clarke's dead.'

'No? I say, how awful!'

'Rotten luck, isn't it?'

'Rotten.'

'Damned good sort.'

'One of the best.'

'It gave me quite a turn when I saw it in the paper just by chance.'

'I don't wonder.'

One man with the paper in his hand went into the billiard-room to break the news. They were playing off the handicap for the Prince of Wales's Cup. That august personage had presented it to the club on the occasion of his visit to Timbang Belud. Tom Saffary was playing against a man called Douglas, and the Resident, who had been beaten in the previous round, was seated with about a dozen others watching the game. The marker was monotonously calling out the score. The newcomer waited for Saffary to finish his break and then called out to him.

'I say, Tom, Knobby's dead.'

'Knobby? It's not true.'

The other handed him the paper. Three or four gathered round to read with him.

'Good God!'

There was a moment's awed silence. The paper was passed from hand to hand. It was odd that none seemed willing to believe till he saw it for himself in black and white.

'Oh, I am sorry.'

'I say, it's awful for his wife,' said Tom Saffary. 'She was going to have a baby. My poor missus'll be upset.'

'Why, it's only a fortnight since he left here.'

'He was all right then.'

'In the pink.'

Saffary, his fat red face sagging a little, went over to a table and, seizing his glass, drank deeply.

'Look here, Tom,' said his opponent, 'would you like to call the game off?'

'Can't very well do that.' Saffary's eye sought the score board and he saw that he was ahead. 'No, let's finish. Then I'll go home and break it to Violet.'

Douglas had his shot and made fourteen. Tom Saffary missed an easy in-off, but left nothing. Douglas played again, but did not score and again Saffary missed a shot that ordinarily he could have been sure of. He frowned a little. He knew his friends had betted on him pretty heavily and he did not like the idea of failing them. Douglas made twenty-two. Saffary emptied his glass and by an effort of will that was quite patent to the sympathetic onlookers settled down to concentrate on the game. He made a break of eighteen and when he just failed to do a long Jenny they gave him a round of applause. He was sure of himself now and began to score quickly. Douglas was playing well too, and the match grew exciting to watch. The few minutes during which Saffary's attention wandered had allowed his opponent to catch up with him, and now it was anybody's game.

'Spot two hundred and thirty-five,' called the Malay, in his queer clipped English. 'Plain two hundred and twenty-eight. Spot to play.'

Douglas made eight, and then Saffary, who was plain, drew up to two hundred and forty. He left his opponent a double balk. Douglas hit neither ball, and so gave Saffary another point.

'Spot two hundred and forty-three,' called the marker. 'Plain two hundred and forty-one. Plain to play.'

Saffary played three beautiful shots off the red and finished the game.

'A popular victory,' the bystanders cried.

'Congratulations, old man,' said Douglas.

'Boy,' called Saffary, 'ask these gentlemen what they'll have. Poor old Knobby.'

He sighed heavily. The drinks were brought and Saffary signed the chit. Then he said he'd be getting along. Two others had already begun to play.

'Sporting of him to go on like that,' said someone when the door was closed on Saffary.

'Yes, it shows grit.'

'For a while I thought his game had gone all to pieces.'

'He pulled himself together in grand style. He knew there were a lot of bets on him. He didn't want to let his backers down.'

'Of course it's a shock, a thing like that.'

'They were great pals. I wonder what he died of.'

'Good shot, sir.'

George Moon, remembering this scene, thought it strange that Tom Saffary, who on hearing of his friend's death had shown such self-control, should now apparently take it so hard. It might be that just as in the war a man when hit often did not know it till some time afterwards, Saffary had not realised how great a blow to him Harold Clarke's death was till he had had time to think it over. It seemed to him, however, more probable that Saffary, left to himself, would have carried on as usual, seeking sympathy for his loss in the company of his fellows, but that his wife's conventional sense of propriety had insisted that it would be bad form to go to a party when the grief they were suffering from made it only decent for them to eschew for a little festive gatherings. Violet Saffary was a nice little woman, three or four years younger than her husband; not very pretty, but pleasant to look at and always becomingly dressed; amiable, ladylike and unassuming. In the days when he had been on friendly terms with the Saffarys the Resident had from time to time dined with them. He had found her agreeable, but not very amusing. They had never talked but of commonplace things. Of late he had seen little of her. When they chanced to meet she always gave him a friendly smile, and on occasion he said one or two civil words to her. But it was only by an effort of memory that he distinguished her from half a dozen of the other ladies in the community whom his official position brought him in contact with.

Saffary had presumably said what he had come to say and the Resident wondered why he did not get up and go. He sat heaped up in his chair oddly, so that it gave you the feeling that his skeleton had ceased to support him and his considerable mass of flesh was falling in on him. He looked dully at the desk that separated him from the Resident. He sighed deeply.

'You must try not to take it too hard, Saffary,' said George Moon. 'You know how uncertain life is in the East. One has to resign oneself to losing people one's fond of.'

Saffary's eyes slowly moved from the desk, and he fixed them on George Moon's. They stared unwinking. George Moon liked people to look him in the eyes. Perhaps he felt that when he thus held their vision he held them in his power. Presently two tears formed themselves in Saffary's blue eyes and slowly ran down his cheeks. He had a strangely puzzled look. Something had frightened him. Was it death? No. Something that he thought worse. He looked cowed. His mien was cringing so that he made you think of a dog unjustly beaten.

'It's not that,' he faltered. 'I could have borne that.'

George Moon did not answer. He held that big, powerful man with his cold level gaze and waited. He was pleasantly conscious of his absolute indifference. Saffary gave a harassed glance at the papers on the desk.

'I'm afraid I'm taking up too much of your time.'

'No, I have nothing to do at the moment.'

Saffary looked out of the window. A little shudder passed between his shoulders. He seemed to hesitate.

'I wonder if I might ask your advice,' he said at last.

'Of course,' said the Resident, with the shadow of a smile, 'that's one of the things I'm here for.'

'It's a purely private matter.'

'You may be quite sure that I shan't betray any confidence you place in me.'

'No, I know you wouldn't do that, but it's rather an awkward thing to speak about, and I shouldn't feel very comfortable meeting you afterwards. But you're going away to-morrow, and that makes it easier, if you understand what I mean.'

'Quite.'

Saffary began to speak, in a low voice, sulkily, as though he were ashamed, and he spoke with the awkwardness of a man unused to words. He went back and said the same thing over again. He got mixed up. He started a long, elaborate sentence and then broke off abruptly because he did not know how to finish it. George Moon listened in silence, his face a mask, smoking, and he only took his eyes off Saffary's face to reach for another cigarette from the box in front of him and light it from the stub of that which he was just finishing. And while he listened he saw, as it were a background, the monotonous round of the planter's life. It was like an accompaniment of muted strings that threw into sharper relief the calculated dissonances of an unexpected melody.

With rubber at so low a price every economy had to be exercised and Tom Saffary, notwithstanding the size of the estate, had to do work which in better times he had had an assistant for. He rose before dawn and went down to the lines where the coolies were assembled. When there was just enough light to see he read out the names, ticking them off according to the answers, and assigned the various squads to their work. Some tapped, some weeded, and others tended the ditches. Saffary went back to his solid breakfast, lit his pipe and sallied forth again to inspect the coolies' quarters. Children were playing and babies sprawling here and there. On the sidewalks Tamil women cooked their rice. Their black skins shone with oil. They were draped about in dull red cotton and wore gold ornaments in their hair. There were handsome creatures among them, upright of carriage, with delicate features and small, exquisite hands; but Saffary looked upon them only with distaste. He set out on his rounds. On his well-grown estate the trees planted in rows gave one a charming feeling of the prim forest of a German fairy-tale. The ground was thick with dead leaves. He was accompanied by a Tamil overseer, his long black hair done in a chignon, barefooted, in sarong and baju, with a showy ring on his finger. Saffary walked hard, jumping the ditches when he came to them, and soon he dripped with sweat. He examined the trees to see that they were properly tapped, and when he came across a coolie at work looked at the shavings and if they were too thick swore at him and docked him half a day's pay. When a tree was not to be tapped any more he told the overseer to take away the cup and the wire that held it to the trunk. The weeders worked in gangs.

At noon Saffary returned to the bungalow and had a drink of beer which, because there was no ice, was lukewarm. He stripped the khaki shorts, the flannel shirt, the heavy boots and stockings in which he had been walking, and shaved and bathed. He lunched in a sarong and baju. He lay off for half an hour, and then went down to his office and worked till five; he had tea and went to the club. About eight he started back for the bungalow, dined, and half an hour after went to bed.

But last night he went home immediately he had finished his match. Violet had not accompanied him that day. When the Clarkes were there they had met at the club every afternoon, but now they had gone home she came less often. She said there was no one there who much amused her and she had heard everything everyone had to say till she was fed to the teeth. She did not play bridge and it was dull for her to wait about while he played. She told Tom he need not mind leaving her alone. She had plenty of things to do in the house.

As soon as she saw him back so early she guessed that he had come to tell her that he had won his match. He was like a child in his self-satisfaction over one of these small triumphs. He was a kindly, simple creature and she knew that his pleasure at winning was not only on his own account, but because he thought it must give her pleasure too. It was rather sweet of him to hurry home in order to tell her all about it without delay.

'Well, how did your match go?' she said as soon as he came lumbering into the sitting-room.

'I won.'

'Easily?'

'Well, not as easily as I should have. I was a bit ahead, and then I stuck, I couldn't do a thing, and you know what Douglas is, not at all showy, but steady, and he pulled up with me. Then I said to myself, well, if I don't buck up I shall get a licking, I had a bit of luck here and there, and then, to cut a long story short, I beat him by seven.'

'Isn't that splendid? You ought to win the cup now, oughtn't you?'

'Well, I've got three matches more. If I can get into the semi-finals I ought to have a chance.'

Violet smiled. She was anxious to show him that she was as much interested as he expected her to be.

'What made you go to pieces when you did?'

His face sagged.

'That's why I came back at once. I'd have scratched only I thought it wasn't fair on the fellows who'd backed me. I don't know how to tell you, Violet.'

She gave him a questioning look.

'Why, what's the matter? Not bad news?'

'Rotten. Knobby's dead.'

For a full minute she stared at him, and her face, her neat friendly little face, grew haggard with horror. At first it seemed as though she could not understand.

'What *do* you mean?' she cried.

'It was in the paper. He died on board. They buried him at sea.'

Suddenly she gave a piercing cry and fell headlong to the floor. She had fainted dead away.

'Violet,' he cried, and threw himself down on his knees and took her head in his arms. 'Boy, boy.'

A boy, startled by the terror in his master's voice, rushed in and Saffary shouted to him to bring brandy. He forced a little between Violet's lips. She opened her eyes, and as she remembered they grew dark with anguish. Her face was screwed up like a little child's when it is just going to burst into tears. He lifted her up in his arms and laid her on the sofa. She turned her head away.

'Oh, Tom, it isn't true. It can't be true.'

'I'm afraid it is.'

'No, no, no.'

She burst into tears. She wept convulsively. It was

dreadful to hear her. Saffary did not know what to do. He knelt beside her and tried to soothe her. He sought to take her in his arms, but with a sudden gesture she repelled him.

'Don't touch me,' she cried, and she said it so sharply that he was startled.

He rose to his feet.

'Try not to take it too hard, sweetie,' he said. 'I know it's been an awful shock. He was one of the best.'

She buried her face in the cushions and wept despairingly. It tortured him to see her body shaken by those uncontrollable sobs. She was beside herself. He put his hand gently on her shoulder.

'Darling, don't give way like that. It's so bad for you.'

She shook herself free from his hand.

'For God's sake leave me alone,' she cried. 'Oh, Hal, Hal.' He had never heard her call the dead man that before. Of course his name was Harold, but everyone called him Knobby. 'What shall I do?' she wailed. 'I can't bear it. I can't bear it.'

Saffary began to grow a trifle impatient. So much grief did seem to him exaggerated. Violet was not normally so emotional. He supposed it was the damned climate. It made women nervous and high-strung. Violet hadn't been home for four years. She was not hiding her face now. She lay, almost falling off the sofa, her mouth open in the extremity of her pain, and the tears streamed from her staring eyes. She was distraught.

'Have a little more brandy,' he said. 'Try and pull yourself together, darling. You can't do Knobby any good by getting in such a state.'

With a sudden gesture she sprang to her feet and pushed him aside. She gave him a look of hatred.

'Go away, Tom. I don't want your sympathy. I want to be left alone.'

She walked swiftly over to an arm-chair and threw

herself down in it. She flung back her head and her poor white face was wrenched into a grimace of agony.

'Oh, it's not fair,' she moaned. 'What's to become of me now? Oh, God, I wish I were dead.'

'Violet.'

His voice quavered with pain. He was very nearly crying too. She stamped her foot impatiently.

'Go away, I tell you. Go away.'

He started. He stared at her and suddenly gasped. A shudder passed through his great bulk. He took a step towards her and stopped, but his eyes never left her white, tortured face; he stared as though he saw in it something that appalled him. Then he dropped his head and without a word walked out of the room. He went into a little sitting-room they had at the back, but seldom used, and sank heavily into a chair. He thought. Presently the gong sounded for dinner. He had not had his bath. He gave his hands a glance. He could not be bothered to wash them. He walked slowly into the dining-room. He told the boy to go and tell Violet that dinner was ready. The boy came back and said she did not want any.

'All right. Let me have mine then,' said Saffary.

He sent Violet in a plate of soup and a piece of toast, and when the fish was served put some on a plate for her and gave it to the boy. But the boy came back with it at once.

'Mem, she say no wantchee,' he said.

Saffary ate his dinner alone. He ate from habit, solidly, through the familiar courses. He drank a bottle of beer. When he had finished the boy brought him a cup of coffee and he lit a cheroot. Saffary sat still till he had finished it. He thought. At last he got up and went back into the large verandah which was where they always sat. Violet was still huddled in the chair in which he had left her. Her eyes were closed, but she opened them when she heard him come. He took a light chair and sat down in front of her.

'What *was* Knobby to you, Violet?' he said.

She gave a slight start. She turned away her eyes, but did not speak.

'I can't quite make out why you should have been so frightfully upset by the news of his death.'

'It was an awful shock.'

'Of course. But it seems very strange that anyone should go simply all to pieces over the death of a friend.'

'I don't understand what you mean,' she said.

She could hardly speak the words and he saw that her lips were trembling.

'I've never heard you call him Hal. Even his wife called him Knobby.'

She did not say anything. Her eyes, heavy with grief, were fixed on vacancy.

'Look at me, Violet.'

She turned her head slightly and listlessly gazed at him.

'Was he your lover?'

She closed her eyes and tears flowed from them. Her mouth was strangely twisted.

'Haven't you got anything to say at all?'

She shook her head.

'You must answer me, Violet.'

'I'm not fit to talk to you now,' she moaned. 'How can you be so heartless?'

'I'm afraid I don't feel very sympathetic at the moment. We must get this straight now. Would you like a drink of water?'

'I don't want anything.'

'Then answer my question.'

'You have no right to ask it. It's insulting.'

'Do you ask me to believe that a woman like you who hears of the death of someone she knew is going to faint dead away and then, when she comes to, is going to cry like that? Why, one wouldn't be so upset over the death of one's only child. When we heard of your mother's death you cried of course, anyone would, and I know you were utterly miserable, but you came to me for comfort and you said you didn't know what you'd have done without me.'

'This was so frightfully sudden.'

'Your mother's death was sudden, too.'

'Naturally I was very fond of Knobby.'

'How fond? So fond that when you heard he was dead you didn't know and you didn't care what you said? Why did you say it wasn't fair? Why did you say, "What's going to become of me now?"'

She sighed deeply. She turned her head this way and that like a sheep trying to avoid the hands of the butcher.

'You mustn't take me for an utter fool, Violet. I tell you it's impossible that you should be so shattered by the blow if there hadn't been something between you.'

'Well, if you think that why do you torture me with questions?'

'My dear, it's no good shilly-shallying. We can't go on like this. What d'you think I'm feeling?'

She looked at him when he said this. She hadn't thought of him at all. She had been too much absorbed in her own misery to be concerned with his.

'I'm so tired,' she sighed.

He leaned forward and roughly seized her wrist.

'Speak,' he cried.

'You're hurting me.'

'And what about me? D'you think you're not hurting me? How can you have the heart to let me suffer like this?'

He let go of her arm and sprang to his feet. He walked to the end of the room and back again. It looked as

278

though the movement had suddenly roused him to fury. He caught her by the shoulders and dragged her to her feet. He shook her.

'If you don't tell me the truth I'll kill you,' he cried.

'I wish you would,' she said.

'He was your lover?'

'Yes.'

'You swine.'

With one hand still on her shoulder so that she could not move he swung back his other arm and with a flat palm struck her repeatedly, with all his strength, on the side of her face. She quivered under the blows, but did not flinch or cry out. He struck her again and again. All at once he felt her strangely inert, he let go of her and she sank unconscious to the floor. Fear seized him. He bent down and touched her, calling her name. She did not move. He lifted her up and put her back into the chair from which a little while before he had pulled her. The brandy that had been brought when first she fainted was still in the room and he fetched it and tried to force it down her throat. She choked and it spilt over her chin and neck. One side of her pale face was livid from the blows of his heavy hand. She sighed a little and opened her eyes. He held the glass again to her lips, supporting her head, and she sipped a little of the neat spirit. He looked at her with penitent, anxious eyes.

'I'm sorry, Violet. I didn't mean to do that. I'm dreadfully ashamed of myself. I never thought I could sink so low as to hit a woman.'

Though she was feeling very weak and her face was hurting, the flicker of a smile crossed her lips. Poor Tom. He did say things like that. He felt like that. And how scandalised he would be if you asked him why a man shouldn't hit a woman. But Saffary, seeing the wan smile, put it down to her indomitable courage. By God, she's a plucky little woman, he thought. Game isn't the word.

'Give me a cigarette,' she said.

He took one out of his case and put it in her mouth. He made two or three ineffectual attempts to strike his lighter. It would not work.

'Hadn't you better get a match?' she said.

For the moment she had forgotten her heart-rending grief and was faintly amused at the situation. He took a box from the table and held the lighted match to her cigarette. She inhaled the first puff with a sense of infinite relief.

'I can't tell you how ashamed I am, Violet,' he said. 'I'm disgusted with myself. I don't know what came over me.'

'Oh, that's all right. It was very natural. Why don't you have a drink? It'll do you good.'

Without a word, his shoulders all hunched up as though the burden that oppressed him were material, he helped himself to a brandy and soda. Then, still silent, he sat down. She watched the blue smoke curl into the air.

'What are you going to do?' she said at last.

He gave a weary gesture of despair.

'We'll talk about that to-morrow. You're not in a fit state tonight. As soon as you've finished your cigarette you'd better go to bed.'

'You know so much, you'd better know everything.'

'Not now, Violet.'

'Yes, now.'

She began to speak. He heard her words, but could hardly make sense of them. He felt like a man who has built himself a house with loving care and thought to live in it all his life, and then, he does not understand why, sees the housebreakers come and with their picks and heavy hammers destroy it room by room, till what was a fair dwelling-place is only a heap of rubble. What made it so awful was that it was Knobby Clarke who had done this thing. They had come out to the F.M.S. on the same ship and had worked at first on the same estate. They call the young planter a creeper and you can tell him in the streets of Singapore by his double felt hat and his khaki coat turned up at the wrists. Callow youths who saunter about staring and are inveigled by wily Chinese into buying worthless truck from Birmingham which they send home as Eastern curios, sit in the lounges of cheap hotels drinking innumerable stengahs, and after an evening at the pictures get into rickshaws and finish the night in the Chinese quarter. Tom and Knobby were inseparable. Tom, a big, powerful fellow, simple, very honest, hardworking; and Knobby, ungainly, but curiously attractive, with his deep-set eyes, hollow cheeks and large humorous mouth. It was Knobby who made the jokes and Tom who laughed at them. Tom married first. He met Violet when he went on leave. The daughter of a doctor killed in the war, she was governess in the house of some people who lived in the same place as his father. He fell in love with her because she was alone in the world, and his tender heart was touched by the thought of the drab life that lay before her. But Knobby married because Tom had and he felt lost without him, a girl who had come East to spend the winter with relations. Enid Clarke had been very pretty then in her blonde way, and full face. She was pretty still, though her skin, once so clear and fresh, was already faded; but she had a very weak, small, insignificant chin and in profile reminded you of a sheep. She had pretty flaxen hair, straight, because in the heat it would not keep its wave, and china-blue eyes. Though but twenty-six, she had already a tired look. A year after marriage she had a baby, but it died when only two years old. It was after this that Tom Saffary managed to get Knobby the post of manager of the estate next his own. The two men pleasantly resumed their old familiarity, and their wives, who till then had not known one another very well, soon made friends. They copied one another's frocks and lent one another servants and crockery when they gave a party. The four of them met every day. They went everywhere together. Tom Saffary thought it grand.

The strange thing was that Violet and Knobby Clarke lived on these terms of close intimacy for three years before they fell in love with one another. Neither saw love approaching. Neither suspected that in the pleasure each took in the other's company there was anything more than the casual friendship of two persons thrown together by the circumstances of life. To be together gave them no particular happiness, but merely a quiet sense of comfort. If by chance a day passed without their meeting they felt unaccountably bored. That seemed very natural. They played games together. They danced together. They chaffed one another. The revelation came to them by what looked like pure accident. They had all been to a dance at the club and were driving home in Saffary's car. The Clarke's estate was on the way and he was dropping them at their bungalow. Violet and Knobby sat in the back. He had had a good deal to drink, but was not drunk; their hands touched by chance, and he took hers and held it. They did not speak. They were all tired. But suddenly the exhilaration of the champagne left him and he was cold sober. They knew in a flash that they were madly in love with one another and at the same moment they realised that they had never been in love before. When they reached the Clarkes's Tom said:

'You'd better hop in beside me, Violet.'

'I'm too exhausted to move,' she said.

Her legs seemed so weak that she thought she would never be able to stand.

When they met next day neither referred to what had happened, but each knew that something inevitable had passed. They behaved to one another as they had always done, they continued to behave so for weeks, but they felt that everything was different. At last flesh and blood could stand it no longer and they became lovers. But the physical tie seemed to them the least important element in their relation, and indeed their way of living made it impossible for them, except very seldom, to enjoy any intimate connection. It was enough that they saw one another, though in the company of others, every day; a glance, a touch of the hand, assured them of their love, and that was all that mattered. The sexual act was no more than an affirmation of the union of their souls.

They very seldom talked of Tom or Enid. If sometimes they laughed together at their foibles it was not unkindly. It might have seemed odd to them to realise how completely these two people whom they saw so constantly had ceased to matter to them if they had given them enough thought to consider the matter. Their relations with them fell into the routine of life that nobody notices, like shaving oneself, dressing and eating three meals a day. They felt tenderly towards them. They even took pains to please them, as you would with a bed-ridden invalid, because their own happiness was so great that in charity they must do what they could for others less fortunate. They had no scruples. They were too much absorbed in one another to be touched even for a moment by remorse. Beauty now excitingly kindled the pleasant humdrum life they had led so long.

But then an event took place that filled them with consternation. The company for which Tom worked entered into negotiations to buy extensive rubber plantations in British North Borneo and invited Tom to manage them. It was a better job than his present one, with a higher salary, and since he would have assistants under him he would not have to work so hard. Saffary welcomed the offer. Both Clarke and Saffary were due for leave and the two couples had arranged to travel home together. They had already booked their passages. This changed everything. Tom would not be able to get away for at least a year. By the time the Clarkes came back the Saffarys would be settled in Borneo. It did not take Violet and Knobby long to decide that there was only one thing to do. They had been willing enough to go on as they were, notwithstanding the hindrances to the enjoyment of their love, when they were certain of seeing one another continually; they felt that they had endless time before them and the future was coloured with a happiness that seemed to have no limit; but neither could suffer for an instant the thought of separation. They made up their minds to run away together, and then it seemed to them on a sudden that every day that passed before they could be together always and all the time was a day lost. Their love took another guise. It flamed into a devouring passion that left them no emotion to waste on others. They cared little for the pain they must cause Tom and Enid. It was unfortunate, but inevitable. They made their plans deliberately. Knobby on the pretence of business would go to Singapore and Violet, telling Tom that she was going to spend a week with friends on an estate down the line, would join him there. They would go over to Java and thence take ship to Sydney. In Sydney Knobby would look for a job. When Violet told Tom that the Mackenzies had asked her to spend a few days with them, he was pleased.

'That's grand. I think you want a change, darling,' he said. 'I've fancied you've been looking a bit peaked lately.'

He stroked her cheek affectionately. The gesture stabbed her heart.

'You've always been awfully good to me, Tom,' she said, her eyes suddenly filled with tears.

'Well, that's the least I could be. You're the best little woman in the world.'

'Have you been happy with me these eight years?'

'Frightfully.'

'Well, that's something, isn't it? No one can ever take that away from you.'

She had told herself that he was the kind of man who would soon console himself. He liked women for themselves and it would not be long after he had regained his freedom before he found someone that he would wish to marry. And he would be just as happy with his new wife as he had been with her. Perhaps he would marry Enid. Enid was one of those dependent little things that somewhat exasperated her and she did not think her capable of deep feeling. Her vanity would be hurt; her heart would not be broken. But now that the die was cast, everything settled and the day fixed, she had a qualm. Remorse beset her. She wished that it had been possible not to cause those two people such fearful distress. She faltered.

'We've had a very good time here, Tom,' she said. 'I wonder if it's wise to leave it all. We're giving up a certainty for we don't know what.'

'My dear child, it's a chance in a million and much better money.'

'Money isn't everything. There's happiness.'

'I know that, but there's no reason why we shouldn't be just as happy in B.N.B. And besides, there was no alternative. I'm not my own master. The directors want me to go and I must, and that's all there is to it.'

She sighed. There was no alternative for her either. She shrugged her shoulders. It was hateful to cause others pain; sometimes you couldn't help yourself. Tom meant no more to her than the casual man on the voyage out who was civil to you: it was absurd that she should be asked to sacrifice her life for him.

The Clarkes were due to sail for England in a fortnight and this determined the date of their elopement. The days passed. Violet was restless and excited. She looked forward with a joy that was almost painful to the peace that she anticipated when they were once on board the ship and could begin the life which she was sure would give her at last perfect happiness.

She began to pack. The friends she was supposed to be going to stay with entertained a good deal and this gave her an excuse to take quite a lot of luggage. She was starting next day. It was eleven o'clock in the morning and Tom was making his round of the estate. One of the boys came to her room and told her that Mrs. Clarke was there and at the same moment she heard Enid calling her. Quickly closing the lid of her trunk, she went out on to the verandah. To her astonishment Enid came up to her, flung her arms round her neck and kissed her eagerly. She looked at Enid and saw that her cheeks, usually pale, were flushed and that her eyes were shining. Enid burst into tears.

'What on earth's the matter, darling?' she cried.

For one moment she was afraid that Enid knew everything. But Enid was flushed with delight and not with jealousy or anger.

'I've just seen Dr. Harrow,' she said. 'I didn't want to say anything about it. I've had two or three false alarms, but this time he says it's all right.'

A sudden coldness pierced Violet's heart.

'What do you mean? You're not going to . . .'

She looked at Enid and Enid nodded.

'Yes, he says there's no doubt about it at all. He thinks I'm at least three months gone. Oh, my dear, I'm so wildly happy.'

She flung herself again into Violet's arms and clung to her, weeping.

'Oh, darling, don't.'

Violet felt herself grow pale as death and knew that if she didn't keep a tight hold of herself she would faint.

'Does Knobby know?'

'No, I didn't say a word. He was so disappointed before. He was so frightfully cut up when baby died. He's wanted me to have another so badly.'

Violet forced herself to say the things that were expected of her, but Enid was not listening. She wanted to tell the whole story of her hopes and fears, of her symptoms, and then of her interview with the doctor. She went on and on.

'When are you going to tell Knobby?' Violet asked at last. 'Now, when he gets in?'

'Oh, no, he's tired and hungry when he gets back from his round. I shall wait till tonight after dinner.'

Violet repressed a movement of exasperation; Enid was going to make a scene of it and was choosing her moment; but after all, it was only natural. It was lucky, for it would give her the chance to see Knobby first. As soon as she was rid of her she rang him up. She knew that he always looked in at his office on his way home, and she left a message asking him to call her. She was only afraid that he would not do so till Tom was back, but she had to take her chance of that. The bell rang and Tom had not yet come in.

'Hal?'

'Yes.'

'Will you be at the hut at three?'

'Yes. Has anything happened?'

'I'll tell you when I see you. Don't worry.'

She rang off. The hut was a little shelter on Knobby's estate which she could get to without difficulty and where they occasionally met. The coolies passed it while they worked and it had no privacy; but it was a convenient place for them without exciting comment to exchange a few minutes' conversation. At three Enid would be resting and Tom at work in his office.

When Violet walked up Knobby was already there. He gave a gasp.

'Violet, how white you are.'

She gave him her hand. They did not know what eyes might be watching them and their behaviour here was always such as anyone could observe.

'Enid came to see me this morning. She's going to tell you tonight. I thought you ought to be warned. She's going to have a baby.'

'Violet!'

He looked at her aghast. She began to cry. They had never talked of the relations they had, he with his wife and she with her husband. They ignored the subject because it was to each exquisitely painful. Violet knew what her own life was; she satisfied her husband's appetite; but, with a woman's strange nonchalance, because to do so gave her no pleasure, attached no importance to it; but somehow she had persuaded herself that with Hal it was different. He felt now instinctively how bitterly what she had learned wounded her. He tried to excuse himself.

'Darling, I couldn't help myself.'

She cried silently and he watched her with miserable eyes.

'I know it seems beastly,' he said, 'but what could I do? It wasn't as if I had any reason to . . .'

She interrupted him.

'I don't blame you. It was inevitable. It's only because I'm stupid that it gives me such a frightful pain in my heart.'

'Darling!'

'We ought to have gone away together two years ago.

It was madness to think we could go on like this.'

'Are you sure Enid's right? She thought she was in the family way three or four years ago.'

'Oh, yes, she's right. She's frightfully happy. She says you wanted a child so badly.'

'It's come as such an awful surprise. I don't seem able to realise it yet.'

She looked at him. He was staring at the leaf-strewn earth with harassed eyes. She smiled a little.

'Poor Hal.' She sighed deeply. 'There's nothing to be done about it. It's the end of us.'

'What do you mean?' he cried.

'Oh, my dear, you can't very well leave her now, can you? It was all right before. She would have been unhappy, but she would have got over it. But now it's different. It's not a very nice time for a woman anyhow. For months she feels more or less ill. She wants affection. She wants to be taken care of. It would be frightful to leave her to bear it all alone. We couldn't be such beasts.'

'Do you mean to say you want me to go back to England with her?'

She nodded gravely.

'It's lucky you're going. It'll be easier when you get away and we don't see one another every day.'

'But I can't live without you now.'

'Oh, yes, you can. You must. I can. And it'll be worse for me, because I stay behind and I shall have nothing.'

'Oh, Violet, it's impossible.'

'My dear, it's no good arguing. The moment she told me I saw it meant that. That's why I wanted to see you first. I thought the shock might lead you to blurt out the whole truth. You know I love you more than anything in the world. She's never done me any harm. I couldn't take you away from her now. It's bad luck on both of us, but there it is, I simply wouldn't dare to do a filthy thing like that.'

'I wish I were dead,' he moaned.

'That wouldn't do her any good, or me either,' she smiled.

'What about the future? Have we got to sacrifice our whole lives?'

'I'm afraid so. It sounds rather grim, darling, but I suppose sooner or later we shall get over it. One gets over everything.'

She looked at her wrist-watch.

'I ought to be getting back. Tom will be in soon. We're all meeting at the club at five.'

'Tom and I are supposed to be playing tennis.' He gave her a pitiful look. 'Oh, Violet, I'm so frightfully unhappy.'

'I know. So am I. But we shan't do any good by talking about it.'

She gave him her hand, but he took her in his arms and kissed her, and when she released herself her cheeks were wet with his tears. But she was so desperate she could not cry.

Ten days later the Clarkes sailed.

While George Moon was listening to as much of this story as Tom Saffary was able to tell him, he reflected in his cool, detached way how odd it was that these commonplace people, leading lives so monotonous, should have been convulsed by such a tragedy. Who would have thought that Violet Saffary, so neat and demure, sitting in the club reading the illustrated papers or chatting with her friends over a lemon squash, should have been eating her heart out for love of that ordinary man? George Moon remembered seeing Knobby at the club the evening before he sailed. He seemed in great spirits. Fellows envied him because he was going home. Those who had recently come back told him by no means to miss the show at the Pavilion. Drink flowed freely. The Resident had not been asked to the farewell party the Saffarys gave for the Clarkes, but he knew very well what it had been like, the good cheer, the cordiality, the chaff, and then after dinner the gramophone turned on and everyone dancing. He wondered what Violet and Clarke had felt as they danced together. It gave him an odd sensation of dismay to think of the despair that must have filled their hearts while they pretended to be so gay.

And with another part of his mind George Moon thought of his own past. Very few knew that story. After all, it had happened twenty-five years ago.

'What are you going to do now, Saffary?' he asked.

'Well, that's what I wanted you to advise me about. Now that Knobby's dead I don't know what's going to happen to Violet if I divorce her. I was wondering if I oughtn't to let her divorce me.'

'Oh, you want to divorce?'

'Well, I must.'

George Moon lit another cigarette and watched for a moment the smoke that curled away into the air.

'Did you ever know that I'd been married?'

'Yes, I think I'd heard. You're a widower, aren't you?'

'No, I divorced my wife. I have a son of twenty-seven. He's farming in New Zealand. I saw my wife the last time I was home on leave. We met at a play. At first we didn't recognise one another. She spoke to me. I asked her to lunch at the Berkeley.'

George Moon chuckled to himself. He was alone. It was a musical comedy. He found himself sitting next to a large fat dark woman whom he vaguely thought he had seen before, but the play was just starting and he did not give her a second look. When the curtain fell after the first act she looked at him with bright eyes and spoke.

'How are you, George?'

It was his wife. She had a bold, friendly manner and

was very much at her ease.

'It's a long time since we met,' she said.

'It is.'

'How has life been treating you?'

'Oh, all right.'

'I suppose you're a Resident now. You're still in the Service, aren't you?'

'Yes. I'm retiring soon, worse luck.'

'Why? You look very fit.'

'I'm reaching the age limit. I'm supposed to be an old buffer and no good any more.'

'You're lucky to have kept so thin. I'm terrible, aren't I?'

'You don't look as though you were wasting away.'

'I know. I'm stout and I'm growing stouter all the time. I can't help it and I love food. I can't resist cream and bread and potatoes.'

George Moon laughed, but not at what she said; at his own thoughts. In years gone by it had sometimes occurred to him that he might meet her, but he had never thought that the meeting would take this turn. When the play was ended and with a smile she bade him good-night, he said:

'I suppose you wouldn't lunch with me one day?'

'Any day you like.'

They arranged a date and duly met. He knew that she had married the man on whose account he had divorced her, and he judged by her clothes that she was in comfortable circumstances. They drank a cocktail. She ate the *hors-d'œuvres* with gusto. She was fifty if she was a day, but she carried her years with spirit. There was something jolly and careless about her, she was quick on the uptake, chatty, and she had the hearty, infectious laugh of the fat woman who has let herself go. If he had not known that her family had for a century been in the Indian Civil Service he would have thought that she had been a chorus girl. She was not flashy, but she had a sort of flamboyance of nature that suggested the stage. She was not in the least embarrassed.

'You never married again, did you?' she asked him.

'No.'

'Pity. Because it wasn't a success the first time there's no reason why it shouldn't have been the second.'

'There's no need for me to ask if you've been happy.'

'I've got nothing to complain of. I think I've got a happy nature. Jim's always been very good to me; he's retired now, you know, and we live in the country, and I adore Betty.'

'Who's Betty?'

'Oh, she's my daughter. She got married two years ago. I'm expecting to be a grandmother almost any day.'

'That ages us a bit.'

She gave a laugh.

'Betty's twenty-two. It was nice of you to ask me to lunch, George. After all, it would be silly to have any feelings about something that happened so long ago as all that.'

'Idiotic.'

'We weren't fitted to one another and it's lucky we found it out before it was too late. Of course I was foolish, but then I was very young. Have you been happy too?'

'I think I can say I've been a success.'

'Oh, well, that's probably all the happiness you were capable of.'

He smiled in appreciation of her shrewdness. And then, putting the whole matter aside easily, she began to talk of other things. Though the courts had given him custody of their son, he, unable to look after him, had allowed his mother to have him. The boy had emigrated at eighteen and was now married. He was a stranger to George Moon, and he was aware that if he met him in the street he would not recognise him. He was too sincere to pretend that he took much interest in him. They talked of him, however, for a while, and then they talked of actors and plays.

'Well,' she said at last, 'I must be running away. I've had a lovely lunch. It's been fun meeting you, George. Thanks so much.'

He put her into a taxi and taking off his hat walked down Piccadilly by himself. He thought her quite a pleasant, amusing woman: he laughed to think that he had ever been madly in love with her. There was a smile on his lips when he spoke again to Tom Saffary.

'She was a damned good-looking girl when I married her. That was the trouble. Though, of course, if she hadn't been I'd never have married her. They were all after her like flies round a honey-pot. We used to have awful rows. And at last I caught her out. Of course I divorced her.'

'Of course.'

'Yes, but I know I was a damned fool to do it.' He leaned forward. 'My dear Saffary, I know now that if I'd had any sense I'd have shut my eyes. She'd have settled down and made me an excellent wife.'

He wished he were able to explain to his visitor how grotesque it had seemed to him when he sat and talked with that jolly, comfortable and good-humoured woman that he should have made so much fuss about what now seemed to him to matter so little.

'But one has one's honour to think of,' said Saffary.

'Honour be damned. One has one's happiness to think of. Is one's honour really concerned because one's wife hops into bed with another man? We're not crusaders, you and I, or Spanish grandees. I *liked* my wife. I don't say I haven't had other women. I have. But she had just that something that none of the others could give me. What a fool I was to throw away what I wanted more than anything in the world because I couldn't enjoy exclusive possession of it!'

'You're the last man I should ever have expected to hear speak like that.'

George Moon smiled thinly at the embarrassment that was so clearly expressed on Saffary's fat troubled face.

'I'm probably the first man you've heard speak the naked truth,' he retorted.

'Do you mean to say that if it were all to do over again you would act differently?'

'If I were twenty-seven again I suppose I should be as big a fool as I was then. But if I had the sense I have now I'll tell you what I'd do if I found my wife had been unfaithful to me. I'd do just what you did last night: I'd give her a damned good hiding and let it go at that.'

'Are you asking me to forgive Violet?'

The Resident shook his head slowly and smiled.

'No. You've forgiven her already. I'm merely advising you not to cut off your nose to spite your face.'

Saffary gave him a worried look. It disconcerted him to know that this cold precise man should see in his heart emotions which seemed so unnatural to himself that he thrust them out of his consciousness.

'You don't know the circumstances,' he said. 'Knobby and I were almost like brothers. I got him this job. He owed everything to me. And except for me Violet might have gone on being a governess for the rest of her life. It seemed such a waste; I couldn't help feeling sorry for her. If you know what I mean, it was pity that first made me take any notice of her. Don't you think it's a bit thick that when you've been thoroughly decent with people they should go out of their way to do the dirty on you? It's such awful ingratitude.'

'Oh, my dear boy, one mustn't expect gratitude. It's a thing that no one has a right to. After all, you do good because it gives you pleasure. It's the purest form of happiness there is. To expect thanks for it is really asking too much. If you get it, well, it's like a bonus on shares on which you've already received a dividend; it's grand, but you mustn't look upon it as your due.'

Saffary frowned. He was perplexed. He could not quite make it out that George Moon should think so oddly about things that it had always seemed to him there were no two ways of thinking about. After all there were limits. I mean, if you had any sense of decency you had to behave like a tuan. There was your own self-respect to think of. It was funny that George Moon should give reasons that looked so damned plausible for doing something that, well, damn it, you had to admit you'd be only too glad to do if you could see your way to it. Of course George Moon was queer. No one ever quite understood him.

'Knobby Clarke is dead, Saffary. You can't be jealous of him any more. No one knows a thing except you and me and your wife, and to-morrow I'm going away for ever. Why don't you let bygones be bygones?'

'Violet would only despise me.'

George Moon smiled, and unexpectedly on that prim, fastidious face, his smile had a singular sweetness.

'I know her very little. I always thought her a very nice woman. Is she as detestable as that?'

Saffary gave a start and reddened to his ears.

'No, she's an angel of goodness. It's me who's detestable for saying that of her.' His voice broke and he gave a little sob. 'God knows I only want to do the right thing.'

'The right thing is the kind thing.'

Saffary covered his face with his hands. He could not curb the emotion that shook him.

'I seem to be giving, giving all the time, and no one does a God-damned thing for me. It doesn't matter if my heart is broken, I must go on.' He drew the back of his hand across his eyes and sighed deeply. 'I'll forgive her.'

George Moon looked at him reflectively for a little.

'I wouldn't make too much of a song and dance about it, if I were you,' he said. 'You'll have to walk warily. She'll have a lot to forgive too.'

'Because I hit her, you mean? I know, that was awful of me.'

'Not a bit. It did her a power of good. I didn't mean that. You're behaving very generously, old boy, and you know, one needs a devil of a lot of tact to get people to forgive one one's generosity. Fortunately women are frivolous and they very quickly forget the benefits conferred upon them. Otherwise, of course, there'd be no living with them.'

Saffary looked at him open-mouthed.

'Upon my word you're a rum 'un, Moon,' he said. 'Sometimes you seem as hard as nails and then you talk so that one thinks you're almost human, and then, just as one thinks one's misjudged you and you have a heart after all, you come out with something that just shocks one. I suppose that's what they call a cynic.'

'I haven't deeply considered the matter,' smiled George Moon, 'but if to look truth in the face and not resent it when it's unpalatable, and take human nature as you find it, smiling when it's absurd and grieved without exaggeration when it's pitiful, is to be cynical, then I suppose I'm a cynic. Mostly human nature is both absurd and pitiful, but if life has taught you tolerance you find in it more to smile at than to weep.'

When Tom Saffary left the room the Resident lit himself with deliberation the last cigarette he meant to smoke before tiffin. It was a new rôle for him to reconcile an angry husband with an erring wife and it caused him a discreet amusement. He continued to reflect upon human nature. A wintry smile hovered upon his thin and pallid lips. He recalled with what interest in the dry creeks of certain places along the coast he had often stood and watched the Jumping Johnnies. There were hundreds of them sometimes, from little things of a couple of inches long to great fat fellows as long as your foot. They were the colour of the mud they lived in. They sat and looked at you with large round eyes and then with a sudden dash buried themselves in their holes. It was extraordinary to see them scudding on their flappers over the surface of the mud. It teemed with them. They gave you a fearful feeling that the mud itself was mysteriously become alive and an atavistic terror froze your heart when you remembered that such creatures, but gigantic and terrible, were once the only inhabitants of the earth. There was something uncanny about them, but something amusing too. They reminded you very much of human beings. It was quite entertaining to stand there for half an hour and observe their gambols.

George Moon took his topee off the peg and not displeased with life stepped out into the sunshine.